PRAISE FOR THE NOVELS
OF JEN McLAUGHLIN

"Sexy, hot chemistry and heroes to die for!"
—*New York Times* bestselling author Laura Kaye

"Jen McLaughlin's books are sexy and satisfying reads."
—*New York Times* bestselling author Jennifer Probst

"I'm a huge Jen McLaughlin fan—she never disappoints."
—*New York Times* bestselling author Monica Murphy

"I devour [Jen McLaughlin's] books no matter what genre
she's writing in."   —Romance for Every World

"A really enjoyable read. No one does angst and romance quite
like Jen McLaughlin does. . . . I laughed, shook my head, and
swooned."   —Once Upon a Book Blog

Also by Jen McLaughlin

DARE TO RUN
DARE TO STAY

DARE
TO
STAY

THE SONS OF STEEL ROW

JEN McLAUGHLIN

A SIGNET ECLIPSE BOOK

SIGNET ECLIPSE
Published by New American Library,
an imprint of Penguin Random House LLC
375 Hudson Street, New York, New York 10014

This book is an original publication of New American Library.

First Printing, August 2016

Copyright © Jen McLaughlin, 2016
Penguin Random House supports copyright. Copyright fuels creativity, encourages diverse
voices, promotes free speech, and creates a vibrant culture. Thank you for buying an authorized
edition of this book and for complying with copyright laws by not reproducing, scanning, or
distributing any part of it in any form without permission. You are supporting writers and
allowing Penguin Random House to continue to publish books for every reader.

Signet Eclipse and the Signet Eclipse colophon are trademarks
of Penguin Random House LLC.

For more information about Penguin Random House, visit penguin.com.

ISBN 9780451477606

Printed in the United States of America
10 9 8 7 6 5 4 3 2 1

Penguin
Random
House

This one goes out to the readers out there
who fell in love with Lucas Donahue in book one.

ACKNOWLEDGMENTS

First and foremost, I'd like to thank you, my readers. Without you, I wouldn't be able to tell stories and live in worlds where Lucas, Chris, and Scotty existed. Without you, I'd be lost.

I'd like to thank my family, like always. Greg, Kaitlyn, Hunter, Gabriel, Emmy, Dad, Mom, Tina, Erick, Danny, Riley, Connor, Cynthia, Ashley, Greg, Carole, MeeMaw, PeePaw, and everyone else in my family, thank you for always being excited to hear about my latest book deal or my newest idea. And for understanding when I'm just too busy to talk.

To my friends Jay, Jen, Brittany, Jill, Tessa, Megan, Liz, Joanne, and every single one of you out there who means something to me, you're my world. My life. Thank you for being there for me whenever I needed you, however I needed you. You rock.

To my agent, Louise, and Kristin and the rest of her team and the Bent Agency, thank you for always working hard to make sure my career goes as far as it has already and for always trying to push it a little bit further, too.

And Kristine, my editor here at Penguin, thanks for loving this book as much as I did! And to everyone who had a hand in this book in any way here at New American

Library/Signet Eclipse, thank you for that, too! You're the best!

To anyone out there who reads books, please keep on reading. Keep on dreaming. And more important, keep on living vicariously through these stories we authors are lucky enough to make up for you. Without you, we wouldn't be who we are.

Thank you.

CHAPTER 1

CHRIS

Sometimes you've got to take a look at your life—a good, hard, brutally honest look—and admit that somewhere along the way, you fucked up *big*-time. Just as importantly, sometimes you had to accept that the reason you were in an alley, bleeding and dying behind a busted-up Laundromat, was because, those choices you made? The screwups, the wrong turns, all the things you wish you could take back?

Yeah. Those were the reasons why you deserved this.

To die alone, as violently as you lived.

I turned my head to spit out blood, painting it across the dirty concrete wall next to me, and laughed at the almost–smiley face it made, because why the hell not? But my laugh made my aching ribs hurt more than before, so it ended on a groan. Clutching my ribs, I gingerly rolled over and glowered up at the sky. The uneven cement under my back dug into my already sore spine. The docks were nearby, the smell of week-old garbage and rotting rat corpses the only thing surrounding me.

The moon was absent tonight, and there wasn't a cloud to be seen in the sky. The stars shone down on me—never changing, always steady—mocking me with their bright futures. While I probably wouldn't last the night.

Because I tried to kill my best friend . . .

And he let me live.

Lucas Donahue should've killed me instead of just shooting me and cracking my ribs. He was the closest thing I had to a brother, and I'd engineered a bloody coup that had nearly cost him everything. He should have shot me down in cold blood, should have put me down like the rabid dog I was. I deserved it. But instead, he showed me mercy. He let me walk away.

What the hell was I supposed to do with *that*?

The moment he let me walk out of his apartment, a crumpled-up, bloody note in my hand giving me everything I wanted, I knew I'd made a huge mistake. I never should have attacked my blood brother to get ahead in a gang that—more likely than not—would end up killing me, anyway. I'd stupidly wanted to show my pops that I could be a harder man than he was. That I could beat him at his own game. Be cold. Ruthless. A killer.

I *was* all those things, but not to Lucas.

Betraying Lucas was the single biggest regret in my life. Normally, I didn't wallow in the what-ifs or the shoulda-beens. I didn't waste my damn time with what I could have done or what I could have been. But if I could go back in time and undo all the shit I'd done to Lucas . . .

Man, I would turn that damn clock back so quickly, it'd snap in half.

The bloodstained note in my pocket burned against my thigh. It named me Lucas's successor, just like I'd wanted. And just like I'd wanted, Lucas was out of the picture, out of the gang. When his younger brother, Scotty, had shown up at his place, gun in hand, I knew that, no matter the outcome, I wouldn't win.

But truth be told, even before that, I knew I'd made a mistake.

Lucas had looked at me with hope, thinking I'd come to help him, and part of me had died back in that apartment with the rest of the men who'd dared to attack Lucas. When he realized *I* was the mastermind all along . . .

There was no coming back from that.

It had been too late.

Too late to say, *"You know what, man? Never mind. We're cool."* The second Lucas found out I was trying to kill him to move up the ranks, I was a dead man, whether he pulled the trigger on his gun or not. All along, I'd thought our friendship was more a friendship of convenience at this point. That Lucas had used his connections to me and Pops to get into the gang, and he'd remained friends with me because he couldn't afford to lose that connection.

But the betrayal Lucas had felt hadn't been feigned, and he'd chosen to let me live even after I'd tried to rid the world of him. My own father would have laughed and shot me in the face, but not Lucas. And that's when I'd realized in trying to prove I was the better man, I'd become my father.

The one thing I despised more than anything.

Angry at what I had become, I'd lashed out at Lucas. Tried to get him to pop me, to put me out of my misery. But he hadn't. He'd done the honorable thing and let me live. He hadn't wanted to kill me, even after all the shit I'd done to him. He'd told Scotty to let me walk away . . . and I had.

Now with Scotty's help, Lucas was gone.

Dead. Only he wasn't. By now, he was probably miles outside of Boston, and away from this slum we called Steel

Row—while I would die in the worst section of Southie, knowing I had put power above brotherhood.

I should have lived the life that Lucas led. He was the type of guy who put friends first. Family first. The type of guy who saved a guy's neck, even if that guy had just tried to kill him, because he'd made a promise he'd be blood brothers with him when they were kids.

And here I was, a fucking fool.

Any minute now, my phone would ring with the news of Lucas's "death," and I would be expected to be shocked. Raging. Grief stricken. And the thing was, even though he was alive and well . . . I *was* all those things.

Because I'd become a monster.

I laughed again. "Rest in peace, Lucas Donahue."

As if on cue, my phone buzzed in my pocket. Wincing, I dug my sore fingers into my pocket and pulled out my iPhone. Squinting at the screen, I sighed. It was Tate, the head of the Sons of Steel Row, my gang. Time to put on a good act. "Hello?"

"Where are you?" Tate asked, his voice hard.

I struggled to sit up, resting my back against the concrete wall, right next to my bloody smiley face. "I ran into some Bitter Hill guys, and they did a number on me. I'm just trying to recover a bit before I head back in. Why? What's wrong, sir?"

"We just got bad news . . . about Lucas."

I rubbed my forehead. It hurt like a bitch. I didn't know what Scotty had or hadn't told him yet, so I didn't want to say too much. "Where is he?"

"I'm sorry, but he's gone." Tate made a growling noise. "Fucking Bitter Hill took him and his girl out. They burned the place down, leaving nothing but bones and ash, but the dental records match. Lucas is dead."

I blinked. How the hell had they managed to pull off a

damn dental records match—and so quickly? I'd hung around after the attack to make sure Lucas and Heidi actually kept their word and left. They had. Scotty had waved them away with a smile. They weren't dead, and yet . . . *oh shit*. Son of a fucking bitch.

It all made sense now.

Scotty had seemed too quick to agree to keeping my secret. And when he came barging into Lucas's apartment, the way he'd held the gun had been telling. It had screamed his true identity, clear as day. And the way he stood, all straight and at attention, with a firm grip on his pistol—like they teach at the academy. Scotty was a fucking cop.

In the eyes of Steel Row, that was worse than what I'd done. It was worse than a betrayal. Beyond a death sentence, it was a *mutilation* sentence.

If I told Tate about this, Scotty would be dead within the hour, and no one would ever find all the pieces that would put him back together. My position in the gang would be more secure than ever before, if I helped take him down. I would successfully take over Lucas's position, and Pops would finally be proud of me.

It was the perfect way to secure my future.

But it was Scotty Donahue, Lucas's little brother . . .

The brother of the man I'd wronged.

"Chris?" Tate said, his voice raised. "Are you there?"

I must've been silent too long. But my shock over Scotty's occupation would double as my grief over Lucas's demise. I cleared my throat. "Y-yeah. I just . . . I can't . . . I'm gonna fucking kill them all. Every last one. Right now."

"No." Something slammed down on wood. More than likely, on Tate's walnut desk. He loved opulence as much as I loved women. "We need to be smart about this. We've got enough cop focus on us right now, and we don't need more by bringing a gang war down on Steel Row. All that'll do is land our asses behind bars. I think we've all done enough time."

There it was. The opening to mention my suspicions about Scotty's side job as an undercover. It would be so easy to do. A hell of a lot easier than shooting Lucas had been. "What am I supposed to do? They killed my best friend. I . . . I . . . *shit*. I can't let that go."

"You have to, until we have a foolproof plan. Until then . . ." Tate slammed something else down, and I heard someone speak in a low voice. "Okay, yeah. Your pops called in from the airport. He suggested you take some time to yourself, and I agree. Lie low. Heal. Drink. Fuck it out of your system. Whatever works for you."

I gritted my teeth. Of course my pops immediately assumed that I was weak and would need time to heal. And worse than that, if he knew I'd tried—and *failed*—to kill Lucas, and that his death was a ruse, he wouldn't be so quick to protect me. "Are you sure? Don't you need me there? I mean . . . Christ. *Lucas*."

"I know." Tate sighed. "You do you; we've got this. We'll make plans, and when we have anything concrete—"

"I'll be the first to pull the trigger."

"I promise," Tate agreed.

"Thank you, sir," I said, glancing down at my blood-soaked T-shirt and brown leather jacket. If I didn't sew that bullet hole up soon, I would go from dying to dead. "I appreciate it."

"Sure thing."

The line went dead, and I dropped my hand to my thigh. Simply holding up the phone took too much effort. Hurt too much. But it was nothing compared to the guilt trying to choke the life out of me. Banging my head on the wall hard enough to see stars all over again, I said, "Son of a bitch, Scotty."

Didn't he know how much danger he was in by doing this? By pretending to be in the gang, while reporting back to the Boys? If Tate found out about Scotty . . .

Gritting my teeth, I struggled to my feet, wavering.

I'd lost a lot of blood, and unless I truly wanted to die in this alley, I needed to get moving. There was a closed pharmacy in the swanky part of town, outside of Steel Row, that Southies generally avoided. But this one was in the Sons' employ, thanks to Pops and his fondness for gambling. If I could get in the back door, I could grab supplies and pain meds, stitch myself up, and then . . .

Then *what*?

Fuck if I knew.

Trust that Scotty, the *cop*, didn't turn me in to Tate? Trust that he wouldn't tell the man of my deceit and betrayal? If he told them, they would kill me, no matter what Pops said. I would be a dead man. And, even worse, what if Scotty used the other side of his advantage—and turned me in to the Boys? Told them all the shit I'd done, and locked me away behind bars? *Or*, conversely, I could tell Tate about Scotty's dirty little secret first, and be responsible for yet another "disappearance" in the Donahue family.

Or . . . I could just hide out.

Wait and see how all this blew over.

Nothing good ever came from rash decisions, and after the death of four Bitter Hill guys, there was more than likely going to be some reaction. And that backlash would come right back to me. I'd sworn Phil and his men to secrecy when I hired them to take Lucas out, but that didn't mean they hadn't blabbed to someone.

Men like them always did.

I stumbled down the alley, each step hurting more than the last. Lucas had kicked my ass within an inch of my life, and he should have killed me. I should have been *dead*. Maybe I'd just lie down and wait to bleed out. It was a fairly peaceful way to go, for a guy like me. I could just let my blackened blood spread across the grimy cement until nothing remained of me but a dried-up shell.

But that damn survival instinct in me refused.

I'd fucked up big-time by betraying my best friend—that much was true. But to just give up and let the devil drag me to hell? I couldn't do it. And Scotty, fool that he was, had a lot riding on this whole affair, too. If he wanted to remain undercover, he would need me to back his story up. Vouch for him.

If he told them I was there, too, I needed to agree.

It was the only way to keep Scotty whole.

I had to play my part. Tate and the rest of the guys at Steel Row would expect me to be vengeful, bitter, and upset. I could do that. I might be too late to make it up to Lucas, to let him know how sorry I was for what I did, but I could save Scotty.

Because I owed it to Lucas.

It was a small thing to do, really. Not even close to big enough to make up for all I'd done, or the lies I'd told in my quest for power and Pops's approval.

But it was *something*.

And it had to be enough.

Rounding the corner, I clutched my bleeding shoulder, breathing heavily. The world spun in front of me, and I rested against the rough brick. I needed a few seconds to gather some strength.

To make sure I didn't pass out—

"Well, well, what do we have here?" a man said from the darkness. I recognized that voice, dammit. Reggie, a lieutenant in Bitter Hill, was the only other man who knew about my plot to kill Lucas. Therefore, he was the only man who knew why Bitter Hill guys had died, and *how*. He probably hadn't shared that information, because working with Steel Row would get him and Phil killed, too. "Chris O'Brien, bleeding and alone."

I smirked. "Reggie, great to see you, man."

"Where are *my* men, O'Brien?"

"Yeah, about that?" I shrugged, ignoring the pain blazing through my shoulder from the small gesture. "Turns out, Lucas isn't as easy to take down as I thought. It got ugly, and there were losses, but he's dead."

Reggie rubbed his jaw and walked closer, his black hair as black as his eyes. He walked behind me, and I stiffened. I didn't like anyone at my back. Especially not guys like him— guys like *me*. "Let me guess. Steel Row thinks we're to blame while you're free and clear of all blame?"

"Shit if I know. Haven't heard word yet. I'm kinda recovering from the op, in case you can't tell." I straightened and pushed off the wall. "But as soon as I hear who they're looking to pop, I'll let you know."

Reggie chuckled. "Yeah. Sure you will. You must think I'm a fucking fool."

Well, actually . . . "Nah, man."

"Why should I believe you?"

I shrugged, even though it hurt. "Why not? You lost some men, but you took down Lucas Donahue. I call that a win."

"Know what I call a *win*?" He flicked a finger, and two guys came out from the darkness. "Kill him, and make it painful."

He walked away, not bothering to turn around to see if his men followed orders. I reached for my gun—till I remembered that Lucas had taken it from me. *"Shit."*

Reggie's guys grinned, and one pulled out a Glock with a silencer on it. "Any last words?"

I'm sorry, Lucas. "Yeah." I inched closer and forced a grin. The man's hold on his weapon trembled, and I knew I could take him. A man who hesitated was a man easily overtaken. "Never fuck with someone who's got nothing to lose."

I threw myself at him, and we hit the ground with a bang— literally. The gun went off, and it miraculously hit the man who'd leapt forward to help his buddy. He hit the ground, convulsing and choking on blood. The guy under me cursed and let loose a mean right hook that solidly connected with my nose. I rolled to the side, blinking away the impending blackness, but I would be too late.

I really was going to die in this alley . . .

And I deserved it.

CHAPTER 2

MOLLY

It's a Saturday afternoon, and you're in school grading papers. What are you doing with your life, Molly? "Teaching, and shaping little lives," I muttered to myself.

While that was true, I also knew I was lying to myself. I was here, on my day off, because I needed a distraction, and being home alone hurt. Blinking, I returned my focus to the papers on my desk. A blue-and-red cat, with bright green eyes, glowered back at me from my desk. I'd told the children to color in the creature to match what they thought a cat should look like, and this was what the adorable little Johnny had drawn. I didn't know whether to be impressed with his open-minded creativity, worried that he'd seen a cat like this at some point, or happy that he'd done such a great job coloring between the lines.

So I drew a smiley face and moved on to the next cat.

It was gray with blue eyes, and perfectly realistic. Another smiley face.

Sighing, I leaned back in my chair and glanced out the window, rubbing my forehead. Well, *crap*. It had gotten dark somewhere between the colorful cat and all the ones before it, and the skies were black without even a hint of color to them.

That meant it was time to head home.

I would pour myself a full glass of Elmo Pio Moscato and forget all about the fact that, five years ago today, I watched my only surviving parent, my *father* . . . die. Force my mind away from the memories of a ruthless gangbanger who had decided to hit up the Quick-E mart where my dad had stopped to pick up milk. And I wouldn't remember that my father had saved the life of a mother and her small child . . . and paid with his *own* in the process.

All because a gangbanger had to prove he was a ruthless killer.

And the ironic thing was, after Mom died from cancer when I was nothing more than a toddler, Dad had spent his life trying to help men like the one who killed him. Trying to rehabilitate them, show them a better way to live.

It had, quite literally, killed him.

Well, point proven. The gunman had taken everything from me that day, and there was nothing I could do to change that. I was alone, and Dad was gone, and . . .

And, yeah.

That pretty much covered it.

A knock sounded on my door, and I glanced up. "Come in."

"Hey," another kindergarten teacher, my friend Hollie Yardley, said. "I wasn't expecting you to still be here. You heading out soon?"

"Yeah, I think so. Now, actually."

She smiled. "Want to go out? Rachel and I are going to the club to dance and to drink a little. Maybe find a hot guy or two to flirt with. You in?"

That was pretty much the *last* thing I wanted to do today, the anniversary of my father's death, but I forced a smile, anyway, because I liked Hollie. "Thanks, but I think I'll head home and catch up on *The Walking Dead* instead."

Hollie didn't lose her smile, but I saw the look in her eyes. The one that said I never did anything but head home to watch TV. But that was my life. It was my happy place, and it was where I wanted to be. Why go out at night, with all the killers and creeps of the world, getting hit on in some shady bar by some shady guy, when I could be tucked in on my couch with a glass of wine and my orange cat on my lap?

No, thank you.

"All right, maybe next time?" Hollie said.

I nodded. "Totally." *Liar.* And we both knew it. "Let me know."

After she left, I rubbed the aching spot between my eyebrows again. Okay, so yeah. Maybe helplessly watching my father bleed out all over a white sidewalk had done things to me. And maybe those things made it hard for me to go out in crowds and have fun, or be outgoing and make lots of friends like Hollie did. And maybe I thought it was crazy to get drunk in public and assume no one would take advantage of a person's slow reflexes and heightened pheromones.

Some people might call it paranoia.

I called it staying *alive*.

Swallowing hard, I pushed away from my desk and stood. I didn't usually come to work on a Saturday, but all the kindergarten teachers had banded together to decorate for spring, since spring break started on the following Wednesday. Since the sun had gone down hours ago, I pulled out my Mace. I wasn't in a bad section of town. In fact, I made it a point to never go *anywhere* near Steel Row, a crappy section of

Southie where murder and mayhem ruled—where my father had been murdered—but still.

You could never be too careful.

Life had taught me that the hard way, in blood. Don't take unnecessary risks. Always think things through. And for the love of God, don't put yourself in dangerous situations or try to be a hero. Being a hero got you killed.

As I walked down the empty, darkened hallway, a door slammed behind me, and I jumped, pulse racing. As I spun to glance behind me, Mace held at the ready, I accidentally dragged my hand across a jagged, broken corner of a cubby, slicing it open.

"Son of a—" I cut myself off. "Beetlecracker."

There might not be kids here on the weekend, but I didn't feel like losing my job because of an ill-timed curse and a shocked first grader. Shaking my stinging hand out, I glanced down at it. Blood dripped from the wound already, so I curled my fist tight. The nurse wasn't in the office on a Saturday evening, and she always locked the door when she left, so I was on my own. Looked like I *would* be making a stop on the way home.

Thanks to my stupidity.

What would Dad say if he knew I'd grown scared of my own shadow? This wasn't the life I wanted or the life he would have wanted me to have. He'd spent his life helping people, and I couldn't even help myself. I needed to stop looking over my shoulder and start looking ahead. Starting now.

"You better be listening, Molly," I whispered to the empty hallway.

Shaking my head at the fact that I was talking to myself, even though I did it all the time, I made it out of the school without any more bodily harm. Sliding into my car, I rested my injured hand on my lap and started the engine. It roared to life, filling the silence that surrounded me. Usually I liked silence. It soothed me. But tonight . . . it didn't.

I should have gone out with Hollie.

The ride to the pharmacy passed quickly. Hopping out of the car, I wrapped an old Burberry scarf around my palm so I wouldn't leave a blood trail all over Doc Rutgers's white tile floor. Leaning down, I reached for my Mace . . . but stopped halfway. Enough being scared because on this night five years ago my father died. Enough with being afraid to take chances, and trying to be half the person my father was.

All being frightened got me was a cut hand.

It was time to make a change in honor of my father.

Slamming my door shut, I walked up the pathway to the front door. The lights were on inside, but the pharmacy appeared to be empty. I paused at the door, the hairs on the back of my neck rising. It felt like . . . like . . . someone was *watching* me. Like somewhere, out in the darkness, someone waited for the most opportune moment to . . . what?

Licking my lips, I called out, "H-hello?"

No one answered. Because no one was there. *Duh*.

Shaking my head at myself, I yanked on the front door, but it didn't budge. Frowning, I cupped my hands around my face, wincing at the pain it caused me, and peered inside. What I saw sent an ice-cold chill racing through my veins and down my spine, paralyzing me momentarily.

Something red was smeared all over the floor by the first aid aisle, looking like one of my students' finger paintings. Gauze was strewn all over the floor, as well as hydrogen peroxide, thread, and . . . a *sewing needle*. Behind that was an open bottle of water and an empty orange pill bottle with the lid off. White pills were spilled out into the blood, like Cheerios in red milk, and all I could do was stare because—

Someone had broken in to Doc Rutgers's pharmacy, bled

all over the place, and stolen drugs. If that person didn't want to go to the hospital to get fixed, that meant one of two things.

Someone wanted by the law, or had been shot by someone who was. After all, no one went to the hospital with a gunshot wound unless that person wanted to be questioned by the police.

And whoever it was might still be here. With *me*.

Covering my mouth, I backed up slowly, breathing heavily. As I moved away, something fell on the road behind me. Gasping, I whirled, automatically reaching for my Mace. It, of course, wasn't there, because I'd picked tonight of all nights to grow a pair of girl balls. *Just great.*

Scanning the shadows surrounding me, I searched for any signs of danger. Aside from the noise—which could have been anything at all—there was nothing. Focused straight ahead, I backed up, hand still over my mouth. If there was a bleeding criminal somewhere out there, well, I didn't want to meet him in a dark alleyway, thank you very much.

As a matter of fact, I didn't want to meet him *at all*.

A groan broke the stillness but quickly was cut off. I froze, heart racing, and didn't move. It didn't take my Harvard education to figure out where that pain-laced groan had come from . . . or from whom. It was directly next to the pharmacy, about three feet away from me. As I watched, eyes wide, a man stepped out.

Well, staggered out was more like it.

He moved forward another step, and another, one unsteady foot in front of the other, holding a scary-looking gun in his right hand. His dark brown hair was the only thing I saw of his features, and he was tall. Easily six foot three. Muscular. Tattoos. Written letters across his knuckles that spelled out *Steel Row* on both hands and that struck a memory that I couldn't quite place. As if that wasn't enough to let me know what gang he belonged to, he wore a dark brown leather jacket that announced him as a member of the Sons of Steel Row as clearly as a red bandanna announced a man as a member of the Bloods. Steel Row was a neighborhood filled with crime and poverty, ruled by a ruthless gang. They called themselves the Sons of Steel Row.

At least I would have an accurate description to give the police . . .

From the afterlife.

Not daring to move, I willed myself into invisibility. He had his head lowered and hadn't turned my way yet. If I was lucky, he wouldn't. He'd stumble off into the darkness and leave me alone. And I could slip away to—

Slowly, the man lifted his head.

It seemed as if it took a lot of effort on his part. Almost too much. And he took so long to do it that by the time he lifted his head completely . . . I knew exactly why those tattoos and that brown hair seemed so familiar. And I also knew why I hadn't turned around and run yet. Instinctively, I must've recognized him.

Chris O'Brien. Killer, gang member, and the devastatingly handsome boy next door.

Despite his ties to Steel Row, his parents lived next door to me. When I was fifteen, they bought the biggest house in my opulent neighborhood—which happened to be the one closest to ours. Everyone knew their money was dirty, just like everyone knew it was best if we all kept our mouths shut about how we felt about that matter. And their son, Chris, was as dangerous as he was sexy—and believe me, that was saying a heck of a lot.

The man was pure sexual tension and hot gazes.

He'd moved out when he turned eighteen, but after my father died, he started showing up on my property whenever he visited his parents on the weekends. Every Sunday afternoon, he did some small favor for me, even though it was quite a hike from my house to theirs. He'd mow the lawn, or wash my car, or pressure wash the windows.

I always thanked him with a smile, but I never encouraged him. Never gave him a reason to think his benevolence would get him anywhere, because it *wouldn't*. Not with me. If I succumbed to the desire he made me feel, it would be like sleeping with the enemy. But still, he was attractive in a way I couldn't deny, no matter his proclivity toward killing people. His dark brown hair and dark brown eyes were haunting in their obvious suggestion of the fact that he wasn't a good man. And his tattoos were stark against his pale skin, as was the scruff that covered his jaw.

His hard, square, *unyielding* jaw.

It would be too hard, though, if it wasn't for the fact that he had a dimple in his chin. Something about that soft dent, that charming little flaw, made him more human. But I knew better. He was more monster than human. All men like him were. Deep down, beneath his acts of neighborhood friendliness and that devastatingly handsome smile . . .

He was a killer. He would always be a killer.

But he was *hurt*.

Blood ran down his arm and soaked the spot on his shoulder where there was a hole in his jacket. He was pale, even in the darkness. Bruises were forming under his eye, and his nose appeared to be broken. He looked like he'd been hit by a truck, and lived to tell. But trucks didn't shoot bullets, so they were innocent of this crime.

He'd been *shot*.

My heart wrenched, and I wanted to help him, but it would break my rule of not letting him get too close. Men like him left devastation in their wake, and I didn't intend to be a part of that. Didn't intend to be yet another victim of his. He lived in his world, and I lived in mine. The two didn't mix. Just like we didn't.

But he was *bleeding*.

Breath held, I backed up a step, hoping he couldn't see me in the darkness. The second I moved, he lifted the gun and pointed it at me. "Whoever you are, get the hell out of here and forget you saw me, or I'll shoot. Go. Now."

I held my hands up, not moving.

I should have done what he said to do. Turn around and walk away. When a man held a gun at you and told you to go? You went, and you didn't look back. You got in your car and drove away before he changed his mind and shot you.

And this wasn't any man. This was Chris O'Brien.

But he was *weak*.

I lifted a foot, about to follow his instructions, but froze. What would my dad have done? Would he have walked away, or would he have helped a man who clearly needed it? Of course, I already knew the answer to that question.

Licking my lips, I did the opposite of what Chris had told me to do. I honored my dad's memory and did what he would have done. I stepped closer. "C-Chris? It's me. Molly Lachlan."

The gun didn't waver. He blinked at me. "Molly?"

"Yeah." Another step. "See? It's me."

Again, the gun held steady. "Shit."

"Are you okay?" I asked, my voice low and as unassuming as I could make it, considering the circumstances. "I mean, I know you're not okay. I can see you're injured and bleeding and you broke in . . . But are you *okay*?"

He laughed, the sound as harsh as the sight of his ashen skin was. "No. I'm not okay at all."

"I'm sorry." I swallowed hard. "Do you need some help?"

"No." He finally lowered the gun. His hand didn't tremble, or shake at all, despite the fact that he seemed seconds from death, and he sagged against the building as if the effort of standing up was too much. "Just go home and forget you saw me."

When he turned to me, my heart sped up. Even weak and bleeding, the man had an irresistible sexual pull that was impossible to deny. I didn't move. "I can't leave you here."

"Sure you can." He gestured toward my car weakly. "You just walk back to your fancy car, start it, step on the gas, and keep going."

I hesitated, but shook my head.

For some reason, I grew surer of my decision to stay. Something instinctively told me that while Chris was a dangerous guy, he wasn't a danger to me. I took another step closer, under the streetlight.

He lifted the gun again, pointing it at me. "Don't make me *make* you leave, Molly. Don't make me threaten you. Just *go*."

Then again . . .

"You're not going to shoot me." I held my hands up, my heart racing so fast it hurt, because even though I was about ninety-nine percent sure he wouldn't, there was that one percent that was screaming at me to hurry up and *run*. "But if you want to, go ahead. Pull the trigger. I can't stop you."

He didn't drop his gaze, and a muscle in his cheek ticked. The gun stayed pointed at me, ever steady, and there was a coldness in him that I'd never seen before that made me fear for my life. Maybe I'd overplayed my hand in an attempt to honor my father's memory. To make him proud of me.

And I might pay the ultimate price.

"Dammit, Princess." But he lowered the gun and shook his head. "Why are you so sure I won't shoot you?"

Princess? Where had that come from? "I don't know. I just am."

"Well—" His gaze fell to my hand. "You're bleeding. Why are you bleeding?"

"What?" I glanced down at it in surprise. Somewhere in between finding the blood smeared all over the store and discovering it was Chris who had done the smearing, I'd forgotten all about the whole reason I'd come to the pharmacy in the first place. "Oh. That. Yeah, I cut myself on the corner of a cubby. I came here to get some gauze and tape."

"Here." Chris tucked the gun into his pocket and reached into the other one. Stepping closer, he held out gauze and medical tape. "Take it. I got the last of it."

I blinked at him, my gaze locked on his blood-covered shoulder and on the red that had seeped all through the front of his shirt and down his hand. He was literally bleeding out, and he was worried about my *hand*? "No offense, but I think you need it more than I do."

"I don't give a damn about me." He shook it, glowering at me. "Take it."

Reaching out, I did as I was told. Our fingers brushed against one another, and I gasped at the surge of electric desire that pulsed through my veins. He stiffened, and I wondered if he'd felt it, too. Jerking back, I put a little more distance between us. Far enough that I couldn't smell his woodsy, manly cologne—or his blood. "Thank you."

He collapsed against the building, a small groan escaping him. "I have a question."

I gripped the tape tighter. "What is it?"

"Do you think all people can be saved?" He frowned up

at the sky. "That they could possibly change for the better after doing horrible things?"

I thought about the man who had killed Dad. I was pretty sure he couldn't be saved. For years, I'd tried to humanize the man. Maybe he had a family he needed to provide for, and the only way he could do so was by joining a gang. Or maybe he was homeless and needed a family, so the gang took him in. I'd thought if I did that, if I made him noble in some way, it would be easier to accept my father's death.

It hadn't been. It had only made it worse.

So my only answer for Chris was "I honestly don't know."

"Yeah." A small laugh escaped him. "Me neither."

He glowered up at the stars. His hard jaw was covered by dark stubble that begged to be touched. I couldn't help but wonder if it would feel soft underneath my fingers, or if it would scrape my skin. And for some reason, I really wanted to find out.

But he was a *killer*.

Finally, he broke the silence. "Go on. Get out of here."

I should go. Take my medical supplies, get in my car, and forget all about Chris O'Brien . . . and the fact that he was clearly too weak to take care of himself. But the thing was, I couldn't stop thinking about his question. If he was wondering if all men could be saved, then maybe he wanted to be saved. Maybe he wanted to be better. I wasn't a huge believer in fate or divine intervention, but maybe my father had guided me to this alley tonight for a reason. Maybe I was supposed to be here, helping this man.

And he was *hurt*.

Tonight, Chris had shared his limited medical supplies with me, and he had spent years doing things for me while asking nothing in return. I guess it was a case of like father, like daughter, because there was no way I was going to turn away from a guy in need. No way I could walk away from Chris. Not when this might be the moment that defined his future choices. All he needed was a little push from someone who cared enough to push. And, inexplicably . . .

That someone was me.

CHAPTER 3

CHRIS

I glared up at the darkness above us, breathing heavily, refusing to look at Molly. Orion and his damn righteous pose, and his fucking club, mocked me from the skies. It reminded me again of Scotty and the fact that he was a cop. He'd stood like that in the door to Lucas's apartment. All authoritative and brave and morally upstanding.

Guys like Orion and Scotty?

They got constellations named after them. People wrote stories about them, sang songs of their bravery for hundreds of years, wrote books about them. They probably always got the girl, too. Girls like Molly Lachlan.

She was everything I knew I could never have.

Wholesome. Beautiful. Successful. Brave. Rich as Croesus, with clean money. Her father had been a doctor, right up until the moment he died in my town. For some reason, that never sat well in the bottom of my gut. And every time I saw her, I tried to atone for that guilt. Even though the guilt wasn't mine.

Sure, I killed without a second thought, but I'd never killed anyone who didn't deserve killing. The men I killed were in the same world as me. They knew what risks they ran by living the life, just like I did. We all knew we would more than likely die in a fight for power and that no one would give a damn once we were gone.

I didn't lose sleep over the lives I took, and I didn't regret my actions in the gang. It was all I knew. All I would ever know. Unlike Lucas, I didn't have some deep-seated desire to escape. In my own way, I was cleaning up the city, too, just like the cops.

I killed men like the ones who'd killed Molly's father.

And the world was a better place for it.

I never took an innocent's life, and I never intentionally would, but if you were shooting at me, it was damn certain I was gonna shoot back. And I didn't miss. Scotty was no different. How many times had he watched one of his "brothers" get taken down, and known it was his fault? How many times had he let his cop buddies gun down a man who'd trusted him with his life . . . and how often did he lose sleep over *that*?

I would wager never. After all, it was just another scumbag crossed off the Boston PD's most wanted list. So, me and the cops? We weren't all that different.

I just didn't have a shiny badge to hide behind.

After giving Orion one last mental *fuck you*, I turned back to Molly. Even in the darkness, her brown hair somehow managed to shine. And even though I couldn't see them, her bright hazel eyes were locked on me. They had little gold flecks in them, with a hint of brown. She had, hands down, the most beautiful eyes I'd ever seen.

The most beautiful everything.

For years now, I'd watched her from afar, silently wishing

I could be good enough for her. That I stood a winter in hell's chance of claiming her as mine someday.

But I didn't, because I wasn't.

And we both were all too aware of that.

So why the hell wasn't she leaving?

"Don't make me point my gun at you again," I said, straightening so I wasn't leaning on the building for support. I didn't want her to see how weak I was.

"We both know you won't use it," she said quickly, biting her lower lip.

I stepped forward, reaching into my pocket. I didn't have a proper holster since I'd taken the gun off the dead Bitter Hill guy I'd left to rot in an alley. If I needed to scare her to get her to leave safely, I would. But she was right; I wouldn't hurt her. I would never hurt her. "Listen here, Princess. I—"

She pointed a finger at me, frowning, not even paying attention to the fact that I was literally about to point a gun in her face and tell her to fuck off. "Don't call me that. I'm *not* a princess."

I released my gun, not taking it out of my pocket. "Just go. Get out of here."

"I can't do that."

I held my hands out at my sides, hiding the grimace at the pain that the movement caused when I pulled on my self-inflicted stitches. "Why the hell not?"

"Because you need help." She stepped closer, still holding the bandage to her chest. "Let me help you."

I honestly didn't get her angle. People weren't inherently altruistic. Why would she want to help me, when I could offer her nothing in return? I wasn't used to people acting this way, especially women. My own mother had watched Pops beat me my whole childhood, and not once had she stepped in to stop it. Not once had she tended my wounds. But now Molly was here, and she wouldn't leave me—

And I didn't *get it*.

"There's nothing you can do to help me."

"I can bring you back to your home," she said, her voice so musically soft that it made me want to close my eyes just so I could savor it properly. But if I did that, I'd lose the fragile hold on consciousness I still grasped. "At least let me do that."

"Bitter Hill ambushed me and did—" I glanced down at myself. I was a wreck, covered in blood and sweat and shame. "Well, this to me. They know where I live, so my house isn't safe anymore. Thanks for the offer, though. Now get."

She came a little closer, those eyes I loved so damn much studying me. Eyes that deserved poetry and songs written about them, and to be captured on paper for all eternity. "Then I'll take you to a hotel."

"I lost my wallet." I had no idea where, but I had a feeling it had been burned in Lucas's apartment, along with the two bodies that had been passed off as Lucas and Heidi. As well as the bodies I'd left there—the Bitter Hill men I'd hired to kill Lucas. He'd killed them, instead, but he hadn't killed me. *Why didn't he kill me?* "So, no dice. Again, thanks for the offer."

"I'll pay for it."

I gritted my teeth. "Hell no. I don't take charity."

"It's not charity. We're frien—" She cut herself off, pressing her lips together. She was right to do so. We weren't friends. "I mean . . ."

She trailed off, since she clearly didn't know what "we" were.

I did.

We were nothing. Passing acquaintances in life.

After all, her real friends didn't bleed out in alleyways because they couldn't show their faces in the hospital. And they didn't kill people for a living and not feel a shred of shame for it. The only thing I regretted was what I'd done to Lucas. The rest? Part of the job.

Including the two men I'd killed just an hour before.

It had been a stroke of pure luck that I'd walked away from that. If the gun of the guy I'd been busily choking out hadn't misfired . . . I'd snapped his neck, taken the gun, and unjammed the bullet from the barrel. If Reggie wanted me dead, he really needed to send more experienced guys my way.

Ones that actually knew how deal with the unexpected.

Because guys like me? We didn't die easily.

Molly finally found her voice again. "I mean . . . I want to help you. You did all that work around my house, never asking for anything in return," she finished.

I shrugged. It stung my fresh stitches like a bitch, so I rested against the building again. I tried to make it look as casual as possible. "I didn't ask for anything because I didn't want anything. Plus, if they tracked me down, your name might be attached to mine, and you could be in danger. Again, thanks but no thanks."

"You can barely stand up," she snapped. I immediately did so just to prove her wrong, because I was a stubborn asshole like that. She scowled. "What about your parents' house?"

"It's not safe, and they're not home." I flexed my jaw. "Even if they were, I wouldn't go there after I . . . I can't face them now that I . . ." I staggered away from her, almost losing my balance. My consciousness was getting more and more fleeting the more I stood there arguing with her, but I didn't think I was strong enough to walk away. "I just can't. Your moral obligation has been met by trying to help me, so just *get the hell out of here already*."

"No."

I cocked a brow. "No?"

"Yeah, that's right." She stalked toward me. *"No."*

"Look, Princess. I don't know what you see when you look at me, but take the worst thing you can imagine, and multiply that by about a million, and that's me in a nutshell." I shoved my hands in my pockets, gripping my gun, but I couldn't bring myself to pull it on her again. "Girls like you look out of the windows of their mansions in their fancy neighborhoods and think they know what it means to be a criminal, out there fighting for your life. If you did, you'd run for your car as fast as those four-inch limited-edition red-soled Louboutins could take you, and trust me. You wouldn't look back."

She blinked at me, then down at her shoes, as if she couldn't figure out how I knew what they were. I knew lots of things. It was my job to know how expensive easily stolen items were. "Are you finished insulting me yet?"

"I've barely started," I said, sarcasm laced in every word. "I can go all night."

She stared at me thoughtfully, and for some reason, heat swept through me at her perusal. It wasn't meant to be seductive, or even sexy, but somehow . . . it was. Because it was *her*, and I wanted her more than I wanted to get out of this hellhole.

But no matter what she made me feel, or made me want, I wouldn't act on it. Girls like her didn't need guys like me fucking up their lives.

She crossed her arms, pushing her breasts higher. "Funny, it doesn't even look like you could last another minute on your feet."

If this were any other night, or if she were any other girl, I would show her how wrong she was. I would say something cocky that made her angry but made her want me, too. I was good at it. I knew women like I knew the back of my hand, and I knew how to play them until they were trembling with pleasure—and wondering how they'd stooped so low as to fall into bed with a Steel Row loser. But I had no intention of messing with Molly Lachlan.

So I just cocked a brow.

After a moment, she flushed and said, "Come home with me, to my place." She reached out and touched my uninjured shoulder. "I'll close all the blinds, and no one will see you. Let me get you set up in a guest room, and you can rest up. Tomorrow's another day."

What is her deal? "Hell no." I backed away from her, shaking her hold off. "Go home. Forget about me. I already forgot all about you."

Too bad I hadn't. And never would.

"Chris—"

I zigzagged down the alley, intending to leave her behind since she clearly wouldn't leave *me*. But I made only a few steps before stars swam in front of me and the blackness crept in. "Son of a bitch."

Blindly, I fell against the wall, luckily close enough that I didn't hit the ground. The second I did so, she rushed toward me, her expensive heels clacking on the cement as she came forward. She wrapped a hand around my waist, supporting me, as if she stood a chance in hell of catching me if I fell.

She didn't. I would crush her like a bug.

"What do you think you're doing?" she snapped.

"Leaving," I slurred, the Vicodin I took hitting me. At least it dulled the pain while dulling my brain, too. If someone found me and finished me off, I'd be too out of it to give a damn. That wasn't such a bad way to go. "Since you won't, because you're a pretty little princess."

"I see the pain meds kicked in," she said, her tone disapproving. She sounded every inch the kindergarten teacher in that moment, scolding a kid who drew on the table and not on the paper. I had been that kid, and Pops had beaten me till I turned black and blue every time. Didn't stop me from doing it, though. I was stubborn like that. "With all that blood loss, and the fact that you probably haven't eaten in a while, you're lucky you're still standing . . . mostly. Let's get you somewhere safe."

"Don't feel bad for me. The whole reason I have nowhere to go is because I did something you'd find horrible. Whatever happens to me, whatever alley I die in, it will be deserved, and the world will be a better place because of my absence. So don't you worry about it."

"Well, you're not dying tonight," she said, her voice tight with anger and maybe . . . worry? I didn't know what to do with that. People didn't worry about guys like me. I deserved to die, unloved and unmissed. "You're coming home with me."

"The hell I am." I pushed free of her hold, and she stumbled back. I shoved off the wall and tried to walk away again, but it just wasn't happening. I wasn't strong enough, or healed enough, to lose her. "Shit, fuck, *shit*."

"Yeah, exactly," she said, her voice raised. "So stop fighting with me, and get in my car! *Now*."

"I'd shoot you before getting in your damn car," I snapped, reaching for my gun. "So fuck off."

She held a gun up, a brow raised. "You looking for this gun, the one you dropped back there when you almost passed out?"

I examined her, unable to look away, because I'd *dropped my gun*, and because I'd finally managed to piss off the angelic Molly. When Molly was happy, she was ethereal and beautiful and should be forever memorialized in pastel watercolors. But when Molly was pissed off, she was captivating and devastatingly seductive and deserved to be caught in charcoals and black shading pencils.

My fingers itched to grab my charcoal set and sketch her face.

Too bad I could barely stand, let alone draw.

"You have two choices," she said, finger pointed at me in anger. The other hand held my gun in the most awkward position ever. It made me worry she might accidentally pull the trigger and shoot herself. "You either get in the car with me and let me bring you to my house, or you pass out in this alley, and I stay here with you and your gun, waiting for the guys who did that to you to show up and try to finish the job. And I fight them off, alone and without your help."

I snorted. "You wouldn't last a second. You'd be dead—if you were lucky."

"I guess you better get in the car, before we find out if I'm lucky or not."

"I know what you're doing. You're trying to save me, and you're wasting your time." I rubbed my face, trying to shake off the impending blackness. "Yeah, I'm beat-up, and yeah, I might die, but the guys who did this to me aren't coming around, because I killed them. The guy who gave me a black eye? I literally snapped his neck. Think on that, Princess, and whether or not you really want me to sleep in your home."

She paled and bit down on her lip. She rested a hand on my chest, holding me up. Or pretending like she could, anyway. "You did what you had to do. Self-defense."

I laughed. I couldn't help it. Because while the murder in the alley might have been self-defense, what I'd done to Lucas hadn't been. I'd taken something that was pure between the two of us, and twisted it into this nasty version of our friendship. And then I'd tried to kill him. If she'd known what I had done to my best friend, she wouldn't look at me as if I could be saved. "You don't know what I've done. You don't know me at all."

"Fine." She gripped my shirt, completely ignoring the fact that my blood stained her hands red. "Then tell me what you did to wind up in this alley, bleeding to death."

I frowned at her, because even high on pain pills, there was no way in hell I was letting that slip. It was my own private shame, and I wasn't sharing it with anyone. Not even her. So I let my silence speak for itself.

"Yeah, that's what I thought," she snapped, nostrils flaring. "Now get in my car before I shoot you and finish the job myself. You're coming home with me for the night, and nothing you say will change my mind."

Guess I could add stubborn to her extremely short list of faults.

Seeing as that was the only thing on it.

I snorted. She was still furiously beautiful, and I still wanted to sketch her more than anything in the world, and I knew when to concede defeat. I wasn't strong enough to fight her off, so for the night, I would go home with her.

She must've taken my silence to be a rejection, because she entwined her fingers with mine. The second she did that, such an innocent gesture, the ground beneath me trembled and shifted. It was as if her touch alone could change the world, or more importantly, me. Maybe I really was about to die. Or maybe it was the Vicodin speaking. Either way, the earth moved—and it was because of *her*.

"Please, Chris," she said, her voice soft and soothing. "I

couldn't live with myself if I left you here to die. You've done stuff for me; now let *me* do something for *you*. Let me help you. Come home with me."

I couldn't say no to that any more than I could shoot her. For some reason, I wanted to be seen as a guy who should be brought into her house and nursed back to health, and that was the worst part of this whole thing. I wasn't that guy, and I shouldn't want to be him. But with her—

I sucked in a breath. It hurt. "Okay."

"And if you don't—" She broke off. "Wait. Okay?"

"You win. I just hope you parked close, because I'm not making it far, and as cute as it is that you think you could catch me if I fell?" I squeezed her hand and tried to smile. "Well, we both know you can't."

She held on to me tightly. "I'm right around the corner. Come on."

Taking a deep breath, I let her guide me toward her Jaguar. But when she swung the gun toward her face, I stiffened and grabbed it. The woman had clearly never held a weapon in her life, and why should she? She was a kindergarten teacher, for fuck's sake.

"Give me that before you kill yourself."

She laughed nervously. "Yeah. Okay. Just don't pull it on me again."

As we staggered toward her luxury sports car, her arm wrapped around me in support, I tucked the gun away. "You were right. I never would have used it on you."

She glanced up at me. This close, I could see those gold specks that I'd been thinking about earlier, staring up at me. And I wanted to hug her close and protect her from the world. From guys like me. Hell, *especially* from *me*. "I know."

We made it the rest of the way to the car in silence, her frail body wrapped around mine, and all I could think about was how good it would feel if she held me like this, but not out of pity. Out of love. Which was the most ridiculous thought ever. Girls like her didn't love guys like me, and guys like me didn't know what love was.

Lucas was the exception with Heidi.

Slumping into the seat, I finally let my guard down as she shut the door for me. Her car smelled good. Like her perfume and cantaloupe, mixed with the beach. It was a calming scent, and I breathed it in with a smile. Her face swam before me as she slid into her seat and started the car. I just needed to rest, so for one second . . .

I let the blackness win.

CHAPTER 4

MOLLY

I cast a quick look at my passed-out companion, my slightly sweaty palms gripping the wheel, stained with Chris's blood and my own. The second he sat down in his seat, he'd passed out cold. I had no clue if that was a good thing or bad, but he wasn't moving, and I was terrified he was going to die. That my best efforts to save his life, to save *him*, would all be for nothing.

What would I do if he didn't wake up?

I'd never harbored a criminal before, and besides those Bitter Hill guys he mentioned, I had no idea who else was looking for him. Or who might hurt him. I couldn't even call his parents because he'd said they weren't safe, so if they were somehow involved in this . . . I'd be killing him by calling them.

I couldn't call the cops. He couldn't go home.

So I just had to hope he didn't die on me.

When I stopped at the red light three streets from my

house, I poked him in the ribs. He didn't move, so I did it harder. He jerked away from me, groaning, and rolled toward me. And I . . .

I couldn't look away.

He had cuts all over his face and bloodstains all over his nose and his chin, like someone had punched him and maybe broken his nose, and he had to be seconds from dying—but even so, he was still the sexiest man I ever saw. Always had been.

That's what made resisting him so freaking hard.

Not that he'd ever hit on me, or made me think he might want more from me than a friendly neighborhood face. But still. He was near impossible to resist, even so.

His nose was imperfectly perfect and looked like it had been broken a handful of times. The bruise forming under and over his eye did nothing to detract from the manly lines of his cheekbones and forehead. And that chin dimple—that chin dimple that never failed to weaken my knees when he smiled—had been affected by his fight, too, and was covered in blood. So was I, after helping him to the car.

For some reason, it didn't bother me.

The car behind us beeped, and I jumped. The light had been green for God knows how long, so I stepped on the gas as hard as I could.

Chris jerked awake, pointing the gun out the window, and said, "What was that?"

Well. Not dead yet.

My cheeks heated, because I didn't want to admit I got honked at because I was too busy admiring his masculine beauty to notice the light had changed. "I was watching the shadows to make sure no one came too close, and missed the light turning green." Yeah. That sounded so much better than *I was admiring your chin dimple. Sorry.*

"Oh."

He sagged against the seat again, resting his gun on his legs. I watched it, swallowing hard, but forced my attention back to the road. I couldn't imagine living like he lived, always ready for the next fight. Always prepared and willing to shoot before getting shot. Never sure if today would be the day when you didn't pull the trigger fast enough. And, truth be told, that gun scared me.

So did he.

I mean, I wasn't scared he'd hurt me, or kill me. It was pretty clear he had no intention of doing so. If he wanted to get rid of me, he would have done it in that alley, with his gun, and he would have taken my car and driven off. He hadn't.

The thing that really scared me was my reaction to him, and the fact that no matter how hard I tried, I couldn't talk myself out of feeling it. Out of wanting him. I was a rational person and was capable of going over the pros and cons of every situation. If the cons outweighed the pros, I moved on and forgot all about what I was deliberating over. I accepted the fact that the risk was not worth the benefit.

But with Chris, when the cons *clearly* outweighed the pros, I couldn't shake off that annoying urge to do it, anyway. He was the first risk I couldn't walk away from.

And that was unsettling, to say the least.

I'd just have to make sure to play it safe. I lived by one rule in my life: Never let anyone in too close. Never care about them enough to let them have power over me. Never love anyone so much that their death would leave a hole in my heart. I already had one of those. I didn't need two.

But something told me my heart would be safe from Chris O'Brien. Despite my desire to help him, and my attraction to him, I wasn't stupid enough to love a criminal.

He'd be lucky if he lived to see thirty-five.

"We're almost there," I said, to fill the silence.

"I know." He rubbed his face with both hands and blinked rapidly, as if trying to stay alert. "I'll be gone by morning."

"That's fine," I said, my voice thick. I wasn't sure why, though, besides the fact that this sexy man was beside me. "I don't mind if you stick around a little longer. My house is always empty, so it's not like anyone will bug you."

He looked at me. Like, really looked at me. And I got the feeling that he saw me better than anyone else had, ever before, in that short, two-second span. "Do you like it that way? Empty?"

"Not really." I tightened my grip on the wheel and turned left into my development. Huge brick mansions and gray stone-front homes were lit up like prizes on a hill, separated enough to provide the luxurious privacy the development's residents expected. Mine would be dark and empty. "I miss Dad, and having people around for holidays and for barbecues . . ."

He turned away from me, gripping his knee so tight that his knuckles went white. "I'm sorry."

"It's okay." I bit my tongue. "You didn't shoot him."

"Someone like me did. Granted, I don't shoot innocent people—just the bad guys like me," he said, his tone casual and unconcerned, as if he weren't talking about, you know, *murders*. "But still. It could have easily been me."

"Yeah, but it wasn't," I said, staring out the windshield.

He didn't say anything to that.

The man who had killed my father had not been from Steel Row. He'd been from another gang outside of Southie, Moss Stones. They wore green. Not brown leather jackets. Chris might be a killer, but he wasn't *my* killer.

He peeked out the window toward my home. "Will a boyfriend be coming around, wondering why there's another guy at your place?"

I glanced, too. It was gray stone and light yellow siding. Big bay windows in the front and white shutters, with a big stone chimney on the side. Pink and red flowers on either side of the porch and nothing but hardwood floors and empty rooms on the inside. "No. I don't have a boyfriend."

He clucked his tongue. "Surprising."

"Why's that?" I asked, frowning. "Because I'm a 'princess' and shouldn't be left alone to do anything for myself?"

He lifted a shoulder. His uninjured one. "If the glass slipper fits . . ."

I hit the open button on the garage door opener. "I am *so* not Cinderella. No one locked me in an attic or made me wash their petticoats."

"Who's Cinderella?" he asked, deadpan.

"Glass slipper. Prince Charming. Evil stepmother." I pulled into the triple garage and shut it behind us. "Two mean stepsisters that she has to wait on hand and foot? Like, the most classic fairy tale ever told? A popular Disney movie? The one you yourself just referenced?"

He gaped at me like I'd grown two heads. "If you say so."

"How—?"

"In my house, we didn't watch Disney movies. I was taught to fight and survive, and how to become a man." He grabbed the door handle and peered over his shoulder at me. "Because life isn't a fairy tale; it's a horror movie."

He climbed out and shut the door behind him.

Shaking my head, I got out of the car, too. "Then how'd you know about the glass slipper?"

He came around the front of the car and grabbed the driver's door. Once I stepped out of the way, he shut it for me. So he was a gentleman *and* a killer. Interesting. "I saw the billboards on the highway exit where I kill people who fuck with what's mine."

"Oh. I see." Shaking off the unwanted lust harder than Taylor Swift shook off her haters, I headed toward the door, and he followed me closely. Too closely. "Do you always kill people in the same spot? Is that your killing ground?"

His gaze briefly traveled down my frame before slamming back into mine. The unmistakable appreciation glowing in those warm brown depths made my heart pick up speed and my thighs press together. "Do you always leave your house pitch-black at night?"

"If I'm not home?" I glanced over my shoulder and slipped the key into the door. "Yeah. Why?"

"Just making sure nothing's out of the ordinary."

"You're worrying too much." I shoved the door open and flicked on the kitchen light. "Why would anyone, anywhere, look for you *here*?"

He shot me a look that said he thought I was off my rocker. "It doesn't matter what you think should happen or will happen. I live in a world where someone's always trying to kill me, or I'm trying to kill someone else before they get to me. It's a dog-eat-dog world, and there's no happy ending for me. I live in a world full of evil stepmothers."

"That's not a fun place to be," I said softly. "And for a guy who doesn't watch Disney movies, you sure know a lot about the plot."

His cheeks flushed red, giving him the only hint of color he'd had all night. He kicked the door shut behind us and collapsed against it. Aside from his cheeks, he was even paler in the bright lights. It was a miracle the man was still standing. "I admit nothing."

I didn't say anything to that, mostly because I didn't know what *to* say. He clearly didn't want me to know he was a closet Disney junkie. Whatever. If he wanted to keep his dirty little secret, I'd let him.

Walking over to my fridge, I yanked it open and pulled out a bottle of orange juice. After filling a glass, I held it out to him. He stared at it, then at me, but didn't take it. I shook it a little bit under his nose. He still didn't budge. "Chris. Drink this."

"I don't like orange juice."

"I don't care," I said, gripping the glass tighter. "I don't need you passing out before we get you cleaned up and in bed."

He took the glass and lifted it to his mouth. He stopped just short of drinking it. "Wait—till *we* get me cleaned up? What the hell is that supposed to mean? Are you giving me a sponge bath? I hope not. I'm not fully able to appreciate those soft hands running all over my body, if you know what I mean."

Even though he was baiting me, my cheeks heated up, anyway. I couldn't help it. The image of me running my hands over his body was . . . *stimulating.* "That's not what I meant, and you know it."

His lips quirked, and he laughed. The orange juice remained untouched. "You sound so serious." He lowered his voice. "So very strict. Do you make all the little kids cry in school when you use that tone of voice?"

"I'll show you how good I am at making little boys cry if you keep it up," I snapped. "Drink. The. Stupid. Juice."

He laughed again, but he did as he was told. Within seconds, the glass was empty. He set it on the gray granite counter and ran the back of his hand across his chiseled lips. "Fuck, that shit's nasty."

A laugh escaped me. He was acting like a petulant child, and it was easier to deal with him like this. I was good at dealing with kids . . . it was my *job.* If he stayed this way, I'd be okay. By the time he got better and left, I'd have worked up immunity to him, and I would stop fantasizing about how amazing those arms would feel wrapped around me. Opening a cabinet, I pulled out another item. "It's over. Now, the good part."

He glanced down at the chocolate chip cookie, slowly lifting his gaze to mine. When he frowned at me, something slammed into my chest. Something real and strong, and a lot like desire . . . "You do realize I'm not one of your students, right?"

"Y-yes, of course," I managed to say, not tearing my glance from his. The thing was, something about him commanded that I meet his stare. That I not back down. "But when you give blood, they give you juice and cookies, and you lost a lot of blood, so . . ."

"So you followed protocol," he finished for me, when it became clear I wasn't going to. He took the cookie out of my hand, and his fingers brushed mine. My breath caught in my throat, and I jerked back right away. He smiled. "Good thinking."

"Thanks," I said distractedly.

I was too busy dealing with the way he made me feel to give him much more of a response. It was like I was a bottle of soda, all shaken up inside. If he twisted my lid, all that pressure would release, and I would explode all over the place. All over him.

Okay, that sounded grosser than it was supposed to.

But *still*.

He might be hurt, but he had a strength and charisma that overshadowed his current weaknesses. I had a sinking suspicion that that's what had gotten him as far as he had gotten already. When Chris O'Brien wanted something, all he had to do was cock a brow and quirk those lips up, and the world gave it to him.

And if it didn't? He took it, anyway.

I'd be smart to remember that.

He finished off his cookie and dusted his hands off. He leaned against my fridge, looking two seconds from sleep. "What next, Ms. Lachlan? Nap time? Story time?"

"Shower time." I eyed his bloody, torn shirt and jacket. His clothes had dried to his skin in some places, so I could only imagine it would hurt as much as ripping off a Band-Aid would . . . if not more. "I think the best way to get that shirt off is scissors. Do you mind?"

His lids drifted closed. "I don't give a damn. Do what you have to do. The quicker, the better, because all I want to do is sleep."

"Okay. Hold on." I pulled the scissors out of the knife block and moved closer to him. So close that to look at him, I had to tip my head back. "Rest against the wall. I have a feeling this might hurt."

He squared his jaw, watching me through his lowered lashes. That shouldn't have sent my pulse skyrocketing . . . but it did. "You won't hurt me. I've been through much worse than removing a dried, bloody shirt, I assure you."

This up close and personal, I could smell his cologne, and the dimple in his chin looked even softer than ever before. I had this insane urge to press my pinkie against it, because I was pretty sure it would fit inside the dimple perfectly. But I didn't. Because that would be insane. Ludicrous, even. And with him staring down at me, I noticed that his brown eyes had flecks of green in them. They were beautiful.

"You ready?" I asked, my voice tight.

"For you to take my clothes off?" A smirk lifted his lips, and the way he examined me—oh my God, the way he *stared* at me—made my heart race and my thighs tremble. He watched me as if I was about to be naked and underneath him. "I think so."

"I don't," I blurted. "I mean . . . okay."

Reaching up, I ran my hands over his shoulders and down his arms, removing his leather jacket. As I dragged my palms over his hard, muscular arms, he watched me, his nostrils flaring slightly. My breath caught in my throat, and I set the jacket aside, touching the hole in the shoulder. I could patch it up for him, if I had the right tools.

And if I, you know, wanted to.

I traced the bullet hole on the soft leather, sucking in a breath. What kind of life did he lead? I mean, I *knew* what kind of life he lived—but I didn't *know* know. It was like watching a TV show or a cops-and-robbers movie . . . only for him? It was real.

And now for me, too.

Because he was in my home.

"It's ruined. There's no way I can fix it without it being obvious." Something in his voice told me he wasn't happy about that. I had a feeling this jacket meant a lot more to him than something to provide him with warmth. "It's trash now."

"Maybe. Maybe not." I stared down at it. "Not everything that is scarred is incapable of being saved."

He watched me with heated eyes, his nostrils flaring, and stepped closer. As he did so, he froze, almost as if he didn't mean to, and clenched his hands into fists. "Yeah, it is. If it's broken and damaged, you can't save it," he growled.

As I laid the jacket on the counter, a bloody piece of paper fell out. It was folded in quarters. Bending, I picked it up. "Do you need this?"

He snatched it out of my fingers and shoved it in his jeans. "Yes. It's mine."

"All right." I bit down on my lip and leaned closer, staring at the gaping hole in his shirt. Moving closer, I eyed his shoulder. I could see the spot where the bullet hit, went through, and didn't come out. The back of his shirt didn't have a hole. "The bullet . . . ?"

"Is gone. I took it out in the pharmacy."

I swallowed the bile trying to rise in my throat. It tasted awful and felt even worse. "You took it out . . . yourself . . ."

A laugh came out of him. Harsh. Hard. Sexy. "Yeah. Not the first time, Princess."

"I told you not to call me that."

"I know." He smirked at me. "But I don't listen to orders well."

Obviously.

I picked up the scissors and grabbed the hem of his cotton shirt. When I did so, my knuckles brushed against the fly of his jeans, and he was hard. Oh God. Not *hard*. But . . . hard. Okay, I know that didn't make any sense, but he was so close, and my knuckles were touching him, and he was *right there* staring at me. Everything about this man was stone. Rock solid. I bet he never even cried as a baby. Just came out, surveyed the world, and settled in for the ride until he was old enough to wreak some havoc.

And he hadn't stopped since.

Taking a deep breath, I positioned the scissors at the center of his shirt. My knuckles brushed against the cool button of his jeans, and my pinkies ran along his . . . yeah. His penis. He jerked a bit, as if he hadn't been expecting it, and I didn't blame him. Neither had I. "I'm so sorry—"

"Shut up; stop apologizing." He clenched his teeth. "And just fucking do it already."

Heat suffused my cheeks. Without another word, I cut right up the center of his shirt. Each squeeze of the scissors had my fingers brushing up against his hard, tattooed skin. I couldn't look away from it as I uncovered it. It was better than unwrapping any present I'd ever gotten . . . and more dangerous, too.

Because this man, this present I unwrapped, was *deadly*.

And when I lifted my face to his, and our eyes met, he watched me like I was the next thing he wanted to wreak havoc on. And that didn't scare me as much as it should.

Instead, it made me feel *alive* in a way I'd never felt before.

"Molly," he breathed, his chest rising and falling.

I swallowed and made one more cut. It had me level with his chest, and I could see his nipples. They, like the rest of him, were hard. Both nipples had silver rings in them, and they matched the one he used to wear in his eyebrow, but he'd taken it out a few months ago. Although in retrospect, it seemed more likely it had been ripped out in a fight, rather than removed of his own free will. I could also make out the black Sons of Steel Row ink above his heart, claiming him for life. "Head back."

He gritted his teeth but tilted his head back, exposing his neck to me. I could see the spot on his eyebrow I'd been thinking of seconds ago, and the angry red scar that had been left behind. I ached to ask him what had happened. I'd liked it on him.

It had been edgy. Sexy.

Just like him.

I took the last cut, which would finish off the shirt, and set the scissors aside. The dark cotton shirt hung open, and I stepped back. Aside from the fact that he was bloody and bruised and a killer . . . he was the prettiest present I'd ever gotten.

Hard muscles. Dark ink. Cold metal. A six-pack that could have been carved by the Roman gods themselves. And as if that wasn't enough, his hard jaw—

A disgruntled sound escaped him. "Princess?"

"Uh . . ." I jerked out of my thoughts, slamming my gaze into his. The heat in his, and the inescapable power, had me stumbling back a step, pressing a hand to my stomach. It hollowed out in response immediately. "Yeah?"

He smirked, and it was, hands down, the sexiest smirk to ever grace this planet. "If you don't stop looking at me like that, I'll show you every damn reason you should—and you'll fucking love it."

CHAPTER 5

CHRIS

Jesus Christ, the woman would try the patience of a damn saint, and I was so far—the furthest thing—from one that it was truly laughable. If I hadn't been in so much pain, I would have laughed my ass off right then. This whole day had been like some alternate reality for me. I'd tried to kill my best friend, realized I'd become something I didn't want to be, and gotten my ass saved by a princess, all in less than twenty-four hours.

My ribs felt like they were split in half, and my shoulder stung like a bitch, and even worse than all that shit? My cock was hard and aching from her soft touches.

And she didn't even have a clue about it.

There was no way she was doing it on purpose, trying to seduce me. And even if she was, despite my words, it would get her nowhere. I refused to dirty her.

She deserved a prince. Not a villain.

That's why I kept calling her *Princess*. Not because I

thought she was spoiled, or a brat, but because it was a constant reminder to myself that she was too good for me and always had been. She was like Rapunzel, at the top of the tower, draped in silks and diamonds and pearls, and I was Flynn, stealing what I could to survive. Rapunzel might end up with Flynn, but that was a fairy tale, not real life. There was no world where the two of us ended up together.

And, yeah. So what if I liked Disney movies? They were a break from my world of death and destruction. But if she thought I'd admit my love for those kid movies . . .

She was sadly mistaken. I'd die first.

She backed up and wrapped her arms around herself, her cheeks bright pink. Even that made her more charming, and more approachable, instead of making me more aware of just how out of my league she was. "You keep saying all these things to me, but I don't think you intend to follow through."

I lifted a shoulder. It hurt like a bitch. "I won't be here long enough to do so, so I guess we'll never find out."

"You don't have to leave first thing," she said, still hugging herself. She'd stopped backing away from me, but she still seemed nervous. Good. She should be. "Take the day to sleep and recover. I won't even be here most of the day tomorrow, so you'll have the place to yourself, and no reason to run off."

I eyed her hand. It still bothered me that she hadn't tended to it yet, and I would be doing it as soon as she stopped fussing over me. "Where are you going?"

"I have some stuff to do," she said evasively, not turning my way. "But I'll be back around four. You could spend the day, maybe another night, and reenter the world of fighting and shoot-outs a bit more rested."

More than likely, I would run for it before Scotty's lies imploded all around me. I wasn't sure what I was doing yet, but if I stayed, I'd more than likely end up dead. I couldn't trust Scotty now that I knew he was a cop. "We'll see," I said.

Biting down on her lip, she came closer again. Her shirt was high necked, so there was no sign of cleavage or even any skin, but I couldn't look away from her chest as it rose and fell. The closer she got to me, the harder it did so. And my own damn body didn't miss that. Too bad I wouldn't give it what it wanted.

Or her.

She might not want to admit it, and might have no intentions of following through on it—much like me—but she wanted me. Everything about her screamed it, from the way she lingered over my chest and abs to the nervous chewing of her bottom lip as she reached out to remove my shirt. Her quick breaths. Her pink cheeks.

It was all there, screaming for me to take her.

But I couldn't. Wouldn't.

Something brushed against my ankle, and I glanced down. It was a little orange fur ball that I would recognize anywhere as hers. It had a smooshed-in face and a heart-shaped nose. It meowed up at me, rubbing its face against my leg. "Cute cat."

A smile lifted her lips, and it was the most beautiful thing I'd ever witnessed. "Thanks. His name is Buttons. He showed up on my doorstep one day, out of the blue."

"Weird," I said, keeping my voice even as she tore the shirt away from my bruised, bleeding skin. "Like a stray?"

"Like a present," she said, her voice softening.

I gritted my teeth. "From who?"

She slowly lifted my shirt away from my skin. It hurt worse than it should have, because she was so damn tender about the whole thing. She should have just ripped it off to get it over with, because tenderness was a luxury I didn't deserve.

"I don't know." She shot me a quick glance. I stared back at her, raising a brow. "Every once in a while, something shows up on my step with a line of a poem. It's been going on for a couple of years now, like a continued, drawn-out love story."

"Love story?" I snorted. "Sounds more like you have a stalker."

"No, I don't think so." She rolled half my shirt down my arm. I hissed because it pulled on the stitches. "It's sweet. He never misses my birthday, or a holiday, and it's become something I really look forward to. I wish I knew who he was."

I didn't reply to that. There was nothing to say.

She moved behind me, not seeming to mind my silence, her shoulder brushing against my bare back as she rolled the remainder of my shirt toward my injured side. I gritted my teeth—not because of the pain, but because her soft touches were going to be the death of me.

After a lifetime of looking only to survive, I didn't know what to do with this softness. No one had ever helped me heal. I'd been on my own for as long as I could remember. Ma hadn't had a soft bone in her body. Half the time, she'd looked as if she enjoyed it when Pops punished me. Like she wanted to see it happen. After what I'd done to Lucas, I was just as bad as they were. I'd become my pops.

How had I let myself fall so far?

"Just pull it off," I gritted out. "I'll be fine."

She trailed her fingers over my back, and I stiffened. "You have so many scars. Are these all from fighting?"

"Yeah." I shrugged. "Most of them were caused by me being a stubborn jackass."

That was a lie.

Most of them were from Pops.

He used to love to beat me when I let him down, or if he was in a bad mood. Hell, he didn't really need a reason, but, lucky for him, I let him down a lot as a kid. Even when I grew enough to fight back, I hadn't. It was all about respect.

In this life, if your lieutenant thought you deserved a beating—you fucking got a beating. And you didn't fight back. Especially not if it was your pops dishing it out.

But I wasn't about to tell her all that. She didn't need to know that Pops's weapon of choice was his steel-tipped wooden cane. Or that for special occasions, he'd used his spiked belt to whip some sense into me.

That was where most of the scars came from.

No one knew who my pops really was, or our fucked-up family dynamics. Not even Lucas. Everyone thought Pops was this easygoing, laid-back asshole who had been in the Sons his whole life and deserved respect. And that wasn't about to change now. I wasn't a pussy-whipped bitch who would cry on someone's shoulder when shown a bit of softness. Life was life. I was me. Pops was Pops. Nothing would change that.

Not even Molly.

The shirt hit the floor, and I stood there, bare chested in her fancy kitchen. She sucked in a breath and pressed her hand against a rigid scar on my back. I remembered that one all too well. I'd been eight, and Pops had had a bad day at work. He came home, found me eating my dinner, and screamed that I'd dropped a noodle on the floor. Next thing I knew, I was bleeding in my room, unable to move because he'd broken one of my ribs.

Ma hadn't even checked on me that night. I'd recovered in my room, alone with nothing but bread and milk for meals, while everyone else was told I had the chicken pox. It still hurt when I twisted too hard to the left. *That* was my life.

"Are you done?" I asked between my clenched teeth, eyeing the opulent kitchen around us. Everything was state-of-the-art, perfectly matched. And lying on the counter—literally just *lying* there—were a diamond necklace and matching earrings.

Easily worth a few grand, and she didn't even lock them up in a safe.

I had money stashed away, a little nest egg in case of emergencies, but it was nothing compared to this. To what she had. If I wanted to, all I had to do was grab a few of her shoes or necklaces, and I could be outta this town so fast, all you'd see would be a blur.

"Yeah. I'm done." She dropped her hand to her side and walked around me, heading for the living room. She didn't glance back at me. She turned the sink on, sticking her hands under the running water. I watched the blood wash off her. If only it was so easy for me. "You're next."

"Huh?"

"To wash." She scrubbed with soap, then backed away from the sink. "Go ahead."

I did as told. When I finished, she handed me a paper towel. I took it, our fingers brushing. "Thank you."

"You're welcome," she said softly. "Come on up. I'll show you to your room and get you a towel and some clean clothes."

I followed her, grabbing the medical supplies off the counter as I did so. "You have men's clothes in your house?"

"Some of Dad's stuff . . . just his things I couldn't bear to get rid of." She climbed the stairs, switching on the hallway light as she got to the top. I glanced behind us at the wooden foyer and the expensive Roman busts on either side of the door. They were probably authentic. "It's nothing great. Just some flannel pajama pants and a T-shirt."

I forced my attention forward again. That wasn't the best idea, though, because I was eye level with her ass—and it was a damn fine ass to be staring at.

Even though I couldn't have it.

"Thank you," I said, my voice coming out a bit rougher than I'd intended. "You don't have to give me your dad's clothes, though. I can just wear what I have."

She turned around and eyed me, her focus dipping low, too low, before shooting back up. I gripped the banister so tight it shoulda broken. "Your shirt is in pieces, and your jeans are covered in blood. Call me crazy, but I think we should at least wash them, since some of the blood probably even isn't yours."

I shot a quick look down. She was right. *Most* of that wasn't mine. Some of it was from the Bitter Hill guys, and some of it was Lucas's. Gritting my teeth, I forced the automatic swell of guilt down. "It's not. How does that make you feel, since you invited me in, anyway?"

"The same as I did before I asked you, and every moment since," she said, her voice even. And she didn't break eye contact. The girl had balls, despite outward appearances and her prissy outfits. "Now let's get you out of those clothes."

"My favorite words to hear from a woman," I murmured. "Especially one as beautiful as you."

She flushed and headed down the hallway. I glanced in the rooms as we walked. Each one was fully furnished, beds made, just waiting for someone to climb on in. We passed a room that was feminine, with clothes tossed over the bed. It had to be hers. Hell, I could smell her perfume wafting into the hallway.

She had one of those huge jewelry boxes that stood six feet tall, and I didn't have a doubt that she had it filled with diamonds, pearls, and God knows what else.

The girl was a prime target and didn't even know it.

Luckily for her, I wouldn't be robbing her. But if she made a habit of inviting guys like me into her home? She wouldn't be so lucky next time.

At the last door on the end of the hallway, she paused. "You can use this room." Turning the knob, she opened it and stepped inside. A flick of her wrist had the room illuminated, and it was fucking perfect. It had dark wooden floors, a king-size bed, and dark, masculine furniture. "This isn't a guest room."

"It was my father's," she said. "But it has its own shower, so it makes sense. You'll need some privacy to attend to"— she glanced at my chest, her cheeks heating—"all that."

"Are you sure?"

"It's been empty for five years," she said, her voice soft as she smiled at a framed picture. It was of her father and what appeared to be a younger version of herself. She had braces, and her hair was shorter than it was now, but besides that, she was still the same fresh-faced and innocent girl she was today. "I'm sure."

"Okay." I gritted my teeth. "Get on the bed."

"W-what?" she asked, mouth ajar. "I—I—I—"

"Not like that." I grabbed her hand and tugged her over to the bed, gently setting her on the edge. She watched me with wide eyes, like she didn't know whether to run, scream, or beg for her life. "Give me your hand."

She held out the uninjured one.

I set it in her lap. "The other one."

Once I picked up her injured hand, she sucked in a breath and fisted the other in her lap. "What are you doing?"

"Taking care of you," I said, staring down at the jagged gash. "It's my turn."

She swallowed but didn't say anything as I worked on her hand. Just watched me fuss over her. Her skin was baby soft and smooth and felt like she'd never done a hard day of work in her life. Maybe she hadn't. After I cleaned and bandaged it, she closed her fingers over the bandage, squeezing. She gave me a small smile. "Thank you."

"You're welcome," I said. After I'd been hunched over her hand, my shoulder ached even more now, but it was worth it. Glancing down at my filthy body, I cringed. "About that shower?"

"Right."

She hopped to her feet and headed toward the closed door on the left wall. She walked past the bed and the dark wood dresser and into the other room. I followed more slowly, because the room was starting to spin, and my eyelids felt like they weighed a million pounds, and if I wasn't careful, I just might fall asleep on my feet.

Water turned on, and I came around the corner, sagging against the wall with a sigh. Yawning, I rubbed my eyes. "This is gonna feel good."

Buttons came in, meowed, and walked over to me again. He rubbed against me, purring almost as loudly as the water. She peeked down at the cat. "He likes you," she said thoughtfully. "He doesn't usually like strangers."

I stared at the cat and undid the button of my fly. "I don't know why."

"Me neither. I—" She turned around broke off. "What are you doing?" she called out, her voice alarmed.

I froze mid-unzip. "Undressing."

"I'm still in here."

"I was just undoing my pants, not getting naked. Have you never seen a guy in his boxers before?" I asked, amused at her reaction. It was no different from seeing me in swim trunks. "I assure you, I'm wearing some."

She closed the curtain, her cheeks red. "Give me a second, and I'll give you some privacy. Go on and get in, and I'll bring in a towel once you're inside the shower with the curtain pulled closed. You're obviously eager to get in."

"I'm fucking tired is what I am," I said.

She slipped past me, her body rigid. I held my jeans in place, since the idea of me in my boxers clearly bothered her. As she passed me, her attention dipped south, and my cock hardened. If she paid attention, she'd see my body react to her scrutiny.

No matter how beat-up I was, or how shitty I felt, nothing would stop me from responding to the heated interest she threw my way. Nothing short of death, anyway.

Maybe not even that.

"Are those from fights, too?"

I glanced down and blinked because my vision was blurring. I saw the knife wound from a fight I'd had when I was sixteen and another scar, courtesy of my father, this one three times bigger than the knife wound. "Some, yes. Some, no."

"You've lived quite the life, haven't you?"

I didn't answer.

What the fuck was I supposed to say to that?

"I'll leave you to get undressed now," she said softly, still studying my scars. I had a lot more, if she had a thing for them.

After she left, I let my remaining clothes hit the floor, wincing as I leaned on the sink to balance myself. Now that I was alone, I stopped hiding the fact that at any minute, I was bound to pass out and maybe never wake up. Somehow, I managed not to.

Breathing heavily, I stepped under the hot water and groaned. I couldn't help it. It felt way too damn good not to appreciate. An hour or two ago, I'd been sure I would die in that alley, alone aside from the rats and the roaches, and no one would care. But now I was showering, and it was warm, and it just went to show that good guys didn't finish first.

They finished last—after the bad guys like me.

No matter how much shit I did wrong, or how many cardinal sins I broke, I just kept coming up clean and grinning, and nothing would stop me. Nothing killed me.

And that kinda pissed me off.

It was time for me to pay my dues.

I placed my face under the water, letting it wash away all the evidence of my wrongdoings into a puddle of dark pink water swirling around my feet. But I knew, even after all the blood, dirt, and sweat washed away, I would still be dirty. I'd never be clean.

Nothing, and no one, could change that. My dirty soul was embedded in my DNA. I had been fucked since the moment I was conceived. Doomed to be a villain.

"Are you in the shower yet?" Molly called out.

"Yeah, you can come in," I said, leaning on the wall and running my hands down my face. I glanced at them. They were stained a wet reddish brown, despite washing them earlier. "Did you bring soap?"

"Yeah, and a washcloth." Her hand popped in, slim, white, and clean. "Shampoo, too. Sorry—I forgot there wasn't any in there."

I took the stuff, leaving dirty streaks on her wrist and hand. "You have nothing to apologize for. I'm the one who—" I broke off, laughing. "I'm the one who's getting your tub all dirty."

"It's just a tub."

"Yeah, and I'm just a guy." I opened the curtain and popped my head out. She gaped at me, her lids dropping as she took in every exposed inch of me as if she'd never seen a wet man before. "You didn't have to save me, and probably shouldn't have, but it's a debt I'll never forget. Thank you."

"You don't owe me anything," she said, rubbing her arms

and backing up. She'd placed a towel and a clean pair of pajamas on the sink counter. "It was the right thing to do."

"Still," I said, squaring my jaw. "I never back down from a favor owed, and if you need something from me, all you have to do is ask."

She shook her head. "I won't be asking."

"If you say so." I closed the curtain and stepped under the water again. "Regardless, I'll be waiting."

"You have a pretty bleak outlook on life."

Unable to resist, I peeked out the curtain at her again. "What tipped you off?"

"You're obviously not all jaded." She bit down on her lip, watching me. "Back at the pharmacy, you could have stolen my car. My purse. My life."

"I'm a shitty person, but I wouldn't do that to you," I said, my voice thick. I probably shouldn't have admitted that, but with her, for some reason, I wanted to be straight, no bullshit. She deserved it. "Never to you."

She rubbed her arm. "Which only goes to prove that no one is all bad, just like no one is all good. I refuse to believe you're as evil as you let on."

I gave her a once-over, lingering over her soft lips and sweet curves. "You're all good."

"Oh God." She laughed. "I'm not. I'm so not."

"I refuse to believe *that*," I said, turning her words back on her.

Silence, and then: "I'm going to let you shower in peace now," she said.

I didn't mind her chatter, which was funny, since on anyone else, I would have found it annoying as hell. But if she wanted to go, I'd let her. "All right."

The door shut behind her, and I sank down in the tub, knees folded in front of me, and stared blankly at the wall, not sure how to feel right now. This woman, this unselfish person, saw *good* in me. I didn't know why, or how, but it didn't change the fact that she *did*. And, God help us both, I wanted it to stay that way. Wanted her to see me as a person worth saving. I didn't want to let her down, like I had everyone else.

For some reason, it mattered to me that she liked me.

When it had never mattered with anyone else before.

I blinked down at the tub, watching as it turned pinkish red with the blood of my sins, and swallowed, dropping my head back against the wall. Quickly, I squeezed my eyes shut, not wanting to watch the evidence of what I'd done to Lucas circle down the drain. If she knew what I did—she would never look at me the same.

I'd tried to *kill* Lucas. My brother. My friend. My partner.

I'd tried to one-up a man who got pleasure out of beating me. A man who would never think I was good enough. Strong enough. Tough enough. Cold enough. And in the process of trying to show him he hadn't broken me, that I was a strong man despite his parenting, I'd somehow become him. How the hell did this become my life?

How the hell did this become *me*?

CHAPTER 6

MOLLY

Last night had been . . . surreal. In lots of ways. Some small part of me had expected to wake up and find out it had all been a crazy dream. Dad's room would be empty, my hand wouldn't be cut, and there wouldn't be a hot, injured, likely *wanted* criminal sleeping under my roof. But I woke up, saw my bandaged hand, and knew none of it had been a dream. It had happened.

I'd saved Chris O'Brien. Dad would be proud of me. But . . .

Now what was I supposed to *do* with him?

True to my word, I left in the morning, tiptoeing outside so as not to wake him up. On Sundays, I went to church and then worked at the shelter for abused women and children, washing sheets and setting up beds for incoming occupants. Today had been a lot harder to get through than normal.

Last night, I'd stayed up late washing his clothes and making sure he got out of the shower okay without passing out or dying. When I heard the water turn off, I waited fifteen minutes before peeking through the door. He'd been fast asleep in Dad's bed, wearing my father's favorite pajamas, a hand flung over his head and his injured arm folded over his chest.

For a second, I stared at him.

And I hadn't been able to look away.

There was something about him, and the way he made me feel, that called to me. That told me not to write him off or send him away. Maybe it was his utter certainty that he was a horrible person or the haunted emptiness in his dark brown eyes that made me want to help him. Heal him. Change him.

I couldn't shake the way he made me feel.

It was like he made me feel alive, or like I was finally doing something that mattered. Like I was finally doing something right. Maybe it was just because I was lonely and no one had stayed with me for a while, but having him under my roof felt . . . *good*. Even if it was dangerous, which there was no denying it was.

I had the undeniable feeling that I'd found him in that alleyway for a reason. Call it fate or destiny or luck. But it seemed like something, or someone, had wanted me to find him. That there was something to be done between the two of us.

Not, like, *sex*, or anything.

Yes, he was attractive. And no, I wasn't going to lie or pretend I didn't want him. I totally did. And he probably knew it. Guys like him always did. But I wouldn't act on it. Heck, I *never* acted on it, so I wasn't about to start now, with *him*. He'd eat me alive, spit me out, and bury me in the backyard when he was finished.

My life hadn't been all that exciting, and I hadn't been in numerous beds with numerous men. The only bed I slept in was my own. And I was always alone . . . unless you counted Buttons. There had been one guy in college. I'd been so sure I was ready. But his groping hands and wet kisses had done nothing to stir any desires, and it had been the worst night, and worst decision, of my life.

If I could take it back, I would. And, God, I wish I could. I would rather be a virgin for the rest of my life than have that memory in my head.

When I pulled into my driveway, I pushed the button and waited for the garage door to open. Either my house would be empty or there would be a man inside. Waiting for me. I wasn't sure yet which I preferred. But after I'd finished up my day at the shelter, I'd bought him some clothes, just in case it was the latter.

After the garage door shut behind me, I grabbed the wine I'd picked up—because, God, I needed some, no matter what waited for me inside—grabbed the bags of clothes, and headed for the door. Before I could open it, it swung inward, and Chris stood there. Barefoot, and still in pajamas. Buttons was behind him, staring up at him lovingly.

Guess I got my answer. He hadn't left.

I tried to ignore the surge of relief as I studied him for any signs of improvement. He still had bruises and scabs, his nose still had that broken look to it and was various shades of yellow and blue, but he was handsome as the devil, smiling, and he acted like a completely different guy from last night. He seemed . . . *normal.*

And my body responded to it.

God, did it respond.

"Hey, Princess." He held the door open, that grin never slipping from his handsome, perfect face. I had a feeling that grin was a façade. A way for him to hide what truly lay beneath . . . whatever that might be. "Welcome home."

I ducked under his hard, muscular arm. He smelled good. Not like the cologne he'd worn the other day, but like coconut shampoo and soap. Like *my* coconut shampoo and soap. "Th-thanks." I walked past him and breathed in deep. The house smelled delicious. Like . . . like . . . "Did you—?"

At the same time he blurted out, "I made dinner for you." He glanced out into the garage, shut the door, and locked it. All the blinds were still drawn, so we had complete privacy. It made sense, since he *was* hiding out and all. "I had to work with what you had, so I went with homemade fettuccine Alfredo."

My jaw dropped. "You . . . *cook*?"

"Yeah. Luc taught me. Since I don't plan on getting married, or ever living with a woman, I figured it was best for me to learn." He scratched the back of his head as if he couldn't believe he'd told me that voluntarily, and rushed forward. When he reached out, he couldn't hide a wince or his furrowed brow as he dropped his arm back to his side. "Here, let me take those."

"Don't hurt yourself," I said quickly, resting a hand on his forearm. "It's heavy."

"I won't. I'm fine." He shot me a quick grin, but his brow was covered in sweat, as if he'd taxed himself too hard. "I'm a quick healer. It hurts, but a good night's sleep did wonders for me. I'll be out of your hair in no time at all. I just wanted to cook for you as a thank-you for all you did. Oh. And I fed your cat."

"Oh. Thanks." I shrugged out of my coat and laid it on the chair by the island, frowning. Buttons stepped between us and meowed. Chris held on to the bags with his good arm, which left only his injured one free. "I'm glad to hear you're better. I got you some clothes. Go on. Take a look."

He stared at me, his jaw flexing, and set the bags down.

Then he rummaged through the one that held the clothes with his good arm, leaving the other hanging limply at his side. "This is all great. Thanks. I'll pay you back."

"You can pay me back by staying here till you're actually better." I took the clothes out of his hand and shoved them back in the bag. "How about that?"

He flexed his jaw, not bothering to deny he wasn't healed yet. "No. I can't stay. It's too dangerous."

"No one knows you're here." I turned back to him and crossed my arms. "And who would think to look for you at my house?"

"Bitter Hill. You can guarantee they've got a guy outside."

"All the more reason to stay here, since they're probably watching next door, not here." I tapped my foot. His gaze dipped down and back up. "I won't tell anyone. I promise, you'll be safe here."

"I'm not worried about me. I'm worried about you. If anyone somehow found out about me staying here, you'd be caught in a shit storm of a war that you have no part in, and I refuse to put you in danger."

I crossed my arms, inspecting him. "I didn't save you only to let you die. You stay. End of story."

He laughed. Actually laughed. "First of all, you 'saving' me doesn't give you any rights over me. And second, I don't know when you got the impression I was a guy easily bossed around, but I'm not. I don't take orders; I give them. So you can—"

"Not here, you don't." I frowned and did my best *I saw you eat that paste* look. "Here, we talk it out. And I say you stay."

Amusement crossed his expression. "No matter how injured I might be, you can't physically stop me from going."

"You're right. I can't win against you." I uncrossed my

arms and walked up to him, resting my hand on his uninjured arm. "But believe it or not, I do like you. And I want to make sure you're okay before you leave. Is that so bad?"

"Yes. It's bad that you like me," he said, his voice gruff. "Liking me will get you nowhere good. Trust me. I would know."

"I'm sure there are people who like you. Like . . . ah, what's his name?" I racked my brain for his friend's name . . . the guy who used to come around with him. He had reddish brown hair and green eyes, and Chris had just said his name . . . "Aha! Lucas, for starters. And his little brother, Scotty."

Something cold and hard slid over his expression. I stumbled back a step, because for the first time since I'd met him, he looked like a killer. I tripped over my purse, and he caught my arm tightly, saving me from going down. "Lucas is gone. Don't bring him up again. Don't even mention his damn name to me."

My mouth dropped open at his angry tone, and I tried to tug free. His grip tightened painfully. "Okay, fine." I tugged again, but he didn't let go. He had a far-off look in his eye that, quite frankly, scared me. Wherever he was, whatever he saw right now, it wasn't me. And it wasn't here. "Chris. You're *hurting* me. Let go."

"I—" He glanced down at his grip on me, his brow furrowed. As soon as he saw how tight he held me, he dropped my arm and paled even more. "Shit. I'm so sorry. I didn't mean—" He cut off and dragged a hand down his face. "I'm going now. Enjoy the dinner, and thanks for the help." He started to walk past me but paused. Gently, he reached out and touched my cheek. "I'm sorry, Princess."

I nodded once, rubbing my arm.

He fisted his hands and started for the door, limping. I watched him go, torn between wanting to stop him and being scared of that icy-coldness I'd just seen. I glanced at the fettuccine cooking on the stove, water bubbling happily, and swallowed hard.

Buttons followed Chris.

"Don't go." I stopped rubbing my arm and stepped closer. "It's okay."

"In no world, in no place, is it okay that I hurt you." He spun on me, his face ravaged, and if there had been any doubt in my mind that he felt bad for grabbing me a little too tightly, it would be gone now. It was written all over his face, clear as day. "That's what guys like me do. We hurt people. And if you let me, I'll hurt you, too—worse than a sore arm. I'm no good for you. Just let me *go*."

"I can't," I whispered, locking eyes with him. "I won't."

"Why the hell not?" he asked, his voice torn. "I'm nobody. Nothing."

"That's not true." The way he watched me—half with fear, and half with something I couldn't name—shook me to my core. "I don't understand it, or the reasons behind it, but I can't let you leave. And it sounds crazy, but I just know, somehow, that you're supposed to be here right now. With *me*."

It sounded crazy when I said it like that, but it didn't make it any less true.

His jaw ticked, and he closed the distance between us, backing me into the wall. I sucked in a breath, but his touch was gentle as he caught my hands and trapped them above my head. "Is that what this is about? You want me to fuck you? Show you what it's like to get in bed with a bad boy before you settle down with another Ivy League graduate like yourself? Take you for a ride on the wild side for a night?"

"I—*no*." I shook my head, but it wasn't entirely true. With his hard body pressed against mine, and his face inches from mine, it would be a lie to say the thought hadn't crossed my mind. But that didn't mean I would *act* on it. "That's not what I meant."

"Then what?" He pressed against me even more, and despite my relative inexperience in this area . . . there was no denying that right now, right here, he wanted me. And knowing that? Yeah, it probably wasn't the best thing for me. "What do you want?"

"Nothing." I licked my lips and a nervous laugh escaped me. "I swear, all I want to do is help you. That's it."

He looked at me as if he didn't understand. As if the mere concept of someone doing something out of the goodness of their heart wasn't real. And in his world, it probably wasn't. "That's it?"

"That's it," I echoed.

Something in him softened, shifted, and his grip on my wrists loosened. He trailed his thumbs over my skin tenderly, but he didn't back off me. If anything, his lower half pressed closer to me, showing me just how hard he was . . . *everywhere.* "You can't be for real. No one is that selfless."

"My dad helped people. Gave them places to go when they needed it. Set up a shelter for homeless women and children." I bit down on my lip, because he was still staring at me as if I was an enigma he couldn't figure out. "I'm simply following in his footsteps by helping you, like he would have. Trying to make him proud, even though he's not here anymore. Can't you understand that?"

His fingers flexed on my wrists. "Yeah. I get that."

"So let me do it."

"You're fucking amazing," he said, his voice low and almost . . . reverent. "You shouldn't waste all that compassion on me."

"I choose who gets it." I wriggled against him, feeling restlessly trapped—but in a *good* way. In a way that made my pulse rush and my thighs ache to be filled with . . . something. Him, maybe. "I choose you, and nothing you say or do will change that."

"Come on, now." He leaned in closer. So close that all it would take was a small movement toward him, and our lips would touch. Neither of us moved. "I bet *that's* not true. What if I kissed you, right here, right now, and showed you just how bad I can be? What if I fucked you against this wall, hard and rough, just the way I like it? How quickly would you push me away after? How fast would you regret letting a guy like me fuck you?"

We wouldn't get that close, and we wouldn't do that, because Chris scared me. He made me feel too much, too strongly, and I wasn't about to let him closer.

Wasn't about to let him make me feel even *more*.

"You're just trying to scare me off again." My breath caught in my throat and a small moan escaped me when he rolled his hips. There was no holding it back. "You have no idea how I would feel afterward. And you never will, because it's a bad idea."

"Most things that feel good are." Slowly, his lids dropped, and he studied the way I bit my lower lip. "That's what makes them so much fun. You know, I've been telling myself not to do this. Not to touch you. But maybe if I do, you'll finally let me go." He did that magical roll of his hips again. "All women do, after they get what they want out of me."

I tried to squeeze my thighs together, but his knee slipped in between them. When he pressed against my core, I gasped. "Chris . . ."

"I can see it in your eyes, you know." He lowered his face to mine. "The desire burning for me, for this. You want me. You want this."

A ragged breath escaped me, and I nodded once. "But—"

"Shh." For a minute—an intoxicating, thrilling, earth-shattering minute—I thought he was going to actually kiss me. He even leaned in, his nose brushing mine, and his warm breath fanned over my mouth. "It'll be okay."

I let my eyelids drift closed, knowing that I could say no but not making a sound.

Some part of me—some deep, dark part that I never listened to—whispered that this was what I'd wanted all along. That he was right. I had an ulterior motive for wanting to be with him. I didn't. But I could still kiss him, couldn't I? Just once, just for this one second, I wanted to see what it felt like to be held, touched, by a man I actually wanted.

Just this once, I wanted to *live*.

A desperate whimper escaped me.

Buttons sat on my foot and meowed.

"Shit." Chris froze, his whole body held stiffly against mine. "I'm sorry, Princess."

I shivered, frustration boiling inside of me until I was sure I would explode. "It's okay. We just got caught up in the moment. No big deal."

"It is." His gaze dipped down to my mouth one last time, stealing my breath away. "It won't happen again. I swear it."

A muscle in his cheek ticked, and he pushed off the wall, letting me go.

I wasn't sure whether to scream, cry, or sag in relief. I settled for collapsing against the wall, my breaths coming fast and uneven. "Now that you know I won't require anything in return, will you stay a little longer?"

He gave me his back, gripping the counter, and laughed. "You're either foolish, too compassionate for your own good, or completely insane. I'm not sure which."

I ignored his possible insult. I wasn't crazy for caring whether he lived or died. I was *human*. That was all. "Is that a yes?"

Shaking his head, he laughed again. "It's a maybe. I'll think about it."

"I suppose that's enough."

Taking a deep breath, he headed for the stove. He still didn't look at me. "It'll have to be, because that's all I have."

"Deal," I said, holding on to the counter behind me. It was the only thing keeping me up, because, oh my God, that *almost* kiss had *almost* floored me. "Dinner smells great. I love Alfredo."

"I hoped as much," he said, watching me as if he half expected me to bite him or something. "It'll be ready in three minutes."

"Great."

We fell silent, and I watched as he stirred the sauce. His dark tattoos swirled down his arms. I saw a dragon and a Chinese symbol and a silhouette of a woman with big boobs. Words were on the backs of his biceps, but I couldn't make them out.

Something about strength, maybe?

The flannel pajamas hugged him in all the right places, showing me just how hard and perfect his rear end was. And for the life of me, I couldn't look away. I mean, it was hard and pert and would probably fill my—

"Molly?" he said, his voice amused.

I jumped. "Yeah?"

"I asked you if you'd like to open the wine," he said, straight-faced but clearly laughing internally. So. He'd caught me admiring his rear. *Greeeat.* "I saw you brought some home?"

"Oh. *Right.* Wine." I nodded a little too enthusiastically. "That's a *great* idea."

He laughed, and his face lit up. I could count on one

hand—maybe one finger—the number of times I'd seen him smile with actual amusement. And when he did—God, he had dimples in his cheeks, too. And he seemed softer. Less scary.

But when he laughed . . .

God, he was like a completely different man.

Like he didn't do what he did for a living, his hands clean of blood, and he was just a normal guy, in a kitchen, cooking dinner. When he laughed, it was as if he wasn't carrying the weight of all the things he'd done in his life on his shoulders in that moment. Something told me he needed that. He needed to forget.

I wanted to make him laugh every day he was here.

Show him what life could be, if you stopped to enjoy it.

"Can you open it yourself?" he asked, still smiling.

If I say no, will I get to watch you flex those muscles for me? "Yes, of course." I opened the drawer that held the corkscrew but didn't get it out. Instead, I shut it again before reopening it. "Huh. That's weird."

"What?" he asked, craning his neck to look down at the floor. Buttons sat behind him, grooming himself. "What's wrong?"

"This drawer always got stuck halfway open."

"Oh. That." He turned back to the stove. "I noticed it was stuck earlier when I was looking for measuring cups, so I fixed it."

I blinked down at it. "Wow. Thank you."

"It was nothing," he said quickly, not meeting my eyes.

But it wasn't nothing. I wasn't handy, and I had no idea how to fix anything, so I'd been putting off calling a guy to come look at it until I had enough projects to make it worth the handyman's time. Knowing Chris had seen it and fixed it for me without being asked made my heart wrench. It wasn't a huge thing. It wasn't much at all, really. But it had been a long time since I'd had a man in the house who would help out, and it showed me just how alone I was, and how long I'd been that way. Five years and one day.

I'd found him yesterday, on the anniversary of my father's death, bleeding in that alley, only because I'd stupidly slashed open my palm. My father had been watching over me last night, and he'd led me straight to Chris . . .

A man clearly in need of some benevolence in his life.

It only made me all the more certain that keeping him around was the right thing to do. That a guy like Chris, who fixed things without being asked, had a softness inside that his life couldn't destroy, no matter how dark it might be. That some way, somehow, my father had led me to him so I could follow in his footsteps and help people like he had when he'd been alive. That Chris could be saved . . .

And *I* would be the one to do it.

CHAPTER 7

CHRIS

Molly sat on the couch, hugging her knees, staring at a couple making out on a beach. I walked into the living room slowly, watching *her* watch *them*. She bit down on her lip, her fingers tightening on her calves, and leaned in, completely enamored with the couple on the screen. When they broke off the kiss, she let out a soft exhalation and leaned back against the couch cushions again.

She kind of *deflated*.

I'd been at her house for two days now, and that was two days too long. All this time to sit here and think had been good for me, but my time at Molly's was drawing to a close. After some deep meditation and lots of internal debating, I'd decided on a course of action that would set me on the path of redemption.

I knew what I had to do.

I was ready.

She glanced over her shoulder, jumping slightly when she saw me standing there. "Geez. You scared me."

"Sorry." I offered her a grin. "I was just watching the show."

"You like *The Bachelor*?"

Hell no. "Yeah."

"Wow." She scooted over and patted the spot on the couch next to her. "Then sit. Watch it with me."

Swearing internally, I walked around the side of the couch and sank into the softness. "Who was just kissing?"

"Aaron and Maggie."

I nodded as if I had an idea who the fuck they were. "Is she your top pick?"

"Yeah. She's a teacher, like me." She looked at me but quickly turned away. "And he's a doctor. They seem like a good fit."

"Is that who you want in your life? A doctor?"

Buttons hopped up on the couch and curled up on my lap. Molly side-eyed the cat and tucked her hair behind her ears. "I don't really think about that much."

"Why not?" I scratched the cat's head, right between his ears, where he liked it. "You seem the type to plan your life out like that. The man. The kids. The school district."

She shook her head. "No. I meant that I don't think about what type of guy I'm going to marry. I obviously haven't met him yet, and might never."

"I wouldn't be so sure. I'm sure your guy is out there." I frowned down at the cat, not liking how murderous the idea of her with another man made me feel. Like I wanted to be a real bad guy and kill a good guy for once. "You just haven't found him yet."

She lifted a shoulder. "I'm not exactly looking, if we're being honest."

"Why not?"

She pursed her lips. "Why aren't you?"

"Have you seen the life I lead?" I asked, raising a brow. "It's not exactly conducive to getting married and starting a family. I'm better off on my own."

"Maybe I feel that way, too."

I snorted. "That your life is too dangerous for a man to handle?"

"No. That life is too dangerous for me to handle." She let out a nervous laugh. "I lost a person I loved once. It hurt. A lot. If I'm going to take that chance on someone again, if I'm going to open myself up to that pain, then it's going to have to be for someone pretty freaking special. I have yet to meet him. That's all I'm saying."

I didn't know what to say to that. It made sense. She'd been hurt before and didn't want to be hurt again. I *got* that. "But that shouldn't make you scared to open yourself up again. The chances of you losing another person that way— they're pretty damn slim. You don't exactly live in Steel Row. Just stay out of there, and keep your man out of there, and you'll be good to go."

She blew out a breath, moving her hair. "Like I said, if I meet someone worth taking a risk on, I'll deliberate on it at that time. But to plan, and worry, and dream about who he might be? What's the point of that?"

I stared at her, my hand on Buttons' back. "That's an awfully bleak outlook on life for you."

"No one can be all sunshiny happy all the time, can they?"

"I always just assumed you were," I answered honestly.

"Well, you assumed wrong." She reached out and patted Buttons on the head. Our hands were so close, yet we didn't touch. It felt like we had. "Ugh. I hate her."

I tore my eyes off Molly and looked back at the screen. A redheaded woman talked animatedly, her hands flying with every word. She looked like she had more silicone than real body parts, and like she was about as deep as a puddle. The guy sat beside her, watching her, but he seemed less than impressed. "Don't worry. He's not into her."

She blinked at me. "How can you be so sure?"

"Look at him." I pointed at the TV. "When he looks at her, there's nothing in his eyes. No desire. No warmth. No heat. It's just a dead stare. And he's leaning away from her, as if he can't wait to walk away." I dropped my hand back to Buttons. "He's got more interest in that couch than he does in her."

Her jaw dropped. "Wow. You're good."

"It's my job to be good. To read people." I shifted uneasily. I failed to mention that I then used the way people reacted against them. That I found their weaknesses and exploited them. Like I had with Lucas. I set Buttons down and stood up. "Want some wine?"

"Sure," she said quickly.

I walked out to the kitchen, needing some space. Sitting on that couch with her, watching some bullshit reality show, had felt way too domestic. Like what we had was real—when it wasn't. I wasn't sticking around, and she wouldn't miss me when I left. I was just some charity case she'd brought into her home in some misguided attempt to be more like her father. Her father had been a good man who helped lots of people—

And look what it had gotten him. An unceremonious death in Steel Row. She was better off keeping to herself, like she'd been doing all along.

After I got us some Red Moscato, I walked back into the living room. The bachelor dude now sat at a romantic dinner with a brunette. She was pretty enough, but something about her was off. As if she was in this only for the fame.

"Dude. This guy gets around."

She glanced over her shoulder at me. "Yeah."

"Who the hell needs to be on a show for an excuse to fuck around?" I handed her a glass and settled back down, crossing an ankle over my thigh. "If you want to play the field, do it without the cameras in your face."

"That's not the point," she argued. "The point is to fall in love and get married."

"Yeah. And I'm the pope."

She choked on her wine. I grinned. "Sure you are."

"Seriously, though, how many of these guys actually get married?"

She set her wine down and wiped her mouth with the back of her hand. "Uh . . ."

"Exactly. They're looking to get fucked, not married." I lifted my glass to the screen. "And they're totally sleeping together."

"What?" She glanced at the screen in horror. *"No."*

I laughed at her horrified expression. I couldn't help it. She acted as if I'd told her he drowned puppies in his spare time. "Yep."

She sank back against the pillow, pouting. "Well, crap."

"Sorry," I said, still chuckling.

"Whatever." The show went to commercial, and she reached for her wine again. "So, you never want to settle down. Have some kids."

I winced. Why the hell would I want to hand my kid the same type of life I led? Like me, he wouldn't have much of a choice when it came to what he did with his life. If you were born into this life, you accepted it. You embraced it. I refused to do that to my kid. Refused to bring another little Son into this life. "Hell no."

"I see." She shifted her weight. Buttons came back on my lap. "What about you? Would you change your mind about being single if you met a girl who changed everything?"

"No."

"How can you be so sure?" She stared at me. "So certain?"

I'd already met that girl, and she sat beside me. But considering my current course of action, and how my plan would more than likely play out, I wouldn't be around long enough for her to make me think I deserved her in my life. "Because I am."

CHAPTER 8

MOLLY

❧

I swallowed a big gulp of wine, not meeting his eyes. Knowing he wasn't even remotely open to the possibility of a relationship wasn't shocking or even surprising. With the life he led, it made perfect sense. But for some reason . . .

It made me sad.

Yeah, I wasn't exactly receptive to the idea of love and marriage myself, but I was at least open to the possibility . . . in theory. But he refused to even think about it and had dedicated himself to a life of solitude. "How does that make you feel?"

He stared at me as if I'd asked him if he liked to suck his own toes, or something equally insulting. "It doesn't make me *feel* anything."

My lips twitched at the way he said that, all deep and manly. "Sorry. I didn't mean to imply you might not be a robot inside."

"Well, don't make that mistake again." He dragged a hand

through his hair. Buttons meowed, and Chris immediately went back to rubbing the cat's head. Those two had bonded something fierce over the past two days. "Did you say something about a spring break over dinner?"

Effective change of topic. "Yeah. It starts Wednesday."

"All right." He pointed at the TV. It was a commercial for a show that took place in Scotland. "That's beautiful. I'd love to go there and draw the landscapes."

Wait. He *drew*? "You—?" Before I could actually ask him about his hobby, he cut me off.

"Now, that?" He frowned at the TV. An ad was playing for Dior cologne. "That shit smells awful. A buddy of mine pours it on like it's bathwater, and it's so strong I smell it for hours after I get home. I swear my body absorbs it and releases it little by little just to fuck with me."

A laugh bubbled out of me. "Somehow I doubt that."

"I don't," he said dismissively. "How long will you be off?"

I blinked at the quick change back to our original topic. "A week and a half."

"Damn." He whistled through his teeth. "All that for Easter?"

"Spring break." I lifted the wineglass to my lips. "We don't call it Easter break anymore."

"Right. I forgot—" He broke off and picked up the remote.

His frown deepened, so I turned back to the TV to see what had him all worked up this time. A news segment was playing. He turned it up.

"Today in South Boston, in what was believed to be a gang-related shoot-out that broke out on Wescott and Bitter Hill Road, three men and a child were gunned down."

Chris sat forward, Buttons forgotten on his lap. "Shit."

"Authorities believe it was a territory dispute between two rival gangs, and the child was not the intended target.

*Three have been taken into custody and are expected to be
charged with murder in the first degree."*

"Son of a bitch." He dragged a hand through his hair again
and turned down the volume. "That was Bitter Hill and Old
Forge. Guaranteed."

"Are you . . . friends with them?"

"Hell no." His forehead wrinkled, and he gripped the glass
tighter. "But I sold them the guns. I gave them the weapons
to gun down children on corners."

I swallowed hard. Sometimes, I forgot what he did. Who
he was. But then he said things like this, and I remembered
all too well what it was he did for a living. "Why do you do it?"

"Because it's my life. That's why. That's what I always
told myself, anyway. That's what I said." He picked Buttons
up and set him on the couch gently, despite the irritation in
his voice. "And it's time I got back to that life."

"N-now?"

"Soon." He set his glass down. "I just need to contact a
few people, set some things in motion, and then I'm back
out there."

"But—"

"It's time to make good. I've done a lot of shit in my life,
and so has everyone in the gang," he said, covering his face.
"I get it now. I understand why Scotty does what he does."

I blinked. "What does Scotty do?"

"He cleans up shit. I thought he was doing wrong, that
he was betraying us, but I was wrong. We're the ones doing
wrong. He's just trying to set it right." He lowered his hands.
The pain and determination I saw in his eyes sent an answering ping of fear through my chest. "And I'm going to help
him. I'm going back in. I'm staying."

Though I wasn't sure exactly what he was talking about
with Scotty and all that, I understood that last part. I lifted my

leg, resting my heel on the couch, and hugged my knee to my chest. "You're ready?"

"Yeah." His jaw flexed. "I'm ready. Now, if you'll excuse me?"

He walked off without another word, heading up the stairs. I listened to his footsteps, waiting to hear the bedroom door shut. Once it did, I let out a sigh. Having him around, acting like a normal guy, had been tough tonight. In a way, I was grateful for that news segment. For that hard, cold reality of what he was.

It made it easier to keep him at arm's length, despite my attraction to him, when the evidence of his crimes was staring me in the face. It reminded me that he wasn't the guy for me. How could I be with someone who *killed* people for a living? Who gave criminals the weapons to cause harm to the city I loved? How could I want him?

And yet . . . I did.

I really did.

CHAPTER 9

CHRIS

"Son of a fucking whoreson *bitch*," I growled.

It was the next day, after that odd night on her couch when I'd watched some corny-ass dating show, and I was still here, lying under Molly's dining room table with sweat pouring down my face. Buttons meowed over my head, batting at my hair, and I flinched at the claws scraping my scalp.

I shook the hand I'd just poked with a screwdriver, glowering at it, and ignored the cat. The table had been wobbling ever since I got here, but it wasn't until today that I felt strong enough to tackle the job. Under Molly's watchful care, my shoulder had gotten better each day, and it was now more of a dull ache than a screaming pain.

Every night, she checked it, cleaned it, and bandaged it up. Even last night, after I'd locked myself away behind her father's door, she'd knocked and asked if she could come in to look at my shoulder. I, of course, had let her in. I didn't

know what to do with her. In all my life, I'd never had someone who cared so much about my well-being.

Yeah, I had Lucas, but we'd been dudes. We didn't call
each other and ask how each other's *boo-boos* were feeling.
We got together. We drank shit. We shot assholes.

And then we went home. Alone.

The past two mornings, she'd woken up at six on the dot.
I'd made sure to be up by quarter of six, and to have a hot mug
of coffee waiting for her. Then she'd left for work, and I'd tried
my hand at fixing shit around the house. When she'd come
home at six, I had dinner and a glass of wine waiting for her.
I tried to take care of her, and she did the same for me. It felt
right. And playing house had taught me something about
myself, too.

I could have been different.

My life didn't need to be all murder, guns, and meaning-
less sex. It could've been more—if I'd been born into another
family. Another life. But I hadn't been.

The longer I stayed with her, the higher the chances got
that I just might dirty that pure heart of hers. And yet, I hadn't
left, because I was still coming up with a game plan—and
putting all my pawns in place on the chessboard. I knew what
I had to do now, and I was prepared to do anything to succeed,
but I had to be careful.

I played a dangerous game.

One wrong move, and *bam*. I'd be off the board too soon.

Tate Daniels, the head of Steel Row, had been texting me
all day long, telling me we were almost ready to take action
against Bitter Hill and that he'd let me know when he was
ready for me to return. I played my part well, slurring my voice
as I told him I was out drinking and fucking Lucas's death out
of my mind.

Scotty had called me a few times, too, wanting to talk. I

didn't answer—I wasn't ready to. He probably wanted to make sure I wasn't going to blow his story or tell anyone Lucas was really alive. I wouldn't. Not that he'd believe me, but it was *true*.

After this short time of normalcy with Molly, I was finally starting to understand the way Lucas had been with Heidi. Why he'd been willing to give up everything, all that power, for a girl. For a shot at a regular life. One that didn't require you to sleep with a gun in your hand, one where your job description didn't include shooting assholes in the head— before you were shot first.

For the first time since being a kid, I wanted a different life than the one I had. I wanted to pretend that I wasn't a killer and that I wasn't unredeemable.

I wanted to believe I could be a *good* guy.

Back when I was still in school, I'd expressed an interest in becoming a doctor to Pops, instead of joining the gang. My grades were good enough to open up a lot of choices to me, and even back then, I'd been the go-to guy for when someone in the gang needed stitching up. I still was.

When I had told Pops of my dream, he laughed in my face and beat the shit outta me. Afterward, he sneered and told me to go fix myself up, if I was such a damn good doctor. Ma had watched as he beat me, her arms crossed as blood poured down my face. That had been the first, and last, time I'd mentioned my dreams.

But I did have hope once.

Dreams about a future that would save lives rather than take them. And it had been glorious. Freeing. I'd forgotten about that, and the way it made me feel, until now.

Here.

With Molly.

And that's why now, more than ever, I wouldn't betray

Lucas. He'd found a way to get that, to escape this life by running, and there was no way I would ruin that for him. And I wouldn't rat out his little brother, either. Lucas loved Scotty, and now that Luc was gone, it was up to me to make sure Scotty didn't get himself killed playing the hero cop.

I couldn't take back what I'd done to Lucas. Couldn't show him how sorry I was. But I could keep his brother alive and make sure that Tate never suspected that Scotty was a Boy, or I could die trying. That was my job. That was my penance.

And I'd see it done.

I glared up at my palm, at the old scar Lucas and I had made when we became blood brothers. I'd broken that vow. I wouldn't break this one. Not this time. Scotty was safe, and Lucas was, too, and I'd keep playing my part till I couldn't play it anymore. It would be up to me to show Scotty I was a changed man, and that he could count on me to have his back. That I was willing and ready to do what it took to keep him alive and to help him clean up Steel Row, one body at a time.

In my opinion, it was a lost cause. You couldn't wash away bloodstains on white shirts, and that's what Steel Row was. It was a permanent, fucked-up stain in Boston's Southie section. But if Scotty believed he could do it, I would believe in it, too. I would be his man. His eyes. His ears. His voice. And if it got me killed?

At least I'd go down doing something good, for once in my life.

That had to count for *something*.

Shaking my sore hand off, I set down the screwdriver, picked up a wrench, and torqued the bolt tight, grinning when it finally slipped into place. "Fuck yeah."

My phone buzzed beside my head, and I glanced over at it. It was from an old buddy from Bitter Hill who often gave me intel. If he was calling me, the news wouldn't be good. Setting the tools down, I picked up my iPhone and swiped my finger across the screen. "Yeah?"

Not wasting time, he said, "Reggie's pissed about what happened to his guys, and he's gonna make a point that his men aren't disposable."

"What's he planning?" I asked quickly. More than likely, it would be a direct attack on me, and if that was the case, there was no way in hell I would be hanging around here anymore. I wouldn't put Molly in more danger than I already had.

He sighed. "They're going after Tommy, Scotty, and a few other lieutenants. And, of course, you. But they can't figure out where you're hiding. Wherever you are, I suggest you stay there."

I gritted my teeth. "Thanks for the heads-up, man."

"Anytime."

I dropped my phone on my chest and rubbed my forehead. Well, shit. Now I had to decide how best to handle this intel and who to give it to. Normally, I would go directly to Tate with it. But now that I owed Scotty, he should be my go-to guy. He had resources I didn't, and bosses to answer to, and lies to maintain.

If I was gonna keep him alive, I had to keep him informed.

I'd already decided on this path last night, while sitting next to Molly, after seeing what had happened to that little boy. But still. This was a big fucking deal. After years of giving my loyalty to Tate Daniels and all the men in the gang . . . I was about to call a Boy. A *cop*. Never before had I trusted one of *those*.

How could I do so now? How could I *not*?

Gritting my teeth, I hovered over Tate but selected Scotty on my phone. He picked up on the second ring. "Where the hell are you?"

I laughed, short and hard. "Like I'm gonna tell a cop?"

"I'm not—" Scotty didn't finish that sentence. After a long pause, he said, "You know?"

"Of course I know." I gripped the phone tighter. "Only a Boy could play off the shit you did, and so fast, too. We both know that the dental records for Lucas and Heidi shouldn't match up, but they do. So tell me how it's possible that I watched them drive off into the sunset, to live happily ever after, and yet the dental records match?"

A door shut. "Maybe I've just got connections."

"Bullshit." I laughed again. "We both know that's not the case, don't we?"

"So if that's true, why haven't you told Tate about me yet?"

I paused, considering my answer carefully. "Because when a man finds himself alone in the world, with a bounty on his head, he starts to reevaluate what's important in life. I never should have turned on Lucas. I—I regret it. All of it."

"That's what any guy in your situation would say," Scotty snapped.

"True." I rubbed my forehead with my free hand. The movement hurt my shoulder, but I didn't even wince. Too much was at stake to be distracted now. "But I could also go to Tate and tell him I know your dirty little secret. I didn't. And I won't. Your secret is safe with me. So is Lucas's."

"So you say." Something shuffled, and I could just picture Scotty sitting at his desk, a case file open in front of him, like a real fucking cop. "For all I know, you showed Tate that bloody note Lucas gave you, and you told Tate the truth about me. The second I show up at Steel Row again, I'm dead, and you win."

I didn't want that note anymore, or the power the note would give me. I'd pulled it out of my jeans pocket and stashed it away in Mr. Lachlan's room, but I had no intention of actually using it. It wouldn't work, and even if it did, I didn't want it. Not anymore.

But Scotty would never believe that.

"The same could be said for me," I argued. "You could have ratted me out, too. What I did is enough to get me jumped out of the gang, at the very least. More than likely, it's a death sentence. One I fully deserve. I should be gutted, dismembered, and burned alive—like the traitor I am. That's what we do to guys like me."

"I agree. You deserve it."

I laughed. What the hell else was I supposed to do when he was right to want me dead? "At least we see eye to eye on one thing."

"The only thing," Scotty said, his voice hard.

"Well, you'll probably get your wish. The night is young yet."

Scotty sighed. "What you did was fucked-up, man. Lucas trusted you. Loved you. And even worse? You led him to believe *I* was trying to kill him. My own brother. And he trusted you enough to believe you over me—his brother."

Guilt, a familiar weight, settled on my shoulders. It would never go away, because I would never forgive myself for it. For any of it. "I know. I'm sorry. I really am. If there was a way for me to let Lucas know I regretted my actions, I would."

"But you can't. Because he's *dead*."

I gritted my teeth. "We both know that's not true."

"As far as the Sons go, it is." Scotty sighed. "We should be in the habit of saying it out loud so we don't slip up."

I snorted. "Real tips from a real cop. I feel honored."

Scotty was silent for a while, and I didn't blame him. He was probably trying to decide whether to trust me or not. I wouldn't blame him if he decided not to. I wouldn't trust me, either. "Why did you call me? Just to tell me you know my secret? To threaten me?"

"No. No threats."

"Then what?" Scotty asked.

"I fucked up, man, but I won't do it again. I know where my loyalties lie now. I heard from a guy in Bitter Hill. He gave me some intel. Reliable shit." I glowered up at the bottom of the table, knowing this was a life-changing moment. That it was the second I changed sides and started working with the "good" guys, but it sure as hell didn't make me good. "I just wanted to warn you—Bitter Hill is coming for you. They can't get Lucas, so they decided you're second best. You, Tommy, and a couple of other lieutenants."

I left out the part about the hit on me. It was redundant to point it out.

We both knew why they wanted me dead.

He cursed under his breath. "And you're telling me this because . . . ?"

"I let down Lucas. Hurt him." I sucked in a deep breath, my heart pounding so loudly in my head I couldn't make out my thoughts. "I can't take it back, but I can do my best to keep his little brother safe for him. From now on, that's what I'm gonna do. From now on, I'm in your pocket."

Silence, followed by: "You can't be serious."

"I am. Dead fucking serious."

"You're willing to turn your back on your pops, who would go down hard as the lieutenant of incoming shipments?"

"Yes." I ground my teeth together. "I meant what I said. I can't make it right, but the least I can do is make sure you're still breathing. So watch your back."

Scotty made a frustrated sound. "This could be a ploy. Another attempt at a power play. Get me to trust you enough to turn my back on you, and you pop me when I'm not looking."

"You're right." I laughed harshly. "It could be, but it's not. If you don't believe me, I understand why. But it's the truth. Stay alive, kid."

I hung up, staring down at the phone I held.

Well, I'd done it. I'd betrayed the man who trusted me, but now I'd turned on my whole gang—including Pops. And you know what? It felt pretty damn good, too.

With one phone call, I'd changed my destiny.

I wasn't so foolish as to think it made me a good guy, or that it meant I could change. After what I did, and who I did it to, I couldn't. There was nothing to be done that could change my course in life. It was time for me to leave this little slice of heaven I'd found, and the softhearted angel who came with it. Molly Lachlan. As if on cue, the door opened and Molly came in, juggling her bag, a purse, and a grocery bag filled with food.

Today she wore a red dress with a belt at the waist, and she was as fresh and clean as always. And just as untouch-able, too. "Chris?"

Every day, she came in and called out my name, as if she expected me to be gone without a proper good-bye. And the thing was, she was right. When I left, there wouldn't be any tender words or soft gestures. No lingering hugs or hesitation. Guys like me didn't deserve that. We just slunk away back into the darkness, where we belonged.

Alone.

"Down here," I said, scooting out from underneath the table.

She scanned the room till she spotted me, and relief filled her features the second she did. I had no idea why, but she

actually wanted me here. She liked me, which was fucked-up.
A smile lit up her beautiful face, and her hazel eyes brightened, and she was even more angelic than ever before.

If she was the angel, I was the devil.

And it was time she booted my ass outta here.

"Oh." She set the bags down and shrugged out of her coat.
Her slim form twisted and turned, and I couldn't look away
from her tiny waist or the soft curves of her body. Perfection.
That's what she was. "What are you doing down there?"

"I was fixing your table." I stood and rubbed my hands
on my jeans, but they didn't come clean. The symbolism of
the moment wasn't lost on me. "It wobbled."

Her soft pink lips curved up into a smile. When she did
that, the freckles on her cheeks danced about her pale skin,
and it was as charming as it was enticing. "You don't have
to fix stuff for me. You know that, right?"

"It's the least I can do, since you let me stay here so long."

Her smile wobbled and faded. "Do I sense a past-tense
tone to that sentence?"

"Molly." I forced a smile and walked over to her, grabbing the grocery bags off the counter and heading for the
fridge. "At some point, I'm gonna have to go. It's not like
I'm moving in permanently as your butler or something."

She blinked at me, not laughing at my attempt at humor.
"Of course not. You're absolutely right."

When she turned away from me, rummaging through
her purse, I studied her profile. As unlikely as it might seem,
I cared about her. Always had. But that was exactly why I
had to go.

I took a step closer to her, my heart pounding. "Princess?"

"God." A laugh escaped her. "You know I hate it when
you call me that."

"Yeah." Another step closer. My palms itched to touch her.

To stroke her soft skin and kiss her until her worries faded away. To protect her from the world. From *me*. To take all the bad I'd done, and all the horrible things I'd learned how to do, and turn them into something good—as a means to keep her alive. "It's why I do it. Gotta keep you on your toes."

"Is that so?"

"Yeah." Another step had me directly behind her. "That's so."

"I—" She turned back to me, gasping when she saw how close I'd gotten. Her lips parted and her pulse raced. I could tell by the way she gripped the table behind her and the way her pupils dilated as her breath quickened. "I got something for you," she finished breathlessly.

I glanced down, tensing when I saw what she held. A drawing pad, some charcoal pencils, and some pastels, too. "Why the hell did you get me those?"

"I—" She flushed. "You mentioned drawing in passing last night, and then I saw you doodling this morning, before you crumpled it up and threw it away. You seemed familiar with a pencil . . . so I thought maybe you might like something to draw with."

I swallowed hard, feeling as if some small part of myself had been exposed. I didn't talk about my hobby, and no one else knew I enjoyed sketching. Drawing, for me, was a cathartic exercise that kept my mind and my hands busy. Without it, I grew on edge. I thought about things I shouldn't. Did things I knew I shouldn't. Made mistakes.

And I'd made enough of those lately.

"I'm sorry if I overstepped my bounds," she said softly, her grip on the pad tight. "You don't have to take them if I'm wrong."

The fact that she'd noticed such an intimate detail that no one else had ever seen before was unsettling, to say the least. It made my chest warm up and my pulse race, and shit, I wanted to . . . to . . . *hug* her. Which was fucking insane. I didn't hug people.

But she had done this, and I needed to show her how much that meant to me. We were a perfectly respectable distance apart—safely in the friend zone, one might say. But with her, it seemed like more, because I wanted her more than I wanted my freedom. I wanted her with a passion and a fiery hell that nothing and no one could ever touch.

Since I couldn't have her, I would take the next best thing. I'd take what she gave me, and draw her. I would try to capture her beauty in charcoal forever, since soon I would be out of her life.

It would be a way for me to remember the time I had, and never ruined, Molly Lachlan. "You're not wrong at all. I do enjoy drawing." Reaching out, I closed my hand around hers and around the pad. "Thank you for thinking of me. No one else—I mean, that was very kind of you. Thanks."

She licked her lips, staring at our joined hands. "May I ask you a question?"

"You can ask me anything you want," I said, smirking, trying to shake the feelings she'd caused by giving me drawing supplies. To her, it was a way of life. For me, it was an anomaly that I didn't know what to do with. "I might not *answer*, but ask away."

"What things do you draw?" She dashed a glance at me, but quickly turned away. It was clear that my being this close to her discomfited her. "I mean, you know, what types of drawings?"

I shrugged as if it wasn't awkward for me to talk about something so private. "Whatever inspires me at the moment." *You.* Her beauty and selflessness—something I never saw much of in the world—needed documentation. I just hoped

I could do her justice. "People. Places. Events. Nature. I do it all. But I'm not very good at any of it."

She watched me skeptically. I wasn't sure why. Maybe she didn't believe I could have an artistic bone in my body. "Can I see some of your work?"

"It's all at my place." I forced a smile, but even though that was true, there was no way in hell I would be showing her my shit. Not even Lucas had been privy to my art. "Sorry."

"You can show me after you draw whatever inspires you now."

I laughed. "No."

"Why not?" she asked, cocking her head to the side. The movement made a lock of hair fall in front of her face. "Are you scared?"

"I don't get scared." Unable to resist, I reached out and tucked the hair behind her ear slowly, savoring the excuse to touch her. Her silky hair teased my fingers, and her cheek was even softer than I'd imagined. Like satin. It would be hard to capture that on paper, but I'd try my damnedest to do so, anyway. "That feeling died long ago."

"Everyone is scared of *something*." Her brow furrowed. "Maybe losing someone you love?"

"There's no one left in my life to love," I said honestly. "If you love nothing, and need nothing, no one can use that against you."

She shook her head. "What about your parents?"

"I—" I hesitated, not sure how much I wanted to tell her. But the truth was, I didn't love them. Pops was an asshole, and Ma was as guilty as he was. With parents like them, I never stood a chance at a normal life. "It's complicated."

"Why?"

Some shit was for me and me only. She didn't need to

know my pops beat me or was an asshole who couldn't accept that I wasn't a carbon copy of him—and never would be, no matter how many times he hit me. Or, at least, I *hadn't* been until I'd betrayed Lucas. "Because it is."

She nodded slowly and rested a hand on my chest. My heart accelerated at her touch, showing her how much she affected me, even though I couldn't tell her. "I'm sorry for that. I truly am."

The thing was, I believed her. No matter what I told her, or how I said it, she seemed to accept me for who and what I was. She invited me into her home. Took care of me. Showed me nothing but compassion. She made me doubt everything I knew about humanity and life and even death.

She made me doubt *myself*.

CHAPTER 10

MOLLY

Chris was hardened, cold, and deadly. There was no denying that, or hiding it. But all that dangerous darkness was entangled with a striking vulnerability that he tried his best to hide from the world. And he was good at it. But now that I'd spent a few days with him, my opinions on him had changed.

And my determination to keep him at arm's length had died a slow, painful death, too. Yes, he was still dangerous, and I wasn't foolish enough to think otherwise, and the stormy, untamed emotion brewing inside him was enough to make any sane woman turn away . . . and yet, I couldn't. Underneath that power and passion was a desire to be accepted for who he was. To be the man he always wanted to be but never stood a chance of becoming. And I wanted to help him find that guy.

I wanted *him*.

Judging from what I'd pieced together and what I'd seen, before I found him in that alley he'd hit rock bottom. I couldn't help but think that it was my duty to help him climb back up. And if I did that, maybe it would help me accept the fact that the man who killed my father, much like Chris, probably hadn't had much of a choice, either. Maybe if someone had taken the time to show *him* he was human, too, my father would still be alive. Or maybe I was just crazy.

His soft touch on my skin was still radiating through my veins, and my body awakened every time he came near me. I couldn't ignore that reaction to him anymore, no matter how hard I tried.

"How's your hand?" he asked, lifting my palm and turning it toward the light. "It looks better. Almost healed."

I forced a smile, but my stomach clenched tight at his lingering touch. This unanswered need he brought to life within me was as unwelcome as it was uncharted. I'd never wanted a man as much as I did him, and I didn't really know what to do with it. Especially since he didn't seem to reciprocate the feeling. The one and only time we'd gotten close to kissing—or at least, the time I *thought* we had—he'd pulled back and acted as if nothing had happened. And he hadn't touched me like that since.

"It's much better. Thank you."

"Good." He ran his thumb over the red gash. I shivered and closed my fingers on him, without really meaning to, but not wanting to let go, either. "It's gonna scar."

I eyed him, knowing that underneath that shirt he wore, he had a lot of scars that couldn't be explained away as battle scars. Something told me they came from someplace darker, which was why he didn't want to talk about them. And I had a pretty good idea where they had come from—or I should say, *whom*. "We all have a few of those, don't we?"

"I would rather you didn't." His grip on me tightened. "You deserve to live a life free of pain."

"But I haven't." I pressed my lips together, thinking of my father. The cold reality of his loss washed over me again and reminded me why it was so important I not give in to the gravitational pull that I felt toward Chris. "No one does. Not in the real world."

"That doesn't stop me from wishing it for you," he said, letting go of me and stepping back. I immediately missed his touch, but I was also relieved it was gone. And, yeah, I knew that didn't make much sense. None of this did. "Roast is in the oven. It'll be ready soon."

"It smells delicious," I said, turning away from him and taking a deep breath. It did nothing to calm my nerves or to ease the hollowness inside me that ached endlessly for his touch. "Is that pie I smell, too?"

"Apple," he answered distractedly as he picked through the bag of art supplies I'd brought home for him. "I remembered it was your favorite."

I blinked. "When did I tell you that?"

"I don't know," he said, pulling out the pad and pencils. "A couple of years ago, I think. When I was painting your shutters blue."

I studied him, because I remembered the conversation now. His mother had been baking cherry pie, and he offered to bring me some, but I had told him I preferred apple. The sun had shone down on him, illuminating his hard brown eyes, and at the time I just wanted to go back inside, to safety, because the man slaving over painting my shutters had *terrified* me.

Now, he did so even more, but in different ways.

I wasn't scared he might somehow snap and hurt me. I wasn't frightened that he'd pull a gun on me and take my money, or my car, or even my life. Now I was frightened of my reaction to him, and worried if I would be able to take what I wanted—him—and not let myself get too close. Not get *hurt*.

And that was a heck of a lot scarier than any uncertainty about my safety.

"Oh. Right." I smiled. "I forgot."

"I didn't." He set the art stuff down and studied me. It made my heart beat faster, and it made the desire I felt for him surge even higher . . . which was a disaster all on its own. "I remember everything you tell me."

I gripped the chair behind me, unable to look away. "Why?"

"Because it's you," he said simply.

It was enough.

And it only made my desire to give in to my, well, *desire* all the more firmly footed. I wouldn't fool myself into thinking that we could live happily ever after, but we could have some fun while we were together. "What are you going to draw?"

"I told you already," he said, his lips tilting up into one of those breathtaking smiles he rarely gave me. "Whatever inspires me."

"I really want to see your work. I bet it's not so bad."

He snorted. "Why?"

"I like art. Someone once drew me a picture." I stepped closer. "That guy I told you about, who gives me things."

"The stalker, you mean?" he asked, opening the oven to peek into it. Buttons took a break from eating, hovering over the bowl to stare at Chris speculatively. "If I were you, I'd stop accepting anything from him. He sounds dangerous."

I shook my head. "I don't think he is, though."

"Seeing as you're the same woman who invited me into her house?" He shut the oven and dusted off his hands. Buttons went back to chowing down on the food Chris had given him. "No offense, but I think your danger radar is a little fucked-up. The guy's a nut."

"I disagree." I paused. "And the drawing was good."

"Then you're lucky I'm not your stalker." He grinned. "If I had been, you would have burned the drawing in the fireplace."

"I doubt that," I murmured. "I think if you drew me something, I would love it."

"That's because you haven't seen my work," he pointed out. "Speaking of work, how was yours today?"

"Good. We were reading today. Tomorrow's the last day before break, so the kids are antsy."

"Oh yeah?" He leaned on the counter and crossed his arms, and he actually acted as if he was interested. "How does that feel, teaching kids how to read?"

"Pretty freaking amazing," I admitted, smiling. "It's my favorite part of the year. It starts with letters and memorizing sight words. But once we get to the part where they can pick up a book and actually read a few words on their own? It's just . . . amazing." I laughed. "I know I already said that, but it's the best word for it, you know?"

"I do." He smiled. It lit up his face. "And that's *definitely* amazing."

I swept my hair out of my face. "I mean, it's not all glamour and reading. There's things about being a kindergarten teacher that really suck."

"Like what?" he asked, crossing his ankles. "The crying and snot?"

"Yeah. Tears over broken crayons, and fights between friends. And the vomiting, and lice." I winced and scratched my head at the mere word. "Those pale little buggers are literally from the devil, I kid you not. I wouldn't wish them on my worst enemy."

He uncrossed his arms. "I would, and I wouldn't even feel bad about it after."

A laugh bubbled out of me. He was nothing if not honest. "Have you ever had them?"

"Yeah." He scrunched his nose. "Once, as a kid." After a second's hesitation, he added, "Pops shaved off my hair, even though I was growing it out, because he didn't want Ma to have to deal with the combing."

"Ah." I studied him. He said it so calmly, like it didn't matter, but something told me there was more to the story than met the naked eye. "Did you ask him not to?"

"I didn't exactly get a say in the matter, Princess," he said, twisting his lips.

I nodded. So his childhood had been one of *those*.

Over the years, I'd seen a lot of kids who felt like they didn't have a voice in their own homes. It never ceased to sadden me. For some reason, I hadn't thought Chris had been one of those kids. He'd always seemed so put together and laid-back. And Mr. O'Brien was always smiling and cracking jokes. Didn't seem to have an exasperated bone in his body. "How'd you feel about that?"

He gaped at me as if I'd magically grown two heads, like he always did when I brought his emotions into the conversation. "I felt fucking fine about it. I was a kid. What the hell did I know about anything?"

"Just because you're young doesn't mean your desires don't count," I said slowly. It was something I said to my kids, in different words, so it was a sentiment I was familiar with expressing. "When you're a kid, you have to bow down to your parents' wishes, obviously, since they're the adults, but it doesn't make your wishes any less important, no matter what your age. You're as much your own person at six as you are at twenty-six."

Not even so much as a hint of emotion crossed his face. "Is that how old you are?"

"I—yes." I frowned at the change of topic. Also, how was it that we hadn't already crossed this territory? Then again, up until I invited him into my home, we hadn't exactly *chatted* a lot. "How old are you?"

"Twenty-eight." He scratched the back of his head and shifted his feet. "Almost twenty-nine."

"When?"

He lifted a shoulder. "Tomorrow, I guess."

"You *guess*?" My jaw dropped. I couldn't help it. He acted like tomorrow was just any other day, and it was his *birthday*. When my father was still alive, he went out of his way to make every single birthday better than the last. It had been the one day I anticipated the most every year. Not because of presents or cake, but because it had always been a wonderful day spent in the company of the person I loved the most: my dad. Since his death, it was the day I felt the absence of his company the most, too. "Is it, or isn't it, your birthday tomorrow?"

"It is." Again, with the shoulder shrug. "It's not a big deal, though. Just another day."

"No, it's not."

His brow furrowed. "Yes. It is."

"What's your favorite cake?"

He blinked. "I don't know. Chocolate, I guess."

"I'm getting you a cake and making *you* dinner tomorrow." I pointed a finger at him. "And you're going to like it. *Capisce?*"

"As much as I like it when you boss me around?" He shoved off the counter and came closer, each step cockier than the last. "What makes you think I'll still be here tomorrow, Princess?"

"Because I refuse to let you leave before we celebrate your birthday." I nibbled on my lower lip. "It's the least I can do after all you've done around here."

"What the—?" Something dark fleeted across his expression. "You've got it all wrong. I'm not the one who's done shit that deserves thanks."

I held my hands out. "But—"

He approached, his shoulders tight. "You're the one who invited me into your home, not the other way around. You *literally* saved my life. What did I do? Fix a few things? Make sure a table didn't wobble? It was nothing in comparison to what you did for me."

I swallowed and shook my head, trying to find the right words to express how I felt. It was a lot harder than it should have been. Tentatively, I placed my hand on his chest, right over his heart, which he was so certain was blackened and dead.

It wasn't. I refused to believe that.

"Chris."

He glanced down at my hand. *"Molly."*

I almost pulled it back, an apology on my lips, but I didn't. "Don't take that tone with me."

"Ah, there's that biting schoolteacher version of you I love so much." His tone was teasing, but his jaw was too tight for me to take his words as a joke. "Careful, though. I'm not one of your kids, and I might bite back."

I rolled my eyes. "Yeah. Sure you will."

"You seem to think I'm not the type of guy to do so." He stepped closer, looming over me. I sucked in a breath, gripping his shirt tighter. "You're so wrong. I'm not your friend, and I'm not being a good guy by staying here. I'm endangering you by my presence. If I was a 'nice' guy, I would have left days ago, but I stayed, because it's nice being in a big house with a big bed and a pretty woman—and I'm a selfish prick who likes the creature comforts of home."

I lifted my chin stubbornly. "I like having you here. I . . . I like *you*."

"Don't. Just fucking don't." He rubbed the back of his neck. "I get paid to kill people, while you teach little kids how to read and make the world a better place one classroom at a time. So, tell me, how in the hell could *you* possibly like *me*?"

When he put it like that, it only drove home the point that my attraction toward him was insane. And that I needed to keep my distance, because no matter how long he stayed, or how much closer we got, *physically*, it wouldn't stop him from leaving. And when he did, I would be alone again. But even knowing that . . .

It wasn't enough to make me stop.

It was too late for that, and it was about time I admitted it, too.

I might regret it when he left, and I might even get hurt, but the thing was, right now, I didn't care. All that mattered to me was helping him. Making sure he was okay. Showing him someone cared about him, even if he didn't want me to, and refusing to let myself waver from that, or regret it.

After all, I'd have plenty of time for regrets once he was gone.

"You only think you like me because of your desire to be the type of person your dad was," he said, his tone even. "You're mistaking compassion for affection."

"You're wrong. This has nothing to do with my dad. Not anymore." I fisted his shirt, not letting him back off this time. "I don't know why I like you, but I know it's not some imagined feeling to be written off by you. And you can't change that."

"Then you're going to get hurt." He covered his hand with mine, and for a second, I thought he would forcibly remove my hand. Instead, he pressed it closer to his chest, and I could feel his racing heart under my palm. "It's what I do. I *hurt* people."

"Not me." I stepped closer, lifting my face to his. "You wouldn't hurt me."

A laugh escaped him. It sounded harsh. "You have no idea just what I could do to you, Princess."

"So show me." My heart picked up speed, but I ignored it. "I'm not scared."

"You should be." He backed me into the counter, his large hard body looming over mine. With his free hand, he gripped my chin and tilted it up to him. His hold was unyielding yet somehow gentle. "You should be fucking *frightened*."

My pulse raced, and I couldn't seem to get enough oxygen to fill my lungs, but I'd never felt more alive than I did in this moment. All my life, I'd been getting by. Going from moment to moment—and this was what I was missing. If he thought I was willing to throw it all away and pretend I didn't want him, he was crazy.

This feeling, this rush, was too intoxicating to deny anymore.

I was done trying.

We might not have long together, and there was no chance for this to be more than just sex, but I was willing to accept that, if he was. "Show me." I lifted my face to his, refusing to cower or shy away. "I dare you."

His fingers shifted on my chin, and he pressed even closer. "You have no idea what the hell you're doing right now. This is all some silly little game to you, and you think you can win. I'll let you in on a secret: I don't play fair. If you go up against me—you'll fucking lose. And it'll hurt."

"Maybe that's a risk I'm willing to take." I gripped his

hip with my other hand but accidentally touched something hard. Something that felt a lot like a gun. "And that's my choice to make."

He gritted his teeth and shook his head. "Yeah, but it's my choice to decide whether or not I'm willing to let you. And I'm not. Keep your distance, Molly. Guys like me aren't made for girls like you. I would rip you apart."

With that, he pushed off me and walked away, not looking back. "Chris—"

"Dinner's ready," he said, his tone final and cold as he opened the oven. "And this discussion is over. I said all I need to say."

I watched him take the roast out, yank off the oven mitts, and cut into the meat with precise strokes. Every single slice was the same size as the last. I wrapped my arms around myself, knowing exactly why he was so comfortable with a knife.

How many people had he killed? Five? Ten? Twenty? A hundred?

I couldn't help but wonder if they haunted him at night. If he ever wished he'd chosen a different life or a different job. Heck, if he ever wished he were a different *person*. I did, sometimes. I was pretty sure most people did, to some degree. But Chris just seemed so . . . so . . . certain who he was, and who he was supposed to be, and he didn't seem to have a single regret. Did he have any dreams? Hopes? Goals?

Did he even dream at night at all?

"I'll stay," he said softly, setting the knife down. "One more day."

I swallowed. "And your birthday dinner?"

"I—" He hesitated and turned to me. He seemed more in control again, and it was as if I hadn't been in his arms moments before, practically begging him to kiss me. "I don't really see the point at all, but if it makes you happy, we can do it. Whatever you want, Princess."

I want you. "Great. What's your favorite meal?"

"I don't have a favorite meal," he said slowly, staring at me oddly.

I crossed my arms. "Chris—"

"Fine. Steak and baked potatoes."

"Good choice." I forced a smile, but my entire body was all wound up into a tight little ball. "Wine? Beer? Whiskey?"

He lifted a shoulder. "Whatever you want."

"It'll be fun. You'll see."

He eyed me like he was torn between kissing me, strangling me, and laughing. Maybe all of the above. "Yeah. Fun."

And I had a feeling, for better or for worse . . .

It was going to be one *hell* of a birthday.

CHAPTER 11

CHRIS

The next evening, I let my fingers and hands do all the work, watching as the black charcoal spread across previously unblemished drawing paper. My strokes were soft and smooth, guided by sheer instinct as I visualized the picture, despite the guilt racking me. I should have left that morning, after she went to work to make the world a better place, and in turn made *her* life a better place.

I should've promised to still be here when she got home, waved good-bye, and broken that promise after I drank some coffee, grabbed my shit, and got the hell outta her life. But when she begged me to stay, so she could make me a *birth-day dinner* of all things, I—like the fucking fool I was—hadn't been able to say no to those bright hazel eyes. Some things would never change.

When it came to Molly Lachlan, I would always be a sucker.

She could ask me to rip the skin off my own back, and I

would do it for her. It was pathetic. My one weakness. And weaknesses could be exploited. Shit, I would know. When Lucas had inexplicably fallen for the lovely Heidi Greene, the first thing I did was use her against him. And it had almost worked.

In my world, weakness was—well, *weakness.*

And it got you killed.

The only reason I was still alive today was because I didn't let anyone get too close, and I didn't give a damn about anyone or anything but myself.

Molly was, and had always been, the exception.

The only reason she was safe was because no one had a clue about it. The only one who had even an inkling of my true feelings for her had been Lucas. And he wouldn't be talking to anyone, because he was "dead."

I stopped my strokes, taking a second to study my work.

Kissable lips that were fully fleshed out pouted up at me, and a soft chin with a hard jawline that hinted of a hidden stubborn streak complemented them as well in charcoal as it did in real life. Wide, hauntingly beautiful eyes watched me with a warmth that I'd managed to get across on paper, and once I colored them in, they would truly represent the life that flowed within them. Sharp cheekbones sliced across the smooth paper, lending a depth to the drawing that complemented the soft waves of hair falling around her fragile, angelic face. It was, in my skeptical opinion, my best work yet.

But that was because it was Molly.

The door opened, and I tore the page out of the book and shoved it behind the pillow, in the crack between the cushion and the couch. Then I slammed the book shut. It was only five, too early for Molly to be back home. Standing, I slowly pulled out my Glock 22. "Molly?"

"Yeah, it's me," she called out, shutting the door behind her with a soft *click*. "Stay in there! Don't come out."

I took a step toward the kitchen, tucking my gun away. "Why? What's wrong?"

"Nothing." She popped her head around the corner, a big grin on her face. "I just have to get everything set up. Happy birthday!"

Her cheeks were flushed, and she was so damn happy and alive it almost hurt to look at her, because I was a dead man walking. Her excitement over my birthday baffled me. My phone had been silent all day, since the only person who'd ever wished me a happy birthday had been Lucas, and he was gone. But she acted like it was this huge thing to be celebrated. As if it should be a big thing. It wasn't. Even when Lucas had been around, we didn't really celebrate. Didn't do presents. We just cracked a few beers, got wasted, and went home with random chicks.

That's what birthdays were.

"Molly—"

"I know." She put on a stern face that I could only assume was supposed to be me, and lowered her voice. "'Nothing too big. It's just another day.'"

I shook my head, but a smile crept out at her adorable representation of me. "That was, quite possibly, the *worst* imitation I've ever seen."

"You're right. Let me try again." She cleared her throat and tapped her chest. "'Princess. Nothing too serious. It's just another fucking day.'"

I laughed. And I laughed *hard*.

Hell, I laughed like I'd never laughed before.

Not because her reenactment of my strict reminder was good—it *wasn't*—but because it was the first time I'd ever heard her curse, and it sounded pretty damn funny coming from those sweet lips of hers.

I bent over, gripping my stomach, because I laughed so hard it hurt.

The whole time, she stared at me like she couldn't stop— and that freaked me out enough to finally make *me* stop. I straightened, the last of my amusement dying in my chest. I glanced down, sure something was wrong, because she was acting so damn *serious* and I was *dying* with laughter. "What?" I pressed a hand to my stomach and glanced down my whole body. It all seemed fine. No open fly. No missing buttons. No torn stitches or bleeding. "What's wrong?"

"Nothing." She gripped the molding of the doorway, her knuckles white. "It's just that when you laugh, I can't look away. It's beautiful." She pressed her lips together and flushed even pinker. "*You're* beautiful."

That definitely killed any remaining laughter, because if there was one thing that I wasn't? Yeah. It was fucking *beautiful*. "The hell I am," I growled.

"But you are. You're not beautiful in a Disney princess kind of way, or even the traditional sense of the word. There's a raw beauty to you that's dangerous, hard, and real . . . but it's there nonetheless. Nothing, and no one, will ever convince me otherwise, so don't waste your breath. Save it for blowing out the candles . . . all *twenty-nine* of them."

I frowned at her, because for the first time in my life, someone had struck me speechless. There was so much I wanted to say to her. Like how she was dead wrong, and I was an ugly man with an ugly soul. Not physically—I scored enough women with my face and body to not feign modesty— but in every other way that counted.

I was a killer. A criminal. A thief. I pushed guns for a living.

That wasn't beautiful. It was *ugly* as hell.

"That's what I thought." She lifted her chin, showing that stubbornness that I'd fought so hard to capture in her drawing. It made me want to rip the picture into shreds, because I hadn't done her justice. Then again, I never could. She was too breathtaking to be accurately duplicated with mere charcoal and paper. "Now stay here. I have stuff to set up before you're allowed in the kitchen or dining room."

Nodding, I still didn't speak.

I should tell her how, right before she found me in that alley, I tried to kill my best friend in some stupid attempt to show Pops I was stronger than him—that I could be a killer, and even more ruthless than him. But then I'd realized what I'd had with Lucas had been real, and he'd really loved me, and all that had changed.

I'd changed.

After spending weeks plotting the best and most painful way to do it—using my intimate knowledge of his strengths and weaknesses against him, because that's who I was—I'd used Heidi against him to get what I wanted. Even though I'd known what I was doing was wrong, and I'd wanted to take it back, I'd kept pushing through. I'd finished what I started, even though I hadn't wanted to, because it was too late to go back.

That was *ugly*. But instead, I let her call me *beautiful*.

And that was ugly as hell, too.

After tonight, I was getting the hell out of her life. She deserved all the best things in life. Flowers. Kittens. Drawings. Tables that didn't wobble. And a real fucking prince.

Not me. Never me.

I liked her thinking of me in a softer light than the cold, hard reality of who I really was.

And it only proved just how ugly I was.

"Okay, you can come out now," she called, her voice a bit softer than earlier. The thing about her was that no matter how angry I made her, she always got over it quickly. It was one of her weaknesses. "I'm ready."

Taking a deep breath, I walked into the room, Buttons trailing behind me like usual, prepared to do my best to show her just how unbeautiful I was—but she ruined it. Because there was wine on the table, my favorite meal was waiting, she was wearing a ridiculous pointed paper hat paired with a huge smile, and she'd gotten me a present.

A *wrapped* present.

With a fucking ribbon on it.

No one ever got me gifts, let alone went to the trouble of making them look pretty. For Christmas, Pops told me when I was five that Santa wasn't real, and bad boys didn't get gifts. I obviously never fell into the "good boys" category, so the tree never had a gift under it for me. And birthdays were just another day. There was no cake, or gifts, or singing.

And we sure as hell didn't wear hats.

I'd told Luc I hated gifts and didn't want any, and he believed me. We fell into a pattern of celebrating without presents, and that was just fine by me.

Molly blew on some weird contraption that shot out straight and was blue. My jaw dropped, and I frowned down at it. "What the fuck is *that*?"

She laughed and took it out of her mouth. "It's a party horn. Surely you've seen them before?"

I blinked at her, not answering.

I felt like I'd stepped into some sort of alternate dimension. One where people smiled and had fun and were happy. And it was all too clear I didn't belong there.

Her smile wobbled a little bit. "Oh. Okay. Guess not. Well, happy birthday!"

I swallowed and tried to force a smile for her, but this show of excitement only served to remind me just how different we were. She was sunshine and blue skies, and I was tornadoes and hurricanes. The two just didn't mix. "Thank you."

She fidgeted with the party horn. "You've seriously never used one of these?"

"No." I eyed it, ignoring Buttons as he purred and sat on my foot. "Never."

She held it out. "Want to?"

"Hell no." I rubbed my head and added, "Thanks, though."

Her smile wobbled more, and she lowered her hand, her fingers tightening on the party favor. "No problem."

Seeing the light fade from her eyes did things to me. Things she had no right doing. Without really intending to, I snatched the toy out of her hand, stuck it in my mouth, and blew. Buttons hissed and took off for the "cat room," as Molly dubbed it. He had his litter box, food, toys, a bed, and water in it. The fucking cat had a bigger room than I did back home. The party horn shot out, and I had no idea what the point of it was . . .

But she smiled again.

And then I knew.

"See? It's not so bad!"

It was stupid—but if it made her smile, I would do it. I set it down, studying the pointy paper cone on her head. "And . . . the hat?"

"Don't tell me you never used those."

I shrugged. I wouldn't complain about the hand I'd been given—it wouldn't change anything—but I might as well be honest with her. It was my last night here, after all. The least I could do, after she went through so much trouble for me, which I still couldn't wrap my brain around—was make it a good one. "Never."

She pressed her lips together, and something crossed her expression. Not pity—thank God, or I would have had to do something that would ruin my streak of good behavior—but sadness. For some reason, it made me want to pull her into my arms to hug it all away. As if I had that power at all. I didn't fix things, or make them better.

Instead, I killed them.

"What childhood did you have?" she asked, her voice so quiet I almost didn't hear her. Maybe I wasn't supposed to. Maybe she was speaking to herself.

I had no clue.

But I answered with an honesty that had no place coming out of my lips. "The kind that didn't have birthday parties, or cake, or even laughter. And it was as far off from your life as you could possibly get." I shrugged. "But that's okay. Not all of us get that life, right? We can't all be princes or princesses. Some of us are just alive, making it by, day by day, every day."

The way she watched me, like I was this broken creature she wanted to patch back together, punched me in the chest like a bullet. "*Chris*. I—"

"Don't. It's fine. I'm fine. It's just a stupid hat."

She swallowed, tears filling her eyes, but she shook it off. "Okay. Let's get this on you."

Crossing the room, she lifted her arms, holding a hat with an elastic band. It said *Birthday Boy* and was in the shape of a crown. A crown I had no right or desire to wear. But *she* wanted me to, so I lowered my head to make it easier for her. "Go for it, Princess. Crown me as your prince."

She shot me a quick glance, still looking seconds from bursting into full-on waterworks. "I'm sorry. I didn't mean to pry earlier."

"You didn't. It's fine."

"I know. It's just—" Pressing her lips together, she shook her head. "Crap. I'm sorry. Ignore me."

Once she settled the hat into place, I shifted on my feet, uncomfortable with this show of emotion. In my world, you didn't *cry*. If you did, you got a worse beating than you would have gotten in the first place for showing softness. So seeing such a blatant display of affection was, quite honestly, alarming and foreign.

And when I locked gazes with her, what I saw there— raw, open, painfully honest feelings that had no place being directed toward *me*—should have had me stepping away.

Instead, I did the unthinkable.

I pulled her into my arms and hugged her.

My arms hovered awkwardly. I didn't really hug women. I either walked right on by them or fucked them—but I didn't *hug* them. And no one hugged me. So at first, I didn't know where to place my arms around her. I settled them around her waist and hauled her closer, like I was going to kiss her, only instead of lowering my mouth to hers, I rested my cheek against the top of her head.

And it felt . . . *good*.

Right, even.

She wrapped her arms around me, too, pulling me even closer, and rested her face right over my heart, which sped up. Breathing in her soft, floral scent, I turned my face toward her hair to get closer. "Shh. It's okay."

I didn't know why I said that, but she seemed to like it.

"I'm sorry." She sniffed. "I don't normally cry. I just . . ."

"I do." I kissed the top of her head. "I cry all the damn time. You should see me. I'm like a blubbering baby on crack."

She choked on a laugh and gripped the back of my shirt with her fists. Her nails dug into my skin a little bit, but it felt good. And it made me think of something that was a hell of a lot more intimate than hugging. Although, in a way, hugging was actually more intimate. I'd fucked lots of women. But comforting them?

Yeah, she was the only one.

"Somehow, I find that hard to believe."

I blinked. "What? Why?"

"Well, you're hardly the crying type." She pulled back a little bit and studied me. I had the urge to push her head back down to my chest, not only because it felt good, but because having her this close to me, watching me, made me uneasy that she might see something I didn't want her to see. "I bet you've never cried a day in your life."

"You'd win." Legend was, even when I was a baby, Pops had taught me that crying was bad, and I'd been the quietest little guy this side of Steel Row. "My secret is out. I'm a cold, heartless man who doesn't know what emotion is."

She laughed.

Funny, she actually thought that was a *joke*.

When I didn't join in, she stopped and nibbled on her lower lip. "You have emotions."

"Not really." I gripped her waist. "I only experience three emotions on any given day: anger, hatred, and lust."

"That's not it," she argued, her pulse racing at the last one I added in.

"Yeah." I spread my hand across her lower back, right

above her ass. She sucked in a breath and placed her hands on my chest, not pushing me away, but not pulling me closer, either. "That's *it*."

She licked her lips and swayed closer, her attention locked on my mouth. "Oh yeah? Funny, because I have yet to see you display any lust . . . and you've been here for almost a week."

Actually, it had been five days—but who was counting?

"Oh, Molly." I moved closer, letting her feel just how wrong she was. It worked. Her mouth formed a perfect little O. "How adorably naïve you are . . ."

Her hands flattened on my pecs, the bottoms of her palms brushing against my nipple rings. I clenched my teeth at the shot of pleasure that sent through me, right down to my already painfully hard cock. She had no idea what she was messing with.

Had no idea what I was capable of.

And I wasn't about to show her.

Some of my knee-jerk reaction to having her in my arms, her innocently touching my nipple rings, showed. Something lit her eyes—something seductive and dangerous—and she slid her hands lower, her fingers tracing the cold, hard hoops.

I bit back a groan, but damned if I didn't press closer to her. Her soft touch was torturous and heavenly, all in one. Mostly because I wanted her more than I'd ever wanted anyone or anything, and I couldn't have her. It would be so easy to take what she offered. I was good at it. I loved fucking, and fucking loved me.

If she were any other woman, she'd be flat on her back, moaning my name as I made her come within a minute of touching her. Of claiming her as mine . . .

Temporarily.

I was good at that, too.

But this was Molly, and she deserved better than that. Better than me, and we both knew it. So she needed to stop looking at me as if she would die if I didn't kiss her. Because I wasn't going to, no matter how damn badly I *wanted* to.

"Chris . . ." She rose on her tiptoes and did it again. Traced my nipples. I gritted my teeth, fighting against every asshole bone in my body that demanded I take her. "Prove it."

I held on to her hips, seconds from pushing her away . . . or doing the unthinkable and pulling her closer. I wasn't a hundred percent sure which at this point. "Prove what?"

She opened her mouth to reply, but before she could, I caught movement out of the corner of my eye. A man dressed in black crept closer, crouched over, and the front door stood open, even though it had been locked earlier.

Someone was in the house.

It took me a second—I'd been too lost in her to be fully alert, which was why I never should have touched her in the first place—but I saw him lift a hand, and then I saw the AR-15 pointed at us.

At *my* Molly.

Before she could so much as blink, I knocked her to the floor and slid my gun out of my pocket as we went down. She hit the floor hard, since I couldn't cushion her, and I hit even harder, barely managing to avoid landing on her. As she skittered across the wood floor, I pulled the trigger in two rapid fires, which hit true in a tight grouping on the other man's chest.

The man barging into Molly's home hit the floor, gurgling on his last breath, blood spraying out of him like a busted fountain, and dropped his weapon. It slid toward Molly, who stared at it—and the dead body—with an open mouth. To her credit, she hadn't screamed. Hadn't even made so much as a peep.

She'd just *stared*.

I army-crawled across the floor, snatched up the AR-15 in case I ran out of ammo on my Glock with a silencer on it, and rolled to my feet in one fluid motion. The quick movement jerked on my still-healing shoulder, but I didn't have time for that shit.

Because where there was one murdering asshat . . . there was another.

And I had to be prepared.

"*Run.* Go hide behind the couch in the living room until I tell you to come out!"

She struggled to her feet, gained solid footing, and did as she was told without asking questions. I watched her go, gun raised to protect her back. Once she was safely tucked away where I'd ordered her to go, I settled myself behind a wall where I could keep an eye on both the front door and the garage door, blinking rapidly, automatic weapon pointed and primed—and ready to kill some assholes.

I was next to the cat room, and Buttons was cowering in the corner, so I quickly shut the door. If he escaped in the fight, Molly would kill me. If, for some reason, it was too much for me to handle on my own, I'd run outside and draw the fire toward myself, giving Molly a chance to escape to safety. "If I run, wait till it's clear, and then run in the opposite direction. Got it?"

"Yes," she called out from behind the couch.

I breathed evenly, but it was harder than normal, considering the pure rage shooting through my veins. These fuckers thought they could threaten my woman—*my woman*—and get away with it? I would show them otherwise, and then I would show them again. No one messed with my Molly and lived to tell.

It wasn't until the thought crossed my mind that I realized I'd made a colossal mistake. Against all reason and logic and history, I'd let myself develop a weakness. I'd let Molly in, and I cared about her. I cared whether she lived or died. If anyone hurt her, I would hurt them back a million times worse. And after this, everyone would know about it, and she'd never be safe again.

This was all my fault.

CHAPTER 12

MOLLY

My heavy breathing was the only sound in my house, *in and out*, *in* and *out*, fast, uneven, and hard. I hid behind the couch, my cheek pressed against the wood floor so I could watch what happened without giving away my position. I knew, more than you would think I might know, that my hiding back here was critical to Chris's concentration. I'd seen enough shoot-out movies to know a man under fire needed all his concentration, and so I needed to hide so Chris would know I was "safe."

But this wasn't a movie, and it was all heart-stoppingly *real*.

As I lay behind the couch, staring at the ever-growing puddle of thick red blood under the intruder's body, bile rose in the back of my throat and tickled my gag reflex. I slammed my hand over my mouth, willing the urge to go away. My heart was pounding so fast it felt like it would surely go right through my ribs and chest and splatter against the back of the sofa.

And Chris . . .

I focused on him, terrified I was about to watch him die.

Just moments before, I had been seconds from kissing him, and now he was fighting to save his life. To save my life. To keep us both *alive*. And I was useless.

I didn't know how to fight.

I'd never even held a gun before that night in the alley when I'd touched his. And I certainly didn't know how to kill a guy. He'd been so fast out there, when the man came in. He'd pushed me out of the way and fired off shots before I even knew what had happened. And the sound that came out of that man . . .

I would never forget it.

Part groan. Part choke. Part dying breath.

Chris pulled the trigger again, and I jumped, smacking the back of my head against the wall behind me so hard it hurt badly enough that I saw stars. For a second, I thought maybe I'd gotten hit. But another man crumbled to the floor, next to the first, and he made the same sickening sound as the other.

His last dying breath.

This one had taken a bullet to the throat, right above the clavicle, and he choked as he tried to breathe and failed. His blood splattered the floor and the wall behind him like a sick, twisted imitation of artwork. And no matter how hard I tried, I couldn't look away from it. It was like staring at a cloud, trying to decipher its shape, because it had to *mean something*.

Like his last message to the world.

Shots fired from outside, and Chris staggered back, so I finally tore my gaze from the sick painting in time to see him curse, almost trip over his own feet, and get another shot off all within the space of a second. The man was like some kind of action hero, and despite the fact that this was life or death, and the fact that there were literally dead men lying on my floors, staining them forever, I couldn't look away from him.

He was beautiful, even now, in this moment.

Growling, he fired the gun again, blood wetting the sleeve of his blue button-up shirt as he did so. He didn't even look fazed. Just kept fighting. Another guy staggered back out the door, falling parallel to it after taking a shot to the chest. He blinked, pain all over his face, and choked on blood. He looked terrified. Terrified and *alone*.

Chris stalked over and stepped on his throat, cutting off his air supply. The man's eyes widened, but he didn't even bother to fight.

Probably because he knew it was pointless.

"Who sent you?" Chris snarled, letting up his pressure on the man's windpipe.

"Go . . . to . . . hell . . ." Then the dying guy laughed, choked on blood . . . and died.

And there it was again.

That *sound*.

"Son of a fucking bitch," Chris growled, rising to his feet and pointing the weapon outside again. He stood there, scanning the perimeter, and ran his hand down his face, still holding the gun. "Shit, shit, *shit*. Stay back there. Don't come out."

I nodded, but he couldn't see me, so I tried to answer.

All that came out was a pathetic squeak.

It was, it appeared, enough. He walked outside, dragging a body with him as he went. After a few minutes, he came back, grabbed another dead guy's foot, and dragged him, too. It was then, in my shock, that I realized what he was doing. After killing those men without a sign of hesitation . . .

He was cleaning up the mess.

But what would he *do* with them?

He came back for the last body, his face a cold, hard mask as he collected that one, too. I couldn't believe he was the same guy who had held me in his arms moments before, or that no one had called the cops or reported the noise. But then again, we lived pretty far apart in this community.

I couldn't see any other houses from mine besides his father's . . .

And no one was there. Even if they were, they certainly wouldn't call the *police*.

Chris disappeared back out into the night again, and a car started and pulled away. It was then that I realized . . . he'd left. He'd left me, and I was alone and too scared to come out, and I couldn't *breathe* back here, because *he'd left me*.

The risk of cops showing up must have been enough to send him running.

I knelt there, hiding, trying not to panic, and attempted to even out my breaths, but they grew faster and more uneven with each inhalation and exhalation. It was like I was those men, about to die, and nothing I did would stop it.

Nothing would give me oxygen.

I was going to suffocate back here, behind my couch, and no one and nothing would ever find me. Because Chris was gone, and I was alone, and *oh my God*.

A hand latched down on my shoulder and yanked me out, and I screamed. A man held me—his front to my back—so I had no way of seeing my attacker, but that didn't stop me from trying to escape. My fists flailed back, and I kicked backward, too, fighting to get away from whoever was trying to finish me off. I refused to go down without a fight, or at least getting some DNA under my—

"Molly, *Jesus*. It's me." Chris didn't let go, but his voice held a new wariness I'd never heard from him before. "It's Chris."

"C-Chris." I stopped fighting immediately, sagging against him. "I thought you left. I thought you were gone."

He tightened his grip on me, and what once felt threatening turned soothing. "I wouldn't leave you with this mess. Are you fucking kidding me?"

I dropped my head against his shoulder, my breathing finally calming. Funny. I had watched Chris literally kill three men, right in front of me, but it was his touch that soothed me and pulled me out of my panic-induced state. In his arms, I felt safe.

"It's just that—" I glanced down and gasped. In all the craziness, I'd forgotten he'd been *shot*. "I . . . You . . . I . . . your arm. It's bleeding."

"It's nothing. Just a graze. It doesn't even need stitches." Gently, he turned me to face him, his face no longer the cold, emotionless mask he wore as a killer. Instead, he appeared to be worried, sad, angry, and maybe . . . *guilty*? He smoothed my hair out of my face, his bloodstained hands impossibly gentle on my skin. "I'm so sorry. I'll clean this up, and I'll go."

"Go?" I shook my head and gripped his wrists. "No. *No.* Why?"

His jaw tightened, and he made an irritated sound. "How can you ask me that?"

"How can I not?" I answered breathlessly, still holding on to him, as if by doing so I could somehow make him stay. "Why?"

"Look around you, Princess," he snarled, his voice harder than I'd ever heard it before. It sent chills down my spine, but not enough to make me afraid of him. I was way beyond that point. He wouldn't hurt me. "See the destruction? The death? The fucking blood? That's my life."

I shook my head again. "You don't know this was because of you. It could have been a random—"

"It wasn't. They're in black with black leather vests, so they're from Bitter Hill." He let me go, and I almost fell over. I hadn't realized how much he was supporting me until he let go. "They came because I'm here, and they'll keep coming unless I leave. So no matter what you say, or how you say it, it won't change my mind. I'm gone."

"You saved my life. If you hadn't done the things you did, I would be dead right now." I lifted my chin. "We'd *both* be dead."

"Jesus Christ. Don't you see? The only reason your life needed to be saved was because of *me*." He held his arms out, chest rising and falling, eyes flashing with anger. "I did this to your home, Molly. *Me*."

"No," I whispered, knowing as I did so that it was useless. He'd made his mind up, and nothing I said would change it. "Please."

He fisted his hands at his sides, looking at me as if I'd shot him instead of asked him to stay. "Stop doing this. Stop asking me to stay, dammit."

My heart wrenched, because I knew he meant it. There was no doubt in my mind. But I didn't want him to go. He might be right, and he might be endangering me by being here, but I didn't *care*. Shaking my head, I threw myself into his arms. *"No."*

He caught me, staggering back, surprise clearly written on his expression. "Molly, I—"

Before he could finish that sentence, which would more than likely be all the reasons why I should hate him and he should go, I kissed him. After days of buildup and thick tension, I finally did it. The second our lips touched, it was like everything in the world became clearer.

Instead of sending me into a panic because I was kissing Chris O'Brien . . .

Everything just made sense. Like it was meant to happen all along.

He growled low in his throat and cupped the back of my head, threading his fingers through my hair as he took over the kiss, splaying his other hand midback, stealing control from me. I didn't mind, though. I was too far gone in the way his lips felt against mine, all powerful and domineering, and the way he held me, like I was some precious, priceless item he was scared to break.

And in his arms, I *felt* that way.

He ended the kiss, resting his forehead on mine, breathing heavily. Knowing I did that to him, made him lose his impervious control, only made me all the hotter for him. "*Shit.* Molly, I can't. We can't."

"Yes." I gripped his shirt with both fists, right above his chest, and tugged him closer. His erection pressed against my stomach, so I knew very well that we *could.* "We can. And we are. Kiss me."

He didn't budge, but his jaw certainly got harder. How did he *do* that? "I don't want to hurt you."

"What makes you think I'm the type of girl to get hurt? I told you the other night that I'm not exactly looking for forever. I meant it," I shot back, licking my lips. Knowing I affected him, made him want me, sent a boldness coursing through my veins that I'd never experienced before. And it felt *good.* "I'll take care of me, and you take care of you."

He shifted his weight a little bit, and he moved toward me as he did so. As clearly as I could feel the hard muscles of his pecs under my fists, I could surely taste victory on the tip of my tongue, but I would rather taste *him.* "I'm no good."

"Let me decide that." I tightened my grip on his shirt, yanking him down again. "I'll let you know once we're finished if I agree."

His lips slid into a familiar smirk, and he gripped my hair with a tight fist, pulling ever so slightly as his hand dipped lower, stopping just short of my butt. "Oh, I have no doubt I'll be good at *that*. That's not what I'm talking about, and you know it."

"No, I don't." I licked my impossibly dry lips. "So show me."

He lowered his face to mine, stopping just short of kissing me. Our breath mingled, and his lips brushed mine in a mockery of a kiss. "You're going to regret this."

"So *let* me."

Something in him seemed to snap, and he closed the distance between us, capturing my mouth in a breathtaking kiss that wiped every other mediocre kiss with mediocre men I'd ever had from my memory. All that remained was this—*us*—and nothing else mattered. Not the past, or even the future. No matter what he said.

He growled deep in his throat, which was easily the most primal, sexy thing I'd ever heard, and backed me against the wall as his mouth devoured mine. When I gasped, his tongue slipped inside, and I did more than gasp that time. Groaning in reply, I slid my hands up his shoulders and buried them in his hair, holding on securely.

I had a feeling I was pulling on it, but at this point I didn't care. I was too far gone, with just a simple kiss and a wall. Which was ridiculous . . .

But *oh so amazing*, as well.

He slammed his hands on my butt, almost slapping it, and lifted me, insinuating himself between my legs with the easiest of gestures. It was so practiced, so natural, that I knew, I just knew, he'd done it a million times before. He was as experienced as I was *in*experienced, and could probably do this with his eyes closed.

That bothered me, but at the same time . . .

I felt like, for him, this was special. Which was so utterly naïve. I wasn't special to him. He didn't give a damn about me, short of the way that most people cared for others. I was just another girl he was going to screw . . .

And oh my God, he *knew* what he was *doing*.

He rolled his hips into me, and even though we both had clothes on, multiple layers between us, it was magical. He deepened the kiss, his hands still gripping my butt, and did it again. It sent a surge of pleasure coursing through me, and I yanked on his hair.

He broke the kiss off, blinking down at me. "What's wrong?"

"Nothing. God, nothing." I tugged again punishingly, my breath escaping in a *whoosh*. "Don't stop. Give me *more*."

He laughed, and it was deeper than I'd ever heard him laugh before. Like, Benedict Cumberbatch deep. "Damn, Princess. You've got a naughty streak a mile wide."

"Chris." I moved my hips in a figure-eight motion, desperate for the release I knew he could give me. "Oh my God, *yes*. Hurry."

The laugh faded away into a smirk, which gave way to such a look of . . . of . . . *possession*, it should have scared the crap out of me. But instead, it sent a surge of answering need and submission inside of me that I didn't know I was capable of.

He slammed me against the wall even more securely, and slid his hand inside my pants, pressing against the spot where I ached for him most. "You have no idea how long I've waited for this. If you had any clue, you wouldn't be telling me to fucking *hurry*."

I let go of his hair and dug my fingers into his shoulders, grasping on to him with all ten nails. He hissed. "It hasn't even been a week," I said, grinning when he pressed into me even harder. I had no idea where this recklessly open side of me came from . . . but I liked it. "Don't be so dramatic."

"A week?" He laughed and ran his thumb over my clitoris. It was so close to what I needed, but not close enough. "Try *years*. Fucking *years*."

"I—"

He kissed me again, taking all words and thoughts out of my head. Pulling back, he ran his finger down my cheek. "I get it. You need satisfaction." He smirked again and traced my clit in one big sweeping circle. "I can give you that, but I'll be damned if I hurry with getting mine. I'm going to explore every"—he pressed his thumb against me—"fucking"—this time he rubbed my clitoris, hard and slow—"inch." He bit down on my neck and moved his fingers in circles, pumping his hips against me at the same time. His hard erection was impossibly huge against me. *"Slowly."*

I sucked in a deep breath, but it wasn't enough.

I needed . . . needed . . .

He thrust against me again, his lips pressed against the side of my throat, right under my ear, kissing me tenderly as his thumb circled my clitoris. It was all I required to go flying . . . right into my first orgasm.

I gasped and clung to Chris, my eyes open but seeing nothing.

My whole body hummed with pleasure, from my toes to the tips of my fingers, releasing this euphoric energy that I'd never even imagined was possible. Arching my back, I rubbed against his erection, which only made the searing pleasure even more amazing. "Oh my God."

"Shit." He buried his face in my neck, his own breathing uneasy, and he pumped against me with his hips. "That was the hottest fucking thing I've ever seen, Princess."

I dropped my head against the wall, still holding on to him for dear life. I didn't say anything, because I didn't know what to say to that. I mean, what do you say to someone who thinks your orgasm is hot? *Thank you?* or *Glad you enjoyed it. Hey, I did, too.*

"Now I'm the one who needs more." He gripped my shirt and tugged it up, but it got stuck under my arms. "I need more of you. All of you. Now. *Lift your arms.*"

I did as I was told, without hesitation.

He pulled my shirt up, slowly, as if he savored the moment.

After he pulled it over my head, he tossed it behind him. His gaze dipped down, taking in my body, and I didn't even think about covering myself up, even though my bra was sheer. If he wanted to look, he could look all he wanted. I wouldn't stop him.

After the way he'd made me feel, I was all his.

He swallowed hard. The heat in his brown eyes burned right through me, leaving marks I had a feeling would never fully go away. The desire made the green flecks in his eyes more visible. Brighter. "You're so fucking beautiful. Way too beautiful for me, but I don't give a damn. I'll take you, anyway, because that's the guy I am."

"No, you're—"

He shook his head, gave me one last lingering look, and kissed me into silence. And that look—God, that look—said I was the only thing he needed or wanted, and I didn't think I was imagining that. In his arms, I felt special. Unique. One of a kind.

Like a princess. And he was my tarnished prince . . .

Whether he liked it or not.

CHAPTER 13

CHRIS

I'd seen a lot of tits. Kissed a lot of lips. Touched a lot of slim, sexy bodies. Fucked a lot of women. Sold a lot of guns that killed a lot of people. Broken a lot of noses. Done a lot of shit that any normal person would regret, but then again, I wasn't *normal*. The thing about my lifestyle was, in a way, it was monotonous. Yes, I got laid. Yes, I killed people. But it was the same thing, every damn day, and all the women and guns faded into one long, boring, repetitive life that did nothing to excite me anymore.

But with Molly—

All that changed.

She was like a breath of fresh air. Her pink, plump lips were parted and soft, making me ache to kiss them. Her firm, perky breasts were tantalizing, and I bet they would fit in my hands perfectly. Her slim body was curved in all the right places, and fit against mine as if she was my other half—and yeah, I knew how damn corny that sounded. I just didn't give a flying fuck anymore. And being with her? Holding her?

It was like all of this was brand-new.

Like *I* could be brand-new.

I closed my hands over her breasts, dragging the sides of my thumbs over her hard nipples. She arched into my hands, her body undulating with pleasure and desire. She held nothing back, and it was a refreshing change from the other women I'd been with. The other women, whom, try as hard as I could, I couldn't remember.

All that existed was Molly.

I deepened the kiss and pinched her nipples between my fingers, pressing more firmly against her hot pussy. I couldn't stop kissing her. Touching her.

Sure, I wanted to fuck her. I would have to be dead not to.

But this was the only time I would have her, so there was no way I wouldn't savor every damn second of her lips. She tasted like a slice of heaven and hell, all wrapped into one. I knew I shouldn't be taking her, and was damning myself by doing so, but, whatever. I was going to hell, anyway.

Might as well be for something good.

Her tongue swirled around mine, and after she undid the first few buttons, she gripped my shirt, lifting it up. I knew she wanted it off, but I didn't want to stop kissing her long enough to oblige her. Growling, I broke off the kiss and let her yank my shirt over my head. After it was gone, I went to kiss her again, needing another taste of her sweet lips.

The look on her face stopped me dead in my tracks.

She watched me with parted lips and rosy cheeks as she reached out with a trembling hand. Running her fingers down my shoulder, over my chest, and around my nipples, she licked her lips and darted a quick glance up at me before focusing on my piercings again. Lucas and I had done it on a dare, years ago. He'd gotten one done, and I'd gotten them both pierced.

They had hurt like a bitch.

Worse than a bullet.

"This is so hot." She ran her finger over the ring, her face glowing with interest and desire—for *me*. And I couldn't look away. "All these tattoos . . ."

I swallowed. They covered me from shoulders to hands and went down my chest and across my back. "Do you have any?"

She traced the cross on my chest, her touch light. "God no. I don't like needles."

"It's not so bad." I skimmed my fingers down her shoulder and over the swell of her breasts. She had the prettiest, smoothest skin I'd ever seen. I lowered my lips to her throat, placing a kiss there. "But to blemish a single inch of this perfect body would surely be a mortal sin."

Her breath hitched in her throat. "Chris—"

I melded my mouth to hers, cutting off whatever she might say. She moaned and played with my nipple rings, tugging gently. The slight pressure sent a knife of pleasure shooting straight to my cock, and I kissed her harder, my teeth digging into her lips. She gave a slight nod and did it again, rolling her hips in a circular motion as she strained to get closer.

"Take me," she whispered against my mouth. "I need you."

I nodded in return, gripping her ass, hauling her into my arms, and kissing her as I walked her up the stairs. I never broke contact, not even as I carefully stepped over the congealed blood on the wood floor. I would clean that up later. Over the years, I'd gotten quite good at it. By the time I was finished, she wouldn't even see a trace of the stains from those lives I'd taken in front of her.

And she wouldn't see a trace of me, either.

I owed her that.

Hands on her ass, supporting her, I stumbled into her room, leaving the door open. I could listen for any more threats that way, even though I was positive I'd killed all the men sent to kill me. It's what I did. Ensured I removed all the threats. I wouldn't be fucking her if I thought our lives were in danger. I knew the ins and outs of Bitter Hill, and we were safe.

Well, as safe as she could be with me here, anyway.

My knees hit her bed, so I lowered her to the mattress, making sure to support her fully. When she hit the soft comforter, I reluctantly let her go. I straightened, watching her as she reached for me with both hands. *"Chris."*

I gripped the waist of my jeans. Even though I tried to keep my cool and treat this like any other sexual encounter I'd ever had, the truth was, it wasn't. Molly was special, this was special, and out of all the shitty things I ever did, I refused to let this be one of them. She had to know what this meant to me, before I left.

"You have no idea how many times I've thought about this. You lying on a bed, naked, or almost naked, watching me as I got ready to fuck you. I never thought it would happen, because I'm me and you're you, and there's no world where the two of us are together." I undid the button of my pants. "But no matter how many times I thought about it, or wanted it, nothing compares to this. To the reality of having you lying there, waiting for *me*."

"I thought about it, too." She focused on my chest and pressed her thighs together. She seemed as obsessed with my nipple rings as I was with—well, *all* of her. "You and me."

I unzipped my jeans. Her gaze dipped down, and her breathing increased. "What did you picture? I want to know every dirty detail."

She rose on her elbows, her focus locked nowhere near my face. "Nothing like this. Just kissing, and you touching me"—she pressed a hand right above her breasts—"here."

I ground my teeth together and grabbed a condom before letting my pants hit the floor. There was no hiding just how much she affected me anymore, even if I wanted to. "Is that all?"

She swallowed. "Yeah. I'm not exactly the most experienced person . . . in . . . bed. And what I've done wasn't all that memorable. So my fantasies aren't all that dirty."

I smirked. I couldn't help it.

Knowing she hadn't been with a lot of men, yet wanted to be with *me*, felt better than winning any other competition ever would. And believe me—I liked to win more than I liked anything else besides her. She was the ultimate prize.

Too bad I couldn't keep her.

I ran my finger down the soft skin of her leg. "That'll change, after me."

"God, I hope so." She squeezed her thighs together even more. "Have you gotten your fill yet? Or do you need more?"

"I'll never, ever, look my fill of you. Not in a million years. Oh, and, Princess?" I stepped closer, unable to look away. "You can press those sweet little thighs together all you want, but it won't change a damn thing—you need me to ease that ache you feel deep inside of you. You need my cock, driving deep into your pussy, until you forget everything and everyone but *us*."

A small moan escaped her.

"So do it already." She undid her pants and yanked them down. I stood there, mesmerized by all the smooth, creamy flesh she uncovered. "Take. Me. Now."

Urgency punched me in the gut. Sucking in a deep, calming breath, I took my boxers off. And I stood there, in front of her, naked. She let out a soft sound of admiration, pressing her thighs together again despite my warning. "Oh my God."

I cocked a brow. "Look your fill yet?"

"Not in a *billion* years." She sat up and scooted to the edge of the bed, licking her lips. "Don't move. I need to touch you. It's my turn now."

Well, hell.

That meant I would be dead by the time she finished with me, because with only a few kisses and a little bit of groping, I was already primed, locked, and loaded.

If *she* touched *me*—I would fucking explode.

But since I refused to tell her no, I nodded and said, "Okay."

"Come here." She took the condom out of my hand, set it on the bed, and spread her thighs. I stepped between them easily, and it felt like home. She skimmed a finger across my stomach, going from one side of the V above my cock to the other. Women loved that spot, and it appeared she was no exception. "You're so beautiful."

I opened my mouth. "The hell—"

"Uh-uh." She held a finger up, dangerously close to the tip of my cock, yet not close enough, her brows slamming down. "Don't even think about telling me you're not, or I'll stop this—right here, right now."

Part of me wanted her to. Giving her control over my body couldn't go anywhere good. But the other, sadistic part of me craved it. So I kept my mouth shut.

She smirked. "Good boy."

Reaching out again, she wrapped her hands behind me, cupping my ass with a firm grip, and pulled me even closer. I sucked in a breath when her nails dug into the skin, and shifted till my knees hit her mattress—less than an inch from her pussy.

I gritted my teeth, because being so close yet so far did things to my self-control. On top of that, I never gave control over my body to another person like this. It was new. And I wasn't sure I liked it. "You've got two minutes. After that, you're mine."

"Authoritative. I like it." She smiled. Even half-naked and eye level with my cock, she managed to toss out big words, all while looking sweet and innocent. "Deal."

Without warning, she leaned in and flicked her tongue over the tip of my cock. I tensed, my abs jerking, and threaded my fingers in her hair. "Jesus Christ."

She didn't say anything, just closed her perfect lips around my cock, sending me straight into heaven or hell—I had no idea which one. She sucked, her cheeks hollowing out, and ran her tongue over me at the same time. Groaning, I cupped the back of her head, watching her, because there was no way in hell I was gonna miss this show.

She moved her mouth down my shaft and back up it, and I was torn between being incalculably thrilled that she was so damn good at that, and angry that she was.

Inexperienced, my ass.

I pumped into her mouth, pleasure punching through me like an iron fist. "Molly, fuck. *More.*"

Moaning, she did as she was told and took more of my cock in her mouth, so deep I was sure I died and impossibly ended up in heaven with a dirty angel. Her nails dug into my ass, but she released the pressure and snaked them around the front of my body. With expert precision, she pulled on my balls, increasing the pleasure she caused with her mouth tenfold.

I gritted my teeth so hard they should've snapped.

And my tenuous hold on restraint did.

"Enough," I rasped, my voice foreign even to my own ears.

I tugged her hair till she released me, inch by torturous inch. If she wrapped those lips around me for another second, this would be over too fast. She released me with a popping sound, staring up at me with warm hazel eyes that seemed as if they stared right into my soul and didn't judge me—

Which was even more impossible than her being in my arms was.

Yet, there she was.

She licked her swollen lips, and with way too much practiced ease, she undid her bra, letting the straps fall down her arms. Latching gazes with me, she shrugged it off, baring her perky, pink-tipped breasts. My fingers itched—physically *itched*—to draw them. The way the light played on her aroused nipples. Her pouted lips. The soft curve of her hip. Hell, I wanted to draw *her*. All of her.

But it would have to wait.

Her hair was messy, and her makeup was smudged, but in this moment, for this short time, against all rhyme or reason, she was all mine.

And I'd never seen anything so unattainably beautiful in my whole life.

"I want to do that to you again," she said, leaning in and licking my cock, watching me the whole time. "And again."

A strangled groan escaped me. She was trying to *kill* me.

"I love watching you fuck me with that sweet mouth of yours, and trust me—it feels amazing. But if you keep licking me and sucking on my cock, I'm gonna come, and I'll be damned if the first time I come, I'm not buried deep in that tight, wet pussy of yours." Gripping her shoulders, I pushed them until she lay on her back, and I stood between her legs, naked and towering over her. "So it's *my* turn, Princess."

I made quick work of rolling the condom on my cock, not wanting to take time to do it later, when I had her naked and panting and screaming my name so loud the neighbors called the cops. The second the protection aspect was taken care of, I dropped to my knees between her legs, my attention firmly set on that tiny strip of red satin that kept me from what I wanted most—to worship her with my mouth until she saw heaven, came back, and went on another trip.

And I wouldn't stop until she did.

Leaning in, I nipped the skin on her soft inner thigh. She tasted sweet, like strawberries. She moaned and arched her back, undulating her hips. "Oh my God, *Chris*."

I bit her other thigh, a little harder. "Yeah, Princess?"

"I need you," she managed to say, her voice strangled and strained. She lifted her hips again, breathing heavily. She still wore her panties, and I couldn't wait to unbury the rest of my treasure. *"Please."*

"Since you asked so nicely"—I grabbed the top of her panties and pulled, tearing them off her in one smooth motion—"how could I say no?"

Burying my face between her thighs, I breathed in her musky scent and closed my mouth over her clit, rolling my tongue over the hard bud in short, firm strokes. She screamed and lifted her hips, her whole body twisting and turning in a desperate attempt to get closer. To get more. *"Chris."*

The way she said my name—part cry, part curse, part admiration, and part fear—struck me all the way to my core. It would have sliced straight through my heart if I'd had one. I deepened my intimate kiss, rolling my tongue over her.

She was so close to coming that I could taste it.

I gripped her thighs, digging my fingertips in so I held her right where I wanted her. She thrashed against me, fighting my hold, but I didn't relent. Didn't back down.

Her back bowed, her mouth opened, she buried her hands in my hair—and she came. She motherfucking came. I thought the last orgasm was the hottest thing I'd ever witnessed? I was wrong. *This* was. Growling deep in my throat, and filled with a deep, searing possession I'd never before felt, I climbed up her body, slid my hand under her head, and kissed her with all the pent-up passion and desire I'd held back for so long.

And she gave it all right back to me.

Holding my cock, I squeezed it to relieve the pressure, and bumped it against her clit once. She screamed into my mouth, nails scraping against my upper back as she held on and came again. While she still trembled from that orgasm, I drove inside of her with a force that I couldn't control. The second I was buried inside her, we both froze.

Breathing heavily, I rested my forehead on hers. "Jesus Christ, you're so fucking tight. You've done this before, right?"

I hadn't felt any signs of her being a virgin . . .

But shit if I knew what those signs were.

"Yes. Once." She wrapped her legs and arms around me, holding me close as she took a deep breath. "Let's make it twice."

I kissed her tenderly, moving my hips as my tongue swirled around hers. I pulled almost all the way out of her, but her body fought me as I did so. Once I was perched at her entrance, at the entryway to heaven, I glided in again, gritting my teeth at the insane amount of pleasure her tight walls gave me. Nothing, and no one, would ever compare to this moment, in this bed, with this woman.

Her lids drifted shut and she clung to me, arching her back. I kept up my smooth, easy strokes, driving her higher and higher with each one. It was clear her last experience had been lackluster—she'd told me as much—so this one had to knock it out of the ball field. It had to be a night to remember after I left.

Even if it killed me . . .

Which it just *might*.

Sweat stung my eyes, and my balls ached with the need to find my own orgasm, but I held it back through some miracle of nature. I had no idea how.

But when her mouth fell open, and her eyes glazed over, and her cheeks blossomed into a rosy red, I was right there with her when she came for the fourth, and final, time. I drove inside her, pleasure taking over my whole body, and collapsed on top of her, making sure to keep my weight off her as I soared into my own orgasm.

Her arms and legs held me just as tight as before, and her breathing matched mine, breath for breath. "Wow. Is it always like that?"

"No." I kissed her forehead and settled on top of her more firmly. "Never."

Satisfaction crossed her eyes before they drifted shut.

I buried my face in her neck and finally let my eyes close, too, needing to savor this moment. In a lifetime of murder, sex, and betrayal—this one second of serenity was the thing that kept me alive. Holding Molly in my arms, my body relaxed, my soul complete, my heart pounding steadily, and my mind numb from pain.

Too bad it didn't last forever, this feeling.

Nothing ever did, except death.

Her breathing settled, her grip on me relaxed, and so I pulled out of her and climbed out of the bed slowly. She didn't awaken, but rolled over on her side, her face lost in peaceful slumber. And she didn't move again. Not even as I removed the condom, collected all my clothes, and dressed.

As I walked out the door, I couldn't resist stealing one last glimpse at the angel I left behind. She was softer in her sleep, her features even more innocent in slumber, but instead of making me hesitate, it only cemented my decision. It was time to go.

Before she *really* got hurt.

I had packed my shit up earlier, so I grabbed the trash bag I'd used from under the bed, setting it down at the bottom of the stairs. I didn't have much, just what she'd bought me, so it was lightweight. I cleaned up the bloodstains, sweating as I did so, but by the time I was finished, there were no signs of the mayhem I'd caused in her life. Once I walked out that door, she'd be free of me and all the shit that came with me.

She'd thank me later.

As I passed the dinner we never ate, and the cake we never cut, I hesitated. There, wrapped in a pretty green bow, was the gift she'd gotten me. Glancing over my shoulder like a guilty kid caught peeking under the tree on Christmas Eve, I stepped closer, sliding it across the table.

With steady hands, I undid the bow carefully, almost sad to destroy it. I never got presents, which meant I certainly didn't get presents this pretty. It was a shame to ruin it.

But as I tore the wrapping paper off, excitement built.

And when I opened the box, heart racing, it was as if the world stood still. There, in the box, was something I'd written off as lost days ago. All my clothes from the night she found me had been thrown out, and I'd assumed she'd tossed my jacket as well.

I'd assumed wrong.

In the box, folded with tender, loving care, was my jacket. It had been repaired in the spot where Lucas's bullet had hit me, and it smelled clean. If it weren't for the fact that I recognized every old stain and every little worn spot on it,

I would have sworn she'd bought me a new one. But even better than that?

She'd repaired mine, knowing how much it meant.

And that was the most thoughtful thing anyone had *ever* done for me.

Swallowing down the surge of emotion that hit me at such a thoughtful gesture, I set my bag down and shrugged into the jacket. It fit me like a glove, as it should, but somehow better. A faint meow caught my attention, so I walked over to the cat room and opened the door. Buttons came charging out, practically throwing himself at my feet and purring.

Bending down, I petted his head and belly, just the way he liked it. He stared up at me with adoring yellow eyes, snorting out of his little heart-shaped nose. I couldn't help but wonder, if I had grown up in a home like hers, with a cat like this, where birthdays mattered, and instead of punches you got hugs—would I be like her? Would I be soft and open-hearted? Would I have been one of the good guys, instead of a killer?

It didn't matter, really, because I hadn't.

And I wasn't.

So I patted the cat one last time, picked up the trash bag, cast one last, longing look around the house I would never see again, and walked out the door. I didn't bother to leave a note or an explanation. It was better this way, like ripping off the tape when someone taped your mouth shut. It hurt like a bitch to remove, but it was a hell of a lot better than dragging it out.

It was over. I was leaving.

And she'd be better off without me.

CHAPTER 14

MOLLY

The early-morning sun shone in through the sheer purple curtains, and they drifted in the breeze from the heat coming out of the floor vent, and there was a stillness in the air that soothed me. I lay there, not moving, just watching the curtains blow, and couldn't help but think that the curtains were a lot like me. Transparent. Vulnerable to the slightest force of movement. But they were strong, too.

Sure, they might get tangled up on something, or tear, but they didn't break. Didn't bend. They stayed steady, doing their thing, and didn't let anything stop them.

And I was crazy because I was literally comparing myself to *curtains*.

But what I was really trying to do was remind myself that I needed to keep Chris at a distance. He couldn't give me what I needed out of life. I wasn't exactly sure what it was I *did* want from a man, but it didn't involve constant worrying, stress, police, and bullet holes. *That* much I knew.

I needed a guy who could give me stability and help me get over my fear of falling in love. I needed a man who would go to work and come home at night . . . without bullet holes. I needed a man who would stay *alive*. Who wouldn't leave me.

He couldn't give me those things. He'd never leave the gang, and I'd never be okay with being with someone who did the things he did. He knew it, and so did I.

I just had to make sure my stupid heart remembered, too.

Slowly, I worked up the nerve to roll over. I'd been trying to think of the perfect thing to say to Chris if I was wrong. I had something witty to say all planned out, something that would show him that the night we'd shared had been amazing but that I wouldn't turn into some crazy chick because he gave me an orgasm or two . . . or more.

Who was keeping track, anyway?

But I shouldn't have bothered. He wasn't there. Not a huge surprise. Something told me he wasn't exactly the stick-around-canoodling type of guy. He probably hit it, then quit it. I was now quit. So he was either in bed in his own room, or hiding downstairs to avoid me until he made up some excuse about why we had to forget that last night ever happened.

Which was okay.

That was fine.

I didn't need him staring at me with heart eyes because we had sex and he gave me the best—and *first*—orgasm of my entire life. I didn't need him sitting on the bed, staring at me as if he'd die if he didn't get another taste *right now*. Sure, maybe I thought staying in bed together all day and getting up only for cake was a great idea, but clearly he felt differently.

More than likely, he was downstairs drinking some coffee, planning on how best to leave me. God knows he hadn't hidden his desire to leave as soon as possible. And he was better now. A guy who could do what he did to me last night? Yeah, he was fighting fit.

A fitting description, really.

I sat up and hugged my knees, resting my cheek on them and staring at those curtains again. They still blew slightly, and the sun still shone, but the room seemed darker.

Quieter.

Too quiet.

Nibbling on my lower lip, I climbed out of bed, threw on my robe, and opened the door. The faint scent of bleach greeted me, and Buttons sat there, staring up at me, looking almost . . . *forlorn.* I scooped him up under the belly and checked his paws for glass. They were clean and dry. In all the craziness of last night, I'd forgotten about the devastation and blood . . . and bodies.

And Buttons.

Hugging him close to my chest, I kissed him, bringing him with me. He snuggled into my chest, not minding the snuggles, for now. Tiptoeing, I made my way to Dad's room. The door was open, and the room was empty. The bed was made, and there was no sign of Chris. Not even a loose article of clothing.

Swallowing, I headed for the stairs, knowing what I would find, but also in denial. I'd known all along how he would do it. How this would end. And yet stupidly . . .

I still hoped to be wrong.

"Chris?" I called out, gripping the banister. "Are you down there?"

Nothing. Just silence.

I paused halfway down the stairs, because the aftermath of last night's gun battle . . . it was gone. My foyer had never been so *clean.* The spot where the blood had congealed on the floor, and a broken vase had been littered around it like a kind of broken crown, was wiped clean. Everything was perfect, as if it had never happened. As if no one had died there.

But they had. I'd watched them.

All three of them.

If not for the fact that I'd woken up naked and pleasantly sore, and for the lingering scent of bleach in the air, I might think I'd dreamt the whole thing. Buttons squirmed, and I set him down, now that I knew it was safe for him to wander the house. He meowed and walked into the kitchen. Hugging my robe tighter, I came down the stairs the rest of the way, walking carefully in case a piece of glass had been missed. I shouldn't have bothered.

My house was spotless.

And completely, heartbreakingly, painfully *empty*.

Chris had left. I was alone again. I should probably be relieved or something, since I'd just been thinking about how he couldn't give me what I wanted out of life, and how it would never work out between us, but whatever. Something about Chris had made me happy, and knowing he was gone *didn't* make me *happy*.

"Chris?" I called out one last time, clinging to that last bit of hope that after last night, he hadn't left without a word. That our night together had meant something to him . . . like it had to me. "Are you here?"

No one answered.

Straightening my spine, I lifted my chin and walked into the kitchen. If I meant nothing to him, and last night had been a good-bye of sorts, then, whatever. If he could walk away so easily, without a doubt or hesitation—heck, without a *good-bye*—I could let him. I'd be fine. Great. Wonderful. Fantastic.

And if I said it in enough ways . . .

Maybe I'd believe it eventually.

Making my way over to my Keurig, I frowned at the food we'd never eaten, which I'd completely forgotten about, and the cake I hadn't even lit up for him. Some birthday.

No dinner. No cake. No presents.

Just sex with a side order of death.

Shaking my head, I ignored the mess. I wasn't cleaning up a thing until I had coffee in me. As I pushed the brew button, I turned around and surveyed the house. Every sign of the fight was gone, and all that remained was . . . nothing. As I turned back around, I noticed the open present. Swallowing, I made my way over, wondering if he'd left me a note there. A good-bye. A thank-you. A hate letter. *Something.*

It was empty.

He'd taken his jacket and left. He was gone.

It wasn't until then, seeing his missing jacket, that I knew I was right. There was no hope for us. With his actions today, he'd made it quite clear that he and I didn't mix. That we could never, would never, work out. But still . . .

Deep down, I hadn't believed him.

Guess I did now.

The Keurig made its last churning sound when it was finished, so I grabbed my coffee and sat down, facing the door. And I stared at it, waiting for . . . for . . .

Nothing. He wouldn't come back.

He was finished with me, and nothing I did would change that. I'd probably never see him again. Never watch that hesitant smile cross his face. Never hear him laugh or see him almost jump in surprise as he did so. As if he couldn't believe that something had caused him to share his amusement with others. Something told me he didn't laugh much in his other life.

The one without me.

And that only made me even sadder.

A guy like Chris, with the life he'd been born into, did he really stand a chance at being happy? At laughing over nothing and walking hand in hand with a woman he loved? Did those guys in that lifestyle get to do that? Or was it all kill or be killed and shoot-outs and bullets? Did he ever get to, I don't know, have *fun*?

He'd never had a birthday party. Didn't even know what a stinking party favor was or what to do with it. What kind of full-grown man had never had those things?

What kind of man lived in darkness, without a sliver of light?

I think that was what bothered me the most.

He didn't know how to be *happy*. The fact that every ounce of humanity I showed him surprised him made me want to cry—and I wasn't much of a crier anymore. But it was like he didn't know life could be enjoyable, or that people could be nice just because they wanted to be. Or that laughter felt good.

That sharing your time with someone could make your heart pound and your pulse quicken, and you didn't need death and blood and adrenaline to feel alive.

Because he'd never had a birthday party, I couldn't help but wonder if some of his behaviors stemmed from his parents. I knew from experience that most children who behaved like Chris—their parents, or whoever was raising them, were abusive. Ninety percent of the time that held true. *Had* he been abused? Was that why he was so alone?

I was alone, too, but for different reasons.

Because I didn't want to lose anyone ever again.

I stared at the door, lost in my thoughts, just thinking about Chris and his life—and mine, too. By the time I came back to myself and became aware of my surroundings, I'd been sitting at my kitchen table long enough that my back hurt, my coffee was as cold as it was untouched, my eyes were heavy, and half of my butt was asleep.

And I was still, predictably, *alone*.

Like always.

Something brushed against my leg, and I glanced down. Buttons stared up at me, tail swishing, and I smiled. Reaching down, I picked him up and hugged him, closing my eyes. He rubbed his face against my shoulder, purring, and I smiled for the first time all day. Because he'd reminded me of something. I wasn't alone. I was never alone.

I had *Buttons*.

"Hey, baby. You'll never leave me, right?" I nuzzled his face with mine, laughing when he snorted. "I know what that noise means. You're hungry. Aren't you?"

He hopped off me, walking toward the cat room, confident in my willingness to follow him. Sighing, I stood up slowly. My lower back pulled in protest, but I kept moving. My vigil over the front door was over. He obviously wasn't coming back. Ever.

Dumping my cold coffee into the sink, I went in the cat room, picked up Buttons' bowl full of food, and set it down on the kitchen floor. As he dug in, my phone buzzed with a text message on the island. I picked it up right away, my heart racing. Maybe Chris—

No. Not Chris. Hollie Yardley. My friend at work.

Hey, I'm with Mary. We're going out to lunch to celebrate freedom with mimosas and copious amounts of food and cake. Want in?

No, thanks. I'll just stay in and— I quit typing, staring at the screen. What was I going to stay in and do? Wait for

Chris to return, when he clearly wasn't going to? Miss him? Miss my dad? Enough already. I deleted the text and quickly typed. Sure! Where and when?

Really? Yay! Frank's. Twelve.

I smiled and typed. I'll be there!

Setting the phone down, I made quick work of throwing away last night's dinner and the untouched cake. I didn't want it or any reminder of what had been. I didn't regret it, or him, but no matter how many times I reminded myself that it was for the better, it hurt that he'd found it so easy to walk away.

I wasn't naïve enough to think that sex had emotional significance to everyone—but for me, against all reason . . . it had. I hadn't given myself to him lightly. I'd shared a part of myself with him that not many people had ever seen, or known, and that *meant something*. To me, anyway. Not to him.

After all traces of last night were gone, including the empty present box, I stood in my kitchen, my breath uneven and my heart empty, and smoothly closed the drawer he'd fixed for me. Dusting my hands off, I headed upstairs and took a shower. As I washed away all traces of his touch, I blinked away tears, refusing to let them fall.

And when I got out of the shower, I took special care with my clothes and makeup. By the time I was finished and walking out the door, on the outside, I looked as if I wasn't missing Chris O'Brien and his soft touch at *all*. On the inside?

Well, that was for me and me alone.

Four hours later, I came home, still smiling from the girls' "night" out I'd just had. After actually, you know, going, it made me wonder what I'd been avoiding for so long. Yes, I was alone, and yes, I had only a cat by my side. But whose fault was that?

Mine.

It was time to let people in, to some extent. Make friends, stop hiding behind closed doors. I'd already made plans with the girls for a night out tomorrow. Dancing. Drinking. Being normal. No shoot-outs or blood. Just normal things normal people do.

I smiled at Buttons, trying to decide what to do with the rest of my day. The sun was setting, and the house was as empty as it had been when I left it, and I . . . I . . . I missed *Chris*. So much.

Shaking my head at my thoughts, I headed into the living room. "Let's see, Buttons. What will we do tonight? I could grade some papers. Plan some lessons. Create some classroom decorations. Watch some zombies kill people . . ."

No, I wasn't ready for that yet.

Too much blood.

Sighing, I settled into the corner of the couch, right in front of where I'd cowered last night. Buttons hopped up on the cushion beside me, eyeing the spot where Chris usually sat. Ignoring the pang that sent through my chest, I searched for the remote, since it was nowhere to be seen.

Reaching into the couch cushions, I frowned when I felt a piece of paper. Pulling it out, I unfolded it slowly—and forgot to *breathe*.

Staring up at me was . . . well, me.

There was no mistaking it. The eyes, the nose, the lips, even the hair. It was a picture-perfect representation of me. He'd even managed to portray the way my eyes slanted up when I smiled. Dad had always told me I was like a cat when I grinned— mischievous, with slightly upturned eyes.

He'd captured *that*.

And so much more.

Running my trembling fingers across it, I stared down at the paper, the tears I'd been holding back all day filling my eyes and threatening to spill over. He'd said he wasn't any good. That what he drew was garbage. He'd lied.

This was *art*.

Standing up, I walked over to the hutch. Opening the drawer on the left, I pulled out another drawing. It was a landscape, and it had trees and a lake. I'd always wondered where this place was. I wanted to see it. That's how pretty it looked on paper. The sun shone down on the small body of water, reflecting the tranquility of the moment, and it had always stolen my breath away.

I stared at the two different drawings, trying to find a similarity between them, but, of course, failed. Chris had drawn the portrait, while the landscape had been left on my porch by my secret admirer. Years ago, I'd wondered if the hardened criminal who helped out around my house could be the same man who gave me presents.

Then I'd laughed, because there was no way.

Chris had seemed more likely to shoot a kitten than to *give* me one so I wouldn't be "lonely at night anymore." But now that I knew him better, I couldn't help but wonder . . .

Someone knocked on the door.

I jumped, dropping the landscape. It fluttered to the floor slowly, before sliding under the table. I set the drawing of me down carefully and walked over to the door, my heart racing, because maybe it was Chris. Maybe he'd come *back* to me.

Of course, maybe it was more of those men, the ones Chris had gotten rid of, coming back to finish the job. And once they found out Chris wasn't here . . .

What would they do to *me*?

I peeked out the curtain carefully, checking to see if it looked like it was someone here to kill me. A bored-looking, skinny, tall, pimply-faced teenager stood there, holding a bouquet of flowers. He checked his phone, rolled his eyes, and knocked again.

Looked pretty harmless.

Then again, appearances could be deceiving.

Hesitantly, I let the curtains drift back into place and unlocked the door, opening it just enough to peek out and say, "Can I help you?"

He tucked his phone away, gave me an appreciative once-over and a full smile. The kid still had braces, and he was already looking at me as if he wanted to see me naked. He would be trouble as an adult. "I have a delivery for a Ms. Lachlan."

"That's me."

He held the flowers out. "Pretty flowers for a pretty lady. I'd like to say they're from me, but I'm just the messenger."

"Thank you." I took them and frowned. "Stop it. You're too young to be flirting with me."

"I doubt that. Sign here, my lady."

I rolled my eyes, signed, and grabbed my purse, pulling out a five. Holding it out, I gave him my best stern-teacher look and said, "Go home and play some Xbox."

Then I shut the door in his face.

After I locked it, I leaned back on it and searched for a card. There it was. Tiny and in a pink envelope. Setting the flowers down, I tore the envelope open and let it fall to the floor. The small card had familiar handwriting on it. Writing I'd seen over the past few years, from my secret admirer. Writing I'd recognize *anywhere*.

But then the sun rose, and I knew there was beauty in this world.

I'm sorry, Princess.
Chris

Staring at the writing and the words, I ran back into the living room, pulse racing, and opened that drawer again. I pulled out the most recent gift I'd gotten—a small cat figurine—and the most recent line of poetry I'd received before today.

Putting the two together, I read them.

I was surrounded by darkness and gloom, sure there was nothing good left.
   But then the sun rose, and I knew there was beauty in this world.

It was *him*. All along, my secret admirer had been *Chris*. The flowers. The poems. The books. The words of love. Everything. All of it. Even Buttons. They'd been from him. *Chris.* "Oh my God."

Buttons groomed himself on the couch but lifted his head at my words.

I smiled at him. "It's him. Chris."

Buttons meowed.

A man who could go through so much thought to give me something so beautiful for so many years was worth the risk. Was worth letting him in. And even if he hurt me? I didn't *care*. I wanted him here, with me, and I refused to let him face his demons alone because he didn't want to put me at risk or because I was too scared to let him in.

I could handle it. I was done being scared. Screw that.

He was safer here. With *me*. And I was going to tell him that, as soon as I managed to find him. I knew exactly where I needed to go to do that . . . Steel Row. The place I normally avoided at all costs.

Where my dad had died.

I hadn't been back since.

Dad had always been looking to help out his fellow man. To save lives. It was my turn now. I needed to save Chris. And if I had to go into hell to do it? So be it.

I'd go.

Setting down the poem, I patted Buttons on the head as I passed and grabbed my keys. "I'm going to bring him home."

Rushing to the garage, I jumped in my car and started the ignition. The ride to Steel Row passed way too quickly, probably because I gripped the wheel so tightly my knuckles hurt and because all I could think about was my dad and what had happened to him. To me.

All around me, dilapidated houses, run-down bars, and vacant shop fronts framed the streets. A small group of kids shared a skateboard, egging one another on, while hard-eyed men watched me from the street corners, assessing my threat potential. There were bars on nearly all the windows, and the street signs looked dingy.

It felt like driving into another world, as the air hung heavy with an undercurrent of danger. This wasn't a world I knew, a world I felt safe in, but real people lived here—real people with real lives, and they *lived* here.

People like Chris.

As I drove by the market where my father died, I gripped the wheel even tighter and stepped on the gas hard. I turned down a quiet street right outside of Steel Row, where it was all trees and no houses, thinking maybe it was a good spot for Chris to hide.

The second I cleared the corner, another car pulled up behind me with one of those red flashing lights the cops used on the dash. I pulled over and stepped on the brake.

"Crap." I cracked the window and waited for the officer in question. He shut off the light and approached my vehicle. My pulse raced, and I hesitated, ready to pull my foot off the brake, because he wasn't in uniform. "Officer?"

"Ms. Lachlan." He stopped outside my window and bent down. He wore a dark hoodie and dark jeans and looked *nothing* like a cop. "How are you tonight?"

"Good . . ." I rested my hand on the shifter, ready to stomp on the gas, because something about the officer was familiar. I just couldn't quite figure out what. "How did you know my name?"

"I ran your plates."

I tightened my hold on the knob of the shifter, easing my foot off the brake ever so slightly. "Already?"

"Yes." He rested a hand on my roof, tapping his fingers. "You were doing twenty over the speed limit."

He was right. I had been. I pressed back down on the brake, since he'd obviously just been doing his job. "I'm sorry. It won't happen again."

"I can't help but think you're lost, Molly." He bent lower, and something about him triggered a long-forgotten memory of Chris sitting on his parents' porch with a few buddies. They'd been drinking beer and laughing loudly. "Girls like you don't belong here."

"Do I know you?" I asked. "How do you know what kind of girl I am, Officer?"

"Besides the expensive car, you mean?" he asked with amusement. "In this area, your type of car is a dead give-away, unless you're a member of the Sons. And since you're a chick, I happen to know for a fact you're not."

"O-of course not." My heart skipped a beat at the mention of Chris's gang from a cop, and my cheeks flushed. When it came to lying, I got an F every time. "I'm looking for a friend, and I thought he might be here. I'm not lost."

"Who's your friend? I might know him."

Oh, he probably did. But not in a good way. "I doubt it," I said simply.

"That might be true, but you're right. I do know you, Molly." He lowered his face to the window, but his hood stayed up. I stared at him, recollection finally hitting. "Scott Donahue, at your service."

Scotty Donahue was Chris's best friend's little brother. *That* was why I recognized him. My jaw dropped, because Scotty wasn't a cop. He was a member of Steel Row, and one of Chris's friends, and just as "bad" as Chris was.

"You're not a cop, Scotty."

He laughed at the nickname. "No one calls me that."

"Chris does."

"Yeah." The laugh died. "He who you're looking for?"

I froze, not sure how to answer that. Yeah, he was a member of the same gang as Chris, but Chris had been hiding from . . . something. What if that *something* was Scotty? "What makes you think that?"

"I have my reasons," he hedged. "You looking for him, Molly?"

"Are you?" I shot back, my hand falling back on the shifter.

"Doesn't matter what I'm doing. You have no place in this world, Molly." He shook his head, rested both hands on my roof, and locked eyes with me. "You have no idea what you're jumping into here, with him, and me, and the rest of the Sons. You're going to get yourself killed if you're not careful. Go home."

"I'm not trying to jump into anything at all," I said quickly. "Like I said, I'm just looking for a friend."

He shook his head. "Do you know why Chris is hiding in the first place? Did he tell you?"

So, he knew that much. The question was . . . how did he know? "I don't even know what you're talking about. Who is hiding from who?"

"Molly . . ." Scotty laughed, tapping his fingers on the metal roof, and repositioned his feet. "You don't know how to play this game you're playing, so I suggest you stop trying. I know he was with you. Just like I know he left, and is currently in an alley, bleeding, and refusing to let me help him."

I stiffened, my heart dropping to my stomach at the idea of Chris lying in an alley injured yet again. *What kind of life did he lead?* "Where is he? And why are you acting like a cop when we both know you're not?"

He hesitated but shrugged. "It's a clever disguise in more ways than one. I'm no stranger to molding a person's perception of me to make my life easier."

"You're clearly a man used to lying. Why should I listen to you now? Maybe it's a trap, to get me to go looking for Chris—which I'm not even doing—so I can be used against him somehow. Maybe you plan on holding me captive to get him to show up, so you can kill him. Problem is, he probably wouldn't show. I'm nothing to him."

Scotty laughed, deeply and richly, and grabbed my steering wheel. "Oh, Molly. If only you knew how ironic those words were."

Dread settled into the bottom of my stomach. "Is this when you try to abduct me? I'll fight back. I might not be used to this type of life, but I won't go down easy."

"No." He sobered and locked eyes with me. "I'm not one

of the bad guys. Not tonight, anyway. If you're looking for him—and I *know* you are, so there's no use denying it—he's behind the Patriot, probably regretting the shit he's done, as he should be, and trying not to get shot again."

I stiffened. "What did he do?" I asked quietly.

"That's for him to tell." He lifted a shoulder. "Not me."

I didn't say anything to that. He was right, after all.

He tapped my wheel. "You should go home, though, instead of going out and searching for him. Forget all about Chris O'Brien. Take it from me: Guys like us only bring pain and death, and you're better off without him."

"Then why tell me where he is at all?"

"Because even though he did something unforgivable, I've known him all my life. There's a good guy buried beneath the asshole, and I don't want to find his corpse in an alley tomorrow morning. He's been crazy about you since we were kids, but he never thought a guy like him could end up with someone like you. He trusts you. If you can help him . . . I'm not gonna stop you. You're a big girl. You can make your own choices." He paused, leveling a gaze on me that felt as if it weighed a thousand pounds. "So tell me. Can you help him?"

I thought driving around trying to find him was helping him, but whatever. Of course I'd be there, provided I could *find* him. And once I did, I wouldn't take no for an answer. He'd come with me, whether he wanted to or not. "How much danger is he in?"

"More than you'd ever understand," Scotty answered gravely.

I swallowed hard. "Where's the Patriot?"

"You have no idea how much danger you're putting yourself in if you go find him." He flexed his jaw. "You have to tell me you understand that you could be hurt."

I might be making the wrong choice in deliberately thrusting myself into a mess that had nothing to do with me, but I was going to do it anyway. He'd spent years making my life a little brighter, asking nothing in return. He might have killed a few men, and he might not be a good guy, but he was *mine*. And I wouldn't let him die in some alley alone because I was too scared to go find him. "Like I said, where's the Patriot?"

CHAPTER 15

CHRIS

It was kinda poetic that I came here, in a way. I hadn't come here to die, but I just might. Bitter Hill had jumped me the second I entered the alley, and now I was right back where I started—bleeding in a fucking alley. If I died here, among the ruins of Lucas's apartment, well, what the fuck ever. Not much I could do besides do my best to stay alive so I could save Scotty's sorry life.

Then I could die with a purpose, at least.

And if that wasn't enough for me anymore, then I needed to get over it.

Grinning, I kicked the body near my feet. Another Bitter Hill guy who'd failed to finish me. At least, if I was gonna go down, I would go down swinging. And at least I'd had a taste of heaven in Molly's arms before going straight to hell, where I belonged.

It had been glorious.

My phone rang, and I dug it out of my pocket, grimacing

at the pain it sent shafting through my ribs. Son of a fucking bitch, that hurt. I glowered at the screen and swiped my finger across it. "What the fuck do you want, Scotty?"

"Hi. Nice to talk to you, too." Scotty paused. "You're still alive?"

"No. I'm talking to you from hell. Satan says hi," I snapped. "He told me he has a hot pike reserved for your ass, so hurry up and come join us."

Scotty snorted. "Glad to see you haven't lost your sense of humor in all this shit."

"Why are you calling me?" I kept my gaze on the opening of the alley, ready to shoot anything that moved. "I'm kind of in the middle of something."

"First of all, Molly is out looking for you."

"Son of a bitch." I let the gun fall to my side, still clutching it, because it took too much effort to hold it up. "Where is she?"

"Heading your way. Don't shoot her."

I gritted my teeth, cursing a million times over in my head. I never should have sent her those damn flowers or let her know I was the guy who'd been sending her romantic and sappy shit for years. It had been a moment of weakness, when I was sure I'd never see her again, or that I might die. But it had been selfish. It had been *me*.

"Stop her. Arrest her. Tie her up in your truck. Ship her off to England. Shit, I don't care what you do, as long as it gets her to forget about me and it's nothing bad." I struggled to my feet. "Just do it."

"Sorry—too late. I already sent her on her way with directions to you. You need to go with her." Scotty paused. "If you don't, she'll just end up getting herself killed looking for me, and we both know it."

"Dammit, Scotty." I closed my eyes because he had a

point. If she kept driving around Steel Row, something or someone would eventually take advantage of that. "I'm going to skin you alive for telling her where I was."

He snorted. "You're welcome to try."

I gritted my teeth.

"Go home with her. Sleep. Heal. And, once all signs of you getting your ass kicked repeatedly are gone, rejoin the gang and help me bring down some assholes. We'll clean up Steel Row together. Make the neighborhood safe again. Take down gang members together. Like you said."

I leaned against the wall, letting out an exhausted breath. "And how the hell am I gonna help you do that? I'm not a cop."

"No, but you said you'd do what it takes to help me."

I did, didn't I? Stupid son of a bitch that I was. "So I'm gonna narc for you? Be a rat?"

"Pretty much." Scotty paused. "That gonna be an issue? Are you changing your mind? We can always come up with a different plan, if you want. One that may or may not involve jail time."

I clenched my jaw at the veiled threat, picturing Lucas. In my mind, he watched Scotty with pride as the kid hit a home run, standing up on the bleachers and cheering loudly as his little brother ran the bases. The pride he had for his brother was something I'd never had or felt in my life. Lucas was such a better guy than me.

And I owed him.

"Nah, man. I'm there." I scratched my head. "But I can't go with Molly. Guys showed up at her place yesterday. Bitter Hill. I hid their bodies in Pops's garage. It's not safe there anymore."

"Then take her somewhere else with you."

"I'll go alone," I gritted.

"And leave her defenseless?" Scotty laughed. "You, of all people, should know how quick the enemy is to use a woman against you."

Even though his words made me feel like shit, since I'd done that to Lucas, I forced a laugh. "All's fair in love and war, man."

"That's what they say," Scotty agreed. "They know she's yours now. They'll use her again, only this time, you won't be there to stop them. You need to protect her till we at least take down Reggie."

Fucking A. He was right.

Me leaving her didn't save her. It was too late for that.

Maybe I could send her away somewhere safe. Tell her to take a vacation till this all blew over . . . which would be never. This wasn't some small battle with a shithead.

This was *war*.

"I have to go. Just pulled up to Tate's." Scotty shut off his truck and sighed. "They took out Artie."

I closed my eyes. He was an older member, like Pops. "Shit. Where?"

"Outside of his place. All of the higher-ups are going into hiding. Taking precautions to stay alive. I told Tate I'd let you know, so you being out of sight will look normal." Scotty cleared his throat. "I'll let Tate know you're laying low as ordered and chasing some pussy, and will be back when he wants you. Hang tight. Keep yourself out of Bitter Hill's grasp. Don't kill anyone else."

I stared down at the corpse at my feet. His red, congealed blood poured out of the perfectly centered chest shot—which I'd been particularly proud of, considering the fact he'd snuck up on me and given me quite the beating before I'd killed him—and soaked the pavement behind Heidi's bar, right below what had once been Lucas's living room window. Now it was the charred remains of what had once been my best friend's home, and a reminder of what I'd done to him. "About that . . . ?"

"*Shit.*" Silence, and then: "How many?"

"One." I paused. "So far."

"Molly will be there any minute. Get the fuck outta there, and I'll have some guys clean it up." He closed a door. "I'll get the guys in your pops's garage, too."

"Be careful no one finds out." I dropped my head on the wall, watching the headlights that approached and slowed. More than likely, my princess was here. "You're playing a dangerous game, Scotty boy."

"Aren't we all?"

Molly came around the corner of the alley, hesitating. "Chris?"

For a second, I debated not answering her. Chances were, she'd get scared and run off, go home, and be fine. Then again, maybe not.

And that was a risk I wasn't willing to take. "Here."

"Chris, I—"

"Is she there?" Scotty asked at the same time.

She came two steps closer, and something caught my eye. Still holding the phone to my ear, I lifted my arm, squeezed the trigger, and shot down the motherfucker creeping up behind my girl. The asshat didn't even see it coming, and he hit the ground convulsing. He'd be dead within seconds, since I'd hit him in the throat. He'd choke on his own blood and die, and I didn't give a damn.

I was a sadistic fucker like that.

He shouldn't have come after my girl if he wanted to live.

Molly, for her part, clapped her hands over her ears and dropped to a crouch, whimpering. Well, if that wasn't enough to scare her off, I didn't know what was.

Lowering my weapon, I said to Scotty, who'd fallen oddly silent on the phone, "Make that two."

"You're *killing* me. Get the fuck outta there *now.*"

I nodded, even though he couldn't see me, and hung up. Sliding the phone in my pocket, I swallowed hard, my heart racing because Molly was staring at me with wide eyes that said she wasn't certain whether or not to be scared of me. Easy answer. She should be. "Are you okay?"

She didn't lower her hands from her ears, but nodded, her gaze drifting to the other dead body in front of her. And she just kept staring.

I glanced down at the first asshole I'd sent to hell tonight. The stiff's eyes were pointed at Molly, as if he watched her. I nudged him in the cheek with my boot until his face was toward the wall instead. "Better?"

She licked her lips. Slowly, her eyes lifted to mine. "What about the guy behind me?"

"Dead."

"I thought . . ." She lowered her hands. "For a second, I thought you were aiming at me."

I stumbled forward, my injured leg dragging behind me so I looked like some kind of demented zombie in a movie. But it was the best I could do. "I would never, *ever* hurt you, Molly. Not like that. Not on purpose. I've done a lot of bad shit, some of which I regret, but I would never aim my gun at you. You have to believe that."

Slowly, she struggled to her feet. When she lifted her face to mine again, the fear was gone, but she still somehow managed to look terrified. "I—I do. I believe you."

"Good."

I closed the distance between us, stuck my newly acquired gun in my pants, since you could never have enough protection, and cupped her face. I stared down at her beauty, her classic and flawless features out of place in this dirty-ass alleyway, and caressed her with my callused thumbs. I left behind trails of blood and dirt. Cursing under my breath, I started to pull away. "I'm sorry. I—"

"Don't." She covered my bloody hands with her clean ones, keeping them in place. "Don't apologize."

I swallowed. "All right. Now listen and listen carefully. We need to get outta here. Now. Before someone else sees us."

She nodded. "Yeah. Right. Of course. The bodies . . ." She stared over my shoulder, presumably at the corpse. "Will you come back to my house with me?"

"Hey. Stop." I urged her face back to mine. She'd seen enough death because of me—she didn't need to keep staring it in the face. "No, we can't go back to your place. It's not safe anymore." I dropped my forehead to hers, breathing in her scent, because for a little while there . . . I thought I never would again. And it had hurt more than the beating I'd gotten from the dead fucker behind me. "We have to grab Buttons and hide out somewhere else."

"I have another house, on the Cape," she said in a rush. "No one else knows about it. Let's go there right now. The kids are on break, so I don't have to work, and we'll hide out. Recover."

I stared at her, still wanting her as far away from me as possible, but knowing the likelihood of that happening was slim to none. "I don't want to get you hurt. Will you go there without me?"

"Nope." She shook her head slightly. "Not a chance."

"Molly . . ."

"You come with me, or I don't go at all." She held a hand out. "What's it going to be, Chris? Do we sit here and wait for more bad guys to come, or do we go to my place on the water?"

Stay, or go. Fight, or run.

Be an informant, or stay loyal to the gang.

Kiss the girl, or don't.

These were all decisions my actions had forced me to make in the last few days. But this one was the hardest. If I was with her, she wasn't safe. If I didn't go with her, she wouldn't go, and she wouldn't be safe. If we stayed here, we'd be dead within the hour. Short of kidnapping her and tying her up in a bedroom on some foreign island and leaving her there—I was outta options here. "I'm a dead man walking, and I don't want to drag you down with me. Don't make me, Princess."

"Then don't make me stay here, where it's dangerous." She twisted her lips. "Come away with me and my cat instead."

"Why are you doing this? Why do you insist on helping me, even when I don't deserve it?" I asked, frustration boiling out of me and showing in my words. "Why care whether I live or die? I'm nobody. No one."

"Because you're someone to *me*." She bit down on her lower lip, and her fingers tightened over mine. "You were always someone to me."

I stared at her, not knowing what to say to that. I could tell her she shouldn't give a shit about me, that I wasn't worth it, but it would be pointless. If she was gonna care, nothing I could say would stop her. She'd regret it eventually, when I somehow ended up breaking her heart. But it was what it was, and I was too greedy to tell her to stop. I'd tried to leave her behind once; it didn't stick, and my store of nobility was exhausted. "You're someone to me, too, and I'm an asshole for admitting that, but it's true. You've always been someone."

A small smile lit up her face. "I know. So follow me."

"Anywhere, Princess." I brushed my lips across hers, keeping it short. "Any. Where."

She wrapped her arm around my waist and helped me to her car, and this time, I let her. My fight with the Bitter Hill asshole lying behind me had done a number on my already bruised body, so for once, I needed a little bit of help. When we got to the second dead body I'd made tonight, she hesitated, swallowing and fisting my jacket. "Is he from that other gang? The one that wants you dead?"

"Yeah."

"Why do they want you dead?" she asked quietly.

"Because I'm an asshole." I swallowed back a groan because standing motherfucking hurt. Bending slightly, I picked up my trash bag full of clothes and extra guns. I'd tucked it away behind the Dumpster earlier. "Ignore him. Come on."

She helped me into the car, slid into the driver's seat, and stared at the alley. At the dead body. "But *why* are they chasing you? What did you do?"

I readjusted myself in the seat and clenched my jaw. "Can we not do this here? We need to get out before more come."

"Oh. Right." She seemed to shake herself, and pulled away from the curb, staring straight ahead at the road. "Do you need anything before we go?"

"No. Just the cat. You?"

She shook her head once. "No. I have clothes and stuff there. Buttons has food and litter and toys, too."

"Good. Then, just drive."

I watched her as she stepped on the gas and drove back to her house, her grip on the wheel so tight I could see the whites of her knuckles shining in the moonlight. I guarded her back as she ran inside and grabbed Buttons, carrying him out in a green carrier in a matter of minutes. And then we were gone, heading toward the highway.

As she drove, I watched the emotions play across her

features. Fear. Worry. Excitement. They were all there—
because of me. The worst thing I ever did in my life, short of
betraying Lucas, was going to her place that night. She was
a fucking kindergarten teacher and had no place in gang wars
and shoot-outs.

I'd done this to her. I'd ruined her.

"I'm sorry," I said, still watching her. "I never should
have dragged you into this mess. I wish I could go back and
pick any other fucking pharmacy to break into that night.
Or that I'd gone thirty minutes later. Or that I'd refused to
go with you, no matter what you said. Anything that would
have stopped you from finding me like you did and bringing
me home with you."

"*I* don't. Not at all. You didn't 'drag' me into anything."
She stopped at the red light and frowned at me. "*I* found you.
I offered to take you home. *I* came out tonight, looking for
you. *I* made my choices, and *I* don't regret a single one of
them. Stop acting like you're the bad kid in class, when you're
clearly the quiet one in the back who has no friends and
doesn't trust anyone. The one who's too scared to put himself
out there."

I choked on a laugh. "I'm not quiet—or scared."

"I bet you were in school." She stepped on the gas heavily,
and I glanced in the rearview mirror. No one was behind us.
"I bet you only had Lucas as a friend, and you always turned
in your assignments on time, or even a little bit early, and at
recess, you sat in the grass plucking a blade and trying to
whistle on it, instead of doing the monkey bars or playing tag.
You're the type of kid who goes home to his room, shuts the
door, and hides from his parents so they don't have a reason
to yell at him again. To hurt him."

Shit.

She was way too damn close to home on that one.

I wasn't sure when she'd figured all this out, but she had, because she was a fucking kindergarten teacher, of all things. She recognized the signs in me, that a little boy had been too scared to admit, like no one else ever had, and that hit me harder than it should have—right in the chest, where my heart had once been.

I tapped my fingers on my thigh. "And if I *was* that kid?"

"Then you were." She lifted a shoulder, eyes on the road as she merged onto the highway. The lights of Fenway Park lit up the sky to the right, and the darkness of Southie—and Steel Row—was directly behind us. "That's nothing to be ashamed of."

Funny, because I'd always felt that if I'd been a better kid, or if I'd been smarter, faster, wittier—maybe I wouldn't have made my pops so angry. Maybe he would have liked me. "If I was that kid in your class, what would you tell me to do?"

"I'd tell you to do whatever makes you happy," she said softly. "And I'd hug you and let you know you aren't alone, that I was here for you, even if no one else was."

I stiffened. "Like you're doing now?"

She didn't say anything. Just stared straight ahead.

"Shit. Is that why you're doing all of this? Out of some misplaced sympathy?"

"Oh God. No. Just . . . no." She laughed and shook her head. "I don't feel *sympathy* for you, Chris."

Resting the gun on my lap, I shifted because my ribs hurt like hell. "What do you feel toward me? What am I to you?"

"You're the guy who sent me presents since my dad died, and made my life brighter, while living in the darkness yourself. You're the guy who writes sweet poems and draws amazing portraits but kills someone in an alley and acts like it doesn't bother him."

I lifted a shoulder. "Because it doesn't. Why should it?"

"You're also the guy who sleeps with me and leaves in the middle of the night without a word because he doesn't want to put me in further danger. You might think you're this bad guy without a redeeming quality to be found, but you're wrong," she said, ignoring my question. She pulled off the highway and stopped at a red light, and turned to me, locking eyes with me for one terrifying second. "I *see* you, Chris. I see who you are. I know you. I see your beauty, and I see your darkness. I see it all. And I am here for you."

My heart pounded so loudly, I didn't hear anything at all.

And I knew, in that moment, that this *woman* of mine was going to be my downfall. From the first moment I saw the teenage version of her, headphones in as she sat with her father on their porch, I'd known she was the girl of my dreams. I'd traveled to the edge of my parents' property, trying to avoid Pops since the Patriots had lost to the Giants, and I'd still been a kid unable to protect myself. Her laugh had rung out through the air, and I'd sat down, staring at her. Even back then, she'd brightened my dark soul with nothing more than a smile. For years, I'd admired her from afar, refusing to cross that line.

Refusing to dirty her with my hands.

But last night, that line had been erased and redrawn, and she was on my side of the line now. I'd touched her. Kissed her. Made her mine. It was up to me to keep her safe, to protect her at all costs. She was mine—

And I fucking loved her.

That's right. *Love*. It might seem weird, such an admission coming from a guy like me who didn't have an ounce of goodness in him, despite what Molly said. But I couldn't think of what else this burning need to make her happy, to keep her safe, to hold her close, to kiss her and hug her, and all that other sappy shit, could be.

Not that I was going to tell her that I loved her, or ever say those three little words that held no meaning. No one ever meant what they said anymore. People lied easier than they blinked, or breathed, or slept. Words were shit.

But I meant *this*.

Growling, I hauled her close and kissed her, putting all those thoughts, all those fucked-up feelings, into that kiss. I might never say the words, and she might never know it, but she held my blackened heart in her hands, and had for years. And no matter what came of this mess, no matter how this whole helping-Scotty-out thing ended, I had to make sure she was okay. I had to keep her alive. Even if *I* ended up dying in the process.

That's what love was.

CHAPTER 16

MOLLY

Two days later, I watched Chris as he drew, his hand flying over the paper with a grace that couldn't be described, his forehead wrinkled as he concentrated, and I'd never seen anything more beautiful. He sat by the open window in the living room, right next to the kitchen, which faced the water, the light blue curtains blowing from the breeze. He wore a button-up plaid shirt that was open and a pair of jeans that hugged his rear perfectly.

Not that I could see his rear, but I knew.

Oh, I *knew*.

His ribs were still bruised, but his stitches were holding tight. He was healing. Almost back to as good as new. But for how long? When would the next beating come? The more time I spent with him, the more I wanted to hide him from the world. Lock him away in a mansion, refuse to let him out. Every time he walked out my door, someone tried to kill him.

And that was *terrifying*.

I wasn't sure how to handle that.

The sun broke out of the clouds, shining down on his dark brown hair. He didn't seem to notice as he sketched, occasionally rubbing his finger over a line he'd drawn to blur it out. Today was a little warmer than it had been the rest of our time here, and Chris told me he was going to enjoy every second of the warmth while he could.

When he talked like that . . .

It was as if he wasn't expecting to be alive much longer.

And that terrified me. A guy like Chris . . . yeah, he played hard and probably fell even harder. He ran risks in his line of work—if you could call what he did *work*—and sometimes those risks caught up with you. But whatever he'd done before I found him in that alley, whatever the reason he felt the need to hide out and wallow in guilt, there just had to be a way to fix it. For him to make good.

We just had to figure it out.

I was *good* at solving problems. I was a kindergarten teacher.

It might not sound like a tough job, but it was. I had to deal with two crying kids who felt wrongs at any given time, or who had hurt hearts, or scraped knees, or bruised souls on a daily basis. I took tiny pieces of information given by five-year-olds, saw the whole picture, and put the puzzle back together until everyone was happy. If he would open up to me, tell me what was wrong, maybe I could help him solve his puzzle.

Maybe I could fix this.

After we got here the other night, he'd showered and collapsed in bed beside me, holding me tight all night long. When I woke up, he was still there, and I'd breathed a sigh of relief. We'd repeated the same course of events the next night, and this morning. He hadn't touched me, aside from that kiss he'd given me in the car, and holding me in his arms as I slept.

I *knew*, at some point, he'd walk away without a word again.

Wrapping my arms around myself, I walked over to him slowly, not wanting to pull him out of his moment of Zen. That's clearly what drawing was to him. An escape of sorts. He might not even realize it, or how badly he wanted out of his way of life, but I saw it with every single stroke he made.

Stopping directly behind him, I watched him in awe as he worked. Buttons lay at his feet, napping. Wherever Chris was, Buttons usually followed. Probably because he'd been the one to find him and give him to me. A small smile played at my lips at the thought of Chris in a shelter or pet store, finding the perfect kitten for me.

I peeked at his drawing. He'd re-created the sun rising on the water perfectly, down to the way the rays reflected off the rooftops across the water and the water itself. Even though there was no color on the page, you could see the depths of the sea through his shading. It was, in short, perfection.

And he didn't even think he was *good*.

He stiffened and glanced over his shoulder, reaching for his gun. When he saw it was only me behind him, he relaxed. Before he could greet me, I said, "Did you ever wish you could be anything else besides what you are? An artist, maybe?"

"Sometimes, when I was a kid. I used to want to be a doctor." His fingers tightened on his pencil. "You?"

"A Broadway actress."

He chuckled and resumed drawing. "I bet you'd be an excellent actress."

"You've never seen me try."

"True." He glanced over his shoulder at me, a small smile on his face. "How long were you standing there behind me?"

"I don't know. Like, five minutes, I guess."

He winced and set the pencil down. "Sorry. I didn't hear you come in."

"It's fine." I tucked my hair behind my ear and rewrapped my arms around myself.

He laughed and set the pad on the table. "If I were you, I'd sit on the porch and watch the sunrise while rocking slowly on a rocking chair instead. It's much more entertaining than me drawing."

"I totally would have, if I had rocking chairs."

"We should fix that," he said lightly. "Then you wouldn't be forced to watch some boring guy put some crappy lines on paper and call it art."

I shook my head. "I enjoy watching you draw." I reached out and stroked my hand through his hair, like I'd wanted to do for so long. It was soft, unlike the man himself. "And it's not crappy at all. It's beautiful . . . like you."

He caught my hand and yanked me into his lap, growling under his breath. I ended up sideways in his lap, and his erection pressed against my butt insistently. And yet, he hadn't touched me since that one night together . . .

"I'm not the beautiful one in here, Molly. You are. It's in the way your hair shines, no matter what time of day it is. And in the kindness and warmth in your eyes that's always there, even in the worst situations. And don't get me started on the way you smile at me, even though I don't deserve such magnificence to be cast my way. It's all you. All perfect. All beautiful."

I locked my wrists behind his neck, my breath hitching in my throat. "I'm just a kindergarten teacher, nothing special."

He buried his face in my neck. "I disagree. Deal with it."

"Fine. You'll have to deal with the fact that I find you beautiful, too." I hesitated, my mind locked on the giant elephant in the room we hadn't really mentioned yet. "I found your drawing of me after you left. And got your flowers . . . and the note inside the flowers. With the poem."

He dropped his forehead on mine and let out a sigh. "I was kinda hoping you hadn't. I shouldn't have sent those. Shouldn't have told you who I was."

I pulled back, wanting to see his face. "Why did you, then?"

"Because I know how this ends. I won't be around much longer, Princess." I opened my mouth to argue, and he placed a gentle finger on it. "Shh. Let me finish. I made certain choices, choices I now regret, and I need to make it right. The way to make it right is dangerous and scary—but it's what I've gotta do. But before I die, before I make things right, I want you to know that someone, a guy who hasn't known a sliver of kindness or love in his life, *cared* about you, and it was because you're just the kind of person that inspires that kind of warmth, even in an unfeeling monster like myself. I didn't want to want you like that, or to need to see you smile so badly I'd do anything to get you there. But you got to me, anyway."

"Why not tell me before?" I asked, staring into those brown eyes of his, which I could get lost in forever and ever. So much lurked there. Pain. Loss. Fear. Hope.

It was all there for me to see, even if he didn't realize it.

"Because I didn't, don't, and will never deserve you. Even now?" He ran his fingers down my cheek almost reverently. "Touching you? It's wrong. It's a fucking sin. You're too good for me. Too pure. And I think that's what draws me in—that pureness. That goodness. It's something I've never had. Never called mine. And, Christ, Molly. I want to call you mine, in every way."

I opened my mouth to reply, even though I wasn't sure what I was going to say, but he cut me off, melding his lips to mine so gently and completely that it stole a part of my soul. I clung to him, letting my eyes close and my mind shut off, and lost myself in his touch. In his arms. In his kiss. In *him*.

He cradled the back of my head and deepened the kiss, pulling me closer to his chest. Again, I couldn't shake that feeling that no matter how much bad he'd done in his life, no matter how many people he'd killed, in his arms . . . I was safe.

In a way I'd never been safe before.

He broke the kiss off, breathing heavily, and laughed. "Shit, I didn't mean to do that. I'm sorry."

"Don't be. I like it when you kiss me."

Shaking his head, he ran his thumb down the line of my jaw. "Even when you kiss me, it's like some part of you is trying to clean me. To make me better. But you can't. I'm not gonna be better. What you see is what you get."

"Well, I just so happen to like what I see," I said breathlessly.

"Bullshit. I'm a killer." His grip on my hair tightened. "No one likes that."

I lifted my chin. "I do. I like *you*."

"Oh, Princess." A hard laugh escaped him. "That's only because you literally have no idea what I've done. What I'm capable of."

"So tell me." I gripped his shirt, my heart thudding loudly in my ears. "What did you do that night I found you in the alley? Tell me, and I can help you fix it."

He squared his jaw. "That's my own personal shame to bear.

Not yours. And I hate to break it to you, but it's not something that can be fixed, either."

"But—"

"No." He cupped my face, his rough palms scraping against my skin. "You have no place in my world, and no reason to try and help me. Just let me deal with it."

I pressed my lips together. "You don't understand. At school, when a kid comes to me with a problem, I—"

"This isn't some bullshit kindergarten problem, Molly. Jesus, you don't get it. I didn't steal some crayons or pull someone's hair." He flexed his jaw and picked me up off his lap, set me down, and stood. "I tried to fucking kill my best friend—and *failed.* Lucas trusted me, called me his brother, and I tried to take him down. How's that for ya? Ready to solve my problems with a Hello Kitty Band-Aid and a fucking smile?"

Oh my God, how could he have done something so awful? Something so . . . so . . . *cold*? That wasn't the Chris I knew. My Chris wouldn't take down his best friend. I didn't know what to think, or feel, or say.

I stared at him. Just *stared.*

"Shit, shit, *shit.*" He covered his face and growled. "I didn't want to tell you that, dammit. You didn't . . . you shouldn't have learned—*fuck.*"

"Yes. I should have." I finally looked away from him. Stopped gaping like a fool. I wasn't sure how I felt about this yet, but I knew one thing. The truth was never a bad thing. Well . . . usually never a bad thing. "I—I—I'm happy you told me."

"Is that so?" He lowered his hands, his eyes narrowed. "And now what?"

I opened my mouth, and closed it, no sound coming out. That was all I was capable of at the moment, because what he said and how he said it—it couldn't be *true.* He just felt guilty over something, some mistake he made, that almost killed Lucas. It had to be something easily explainable like that. "Sometimes, we make mistakes, and people get hurt. But that doesn't make it your—"

"Jesus Christ." He dragged his hand through his hair and stalked toward me, anger vibrating off him. "You're still trying to make excuses for me. Aren't you?"

I refused to back away, even though he looked seconds away from walking out the door again. "So what if I am?"

"Then you're even more of a fool than I originally thought." He flexed his jaw. "I tried to kill my best friend. There's no excusing that, Molly. *None.*"

Shaking my head, I said, "Just because someone almost dies on your watch doesn't make it your fault. That's all I'm saying."

He laughed. Actually laughed. "It wasn't a mistake I made that I'm nobly punishing myself for, Princess. I actually, physically, tried to *kill* him. With a gun. Several times. I had a whole plan. A plan that almost succeeded."

I took a step back, shaking my head, unable to believe it. That Chris, the guy who drew pictures so breathtaking that I couldn't look away, the same man who wrote me poems and courted me for years, could *possibly* be the same guy looking at me now, admitting he tried to kill his best friend with a hard glint in his eye.

"Why?" I backed up another step. "What did he do to you?"

"Nothing. Abso-fucking-lutely nothing."

Another step had my back against the wall, and there was nowhere else to go. Fear crept into me, claiming the dark corners of my mind that had whispered all along that I never should have let him in. "So why did you do it?"

"Because he was promoted before me. He wasn't blood. He wasn't better than me. He'd been in lockup and came out, and just like that—he was promoted." He stalked closer to me, his whole body hard, and there was nowhere for me to retreat. I was stuck there, in the room with Chris, and I wasn't sure how I felt about that yet. I'd thought I'd known him . . . but did I *really* know him at all? "It wasn't fair, so I decided to do something about it. I decided to kill him and take his position, since it should have been mine, anyway. How's that for beautiful, Molly?"

"So what—?" I broke off, because my voice cracked. I placed my hands on the wall, trying my best not to cower from him when he stopped directly in front of me, looming over me. I tried to focus on the cold, hard facts. "How did you escape him? Is he the one trying to kill you?"

"No. He let me go." He laughed again, resting a hand on the side of my head against the drywall. "He *forgave* me. Set me free. Gave me what I wanted and skipped town with his girl—who I also tried to kill, by the way."

I let out a small broken sound. "No."

"Yes." His eyes hardened. "They're gone, and everyone thinks they're dead, and *he forgave me*. That's the kind of guy he is."

I sucked in a deep breath, holding it in till the room swam all around us and my eyes filled with tears. Tears I hadn't shed for way too long. "So . . . he's still alive?"

"For all intents and purposes—he's dead."

I opened my mouth. "But—"

"He's *gone*." He slammed his other hand on the other side of my head. "He's fucking gone, and so is she, and it's all my fault. I have to fix it. I *will* fix it."

"How?" I asked, resting my palms on his chest. I wasn't sure yet if I placed them there to keep him at a distance or so he didn't run. Because I had a feeling, him telling me this stuff, it wasn't easy. And he didn't do it lightly. "What are you going to do?"

"Not what. Who. Scotty." His jaw flexed. "I'm gonna keep him alive for Lucas. With all the shit he's in, he'll need all the help he can get."

For the second time now, he mentioned helping Scotty. It was time to get some answers. "Why does Scotty need your help? He's—" My heart quickened and thumped against my ribs. The scene outside of Steel Row replayed in my head, how he'd had the flashing red light, and his reply when I'd asked him why he was pretending to be a cop. He'd called it a clever disguise, in more ways than one. I'd shrugged it off then, but now it made perfect sense. "Oh God. He's actually a cop, isn't he?"

He didn't answer. He didn't need to.

"What happens with the gang, if they find out?" I asked slowly. "What happens to him?"

He tapped his fingers on the wall, right next to my head. "Nothing good, and nothing he'll recover from. Which is why I have to make sure they never suspect him. If they think there's a cop in their midst, I'll make sure suspicion doesn't fall on him. To draw the attention elsewhere. I'll keep his cover *and* him safe, no matter—" He broke off, gritting his teeth.

"No matter the cost," I finished for him in a whisper. "You're going to die protecting him."

He lifted a shoulder, not meeting my eyes. "It's my penance."

"Are you becoming a cop?"

He snorted. "With my record? Not fucking likely."

"Then why would you need to die to protect him? Why would you have to?" I fisted his shirt. "Are you going to pretend to be in the gang, while feeding information to the cops on the side and hoping not to get caught?"

"Pretty much," he said dryly. "That's my plan."

I stared at him, knowing he was hiding something else. It was like a sixth sense of mine—spotting half-truths. "There's more to it than just helping Scotty get information, isn't there?"

He laughed. "Does there need to be?"

"You're so sure you're going to die. That there's no way out of this." I stared at him, watching as he shifted on his feet nervously. "Why?"

The only possible way I could think of him being so certain there was no way out, that his helping Scotty was a death sentence was if . . . if . . .

"Because guys like me—"

"Oh my God. I know what it is. You freaking *idiot*." I shoved his chest as hard as I could. He didn't budge, or pretend to budge. "At some point, someone is going to suspect there's a cop in their midst. They'll figure it out. They always do."

He flexed his jaw. "Leave it alone, Molly."

"You plan on making sure if they think there's a cop in their midst, that they suspect *you*. You're going to . . . what? Layer in the suspicion? Take the fall? Take the kill for him?"

He curled his hands into fists against the wall. *"Molly."*

"Don't *Molly* me." I shoved him again. "You're going to take the fall for him. Aren't you? Be the sacrificial lamb, because if they find out you're a cop, they won't look at him twice. They'll think they're safe after they take you down. It'll give them a false sense of security."

He laughed and shook his head, but it wasn't a laugh. Not really. He looked the opposite of amused. "You're too damn smart for your own good, Princess. Maybe you should've been a fed instead of a teacher. You missed your calling."

"You can't do this. I won't allow it."

He spluttered. "You won't allow it? I don't know who you think you are, but I don't take orders from you—or *anyone*."

"Shut up." I pushed him again. "There's another way. There's *always* another way."

He shook his head again, still leaning on the wall. "No. There's not. I have to do this."

I punched his chest as hard as I could. He didn't even flinch. "You don't have to *die*. You can help him without endangering yourself or throwing yourself into a bottomless pit. Do it in a way that doesn't make you—"

"The only other option is for me to run and leave Scotty to deal with this mess—the mess *I* fucking made—all by himself." He lowered his face to mine, not giving me breathing room. "Should I betray the whole Donahue family? Let Lucas's little brother die, after *he* let *me* live, and run out of town? Is that the *right* thing to do, Molly?"

I shook my head, tears blurring my vision. "No!"

"What do you suggest I do? Do you have some great idea for me?"

"I—I—" I broke off, because I had nothing.

"Exactly." He slid his hand into my hair, cupping the back of my head tenderly, which was so at odds with our conversation that it brought tears to my eyes. "What should I do? Run? Stay? Fight? Hide? Live? Kill?"

"I don't know!" I cried out, a tear escaping, and gripped his shirt, shaking my head. "But you can't just *die*. You don't make them think you're a cop and take the punishment that should have been another man's. You can't just—*no*."

Some of the anger left him, and he looked at me with resignation in his eyes. It was that resignation that scared me the most. Even more than his words. He dropped his forehead on mine. "I'll do what must be done to make this right."

"Get out." I let him go. "I refuse to watch you kill your-self. I won't stand here when you set yourself up for a fall that isn't yours out of guilt for something that you tried to do but failed. Lucas is alive, and your death isn't an even trade."

His grip on me flexed. "It's not that easy."

"Yeah. It is." I shoved his shoulders again. "Go. Get out of here!"

"But I—" For a second, just a second, agony showed on his face. He let me see the pain I caused him by pushing him away. He let me in. "All right. I'm gone."

I crossed my arms and tried to hold the tears back. "Good."

As he dropped his hold on me and stepped back, he swallowed hard, and that pain didn't fade. He nodded once, turned on his heel, and started to walk away.

If I let him leave, I'd never see him again.

Not until he was a story in the news, another criminal crossed off the list as the cops celebrated his death or his arrest. I'd never again hear him laugh or see him sketch or feel his soft touch on my skin. I'd never feel his arms around me again or smell his woodsy cologne. I'd never get to feel his five-o'clock shadow scrape my cheek or wake up next to him smiling at me. He bent down, picked up his trash bag, which he hadn't unpacked—*a freaking trash bag*—as if he'd known this was going to happen all along. And he walked toward the door.

It felt like he tore my heart out of my chest and took it with him.

"Wait—*no!*" I called.

He tensed and turned around, that pain still written all over his face.

He didn't say anything. He didn't need to.

I flung myself at him, and he caught me, wrapping his arms around me securely. Just like he always did. I kissed him with all the anger and fear and pain he brought out in me—and so much more that I didn't want to examine yet.

Like *I* always did.

CHAPTER 17

CHRIS

I'd thought she had finally given up on me, that the truth—however ugly it might be—had finally been enough to push her away. The time had come for her to hear it, despite my reluctance to tell her, and the look on her face when I told her what I'd done—the disgust and horror—had been enough to break my heart.

She'd told me to leave, ordered me out of her life, and I found out what real pain was. What real loss was. I'd never felt it before. Not like this. Not so strong.

I'd never really had her, but suddenly I was losing her.

And that hurt.

But she called me back and kissed me, and there was no way in hell I was going to let that go to waste. I needed her too damn badly to be noble like that. I growled and backed her against a wall, kissing her like I was a starving man and she was my last meal before my execution—because she just might be.

The fact that she'd figured out my endgame, my plans, before even Scotty did, blew me away. It shouldn't have. She was as brilliant as she was kind, which was why I shouldn't have been doing this. Loving her. Kissing her. Dragging her down with me.

And yet, I couldn't stop.

I loved her, and if she was willing to give herself to me, I wasn't a strong enough man to turn her away. I wasn't that guy. I traced her curves with both hands, memorizing the way her breasts swelled out, and the gentle indent of her waist right before her hip, and how right she felt when I grabbed the sides of her ass and rolled my hips against her.

It was all perfect. Too perfect for me.

And I was gonna fight like hell to keep it.

Deepening the kiss, I swept my tongue through her mouth and palmed her ass, pulling her closer to my cock. She moaned and lifted her leg, wrapping it around my waist, and that was all the invitation I needed. I hoisted her up with both hands, slamming her against the wall exactly where I wanted her.

With her hot pussy pressed against my hard cock, and the warming breeze coming off the water, I finally believed heaven existed. But it wasn't a place.

It was a feeling. A thing.

This feeling. *This* woman.

Her hands fell to my shirt, and she gripped it with trembling fingers. I eased back a bit to aid her, but didn't stop kissing or touching her. I couldn't. I gripped her shirt and fisted it at the bottom, breaking off the kiss long enough to yank it over her head before recapturing her mouth like some sort of Viking king claiming his woman.

And with her in my arms, I felt like one.

"Chris," she whispered against my mouth, shoving my

shirt off my shoulders—making us both bare chested since she hadn't been wearing a bra. It fluttered to the floor behind me, and she skimmed her thumbnail across my nipple ring, tugging it slightly. I hissed. "I need you."

"You have me," I growled back, pumping my hips against her again.

She arched her back, her eyes rolling back in her head, and dug her nails into my chest. "I need more. So much more."

"What my princess wants?" I let her feet fall to the floor and dropped to my knees in front of her. I gripped the waist of her pants, undoing the button. "My princess gets."

"Yes." She let her head fall back on the wall. "God, yes."

I unzipped her jeans slowly, feeling like I was unwrapping that present she'd given me all over again. The one I'd never even thanked her for. I would. Right now.

But not with words.

Words were useless in a world like mine. Empty promises made by empty people. It was actions that counted. Actions that really told a person how you felt.

And I was gonna show her.

I kissed her belly, right above the button of her pants, and rolled them down her legs. They fell to the floor, tangling around her feet, so she kicked them off. All she had on now was a pair of sheer pink satin panties, and her long brown hair played peekaboo with the hard pink tips of her breasts—and it was the sexiest thing I'd ever seen.

I nipped the skin directly above the pink bow on her underwear, and spread her legs forcibly with my hands on her thighs. She gasped and grabbed on to my hair, tugging as she fought to gain balance. "You're so fucking gorgeous."

She bit down on her lip, chest rising and falling, teasing me with those brief glimpses of her nipples through her hair. *"Chris."*

"Yeah?" I flicked my tongue over her clit through the panties, grinning when she moaned and strained to get closer. She failed, because I held her right where I wanted her—and I wasn't letting go anytime soon. "What's wrong?"

She glowered down at me, frustration and need blazing out of those hazel eyes of hers without any restraint. Now, *that* was a scene I needed to draw. "I need you *now.*"

I let go of her thighs and tore her panties off, baring her smooth, wet skin. She dropped her head back on the wall again, moving restlessly as she pulled on my hair. I didn't tease her anymore—I took what I fucking wanted. Her.

Always her.

Closing my mouth around her clit, I rolled my tongue and sucked. She tasted so fucking good. Like an angel come to earth, just for me. My hands slid behind her to cup her ass and hold her in place, and I thrust my tongue inside of her. She dug her fingers into my scalp, not releasing my hair, and threw a leg over my shoulder.

Pushing against my mouth, she screamed my name and slammed her heel into my back to pull me closer, desperation taking over her body.

A desperation I understood all too well.

"That feels so good," she breathed, rolling her hips in a figure-eight motion. Pulling back, I captured her clit with my mouth again and thrust two fingers inside her at the same time, crooking it just right. "Too good. I'm so close. So— *Chris.*"

Her whole body stiffened and almost immediately went lax. I didn't stop there, though, even though she came and I had the green light to bury my cock inside her tight pussy. She needed more. More pleasure. More tension. More me.

Just . . . *more.*

Growling, I thrust my tongue inside her again, knowing

I'd never get enough of her. She stiffened, as if surprised I hadn't stopped, but buried her hands in my hair again, straining to get closer before pulling away. "N-no more. You need to stop right—now—*oh my God*, don't stop."

She dug her heel into my upper back again, fucking my mouth with an abandon I'd never seen before. It was addicting. I dug my fingers into the soft flesh of her ass, deepening my intimate kiss, and she let out a frustrated scream, her tits rising and falling with each ragged breath she took.

Her hair was behind her now, so there was nothing obstructing me from that view. I stared up at her, watching the emotions cross her face. Her eyes were closed, and she bit down on her lip so hard it was a miracle she didn't break the skin. Her hips undulated wildly, and her cheeks were rosy pink. I couldn't look away.

She was utterly beautiful.

"Chris."

I scraped my teeth across her clit gently, and licked it. With a ragged cry, she came, her whole body sagging and going limp. If not for the way I held her up, she would've hit the floor. I finally pulled back, knowing if I continued my gentle assault on her, she'd combust before I could make love to her. "You have no idea how good you taste, Princess."

Her eyes drifted open, and she licked her lips. "Take me."

"I will." I set her so she rested against the wall, facing it, and splayed her hands out above her head. Tracing the curve of her ass, I stepped closer, letting my hard cock press against her bare skin. I still wore jeans, so the rough denim should have teased her soft skin. From behind, I cupped her tits and rolled her nipples between my fingers. "When I'm ready to."

She dropped her forehead on the wall, shivering. "You're going to kill me."

"Never." I nibbled her shoulder before circling my tongue over the love bite. "I only want to make you feel good, Molly. I just want to worship every inch of your perfect body, one lick at a time, till you're quivering in my arms and unable to move because you just feel too damn good. I just want to show you how beautiful you are, and how good you make me feel, by returning the favor. That's all, Princess."

She let out an unintelligible sound. I took it as a *yes, please.*

Undoing my pants, I let them hit the floor and kicked them aside, unable to tear my gaze from her naked body. Every single inch of her skin was like artwork, and I wanted to draw her like this. Trembling, naked, filled with need.

I *needed* to draw her like this.

After removing my boxers, I took care of the condom and stepped up behind her again. She still hadn't moved. Just stood there, waiting for me to make love to her. Gently, I pulled her hair away from her face, sweeping it to the side and over her left shoulder.

I kissed her temple and pressed my cock between her legs, teasing her slit. "You have no clue how much I want you. How long I've waited for this. Years, Princess. Fucking *years.*"

A small whimper escaped her, and she arched her back while spreading her legs so her ass was positioned just right for me to enter her. It would be so easy to slip my cock inside her, to forget about worshipping her body—and her—and just take what she offered. But like I said, actions spoke louder than words, and by the time I was finished with her, she'd know exactly where she stood with me.

I kissed her cheek and reached around her front, teasing her clit with my thumb. "You're so soft. So sweet."

"God, *Chris.*" She pressed her ass against my cock again,

and I gritted my teeth because her soft skin pressed up against mine was pure heaven. "Please."

"Shh." I played with her nipple as I pinched her clit, rocking my hips so my cock teased her entrance. "I'm here. I'm not leaving you."

Her hands fisted on the wall, as if seeking something to grab but coming up empty. I held on to her tightly, showing her I had her, and rolled my hips one more time.

She dropped her head back against the front of my shoulder and gasped. "Fuck me. God, please, just fuck me."

I shook my head. "No."

"Wh-what?" She stiffened and glanced over her shoulder at me. "Why not?"

"I refuse to fuck you like you're just some girl to get off and forget. I refuse to treat you like some faceless woman I won't remember come the morning." I turned her slowly, fisting her hair and guiding her exactly where I wanted her. She fell back against the wall, chest rising and falling, cheeks even pinker than before. "Don't get me wrong—I'll make you feel good. I'll take you hard, and rough, and from behind, and I won't stop till you think you'll die from the pleasure, or until you've lost count how many times you've come. But I won't be fucking you, Molly. I'll be making love to you."

Her eyes widened, but before she could reply, I captured her mouth with mine, lifting her in my arms and slamming her against the wall. Before she could so much as wrap her legs around my waist, I thrust inside her tight pussy, sheathing myself completely. She screamed into my mouth, her whole body tensing as she came again, and buried her hands in my hair securely, just like I held on to hers.

Without breaking stride, I moved my hips. Hard. Fast. Just like I promised. And each pump of my hips drove us both higher, until I was breathing heavily and there was nothing in the world but this. *Us.* I drove into her again, and she screamed, yanking on my hair so hard it brought tears to my eyes—and almost made me come.

Growling, I broke the kiss off, let her hit the floor, spun her so she faced the wall, and spread her thighs. She gasped, her whole body trembling. I fisted her hair, gripped her hip, and drove into her from behind. "Jesus, Molly."

She nodded frantically, pushing her forehead against the wall. "I know. God, I know. Don't stop."

"Never," I promised, melding my body to hers. I kissed her neck and pushed inside her again, even deeper. "Not till the day I die. That's a promise."

She hesitated, and nodded.

And I lost control.

Every thrust I made, every movement, shoved me higher until I knew, no matter what became of us, that nothing and no one would ever be able to fill the void inside of me that losing her would leave behind.

And I would. Lose her.

One way or another.

I moved my hips frantically, seeking the release only she could give me—the acceptance only she ever showed me.

She screamed out, "Yes. *Harder.*"

Gritting my teeth, I gave her what she wanted, and I gave her even more. The second the walls of her pussy tightened around my cock, I joined her, letting out a long, predatory growl as I came, too. Dropping my head on the wall, right above hers, I let out a long breath, blinking away the sweat that stung my eyes. "Molly."

So much was in that simple word. The way she made me feel. What I wished I could have. What I wished I could give her, if I hadn't already promised my life to another man. But I knew what had to be done. What I would do. When it came to saving Scotty, there was no question of how far I would go. Not anymore.

She nodded, not speaking.

It was enough.

By the time I pulled out, the bliss had worn off, and I was replaying our conversation from right before we made love. She'd told me to leave.

I stepped back, running my arm across my forehead. "Molly, I—"

"Are you—?" Molly asked at the same time.

We both broke off.

She laughed nervously. "You go first."

"I might not be a gentleman, but even I know ladies go first." I gestured her forward as I went to the trash can to remove the condom. "Go ahead."

Her eyes shifted to the door and back to me. "I was just going to ask you if you wanted coffee," she said lamely.

Bullshit. "Do you still want me to leave?"

She bit down on her lip, staring at me. "Are you still going to die for him?"

"If that's what it comes to?" I lifted a shoulder and stepped into my boxers. "Yeah. I would. But I'd do the same for you."

She paled. "Don't say that."

"It's true." I stepped closer, locking gazes with her. "I might not be a good man, or even a half-decent one, but I swear to you, right here, right now, that I will lay down my life to protect yours. I would do anything—kill *anyone*—if it meant keeping you safe. I wouldn't hesitate. I wouldn't show mercy." I paused, letting that sink in before adding, "I'd blow my own fucking brains out before letting anyone lay a finger on you, including myself. This I swear to you."

Tears rolled down her face, and she bit her lip. "I don't want that. I'd never want you to give your life for mine."

"Tough shit." I stepped closer and slid my hand into her hair, resting my thumb against the spot on her lip she'd just bitten. "I didn't ask for your permission."

Her eyes narrowed. "Well, maybe I'd give my life for yours, too."

"That would be a tragedy." I ran my thumb over her lip, ignoring the pain that sliced through me at the idea of her dying. A world with no Molly was no world at all. "My life in comparison to yours is *nothing*. It's a drop in the ocean. You make the world a brighter, better place. I don't. *Never* think your life is a reasonable forfeit for mine. You're wrong."

"No. You are." She lifted her chin stubbornly, completely naked and obviously okay with that. "And I'm not okay with you taking the fall for another guy, or with you throwing your life away like it means nothing."

I shook my head sadly. "But it's my life to give. My choice to make. I won't apologize for what I have to do. I won't act like I'm sorry when I'm not. If there's a way for us both to walk away from this alive, obviously I'll take it. I'm not looking to die for the sake of dying. I'm not a damn martyr. But if it comes to me or Scotty living—I'll choose him. Nothing, and no one, will stop me. Not even you, Princess."

Tears rolled down her cheeks. "You can't."

"I can. And I will." I let her go, as hard as it was. "Do you still want me to leave?"

She stared at me, not speaking, tears wetting her cheeks.

I stared right back at her, waiting for her to tell me to get the hell out of her house and her life. Eventually I'd hear those words. Eventually she'd realize how much better she was than me, and she'd tell me to go and actually mean it.

And I needed to never forget that.

What we had here, as much as I loved her, it was temporary.

She shook her head and stepped closer. "Stay."

She was killing herself, and me, with her loyalty . . .

And I was gonna let her.

CHAPTER 18

MOLLY

The next morning, I woke up alone in bed. I wondered if this was the day he left me . . . again. He would leave again. I knew it, just like I understood his need to save Scotty, even if I didn't agree with it. Yes, he'd done a horrible thing to Lucas. An unspeakable betrayal lay at his feet, and he shouldered that blame. It made me sick to my stomach, knowing he'd done that to his best friend. That he was capable of such a horrible thing. And now Chris was ready to die to atone for his wrongs, and there was no way he was going to change his mind.

I said I was good at fixing problems, but how did I fix *this*?

At some point, the head of the gang would probably figure out he had an undercover cop in his midst. I didn't know how the whole gang hierarchy worked, or how high up Chris was on the totem pole, but I was pretty sure if the gang leader suspected a cop hid in their midst, Chris would be one of the ones to hear about it . . . which gave him a prime opportunity to confess before Scotty even suspected he was caught.

And he'd lay the groundwork to make the men suspect him, too. Little by little. A word here. A sentence there. Just enough to layer suspicion in their minds so when they suspected someone might not be a team player . . . Chris would be the logical choice.

I should send him away. Let him go on his suicide mission alone.

And, yet, I couldn't.

It was like a sickness, my need to keep Chris close, and there was no cure I could take. I was my own worst enemy in this situation. I didn't want to let him hurt me like he inevitably would, but I didn't want him to leave me, either. I wanted to keep Chris at arm's length so I wouldn't go through what I did when Dad died, but I was apparently all too willing to be brave for the sake of love. I knew he was going to hurt me in the end, but being with him for however long I had him was better than being without him at all.

I was like one of those hamsters in a wheel, running and running, never stopping, and I never got anywhere. Just kept running and trying to figure out what life I led. Sometimes, the fear of how much he would destroy me overcame the desire to keep him at my side. One of these times, I just might come to my senses.

And that scared me even more.

The bedroom door opened, and in came the object of my pain . . . and happiness. "Morning, sleepyhead," he said, holding two mugs. He kicked the door shut before Buttons could follow him in. He wore a pair of sweats I'd bought him and no shirt, leaving all the delectable ink and hard muscles hanging out for me to drool over. He sure knew how to wake a girl up. "I made coffee and chocolate chip pancakes."

Sitting up, I held a hand out for the coffee, my gaze hanging around on his pecs and nipple rings before drifting down south to his happy trail. "Yummy."

He slipped the mug to me and sat on the edge of the bed, watching me with those dark brown eyes of his. When he sat this close and the sunlight filtered in, I saw the green flecks in those brown depths. He had the prettiest eyes I'd ever seen, but I wasn't about to tell him that. He got crankier than a five-year-old coming down off a sugar rush when I told him he was beautiful.

Reaching out, he traced my cheekbone with the backs of his knuckles, his touch almost nonexistent. "This spot? Right here? I struggled with that the other day. With capturing it on paper."

I swallowed a sip of coffee. "I thought it looked good."

"It was shit." He flexed his jaw, withdrawing his touch. "Probably because I had to do it from memory, instead of with you there."

I scrunched my nose. "I don't know if I could sit still long enough for one of those portraits, if that's what you're hinting at."

"But I want to draw you."

"Oh really?" I blew on my coffee. "Like one of your French girls?"

He frowned. "What French girls?"

"From the *Titanic*."

"The sunken ship?" He cocked his head. "What the hell does that have to do with my drawing?"

"Not the ship. The film."

"But the movie is about the ship."

"Yes, I know," I said, laughing a little. "But I was specifically talking about the movie, and Jack . . . aka Leonardo DiCaprio."

He shrugged. "Didn't see it."

"Seriously? Why? *How?*"

"Because I already know how it ends." He smirked. "The ship hits an iceberg and they all die. Why do I need to lose three hours of my life to see a movie where I already know the ending?"

"Because it's a classic," I argued. "And Leo draws in it, just like you. He draws Kate Winslet's character naked, with nothing but a big diamond heart necklace on, and he—"

He choked on his coffee, set it down, and eyed me with a dark, hot gaze all within the span of ten seconds. "Hold the fuck up. Are you telling me you want me to draw you naked, wearing a necklace? Because I'm so on board with that, Princess."

My cheeks heated. The idea of lying in bed naked while my lover drew me . . . it wasn't exactly a *bad* one. What girl didn't want to be Kate's Rose when watching that movie? "N-noooo . . ."

"Was that a question?" He cocked a brow. "Or an answer? I couldn't tell."

I just stared back and sipped my coffee.

He hopped off the bed comically fast. "Oh hell yeah. Let me get my pencils and my—" The phone in his pocket rang, cutting him off, and he stiffened. After a second, he pulled it out and stared at it. "Shit."

"Who is it?"

"Scotty." He shot me a quick look. "Hold that thought." Giving me his back, he said, "Hello?" A pause, then: "Yeah. I know a way in. Why?" Too much of a pause. "Seriously? You just told me to hide out, and now I'm supposed to come back?" More silence, as he paced. "He said that?" A short break. "Fuck

me. All right." A few seconds, then: "What time?" He nodded.
"I'll be there."

He hung up, staring out the window, his shoulders tense.
After taking a deep breath, he loosened them up and turned
to me with a grin. I recognized it for what it was.

His *everything is great* mask. He wore that as well as I
wore my *I'm spontaneous and cool with all this* mask.

"Looks like that drawing will have to wait, Princess."

I gripped my mug like it would save me from the worrying I was about to go through. It wouldn't. Nothing would,
short of chaining Chris up in my room so he couldn't go
back out there ever again. "Where are you going?"

"To a meeting." He leaned on the wall and crossed his
ankles. "Tate wants a way into Bitter Hill, and I'm just the
guy to give him one."

"Tate?"

He eyed me. "My boss."

Oh. The head of the Sons of Steel Row. The same one who
would probably kill him one day. He sounded lovely. "I didn't
know his name."

"You don't need to, really," he said softly. "You'll never
meet him."

"Why not?"

"Because you won't," he said, his voice final.

I stared at him.

He stared back, his jaw ticking.

After a few seconds, he sighed and dragged his hands down
his face. After he dropped them back to his sides, he came
across the room and sat at my feet. "Look. The last thing you
need is to meet the guys I work with, who literally kill people
every damn day—just like me."

I swallowed. "Where is the meeting?"

"At Tate's office." He held a hand up. "And before you

ask, no, I'm not telling you where that is. You don't need to know."

The all-too-familiar panic crept in. "What if something happens to you? I'll have no idea where to look for you."

"Good." He rubbed his jaw. "You don't need to be out looking for me in the first place. Just stay here, where it's safe."

"No way." I set my coffee down and grabbed his hands. "Let me come. I'll stay in the car, and no one will know I'm there."

"Hell no." He shook me off and stood. "First of all, they have cameras and security guys everywhere. I assure you that you'd be seen. Second of all, we're literally in the middle of a gang war with Bitter Hill—because of the things Lucas and me did—and the last place you need to be is sitting outside of a high-target area. Are you fucking insane?"

I crossed my arms. "So I'm just supposed to sit here and wait to see if you died or not?"

"Yes."

My jaw dropped. "But—"

"How is that different from any other couple, really?" He paced back and forth in front of me, his coffee sitting on my nightstand untouched. "It's kind of what couples do, right? One leaves. One goes somewhere else. They both go home to the same place."

I swallowed. He had a point, but most couples didn't have a member who was a freaking gang member, determined to die for his best friend's brother. But I had a feeling if I pushed too hard, made too big of a deal out of this . . . he'd run away again.

And this time he wouldn't come back.

"Of course," I said gently. "You're right."

"I know I am." He sat again and cupped my face. "Look. I waited years to be able to do this." Leaning in, he pressed his lips to mine, kissing me sweetly as he ran his thumb over my jaw. Pulling back, he gave me a tender smile. "You can bet your bottom dollar that I'll be coming back tonight. Nothing short of a bullet to the brain will stop me."

A smile slipped into place despite my fears—which were huge. Like, *Titanic* iceberg huge. "Is that a movie reference you actually know?"

"Annie. Ma liked it."

"It's a miracle," I said, trying to lighten the moment, since he so clearly wanted to. "I still think you know all about *Cinderella*, though."

He lifted a shoulder. "I'm sure I don't know what you're talking about."

"All right. Keep your secret." I smiled. "You go. Take my car. I'll wait here."

"And you'll be okay?"

I nodded, even though I wasn't sure I would be. Not really. "Of course. I'll make something for dinner while you're gone. Maybe roast."

"That sounds delicious." He leaned in and kissed me again, his lips lingering longer this time. "But you're the tastiest thing I've ever had."

My cheeks heated, and I curled my hands over his bare shoulders, pulling him closer. He groaned and yanked my legs so I laid flat on the bed, before lying his whole body over mine. Just like I'd wanted. I didn't waste any time in wrapping my legs around his waist, locking my ankles securely. I wore only a pair of panties under a shirt of his I'd thrown on, so not much stood between him and me.

Burying my hand in his hair, I sought out and found his tongue. At the same time, I traced the curve of his shoulder and played with his nipple ring, tugging it gently. He seemed to like that. I wondered what it felt like when I did that.

Did it hurt? Feel good? Both?

Breaking off the kiss, he rested his forehead on mine. His breathing was ragged and soft, and his grip on me tightened, as if he was about to let go. "Molly, I—"

"Shh." I kissed him again, quickly. "I don't want to talk. I want to *feel.*"

Nodding, he slid his hand under my butt, pulling me against his erection even more. I could feel him, all of him, touching me where I needed him most. Something about knowing he was going out there, where he could be hurt, made me desperate to touch him. To have him. As if that would help me. "I can help you with that."

He kissed me again, rocking his erection against my core with the perfect amount of pressure. He skimmed his hand up my stomach and under my shirt, closing over my breast— right when his phone rang. Again. He broke the kiss off, cursing.

"No. Don't."

"Molly—"

Shaking my head, I pulled his mouth back to mine, kissing him desperately. He gave in, ignoring his phone until it finally shut up, dragging his thumbnail over my nipple. My stomach tightened, and he kissed his way down my body, lifting the shirt I wore so he could actually touch skin.

When he dropped a kiss right over my panties, below my belly button, I arched my hips up and closed my eyes, my whole body tightening in excitement. After the past few times with him, I knew exactly how this ended—and I needed it.

Needed him.

His phone rang again, and I stiffened.

Ignoring it, he buried his face between my legs, flicking his tongue over me. Even through the satin of my panties, it lit me on fire. *"Chris."*

Growling, he ripped my panties off and tossed them over his shoulder. His phone finally stopped ringing, and he closed his mouth around me. I cried out, dropping my legs to the sides, and dug my nails into his scalp. He groaned, sucking and rolling his tongue over me until I was trembling and shaking and seconds from seeing stars. And when he brought me there, and pleasure burst over my whole body, he was there, holding me while I came back down.

"Oh my God," I breathed, collapsing to the mattress, breathing heavily.

"Molly . . ." He nipped at my thigh and ran his tongue over it. He stared up at me from between my legs, his gaze somehow serious and almost . . . scared. He started to speak, but his words became drowned out by the sound of the doorbell. "I love y—" Chris froze, his head still between my thighs, for two seconds. Maybe less. Then he was on his feet, I was alone in the bed, and he had a gun in his hand before I could even move. "Don't leave this room, no matter what you hear. And get in the closet."

The door shut behind him, and I sprang into action.

It didn't even occur to me to disobey him. When it came to fighting a man with a gun, or twelve of them, I wasn't any help. I was a liability, and we both knew it.

Closing the closet door, I left it cracked so I could watch and see who entered. If it wasn't Chris, I would . . . God, I don't know what I would do. I didn't have a gun, and even if I did, I had no idea how to shoot it. I didn't have a weapon of any sort. Breathing heavily, I scanned the closet in the dark, feeling around for anything solid. The best I could find in here was a high-heeled shoe . . . and a wire hanger.

I could poke an attacker's eye out, I guessed.

If he didn't, you know, shoot me first.

A million images ran through my head. Chris being shot

in the chest the second he opened the door. A man dragging him out by his feet, leaving nothing but a bloody trail and a few memories of the real man he was—the man only *I* really knew.

The killer? The guy who shot people for a living?

That wasn't the *real* Chris.

The real Chris drew gorgeous landscapes and portraits. The real Chris woke me up with soft kisses, coffee, and pancakes. The real Chris spent years showing a woman how special she was, never intending to let her know it was him, and put her first, above all other things, no matter what he said.

And the real Chris was *mine.*

The door opened, and my heart sped up painfully. I gripped my wire hanger and shoe, knowing I was helpless to save myself but hoping I wouldn't have to. Chris walked in, looking perfectly healthy, still holding his gun, and I let out a sigh of relief. "You can come out."

Pushing through the closet, I stumbled out into the brightness. "Who was it? Are you okay?"

"It was Scotty. He came to get me. That's who kept calling. Apparently he never planned on meeting me there like he said, so he was already halfway here when he—" He set the gun down on the bed and frowned at me. "Why the hell are you holding a shoe and a hanger?"

"I figured if it wasn't you who came through the door . . ." I faded off, knowing it was stupid, because nothing would have stopped one of those men from the other night.

"You'd what? Force them to wear heels and hang up your clothes?" He flexed his jaw. "What the actual fuck—?"

"It has potential," Scotty said from behind Chris. I hadn't even seen him there. "She worked with what she had, right?"

Chris said nothing. Just grabbed his pistol again, casually tucking it in his sweats. Only, it was anything but *casual.*

"Why did you follow me up here? I told you to wait down-stairs."

Scotty laughed. "Having a sense of déjà vu, are you?"

Chris tightened his fists.

"Easy." Scotty backed up a step, rubbing his jaw. He wore the dark brown leather jacket that the Sons always wore, and an easy grin. Too easy. "I just wanted to assure Molly here that I'd take good care of you. That nothing would happen to you."

I stared at Scotty, taking him in. He had bright green eyes, reddish hair, and a square jaw that rivaled Chris's for hardness. He didn't have a dimple in his chin, like Chris, so he looked even tougher. He seemed ruthless. Cold.

Like he would stop at nothing to get his way.

Swallowing hard, I held on to the hanger tighter, all too aware of my lack of clothing. Thanks to Chris, I didn't even have any panties on anymore. "Good. I'll hold you to that promise."

He inclined his head.

Chris flexed his jaw. "Assurances have been given. Can you go wait for me downstairs now?"

"Yeah." Scotty backed up. "Sure."

The second he walked out the door, Chris shut it. "Son of a fucking bitch."

"What? What's wrong?"

"Him." He slammed a hand on the door, his body trembling with rage. "Don't mistake this for anything other than what it is. A reminder that he can get to you anytime he wants."

"Why would he want to hurt me?"

"He doesn't." He gritted his teeth. "Not yet, anyway."

I hugged myself, still holding my "weapons," and tried to make sense of all this. I failed. "But he's a cop. A good guy."

"Just because he's a cop doesn't make him a good guy,

Princess." He turned and faced me, and what I saw in his eyes—fear, anger, and resignation—chilled me to the bone. "Don't be so naïve to think it does. He was reminding me that I had to cooperate with his plans or pay the price. He doesn't trust me."

"But you'll die for him, anyway?"

A muscle in his jaw ticked. "Yep."

"That's so—" I swallowed hard, dropping the crap in my hands, and stopped my argument. It was one I wouldn't win. The hanger and shoe hit the floor, and I closed the distance between us, hugging him close. "Be safe out there. Come home to me."

He closed his arms around me, hugging me so tight it almost cracked my ribs. Still, it wasn't enough. I closed my eyes and breathed in his masculine scent—a combination of soap, woodsy cologne, and *him*. "What did I tell you?"

"That nothing short of a bullet to the head would stop you."

He kissed my temple. "And I meant it. I'll come home."

I watched him dress and get ready to go, trying my best to act like I was okay with this, when I was the furthest thing from okay. As he shrugged into his leather jacket, I smiled and waved good-bye. He nodded, closing the door behind him after letting Buttons in. After the bedroom door closed, I sat down on the edge of the bed, feeling empty.

Then, and only then, I said what had been sitting on the tip of my tongue that whole time. "But you see, that bullet is exactly what I'm worried about."

CHAPTER 19

CHRIS

I sat silently in Scotty's car the whole way to Tate's downtown office, cursing myself out for telling Molly I loved her. Had she heard me? The bell had rung at the same time as I said it. Maybe I'd lucked out and it had washed out my idiotic confession. What the hell had I been thinking, telling her that I loved her? Love wasn't something to be admitted. It wasn't something you told someone else. It was something you hid deep down, like a shoe box in a closet filled with memories you didn't want anyone to see.

No one had ever loved me back. Not Molly. Certainly not my pops. And if Ma loved me, she would have stopped him from beating the hell out of me.

She would have saved me.

I wasn't supposed to love anyone. But I did. I loved her. And I'd told her like the fucking idiot I was. Now she was going to leave me. That's what love did.

It drove people away.

Shaking my head, I tried to pay attention to Scotty again, but he wouldn't shut up. He'd been going on and on about all the shit we were going to say and all the things I needed to know, so there hadn't been much room for talking on my part. And that was just fine by me, after that little stunt Scotty had pulled by coming into our bedroom.

Considering the fact that I'd done that same thing to Lucas and threatened his girl, the message wasn't lost on me. If I dared to fuck over Scotty and his operation, Molly wouldn't be safe from retribution. Whether she'd have the cops or the Sons coming after her, I didn't have a clue.

And I wasn't sure if one was necessarily better than the other, either.

Scotty glared at me. "Are you paying attention to a word I'm saying?"

I tapped my knee. Apparently it was finally my turn to speak. "Yeah. We go in, you're gonna tell them you picked me up on the way in—not a lie. You'll say I was in some bar in Southie with a whore on my lap—which is a lie. I smirk and say I was celebrating Lucas's life the way he would want me to, and not mourning his death—not sure if that's a lie. When Tate asks me if I was having fun, I tell him I was running recon, and I know a way in Bitter Hill's clubhouse— again, not a lie. At which point we lead them into an ambush, without letting them know you're a Boy—which we both know isn't a lie."

Scotty turned onto Birch Street, his grip on the wheel tight. "Do I sense sarcasm here, Chris?"

"No, you sense anger." I stopped tapping my fingers on my knee. "I made it very clear I'm here to help you, so you didn't need the veiled threats about Molly."

Scotty stopped at a red light, tugging on his leather sleeves. "I didn't threaten her. I was reassuring her."

"Yeah. Sure." I looked out the window. "You're just a fucking saint, right?"

Scotty didn't answer that. "Look, I need to know that you're in this. If we go over there and you screw me over, I'm not only a dead man, but you are, too. And, yes, the cops know about you and Molly, and they know she's been hiding you. They also know you're supposedly helping me, so if shit goes south, the eyes will be turned toward you and her. That's called assurance, not threats."

"Funny. It feels the same to me."

Scotty shrugged. "Call it what you want. You're a guy that isn't exactly the most reliable person to have in your corner. I've seen firsthand how you treat friends."

I gritted my teeth and continued staring out the window.

Really, what could I say to that? Never mind that I'd been the one who went to see Lucas in jail every week, while his little brother had been too busy playing superspy.

I'd fucked it all up with one mistake, trying to be something I wasn't.

My pops.

"I get that you don't like me. I respect it, even." I gritted my teeth. "But you need to leave Molly out of this. She has nothing to do with our agreement."

"You're wrong." Scotty looked at me. The seriousness in his gaze wasn't missed. "If she's with you, she has everything to do with this. And you *know* it."

I tensed, because he was right. And that was one of the million reasons why I shouldn't be with her. But at least if I was by her side, I could protect her—or so I kept telling myself, anyway.

When Scotty turned down the road that led to the Sons of Steel Row clubhouse, instead of the swanky downtown office where the more formal meetings were held, I rested my hand on my gun. "I thought we were going to the office."

"I lied." Scotty side-eyed me. "Had to make sure I'd be avoiding an ambush. I need to ensure I'm not going to show up to a crew of Bitter Hill waiting to pop me. Forgive me if I'm not totally on board with the idea of you as a team player yet."

I flexed my jaw. "I told you I'm in, and I'm fucking in. If I wanted to rat on you to Tate and get a promotion, I'd have done it by now."

"So you keep saying."

Being in this position, with one of my brothers not trusting me, only made me even more regretful over what I'd done. Why had I let my deeply ingrained need to prove to my pops that I was a bigger man than he was, no matter how many times he beat me or told me I was weak, sway my beliefs of right and wrong? How had I fallen so far, so fast, and not noticed? How had I let it get that far?

No matter what Scotty said, I had no way of knowing if he told the truth about not wanting to risk me letting Bitter Hill know who Scotty really was, or if he was about to turn me in to Tate for what I'd done to Lucas. If it was the latter option, I'd be breaking my promise to Molly. I wouldn't be coming home.

"Is the rest of our story staying the same?" I finally asked.

"Yeah." He turned to me. "You still have that bloody paper you fought so hard to get from Lucas? The will he signed?"

The one that claimed Lucas named me as his heir. The one that I almost killed my best friend for. Yeah, I had it. It currently burned a hole in my jacket pocket. "I have no intentions of using it. I don't want it."

"Bullshit." Scotty stepped on the gas when the light turned green. "You killed Lucas for it."

Every time he said that, I hated myself more—even though Lucas was actually alive and well. "Yeah. And now I don't want it. You take his position, as you should. I'll hang back and do my thing from where I currently stand."

Scotty eyed me like he couldn't tell if I was serious or not. "Why?"

"It's blood money." I lifted a shoulder. "And the position isn't mine. It should be yours. You're his brother, and it'll help you gather more intel for your bosses. It's win-win."

Scotty clicked his tongue and pulled into the clubhouse parking lot. We both scanned it for anything out of the ordinary. All was quiet on the western front. "You're sure? I mean, it was part of our deal. You getting this promotion. The fact that you're reneging on the part of the deal that actually *gives* you something doesn't sit well with me. You've got nothing to gain anymore."

"It's just a reminder of what I did to Lucas. I have enough of those." Reaching into my pocket, I pulled the bloodstained note out and handed it over to Scotty. "Burn it. Keep it. Show it to Tate and tell him what I did, and laugh as they rip me to shreds or jump me out. I don't give a damn what you say or do. No matter what you do in there, your secret is safe with me."

With that, I opened my car door and got out, smoothing my leather jacket. I glanced at the spot on my shoulder where Luc had shot me, another constant reminder of the wrong I'd done. But I was setting it right. And that's the best I could do, dammit.

It was all I had.

"You can't be serious," Scotty said under his breath,

closing his door of the Escalade. "If I turned you in, you'd rat on me in a second."

"I'm not a rat," I said through clenched teeth. "I made a mistake when I did what I did, and I'm making up for it. I shouldn't have tried to prove"—*that I was better than Pops*; that's what I'd been about to say—"take what wasn't mine. I won't do it again."

Scotty walked beside me, scanning the parking lot the whole time. "All right."

"You believe me?" I asked.

"Maybe." He mussed up his hair, leaving it sticking up and sloppy looking—which made him seem a hell of a lot more boyish and innocent than he had moments before, when it had been slicked back and in perfect order. He was *good*. "Time will tell."

"Yeah, it— What the fuck?" I waved a hand in front of me, coughing. "What the hell did you just spray on me?"

"Perfume." Scotty grinned, tucking the small vial in his pocket. "If you've been fucking your way through Southie, you'd smell like it. You smell too clean. Like flowery fabric softener."

My cheeks heated. "Fuck you."

"Maybe later," he said quickly.

His square jaw and red hair reminded me of Lucas. I missed him, and knowing he was out there somewhere, hating me, hurt. "Did Luc know about you?"

"At the end he did." Scotty stood the collar of his jacket up, giving him a rakish appearance. He didn't look anything like a cop anymore. "Not before."

I nodded once. "Was he proud?"

"Yeah. I think so." Scotty shoved his hands in his pockets, his gaze locked on the *Members Only* door straight ahead. "Try your best to look hungover and overfucked."

I smirked. "I was hungover before you were out of diapers. I got this."

"You're four years older than me."

"I know." I stopped at the door and knocked three times, in quick succession, before opening it. "I stand by my words."

We moved inside. The second we walked into the dark clubhouse, I felt . . . *I don't know*. The same familiar dark wood-paneled walls greeted me, with the dark wood floors, but they felt different. And there were still three pool tables in the hall, a long, square bar off to the left with padded stools surrounding it, and a mirrored wall behind it. The same voices filled the silence, and familiar laughter rang out along with a few curses every couple of seconds.

In the past, coming here had felt like coming home.

The smoky room, with easy girls and even more easily accessible booze and smokes, had always been the one place I could go to when I needed to clear my head. When I needed to escape Pops and his never-ending beatings—and my *life*.

Even as a kid, I would come here and sit at the bar, my legs swinging in the air as the bartender told me crazy, far-fetched stories about all the men he'd killed in his day. I'd sat there, fantasizing about when it would be my turn, till Pops showed up, grabbed me by the ear, and made me leave. Then I went to Lucas's until I *had* to go home.

This was my true home. My real family.

Yet now, I found myself craving a quieter home. One by the waterfront, with sunshine and coffee and pancakes—and my sweet Molly. That was what I truly wanted. What I craved most, above anything else. Power. Greed. Sex. I didn't need any of it anymore. All I needed was *her*.

What the hell had happened to me?

"Phones," Brian, Tate's right-hand man, said, holding out

a basket filled with iPhones and Samsung Galaxies. He eyed me as I slid my iPhone into the pile. "You look like shit, O'Brien."

"Haven't been sleeping much," I said, not smiling. I had to play the part of the lost best friend, after all. "Been busy."

Brian frowned. His light blond hair and dark brown eyes were always an unsettling mix, but today he seemed even more focused on me, and that couldn't be good. He was a year older than me and was one of those guys who never let on what he was thinking. He barely fucked women, even though they all threw themselves at him, and seemed to care about one thing and one thing only—keeping his boss alive. "Doing . . . ?"

"Women. Lots of them. Some at the same time." I clapped him on the shoulder. Scotty watched from behind me, like a hawk. "You should try it sometime, man."

"What makes you think I don't?" He relaxed and even smiled a little bit. "Some people just don't feel the need to announce it every time they eat a pussy. You should try *that* sometime, O'Brien. And you need to shower. You smell like a chick."

Scotty snorted. "You know how he is, always chasing his next conquest. Hell, he's worse than I am, and that's saying a lot. But right now, he's fucking his way through his grief. It's a coping mechanism I can't recommend. Too many pussies too close together is never a good thing."

I glared at him, pretending to be affronted. There was only one woman I wanted now, but I wasn't about to admit that. "How many chicks were in your bed last night when I stopped by?"

"Three. Just your typical weekend for me, my friend." Scotty shrugged, playing the art like a damn pro. "But not all men can handle the responsibility like me. I have it down to a science."

Brian held his phone basket out to Scotty. "Well, Mr. Scientist, put your damn phone in the basket."

"Gladly." He tossed his iPhone in, too, and ran his hand through his red-brown hair. "Any word on Bitter Hill?"

"We'll get to that. Right now, we're drinking in Lucas's honor."

"I can be down with that," I said, watching the men at the bar. There were no women tonight, which meant we'd be talking here, in the main room. Tate was nowhere to be seen, but Tommy and Frank were sitting at the bar, drinking whiskey.

"I'm sure." Brian set the basket down. "Hands up, boys."

I lifted my arms, letting Brian feel me down for wires. When he slapped my ass, I walked past him, heading for Tommy. He was a lieutenant, like me. So was Frank. "Boys."

Frank nodded to me. His blond hair and blue eyes were as bright as ever, but he looked somber today. He'd gone to school with me and Luc and had also gotten good grades in school. But, like me, he was in a gang, instead of out in the world making a difference. We hadn't really had a choice. "Sorry for your loss, man."

"Yeah." Tommy poured me a whiskey and handed it over. He had brown hair and green eyes, was the same age as me, and had more ink than me—which was saying a lot. His father was Tate's father's cousin, so he was pretty high up on the food chain. "He was a good brother and will be missed."

I took the glass, gripping it hard enough that it should have shattered. This was all so fucked-up—and all my fault. Lucas should be here with us, and he was gone. Forever. I'd never stop regretting that. What would I have done if I'd succeeded in my plan to *kill* him? How would I have handled this damn guilt? I'd underestimated him when I thought he was friends with me only because of my connections, and that pissed me off even more than this farce did. "I miss him already."

"Me, too," Scotty said, sitting next to Tommy. "And I'm ready to get some revenge."

"We all are," Frank said, sliding a glass of whiskey to Scotty. "And we *will* get it."

"Good." I leaned against the bar and faced the room, eyeing the guys there. I stiffened when I saw Pops in the corner, talking to Tommy's dad. "Shit. When did he get home?"

"Today." Frank laughed. "You didn't know your own father was back?"

"Been kinda busy," I said through clenched teeth. If he was here, I had to go over and greet him or he'd chew me out later. "I'll be right back."

Scotty watched me go, his eyes narrowed. As I crossed the room, my brothers clapped me on the back as I went, each offering up sympathy. By the time I made it to my pops, I was ready to tell everyone to kiss their asses, that I didn't need any sympathy. That it was my fault Lucas was gone, and they needed to take action against me.

I couldn't *do* this shit.

This wasn't me.

Walking up behind Pops, I waited until he deigned to notice me, even though he'd spotted me the second I started heading his way. The way he acted around everyone but me—friendly, laughing the loudest, first to crack a joke— was always weird to witness. Around me, he was first to crack my ribs, not a fucking joke.

He talked to Gus, Tommy's dad, for another couple of minutes and finally turned to me once my whiskey was gone. Gus gave me a sympathetic nod and headed over to another older club member. Pops watched him go, letting the smile fade once he was out of earshot. "I hear you've been out fucking your grief away."

"Yep." I nodded once, gripping my empty glass. "Pops."

He stepped closer and lowered his voice. "Care to explain the corpses I saw Scotty Donahue dragging out of my garage when I got home?"

I stiffened, having forgotten about them. When I was with Molly, that part of my life kind of faded away. "Shit."

"Yeah." He stared at my jacket before he rested a hand on my shoulder. "You get yourself shot up again, son? That's a good repair, but I know how to spot a bullet hole when I see one."

I stiffened. "Yeah. It's healing, though."

"Is that so?" He dug his fingers in more and smirked. To an outsider, it probably looked like an emotional father-son moment. But his fingers were directly over my wound, and he wasn't letting go. It hurt like a bitch. "You're lucky your mother didn't see those men. Then you'd be answering to me, boy."

I was well past the age of ass whooping, and if he tried, I could kill him with one hand tied behind my back, if I wanted to. But that didn't stop him from threatening me, anyway.

Or from being an asshole.

"I'm sorry," I said simply, raising a brow. "It was Bitter Hill. They struck me when I was down, and I had to hide the bodies. Scotty was helping me out."

He dug his thumb in more. I clenched my jaw, refusing to react as he guided me into a quiet corner, our backs to the other men in the room. He patted my back with his free hand, making it look as if he comforted me. What a fucking joke. "And with Lucas. What happened there? Where did you get this new bullet hole from? Him?"

He must've put two and two together. Pops was a smart one like that. If I didn't come clean, he'd suspect something was up and ruin everything I'd been so carefully building. *Dammit.* "What do you think happened?" I said casually.

"I took care of business."

Pops's eyes widened, and they lit up with appreciation. For the first time in my life, it was directed toward me. "No shit. Really?"

I nodded once, shoving my hands into my pockets.

He laughed. "Fucking brilliant. Keep up the show. Act sad. Fuck a lot of whores. But whatever you do, don't get caught." He clapped me on the cheek, smiling. "Good job, son. Way to fight your way up to the top. That's my boy."

There it was. The acceptance I'd never gotten from him.

It settled like an anvil at the bottom of my stomach, making me feel like I'd swallowed a Lucas-size brick. If Pops knew I hadn't *actually* killed him, he wouldn't be so quick to show pride. But the thing was, I didn't regret failing. I looked at it now like some sort of divine intervention. I didn't believe in God. Didn't think there was some benign leader that kept watch over us and led us down a good path.

If he existed, he'd never shown himself to me.

But in that apartment, the day I failed in killing my best friend, that was the closest I'd ever gotten to believing in a higher being. In heaven and hell.

Well, I believed in *hell.* I saw it every day.

And I had no doubt that's where I would end up.

Pops walked over to Gus again, and I went back to Scotty, who now sat alone at the bar. Dropping my head and my voice, I said, "Pops figured out I popped Lucas. I had to play along."

"Shit." Scotty slammed his glass down. "How did he know?"

"I don't know. He's good like that."

"How convenient for you," Scotty said, watching me with

a frown. "Looks like you get the position after all. If you didn't, your pops would know we were full of shit. There you go again, getting your way like always while appearing as if you didn't choose to win . . . but did anyway."

I stiffened, because he was right, but I had my own game to play, and if I rejected a promotion, it would further my position on the board. Rejecting advancement was the best way to take any light off Scotty and his secret life before it got too intense. Time to move my pieces.

Let the games begin.

CHAPTER 20

MOLLY

I sat at the dining room table, biting my lip as I slid the drawing into the wood picture frame I'd pulled out of my attic. As I set the cardboard backing into place, I glanced over my shoulder at the front door. It still hadn't opened. Chris had been gone for only two hours, and already I was going insane with worry.

It only went to prove I wasn't cut out for this way of life.

What was I *doing*?

When my dad died, I swore not to let myself feel that kind of pain again. To never care about someone enough that their death left a gaping hole in my heart for all time. To never feel so alone, so lost, and to never love anyone again.

I was good at it. At keeping a distance.

But with Chris, it was next to impossible.

Something I was only just realizing, now that I was alone and terrified for his life, was that I'd broken my rules. I'd let him in. I'd let him matter to me. If he died like my dad . . .

I wouldn't be *okay*.

Really, I needed to take a step back. To remind myself that the way I'd felt after I lost my father, the pain and grief that had almost killed me, could come back if I let it. Dad had been a doctor who helped people who needed it; he hadn't lived a dangerous life at all. Still, he'd died. He'd left me alone. And I'd fallen apart without him.

Chris was *literally* a killer and a member of a *gang*, and he probably got shot at every single *day*. More than once. The chances of him ending up in a morgue from a bullet were pretty high. He knew it. I knew it. And if he died . . .

I'd fall apart all over again.

And this time, I might not get put back together.

Flipping the frame faceup, I ignored the sinking suspicion in my stomach that I was too late to avoid that pain. Ignored all the signs that told me no matter what I did . . .

I'd be suffering.

Chris's drawing stared up at me. It was the one he'd done yesterday, before he told me his secret shame. I still couldn't believe that the Chris I knew would do that to Lucas. That the same Chris who cradled me all night long, intermittently kissing my temple even while asleep, could be the same guy who'd coldly plotted his friend's death.

Who *did* that?

A knock sounded on the door, and I jumped to my feet, pulse racing. Was it the cops, coming to tell me he was dead? Or maybe another one of those bad guys, come to finish the job they started back at my house in Boston? Or, you know, maybe just a person knocking because they wanted to say hi. That was possible, too.

Before Chris came into my life, a knock on the door hadn't been much of a thing at all.

How had my life come to this?

How did I get *here*?

Grabbing the knife off the counter that I'd pulled out for this type of thing, since a shoe and a hanger weren't going to cut it with professional killers, I tiptoed to the door. Peeking out the window, I relaxed slightly when I saw who it was.

It was Mitchell Myers, who lived next door.

I'd known him for three years, and he was a great friend. We often spent hours together, drinking wine and sharing stories. He'd never been anything but good to me. He wore polo shirts and pleated khaki shorts, was a vegetarian who wouldn't harm a fly. He was a handsome guy. He had blond hair and gorgeous blue eyes. He was always immaculately groomed and had a nice body that clearly saw a lot of gym time to keep it that way. He was also a doctor. Rich. Successful. Caring. He was the picture of the harmless suburban preppy . . .

And yet, still I hesitated to let him in.

I'd always suspected he wanted to be more than friends, but he'd never made a move . . . which was just as well. He wasn't my type. Turned out, I preferred inked-up guys with guns and nipple rings. Go figure. Swallowing hard, I opened the door a crack, pushed Buttons back with my foot, and forced a smile. "Oh. Hey. How are you doing?"

"Great, now that you're here." His gaze slid down and widened. "What's with the knife?"

"Huh?" I glanced down, having forgotten I was still holding it. "I . . . uh . . . was cooking. Forgot I had it."

"Oh. Okay. Want some wine to go with whatever you're cooking?" He held up a bottle of red wine. "I brought my best pinot noir and three months' worth of life stories." When I didn't open the door right away, his smile faded a bit. "Can I come in, Molly?"

If I didn't let him in, it would seem out of character. We had a tradition of drinking together every time I was at the Cape. I might not know a lot about hiding out or keeping a low profile, but I was pretty sure you were supposed to act normal to avoid suspicion being cast your way. Normally, I wouldn't hesitate to invite him inside, and I'd drink a whole bottle with him while catching up on lost time.

I'd have to do the same now.

Opening the door, I stepped back and scooped up Buttons so he didn't slip out the door. "Of course you can. You know I love pinot noir."

Laughing, he came inside and kicked off his sandals. He didn't pet Buttons, or even look at him. He was too busy staring at me. "How have you been? I didn't know you were coming this week. I couldn't believe it when I saw your car in the driveway."

"The kids are on spring break," I said, peeking outside. A black car with tinted windows was parked down the road. It hadn't been there before. When I stared at it, the engine started, and whoever was inside it drove off. Swallowing hard, I shut and locked the door. "Figured I'd get some relaxation in by the water, since it's actually supposed to be warm for once."

"I, for one, am glad you did." He studied me. "Are you okay?"

"Yeah. Of course." I let out a nervous laugh and set Buttons on his feet. He sauntered off to hide, like he always did when Mitchell came by. "Why wouldn't I be?"

"I don't know," he said slowly. "You just seem like you're upset about something."

Plastering on a fake smile, I shook my head, my mind still on that car. Why had it left when I looked at it? It could just be a car, of course, or it could be something more. "Nope. There's nothing for me to be upset about. I'm fine."

"Good." He wiggled the wine bottle. "If you're not, I'm sure this will help loosen you up a bit until you're ready to talk."

I made a mental note to not drink more than a glass. "Undoubtedly."

"Glasses?" he asked, walking into my kitchen. "I think I remember where they are, but—" He broke off, staring at the kitchen table. He bent his head. "New artwork purchase?"

Heart pounding, I walked over to him. "Y-yeah. Well, not a purchase, exactly. A friend drew it. He's a . . . an up-and-coming artist. Just getting started."

Mitchell stared at Chris's drawing, set down the wine, and looked toward the water. "This was drawn here? I see my house right there." He touched the drawing, pointing to the building next to mine—which was indeed his house. "It's an incredible re-creation. This artist is amazingly talented. What school did he go to?"

I hugged myself and smiled. "None."

"Seriously?" He blinked at me. "That's all just raw talent?"

"Yeah . . ."

"Is he still here? I'd love to meet him. Maybe talk to him about purchasing a drawing from him, only the view from my house." Mitchell picked up the frame and walked to the window, comparing. "I mean, he even caught the way the water reflects the sun. That's true talent. I *must* speak with him before he's too famous to take commissions."

My heart picked up speed, because this, *right here*, was what I'd been searching for. The solution I hadn't seen, even though it stared me right in the eye. If Chris took the talent that God had given him and used it for profit . . . could he make enough money to live a normal life? One that didn't include guns and death?

Would he get out of the gang if he had another option?

"I'll ask him if he's interested," I said in a rush. "He might be."

"If he's not, I'll throw money at him until he is." Mitchell put down the drawing and picked up the wine again. "Artists are never too proud to take a wad of cash."

I walked into the kitchen and pulled out two glasses. "This one might be. He's not exactly hurting for money."

"You know him personally."

It wasn't a question, but I nodded, anyway.

"I . . . see." He set the bottle on the granite kitchen island. "Will he be back?"

"Yeah." I shrugged, set the glasses down, and pulled out the corkscrew. "Maybe."

He stared at me. After a few seconds, he picked up the wine and the corkscrew I'd laid down. "Is it serious?"

"Is what serious?" I asked quickly, my cheeks heating up.

"The two of you." He pulled the cork out and set it down gently. "I'm not an idiot. You're blushing. He's clearly more than a friend."

"I don't know what we are to one another, honestly." I picked up the bottle and poured the red wine into two glasses. When I was done, I sighed. "It's . . . new. Very new."

"Ah." He picked up his drink and held it out to me. "To new relationships?"

I clinked my glass on his. "Does that mean you're in one, too?"

"Nah." He side-eyed me as he took a drink. "I'm still looking for the perfect woman."

I drank my wine, avoiding his stare. "You'll find her."

"No doubt."

Setting my wine down, I cleared my throat. "How's work been?"

"Good. The hospital's been busy." He smiled. "Lots of surgeries. Lots of work. Not much of a life. You know, the usual."

"You need to get out there more. You won't find a girl sitting at home on your deck watching the water."

"You never know." He laughed. "You don't exactly go out much, yet you found someone."

I flinched. "Mine was not your typical meet cute with a guy. You don't want to use me as an example."

"Still." He lifted a shoulder. "If it's meant to be, it'll happen."

"I guess so."

We fell silent, sipping our wine. He eyed me over his glass, clearly about to speak. I tensed, bracing myself. "This guy. Is he treating you well?"

"Yes. Of course."

"Good." He smirked. "If he wasn't, I'd have to do something about it."

The image of a harmless guy like Mitchell going up against Chris wasn't a pretty one. Chris would chew him up and spit him out like a bug. "Don't worry. I'm fine. He's a good guy."

"I can't wait to meet him." He took another sip of wine. "We could do dinner. I could grill, and we could crack open a few beers."

I might not know a lot about lying low, but I had a feeling an outdoor barbecue with the neighbor didn't fit into that description. "I don't think that's a good idea. He's kind of shy. You know how those artistic types can be. Maybe another night?"

Mitchell stared at me. "Yeah. That would be fine."

I blushed more. I couldn't help it. He suspected I was hiding something, I could see it in his eyes, and he was *right*.

I was. Groaning inwardly, I gulped back the remainder of my wine. "You'll meet him eventually. I promise."

If Chris actually stuck around, and, you know, lived.

"Can't wait." He finished off his drink, too. Almost immediately, he poured us both some more. "How did you two meet?"

I watched the red liquid fill up the glass. It occurred to me that I hadn't eaten all day. Chris had made pancakes, but we'd never actually sat down to enjoy them. By the time I came down the stairs, after a long, frustrated shower, they'd been hard and cold, so I'd tossed them. My stomach growled in protest.

"I've known him for years, but we just recently got to know each other better." I picked up the wine and stared down at it, not drinking it. "His parents are my neighbors, so he's been around for a while. Whenever he comes by, he always does something nice for me. Stops by to say hello. Kind of like you and me, only in the city."

His jaw flexed. "Cool."

"Yeah . . ."

He stared out the window. "What does he do for a living? I'm assuming he doesn't just draw, since you said he's new to the scene?"

"He . . . uh . . ."

God. I wasn't ready for this. I didn't know what to say to these questions. How to answer. Obviously, I couldn't tell him the truth. *He's in a gang and sells guns, and he shoots people with those guns.* In the city, people might understand— maybe. But out here? Yeah. He wouldn't get it, or why I was with a guy like Chris.

It was a rude awakening.

One I didn't entirely welcome.

Mitchell frowned. "It's okay. You don't have to answer. I shouldn't be prying."

"You're not. It's just . . . it's hard to explain, is all." I set my glass down, the room spinning. "He's in sales, kind of."

He cocked a brow. He kind of looked like Chris when he did that. All cocky-arrogant and self-assured. "Kind of?"

"Yeah." I walked over to the fridge and opened it, pulling out some mozzarella and tomatoes. I set balsamic vinegar next to it. "Hungry?"

"Sure." He sat down at the stool by the island. "What kind of sales is he in?"

I closed my eyes and counted to three. Mitchell meant well, and we always talked like this when he came over to visit, but today, it was too much. "I'm *starving*. I haven't eaten yet today."

He seemed to get the point. Coming around the island, he pulled two bowls out of the cabinet. "Well, let's fix that. Can't have you drinking on an empty stomach. So, how goes life as a kindergarten teacher?"

I picked the knife up off the counter and started slicing tomatoes. "It's great. I love the kids."

"You want some of your own someday?" he asked, opening the cheese.

I froze, the knife still halfway buried in a tomato. To be honest, I hadn't really thought about it. To have kids, traditionally speaking, I'd have to have a husband or a lover. And to have a husband, chances were, I'd have to care about someone, and that broke my rules. Loving someone else opened me up to pain and loss. "I . . . I don't know."

"Sorry." He laughed uneasily. "Didn't mean to make you panic. I was just curious. You seem like you'd be a good mom."

"I mean, yeah. I guess I want kids. Someday. Maybe."

Mitchell laughed. "Give it time. You'll know when you're ready. I give it five years before you've got a bunch of little Mollys running around this house."

I tried to picture it. Some faceless guy and me married, with a couple of little kids. But the faceless guy? He wasn't so faceless after all. He was *Chris*. And instead of terrifying me, like this should, it felt . . . good. Like it was something I wanted, even.

Oh God.

Was I falling in love with *Chris*?

CHAPTER 21

CHRIS

"This is the trick to winning." I leaned forward, pointing at the drawing I'd made of Bitter Hill's clubhouse. "Back here."

Tate frowned. "A door?"

It was a rudimentary sketch, but it had all the doors and windows represented accurately. Tate leaned in, too, and so did Tommy, Brian, and Scotty. I'd asked if he could sit in, since he was Lucas's brother and his heir apparent. Plus, I needed him there so I could give him my position.

"Here, behind the Dumpster, is a door that only the club members know about. They keep it hidden for a quick escape, if need be. The Dumpster is always empty, so it can be pushed out of the way." I tapped the square I'd drawn for the Dumpster. "So the way I see it, we have two good options. Either block the door so they can't get out and attack from the front, or attack from the back, since they won't know that we know about it. Or we could even pay the Boys on our payroll to keep people out of the area, and then we'll set fire to the building. We could barricade the doors and pick off the survivors as they escape."

Tate nodded, running his thumb over his chin. His hair was freshly cut, and his blue eyes were narrowed as he studied the replica of the target. He was young, only twenty-nine, and he was the type of guy who women flocked to, never realizing how dangerous he was beneath those designer suits and charming smiles. "I like the last plan. They'll all run for their escape hatch, only to be trapped against a wall. And the ones who head for the front? We can mow them down like the cowards they are."

I nodded. "Exactly."

"Wow." Scotty shifted in his seat. "That's risky, but it could work."

Tate eyed him. "Are you okay with this? As his heir, you have first say."

"Well, actually." Scotty eyed me and pulled Lucas's note out of his pocket. "I found this, and it seems like Lucas had other plans. He named Chris as his heir."

I snatched it out of his hand. "It doesn't matter. I don't think Lucas was right. Scotty should be his successor. Not me. It's only right."

Scotty looked two seconds from murdering me, since this wasn't what we'd agreed upon, but he quickly lost the anger—outwardly, at least. "It's what Lucas wanted."

"I know, but it doesn't feel right," I said slowly.

Yeah, I was supposed to graciously accept the position. But Scotty would get a hell of a lot more intel if he was in the inner circle, and me turning down a promotion was a great way for me to lay the foundation in Tate's head as a Boy. No one turned down jobs in this gang unless they were hiding something. But I couldn't refuse it too adamantly, since Pops knew about my betrayal and could ruin everything before I came out as the rat in their midst.

I walked a fine line here.

Tate didn't show any reaction. Just held his hand out and stared at me with those bright blue eyes of his that looked way too innocent on such a ruthless leader.

Pulse racing, I passed it over. "Like I said, it's not right."

"I heard you the first time." Tate opened it, scanning it. "Where did you find this, Scott?"

"In Heidi's bar. Lucas told me if anything happened to him, to look in the top drawer of Heidi's desk after he was gone." Scotty rested his elbows on his thighs. "That's what I found when I broke in."

Tate rotated it, holding it in the corner with two fingers. "It's bloody. Why?"

"I don't know." Scotty dragged a hand through his hair. "I found it that way."

Tate frowned. Brian leaned in and said something quietly in his ear, and he nodded in return. Then he turned back to me. "You're rejecting this promotion, O'Brien?"

I swallowed hard, knowing I couldn't actually do so. If I did, they'd suspect something was off too soon for my plans, so I had to play this out right, or pay the price. "No. Not at all. I'm honored and would accept the position if you feel it's best. But since Scotty is his little brother, his blood, I'm simply pointing out that it might be best to follow that. Who knows what kind of mind frame Lucas was in when he wrote this? There's *blood* on it. Obviously some shit went down."

Tate looked down at the paper again. "Indeed."

We all sat there silently, waiting for Tate to speak.

Brian settled back in his chair. "If your father knew you

were saying this, he wouldn't be pleased. He's not the type to turn down advancement."

"I know." I lifted a shoulder. "I'm not my father. I'm loyal to the gang, and I like promotions as much as the next guy, but I prefer to earn them on my merit and hard work, rather than from someone else's loss."

Tate eyed me with new respect.

Scotty picked up his whiskey and took a long drink.

Brian nodded. "Well said, O'Brien."

"I agree. It shows how good of a leader you truly are." Tate looked at Scotty, frowning. "What do you think? Would you like to disregard these last wishes of your brother and take the position, or do you think Chris should have it?"

Scotty set his glass down. "Whatever you think is best, sir. I, like Chris, am still mourning my brother's passing. In this instance, I think your opinion on this should decide the matter."

Tate nodded in appreciation. "Well said, as well."

"What's it going to be, boss?" Brian asked. "Scott or Chris?"

"How about this? Scott, you take over your brother's position, and Chris oversees you to make sure no mistakes are made as you learn the ins and outs of leadership. Think of it as an internship of sorts. If you prove capable of the power?" Tate placed the note in his suit jacket breast pocket. "It's yours. If not, Chris gets it. Does that sound like a fair plan to the two of you?"

"Better than fair." It gave us an excuse to spend a lot of time together, which was what I'd been hoping for. For my plan to work, I had to be close to him at all times. "Scotty?"

He nodded once. The way he looked at me—half respect, half hesitation—pretty much summed up his feelings for me. He still wasn't sure if I was playing an angle or not. He'd probably never be certain until this was over. "Yeah. I can work with that, sir."

"Great." He leaned in again and stared down at the map I'd made. "Where did you get this intel, Chris? Is it reliable?"

"Very. It's from an old buddy of mine who got jumped out of Bitter Hill." I shrugged. "I try to keep lots of connections in lots of places. It helps when you need intel that you can't get from the usual avenues."

Tate rubbed his jaw, nodding, but stared at me as if he wasn't exactly sure what kind of connections I had. Again. Part of my plan. It was almost too easy—like taking candy from a baby. "Excellent."

"Should we fill the rest of the men in on the plan?" Brian asked.

"Yes." He stood and eyed both Scotty and me, still looking less than thrilled. "In light of our new arrangements, I want you two to head up the sale tomorrow at ten in the morning on the lower docks. Show Scotty how it's done. You were with Lucas at the last one, right?"

I nodded. "Yes, sir."

"Okay. I leave it in your hands." He picked up the drawing, staring down at it. "Head on out and show him the area. Go over how it works, so there are no hiccups during the real thing tomorrow. We don't want our buyers getting antsy over yet another man handling the sale. Come by my office after it's done. I'll expect a full report."

I shook his hand and repeated, "Yes, sir."

"Thank you." Scotty also shook his hand. "I appreciate the opportunity to prove myself."

Tate nodded and walked to the bar.

Scotty watched him go. As soon as Tate was out of earshot, he clapped me on the shoulder in what probably looked like a comradely fashion, and hissed, "Outside. Now."

We headed for the door, and I rolled my hands into fists. He could rip me a new one all he wanted, but my play had ended exactly the way I'd wanted it to.

All's well that ends well.

Pops stepped in front of me. "Can I have a minute, son?"

"Sure." Scotty gave me a warning look. "I'll wait for you outside."

"What's up?" I asked as Scotty walked through the door.

"Did you get the position?" he asked quietly.

"No." I gritted my teeth and glanced over my shoulder, worried someone might overhear us. "I'm helping Scotty, though, and teaching him how to do Lucas's job. I can ruin all his best efforts, and the position is mine, even more securely than before."

Pops grinned. His weathered, rough skin crinkled, and his brown eyes shone with pride. "Excellent. Make it realistic, though. Don't get too overeager."

"I won't. Don't worry—I know how to play the game. You taught me well." I cocked my head. "Tate wants me to show him the ropes now, so I better go."

He nodded and walked off without another word.

As soon as I faced the door, I ran my hands down my face and took a deep breath. Because, fuck, I needed a deep breath. This game of push and pull, and living a double life? It was exhausting. I'd gotten a small taste of it while I'd been plotting Lucas's death, but now I was lying to a whole fucking gang, and these men were my *brothers*.

I didn't know how Scotty did it.

This double life.

Shaking my head, I pulled the door open. The second I stepped outside, I heard the unmistakable sound of a fist hitting bone and flesh to my left.

"Fucker," Scotty growled. "Come at me."

I grabbed the door before it could shut loudly, slowly letting it latch. To the side of the door, around the corner of the building, Scotty struggled with three other men, who were taking turns punching him. He was putting up a good fight, but he was losing. The men were all bigger than him and were from Bitter Hill.

I recognized the biggest guy as one of Reggie's men.

For once, their fight wasn't focused on *me*.

Cursing inwardly, I stepped back in the shadows, watching. I wasn't about to go charging out there without knowing exactly what I was up against. That wouldn't do any good.

"Did your mama teach you how to punch, little kid?" one of the Bitter Hill guys taunted.

"No. Your mom did last night." Scotty spit out a mouthful of blood. "Right before she took it up the ass."

"I'll *kill* you for that!" one of the bigger guys growled, launching himself at Scotty.

"Shh," the biggest guy said, grabbing him before he could make contact. "We don't want his buddies coming out to help. Take him down quieter."

"Fuck you." Scotty punched the leader in the nose, and blood squirted out. The man stumbled backward, his hand plastered to his nose. Scotty made eye contact with me briefly but quickly looked away. Something told me he didn't expect me to help him. Laughing, he held his arms out to the side. "Who's next?"

One man stepped back and pulled out a switchblade. He flicked it open with a swing of his wrist. "Me."

Scotty eyed the knife. "Coward."

And then he spat at his feet.

The man growled and leapt at Scotty, and they went to the pavement in a tangled mess of fists and legs . . . and one knife. The other men watched, grinning.

"Hurry up," the leader hissed, glancing over his shoulder at the main door.

They obviously sought to take down a gang member right outside the clubhouse, to send a message to Tate. To show them that no one was safe, no matter who they were or where we were. I could walk away. Let the Bitter Hill guys take Scotty out of the equation for me, take over his position, and forget all about betraying my brothers. Forget all about the Donahues and everything they stood for. Move on.

Or I could do the *right* thing.

The thing is, sometimes the *right* thing wasn't so clear-cut. And sometimes it didn't feel good. Not much in this world ever made sense. Nothing was held at face value.

Not anymore.

Pulling my gun out of my holster, I crept around the corner, aimed, and fired off a shot at the grinning asshole. He was still grinning as his blood and brains exploded all over the brick wall behind him in a giant splattered circle. He crumbled to the black pavement like a broken marionette, his knees folding beneath him as his skull hit the pavement with a sick thud.

Scotty looked up briefly, shock written all over his face, but recovered quickly enough to punch the guy who was straddling him in the gut. He fell to the side, slashing out at Scotty as he went, but I had to focus on the other standing man—the leader.

I pointed my gun at him and started to squeeze the trigger when something hit me from behind, slamming into the back of my skull. I hit the ground hard, face-first, stars swimming in front of my eyes, and struggled to roll over and shoot. The second I was on my back, a foot slammed into my nose, snapping it, and I couldn't see a damn thing.

I was blinded by pain and stars, but I still lifted the gun.

Even though I couldn't see where to aim.

"Chris, shoot!" Scotty yelled. *"Now!"*

Trusting him, I pulled the trigger and hoped to hell I hit someone. A strangled moan followed the boom of my gun, and a dead weight fell on top of me, soaking me with warm, sticky blood. I might not be able to see my attacker, but I'd say my aim had been true. And now he was bleeding all over me.

That's what I got for telling Molly I loved her, like a fool.

A corpse and a fucking broken nose.

The door to the clubhouse slammed open, a flurry of shots and cursing took over the quiet of the night, and I stayed under the cover of the corpse, breathing heavily. Gingerly, I touched my nose, wincing, and groaned. "Motherfucker."

When things calmed down, I tried to push the corpse off me, but it was too heavy, and I was too weak. One last shot sounded, and someone crouched beside me. The dead weight crushing my chest was dragged off me, and I inhaled deeply. The air filled my lungs, and my vision cleared a little. I blinked up at the person next to me. Scotty knelt there, blood running down his face and a bruise already forming under his eye. "Shit. Are you okay?"

"I'm fine." Rolling over, I spit out blood. It tasted like metal, a flavor I was all too familiar with. "Are they all dead?"

"Yeah." He pinched his nose and winced. "You got two, I got one, and Brian got the other."

"Good. Assholes."

Tate knelt beside Scotty. "You all right, O'Brien?"

"Yeah." I struggled to sit up, blinking away the lingering blurry vision. "I'm good."

"What happened?" he asked, his attention locked on my nose.

"I stayed back to talk to Pops, and when I came outside, Scotty was surrounded by Bitter Hill guys. It was pretty clear they meant to take him out." I glanced at Pops, who frowned at me. He probably thought I should have let them finish the job. "I jumped in and shot one. I didn't hear the other guy come up behind me, so they took me down."

"That right?" Tate asked Scotty.

He nodded. "Yeah. They jumped me the second I was out the door. I didn't see them coming, so I didn't stand a chance in fighting them off. If not for Chris, I'd be dead right now, and they'd be laughing because they won."

"Well, they didn't win." Tate smiled and rocked back on his heels. "Good job, boys. Do you need that nose looked at, O'Brien?"

Scotty nodded. "He does."

"Nah. It's broken." I struggled to my feet, refusing to take any of the hands that were offered to me. O'Briens didn't need help. They took care of themselves. "All it needs is to be repositioned, and some time to heal."

"But—" Tate's forehead wrinkled. "You need help repositioning it, though."

I rolled my shoulders. "I've got it. I'm fine."

"All right." Tate stared at me with respect and stood. "If you say so."

"Damn." Brian shook his head. "Fucking O'Briens."

"Hey." Pops laughed and crossed his arms over his chest. He might be pushing sixty-three, but he was still harder than a wall. "I'm right here."

"Yeah, I know." Brian walked past him. "And you're all insane."

I forced a grin. "We're just tough. I got this. I had worse before I could even walk."

"Yeah." Scotty frowned at Pops. "We know."

Pops shifted on his feet. "Always was a clumsy kid."

"Come on." Scotty side-eyed me. "Let's get you home so we can set the bones properly. Are you good with this mess, sir?"

"Assholes." Tate glowered at the corpse at his feet and kicked it. "Yeah. Go ahead. We'll clean this up, and send Bitter Hill a nice little message back."

I gave Tate a nod and walked with Scotty to his Escalade. The second I was in the passenger seat, I pulled the visor down and looked in the mirror. Bruises were already forming all across my cheekbones, in browns and yellows, and my septum was clearly crooked. It would need to be reset and taped.

Molly was going to flip her shit when she saw me.

Scotty got into the car and started it, not speaking. I poked at the side of my nose, cringing when it sent a throbbing shaft of pain piercing through my skull. "Son of a bitch."

"You look awful."

"Thanks," I said dryly.

"Anytime." He started the car and backed out almost immediately, stealing glances at me every so often as he steered toward the exit of the parking lot. "Why did you do it?"

I poked the left side of my nose. It hurt just as bad as the right. I took a deep breath through it. I could, so that was a good sign. "Why did I do what?"

"Save me." He pulled onto the highway, his white knuckles moving on the wheel. "You could have let them kill me, and no one would know. Or you could have taken me out, blamed them, and been free. You didn't have to do that. Save me."

"I told you. I know what I'm supposed to do now. I know

it sounds stupid, but I want to help. From the inside." I closed the visor and shrugged. "I want to make the city cleaner, too."

"Bullshit," Scotty said, snorting.

I didn't say anything back.

"You're kidding, right?" he asked.

Again, I said nothing.

Scotty stared at me for so long I shifted in my seat.

"Dude. Watch the fucking road," I snapped.

Scotty slammed his gaze back to the windshield. "You continue to surprise me, Chris."

"Yeah. I'm good at that," I muttered.

"Thank you."

I nodded once, not meeting his eyes. I was as uncomfortable with thanks as I was with mercy. I didn't know either one. "Whatever. I was just doing my job."

Scotty stepped on the gas and flexed his jaw. "And what, exactly, *is* your job?"

"Keep you alive. Give you reliable intel. Hide your secret at all costs." I tapped my fingers on the door, right next to the window. My nose hurt like a bitch, and all I wanted was Molly's sweet touch to make it all better. "Keep my mouth shut."

"At all costs?" Scotty stiffened. "What the hell does that mean?"

I closed my eyes. "Exactly what it sounds like it means. That I'll do what has to be done to keep you breathing."

"Why is it so important to you I stay alive?"

"Why the fuck do you think it's important?" I snapped. "You're Lucas's baby brother."

I watched the restaurant we passed off the highway. A man in a blue dress shirt, black trousers, and suspenders came out holding a little girl's hand. She looked up at the man with so much love you could literally *feel* her adoration in your chest. It was warm, and it spread slowly, taking over until suddenly you felt happy for no fucking reason at all, just watching it.

"Yeah." Scotty switched lanes and stepped on the gas. "And?"

"And I'm going to keep you alive, no matter what I have to do." I ran my fingers over my nose again. "Is that going to be a problem?"

"No." Scotty shook his head and let out a long breath. "But you know you don't owe anything to Lucas, right?"

I froze, my hand hovering in front of my face. I'd only told one person I felt like I did, and I didn't like to think she was spilling information to the Boys, but he had to have heard that *somewhere*. "Who said I thought I did?"

"No one." He pulled off the exit that led toward the Cape—toward my Molly. "I'm just taking guesses. Something tells me I hit too close to home for you."

"You don't know shit," I snapped.

"How far are you willing to go to keep me alive?" he asked quietly.

"As far as I need to go," I said quickly.

"Back there, at the clubhouse, it was almost as if you were trying to make Tate suspect you." He stole a quick look my way. "Like you wanted him to think you were playing him, or me, or both."

I lifted a shoulder. "Why would I do that? If he thinks I'm a narc, he'll kill me."

"Yeah." His fingers tightened. "You keep playing games like that, and he'll start thinking you're the Boy, not me."

I said nothing to that.

"I had guys out there, you know." He glanced at me. "Listening in. If it got too bad, they would have come out. I always have a team with me. So . . . be careful next time. Don't do anything stupid to save me."

My jaw dropped. "'If it got too bad?' That looked pretty fucking bad to me. What were they waiting for before jumping in to help you? A handwritten invitation signed by the president?"

"I had it under control. I have a code word. Once I say my word, they'll come out of the woodwork. They're everywhere. Places you'd never—" He gripped the wheel. "Never mind. You don't need to know how it all works, but I'm just trying to tell you not to endanger yourself too badly next time. I've got guys for that."

"I thought that was a fed thing." I narrowed my eyes. "Not a cop thing."

"I never said I was a Boy, did I?" He shifted his hands on the wheel. "You assumed that's what I was, and so did Lucas. But I never said those words."

Well, shit. That changed things. If he was a fed, he had men in vans watching his every move. And that meant anything they saw me do . . . was now on record. "Shit."

Scotty didn't say anything.

"Are you going to tell me what you are?"

Scotty let out a breath. "Does it really matter?"

"What happens if Tate makes you?"

"We've got stuff in place for that, too." Scotty swallowed. "I can't tell you anything more than that. But I'm relatively safe, so you don't need to worry."

So I might not actually have to *die* to keep Scotty safe. Stupid, ridiculous hope flooded into my chest. If I didn't have to die to save Scotty, if I didn't have to sacrifice myself, I could keep Molly. I could start planning for the future—a future with her by my side. If I played my cards right, we could be *happy*.

In my life, I'd never once let myself think I could have that. Real happiness. But Molly, for whatever reason, seemed to accept me as I was. Flaws and all. And I certainly more than accepted her. If I wasn't going to die . . .

Could I get that? Could I get *her*?

CHAPTER 22

MOLLY

A lot of hours and a bottle of wine later, I opened the front door, smiling at Mitchell as he passed through it. It was dark now, and Chris had been gone all day. "Thanks for keeping me occupied. You helped pass the time for me, and believe me, I needed that distraction."

"Anytime." Mitchell laid a hand on my shoulder and gave me a gentle smile. "And hey. You know I'm here for you, if you ever want to talk. I'm a good listener."

He was. That was one of his best qualities. I placed my hand on his, squeezing. "Thanks. I—" Headlights pulled up the driveway. It was a black Escalade. "Oh God."

Relief punched me in the chest.

That was Scotty's car.

"What's wrong?" Mitchell asked, frowning toward the truck.

"Nothing. It's just . . ." I motioned toward it. "That's him."

"Your boyfriend?" Mitchell asked.

I let him go and nodded. "I think so. I have to—"

"I'll go. Give you two your privacy." He stared at the car, then me. "Be careful, though. Please."

I blinked at him. Why would he say that now, of all times? Did he know more than he was letting on? "Of course."

He walked past the truck, nodding at the tinted windows as he passed.

Once he was gone, Chris opened the passenger door and came out. The second I saw him, I gasped. His face was covered in blood—*his* blood, from what I could tell. He'd removed his shirt, but it was balled up in his fists and was clearly soaked in even more blood—not sure whose.

I lifted my hand to cover my mouth, my heart pounding so hard it was a miracle it didn't pop right out of my chest. "Oh my God."

Chris leaned in the car, said a few things to Scotty, closed the door, and tapped the hood of the truck as he walked toward me. His eyes were hard and angry. "Who the hell was that?"

"What happened to your nose?" I asked, ignoring him.

"A foot slammed down on it. It's broken." He grabbed my arm as he passed, tugging me behind him into my house. "Who the hell just left your house? He looked like a fed."

"He's not." I swallowed hard, staring at what used to be his nose but was now a broken mess. "God. That looks . . . We have to take you to the hospital."

He snorted, letting me go and urging me inside the house with a hand across my lower back. "No."

Once we were inside, he kicked the door shut and locked it, tossed his shirt to the side, and leaned back against the door. For a second, he let his guard down, and he looked . . . *tired.* Like if he had to endure yet another fight, he would crumble.

And, God, I was terrified that he just might.

"Son of a—," he said under his breath, breathing heavily. "This is gonna hurt."

"All that blood." I swallowed, eyeing the shirt, and stepped back. He looked so different, standing there shirtless, with blood literally all over his hands. "Is it yours?"

"No." He gestured toward the shirt. "None of that is mine. Just the stuff on my face. Who the hell was in the house, and why was he touching you?"

"That's just Mitchell. He lives next door. He stopped by—" I broke off and closed the distance between us. "Hey. He's a doctor. We should ask him to look you over. You could have a concussion."

"A *doctor.*" He shook his head, a muscle in his jaw ticking. "No."

"But—"

"I said *no.*" He pushed off the door and caught my chin. Looking up at him, with his bloody and discolored face, sent chills down my spine. "You shouldn't have brought him in here. What if he noticed something was off? What if he calls the Boys?"

I blinked. "The what?"

"Cops," he said from between gritted teeth.

"Oh." I tried to back up, but his hold on me didn't budge. "He wouldn't. Besides, what harm would calling the cops do? You're not a fugitive."

"No, but Bitter Hill might have guys on the payroll." He let go of me and dragged a hand through his hair before stalking up the stairs. "This was supposed to be a secret, us being here. You never should have opened the fucking door."

I followed him slowly. "He knew I was here. If I didn't let him in, that would have raised a flag."

"So did letting the preppy asshole in," he snapped. He

pushed into the bathroom and stood in front of the sink, staring at himself in the mirror. He slammed his hand down on the counter. "Son of a bitch."

I flinched. "Why are you so angry?"

"Who the hell is he to you?" He stared back at me in the mirror, eyes flashing. "He looked at you like he's fucked you—or wants to fuck you."

"Mitchell?" I let out a nervous laugh. "I didn't . . . no. I told you, I don't get around much. And he was not the guy I was with—not that it's any of your business if I was. I'm sure you weren't a monk when we weren't together."

He gripped the edges of the sink, his head lowered, shoulders heaving with each breath he took. "Shit. I'm sorry. I'm being an asshole. I don't know what's wrong with me."

He was jealous. *That's* what was wrong with him. "Your nose is broken, for starters," I said gently, taking a step toward him, trying to be okay with this whole mess. I wasn't okay at all. Not with his broken nose. Not with the blood. "What happened?"

"Scotty got jumped outside of the club. I was the only one out there with him, so I jumped in. Got a broken nose for my efforts but took two of them down." He gestured down to his bare chest. "The fucker that fell on me was a bleeder."

He spoke of killing people like it was nothing.

Just another day on the job.

He killed people, yes, and I'd even seen him do it, but seeing him act like it was *nothing*—like those lives he took were inconsequential—it was chilling, to put it lightly. Like the lives lost didn't matter to him at all. "Do you ever feel bad?"

"No. Why should I?" He snorted. "They were trying to kill me. It was me or them. I chose them. Would you have rather I chose me?"

"Of course not. But they were someone's person." I hugged myself. "A son. A father. A brother. A husband. They were *someone*."

"Then they shouldn't have been there, trying to kill me." He locked eyes with me. "If you're in this life, you don't form attachments, and you don't let people need you. All that does is lead to heartbreak and pain when you're found dead in an alley. Why do you think I don't date women seriously?"

If he didn't date, what were *we* doing? When we were together, he acted like he cared about me. Like I was special. But his words told another story . . . and it was time I started listening to those instead of what I *thought* his actions meant. "You've never been upset to lose someone?"

"Nope. Never." He tensed, still staring at me in the mirror. "Life sucks, and then you die. The person that died goes wherever dead people go, and you're still alive. Why bother with being sad when it won't change a damn thing? It's easier not to feel anything. To never love anyone or anything. Makes more sense, too."

He gripped his nose, took a deep breath, and . . .

Snapped it back in place.

I covered my mouth, choking on bile. My stomach roiled in protest, and I backed up as more blood came gushing out of his nose. "I—I—"

Pressing my hand against my mouth more firmly, I shook my head and ran for the toilet on the other side of the bathroom. I barely hit the floor on my knees before the vomit came, *Exorcist*-style. Chris cursed and followed me, crouching to hold my hair out of my face. I clung to the toilet, trembling, and stared down at the contents of my stomach.

This was it.

This was my life now.

Watching my lover snap his nose back into place after casually telling me I meant nothing to him—and never would. He knelt behind me, smoothing my hair out of my face. The same hand that had killed two men and had snapped his nose into place was gently holding my hair.

It was too much. It was all too much.

I gripped the toilet harder, trembling for another reason now. My entire body ached and hurt, but it was nothing in comparison to my heart. "I can't do this. I can't . . ."

"Shh." He reached past me, closed the lid, and flushed. "I'm sorry. I should have warned you. I didn't know you were squeamish. You helped patch me up the other day, so I didn't even think."

I closed my eyes, breathing heavily. I still couldn't catch my breath. It hurt more than I'd have ever thought possible, but it was time to end this. *"Chris."*

He hugged me from behind, his arms around me secure. And so tender it *hurt*. "It's okay. You don't have to. Go downstairs. I'll finish up in here, and when I'm done, we can have dinner. It's—"

"No." I shrugged his hold off and stood up unsteadily. My chest ached from the sobs I held back. My throat throbbed. My eyes stung. But I held it together. I backed up toward the shower until I couldn't back up anymore. It put a few feet between us. It wasn't enough. "I mean I can't do this anymore. Be with you. I can't."

He stared up at me, not a hint of emotion fleeting across his face, and didn't move. Simply stood there, looking as frozen as ice, and just as cold. "Why not?"

"No matter what you do, who you become, you're always going to come home bleeding . . . and covered in other people's blood." I wrapped my arms around myself and swallowed

back a sob. "I'm a teacher. I work with kids, not guns. I can't
live like this. I can't—" I broke off, tears running down my
face. "You have to go."

Before I back down again.

He didn't even flinch. Just stared back at me like he didn't
care whether or not I could handle being with him. "Right
now?"

I nodded once.

"Jesus." He dragged a hand through his hair and swiped
the back of his palm across his face. He took a step toward
me. "Is this because of what I said earlier? I didn't mean it.
I don't love you, so you don't have to leave me. I swear it. *I
don't love you.*"

What had he said earlier? I must've missed it. "Yeah. I
know." I held a shaky hand out to stop him. He listened.
"You should shower and everything first, but . . . you need
to leave."

Turning on my heel, I bolted from the room.

There was no other word for it.

I barely saw anything as I sprinted across the hallway and
into the guest room. All of Chris's stuff was in the bedroom
we shared, so I couldn't hide out in there. Heck, I might never
be able to enter that room again. Too many memories. Too
much pain.

Trembling, I sat on the edge of the bed and stared at the
closed door.

It was weird. So much pain rocked through me that it hurt
to even think about moving. About living every day without
Chris by my side. Without knowing if he was alive, or shot,
or dead in an alley. Not knowing if he was *okay*.

How was *I* supposed to be okay with that?

I might have only been dating him—if we could even

call it that—for a short time, but with all the courting he'd done, and the danger and the amazing sex . . . it felt like a *lifetime*.

Losing him was like losing that last hope I had that maybe, just maybe, I could live a normal life. That I could fall in love, get married, and have babies.

That dream was dead.

The only man I wanted was Chris . . .

And he couldn't live a normal life even if he wanted to.

Tears rolled down my cheeks, and I lifted my feet up on the bed, bending at the knee and hugging my legs tightly. Still. I just sat there. Numb. Staring at a closed door. Until . . .

It opened, and Chris came in wearing nothing but a towel. He'd showered and had tape across his broken nose. All evidence of blood was gone, but I could still see it.

I'd always see it.

It was that blood, that *life*, that kept us apart.

There was no happy ending for us. Just pain.

He started talking before he located me on the bed. "I thought about it, and you know what? Fuck no. I'm not going. You had your chance, and you passed on it, so I'm staying. Tell me what you need me to do and I'll do—" He took one look at me and my wet cheeks and staggered forward. "Molly, don't. Don't fucking cry over me. Don't you *dare*."

I bit down on my lip hard, but a sob still escaped.

Nothing would hold it back now.

"Shit." He closed the distance between us and pulled me into his arms. The second he hugged me, I knew that nothing would save me. I'd feel his loss just as strongly now as I would if he stuck around. And it wasn't *fair*. "I'll go. I promise. Just stop crying."

The pain in his voice was impossible to miss.

I looked up at him, and he stared down at me with a

haunting emptiness in his gaze. Like he knew nothing he said or did would actually fix what was wrong with me, and that terrified him. And he was right. Nothing would fix me. I was broken.

No matter what I did . . .

I was losing him.

CHAPTER 23

CHRIS

Holding her in my arms as she cried over me, over what *I'd* done to her, hurt more than any kind of torture I'd ever had inflicted upon me. She was the one light in my life, the one shining beacon of happiness, and I'd fucking ruined it.

Ruined her.

And she'd ruined me, too.

That's what love really was.

I never should have let it get this far. All along, I knew how this ended. It ended with her telling me to get the hell out of her life. With me slinking away back into the darkness, with nothing and no one there by my side, like the monster I was.

And still, I'd sought her out again.

Like a moth drawn to a flame, I couldn't quit her. But she needed a man who didn't come home with someone else's blood all over him, and who didn't need to snap his own nose back into place. She needed a dude who worked normal workday hours, like clockwork. She needed a guy who wore suspenders and dress shirts and who held their little girl—

Instead of a gun.

What she needed was a guy like Mitchell. The fucker who'd been here earlier. He was perfect for her. She'd even said so herself, back when we'd watched that dating show. The doctor and the teacher. Mitchell was the type of man a woman could rely on. He wouldn't break her heart. He wouldn't leave her mourning him over his grave at an early age. He would make her happy. They could have kids and a happy home. He could make her smile and laugh and maybe even scream out in pleasure. He could give her everything she deserved.

And I fucking *hated* him for it.

Her bright hazel eyes shone with tears I'd caused, and it killed me. The guilt choked me. I had to go. Put her out of her misery. But she was *crying*.

Because of me.

For the first time in my life, I wanted to put someone else's well-being before my own. For the first time, I wanted to be the guy who walked away.

"Shh." I cradled her head and kissed her temple. I closed my eyes, a shaft of pain piercing through the shield of armor I wore around myself, because this was the last time I was going to get to hold her. The last time I got to touch her. "Don't cry."

Her hand fisted on my bare shoulder. *"Chris."*

I closed the distance between us, kissing her. She tasted like tears, pain, and loss. Like everything I wanted was slipping through my fingers, because it was. I let my eyes close and pressed her back against the mattress, covering her body with mine.

Being here, with her, was the only thing that felt right

anymore. The only place I felt whole. We didn't make sense. She could do better than me. Pretty much any other guy in the world was a smarter choice than me. But against all odds and all logic, I didn't want to accept that. Didn't want to lose her.

And I wanted *her* to want *me* against all logic, too.

To love me like she'd never loved another man.

Which was stupid, since no one had ever cared about me that much before. I wasn't the type of guy who inspired that kind of love and devotion. I wasn't Lucas.

Not even my own parents loved me.

Why should she?

Burying my hands in her hair, I slipped between her thighs, putting all the fucked-up emotions rolling through me into that simple gesture. Our lips melded together perfectly, and I wished that was a sign that we were meant to be. That it proved we could be together, against all odds.

It wasn't.

Not anymore.

She wrapped her legs around my waist, holding me in place, and trailed her hands down my back. The touch was gentle, but there was a franticness behind it that couldn't be ignored. She trembled beneath me, and her tongue curled around mine as she rocked her hips. I knew what she needed. Could get her off in seconds.

I traced the curve of her hip, skipping over her ass and sliding down her outer thigh. As I came back up, I skimmed inward, teasing her but not touching. When I went back down her leg, I grabbed ahold of her ankle and tugged. She resisted at first but gave in when I tightened my grip on her.

Through it all, I didn't stop kissing her. I couldn't.

She broke free, gasping for air as I lowered her foot to the mattress, leaving her leg bent at the knee. "I—I need you. *Please.*"

"You had me." I kissed her again, gently, as I placed her other foot on the other side of my body. "You had all of me."

Her lips parted, and she tightened her grip on my shoulders. "I—"

Before she could say something back, I kissed her again, burying my hand between her thighs. I kissed her like I was a dying man and she was my last chance at salvation. And she was. She'd been my last chance at being a man who lived.

I'd miss her for the rest of my life, no matter how short that might be.

I deepened the kiss when she tried to pull back, sliding my hand under her underwear and thrusting two fingers inside her tight pussy at the same time. Whatever she'd been about to say faded away, and she clung to me, crying out into my mouth. I was good at this part. At making a woman scream.

I just didn't know how to make her happy.

How to make her love me back.

"Shit." I froze, my fingers still inside her. Slowly, I pulled back, staring down at her. "No."

She lifted her lids, staring up at me in confusion. "Chris?"

"No." I pulled out of her, pushed off the mattress, and stood, covering my face. I could smell her all over me. Everywhere. "I can't do this."

She sat up, pushing the sleeve of her dress back up on her small shoulder. She looked so beautiful sitting there, staring at me with plump lips and rosy cheeks. So perfect. So fragile. So *not* mine. "What's wrong?"

"You told me to leave."

She swallowed. "I know."

"So I need to leave. I can't keep playing this game where you tell me I should go, I agree, and then you kiss me and I stay." I shook my head and backed up. The towel still clung to my hips, but I didn't know how. I held it as tightly as I should have held on to her. "You might think I'm an emotionless asshole, but I'm not. If you don't want me here, I need to go. It's that simple."

"It's not that I want you to go. It's that I don't see another option." She struggled to her feet, wringing her hands in front of her, her soft gray knit dress falling back into place. "You're going to die."

I tightened my hold on the towel. "Yeah. I know. We all are. So what?"

"Yeah, but you're literally *planning* your death. I thought I could handle it, take what little time I could get with you while I could get it, but I can't watch you die." She held her hands out. "Don't you see? I did that already. I don't want to do it again."

"So you want to spend the rest of your life alone? Hiding behind closed doors?" I flexed my jaw. "Or what? You just need someone who isn't me? Is that it?"

She flinched. "That's not it."

"What do you want from me? Leaving you, having you, losing you, it's all killing me." I took a step toward her, every fiber in my being aching to pull her back into my arms, where she belonged. "*You're* killing me."

She closed her eyes and tears rolled out again. "I don't want to do that."

"Then don't." I stared her down, breathing unevenly because being so honest wasn't easy for me. I didn't talk about my emotions or sit here and confess what was *really* in my heart. I loved her. I'd shown her that. I'd even told her, if she'd been listening. If that wasn't enough, I didn't know what to say. "Tell me what you want. Anything. I'll give it to you. The stars. The moon. Hell, the world. Just ask."

"You said you don't form attachments. Don't care about people."

I stiffened, knowing where she was going with this. "Yeah. I did."

"Is that true of everything?" She glanced at me through her lashes nervously, her cheeks pinking. "With every*one*?"

I had two options here.

I could be honest with her and tell her I loved her. Maybe she hadn't heard me earlier when I'd slipped, or maybe she just didn't realize what I'd been about to say. Or maybe she wanted me to say it again, to prove it was true. But if I told her I loved her, we'd stay together, and she would be a target, and there was no escaping that.

My other option was that I could lie.

Tell her I meant every word I said and there was no way I would ever love her the way she deserved to be loved. In a way, it was true. I loved her, yes. But getting love from a guy like me was like scoring a bargain at the dollar store and saving a penny on a dollar item.

· It didn't really give you a damn thing at all.

Now I knew what it felt like to love someone more than I loved myself. What it was to love someone enough to put her safety first. I wanted her to *live* and be *happy*, even if it wasn't with me. She'd given me that. Shown me what love felt like, how it changed a person. *She'd* changed *me* for the better.

But I didn't want to change her. I'd only make her worse.

It was time to let her go.

I squared my jaw and braced myself. "I meant every word I said. I don't do love. It's not worth it. I don't know what it's like to put someone first. I will never love another person the way they deserve to be loved."

She gritted her teeth. "You're lying. No one spends years courting someone when they don't care. When they're dead inside."

I didn't correct her, but I also didn't tell her she was right. Instead, I settled for: "Guys like me can't afford to have weaknesses, and that's what love is. Weakness."

"All right. Whatever." She took a deep breath, lifted those long, wet lashes of hers that I loved so much, and glowered at me. "Can I ask you for one last favor, though, before you take your ice-cold heart and leave again?"

I forced my feet to stay still, even though I wanted to pull her into my arms and tell her she was right. That I loved her with all my heart and soul. "Anything."

"I want you to leave the gang. Leave Boston." She swiped her hands across her cheeks. "Run away. Get a job. Live a normal life."

I took a second to form a response, because she'd asked for the *one* thing I couldn't give her. "I can't do that, even if I wanted to. The only way I'd get out of the gang is in a body bag. You don't just *leave*."

"That's not true. Lucas did it." She grabbed the hem of her dress, wringing it between her hands nervously. "He faked his death. You could do that, too."

"Yeah. He did. With the help of his cop brother." I gritted my teeth. "The same brother who knows exactly what I did to Lucas, and *why*."

"Then just walk away. Or buy your way out. Throw a bunch of cash at them. I don't care, as long as you *leave*." She closed the distance between us and pushed my good shoulder. "Stop making excuses and just *go*."

I squared my jaw, glaring down at her. "I'm not going."

"Why not?" She stilled, her face flushing with color. "Is

it a money thing? I have money. Lots of it. I'll give it to you. All of it. You could—"

"Jesus." I backed up, staring down at her with clenched fists. "I don't want your damn money, Molly. I just wanted—" I broke off and laughed, rubbing my jaw. *"Shit."*

"What?" She stared at me, tears still wetting her cheeks. "What do you want?"

You. Only you.

All I wanted to do was make her happy—and I'd even managed to screw that up. But I didn't want to run and hide. Didn't want to be that guy anymore.

I was staying. Fighting. Without her.

Princesses weren't supposed to choose the black knights.

"It doesn't matter what I wanted." I backed toward the door, staring at her one last time. Memorizing how beautiful she looked, even with a red-tipped nose and puffy eyes from crying. "Good-bye, Princess."

And I walked away before I did something foolish.

Like beg her to love me.

She stumbled after me, choking on a sob. "Wait! Please. You have to leave this city. You have to *live.*"

"No. I *don't."* I didn't pause. Just went into the bedroom and grabbed a pair of jeans off the floor. "I'm not leaving the gang. Not even for you."

I'd texted Scotty before I got in the shower, so he would probably be waiting outside for me by now, if he'd turned around and headed back right away. I tossed the towel across the room and stepped into the jeans, not bothering to put on underwear. I needed to get the hell out of here before I broke down. Before I forgot why it was better for her if I left.

She came around the side of the bed. "But where will you go?"

"Home. I'm back in the game." I yanked a shirt over my head, ignoring the pain that rocketed through me when the hem hit my nose. "I've got no reason to play it safe anymore."

"Bitter Hill is still trying to kill you," she said softly.

"Someone is *always* trying to kill me," I pointed out, shoving my belongings into the same damn trash bag my shit had been in before. I really needed to buy a damn duffel bag. I made sure to keep my voice perfectly even. To pretend like my heart wasn't breaking. "That's my life, Princess. But it's not yours. Not anymore. Go back to teaching kids and making the world a happier place. You're good at it."

She bit down on her lip. It didn't stop the trembling. "Chris . . ."

"Don't." I picked up my bag and slung it over my shoulder. "Just don't. You're you, and I'm me, and we both know this could never work out. I'm leaving, and this time—I'm not coming back. That's a promise."

"I'm sorry," she whispered. "I just can't be with you if you refuse to leave the gang. I can't do it."

"You don't have anything to be sorry for," I snapped, angry that she felt like she did. No one would blame her for not wanting to be with me. Not even me. "Don't apologize for being smart."

She bit down on her lip harder.

I walked around the bed, pausing when I reached her. Closing my eyes, I reached out, wrapped my hand around the back of her head, and pulled her into my arms, hugging her close. For a second, the world felt right. She was soft and warm and everything I couldn't have. "You're doing the right thing. Trust me."

She fisted my shirt, right over my heart, not letting go. "It doesn't feel right."

"Most of the time, the right thing feels wrong." I ground

my teeth together and let go of her, and the world went right back to being a shitty place. "Trust me. I'd know."

And I walked out of her life without telling her how much I loved her. It was, hands down, the nicest thing I'd ever done for someone else. The single best thing I'd ever done. Hopefully the first in a line of good things.

This was my new beginning.

I had to make sure not to waste it.

CHAPTER 24

MOLLY

Four days later, I sat on the porch of my Cape house, rocking in the off-white wooden rocking chair that had been placed there two days after Chris left, and watched the sunrise. He'd left a card on the chair, but I hadn't read it yet. Just seeing that envelope, with the familiar sloppy handwriting on it, had been enough to bring me to tears. That was all I could handle right now.

I rested my head on the chair and closed my eyes, a tear trickling down my cheek. It was stupid, really. I used to think losing my father had used up all my tears. That I didn't have any left. Turned out, I was saving them all for this. For losing the second man in my life I loved and lost. Chris O'Brien.

Tires crunched on gravel, and I opened my eyes, my heart picking up speed when I saw the car. It was a black Escalade. Scotty. I stood up unsteadily, not sure whether his arrival was a good or bad thing. After all, he was the only one who knew who I was, or that Chris had been here. If he was here . . .

Please, God, let Chris be okay.

I went down the steps of my porch as he got out of his car. He smoothed his leather jacket, pushed his sunglasses into place, and shut the door.

No one else came out.

I stopped walking, pressing a hand to my chest. "Is he . . . ?"

"No." He dragged a hand through his hair, messing it up, and walked over to me. He had this way of walking that made him look as if he didn't have a care in the world, but we both knew that wasn't the case. "He's not dead, if that's what you're asking."

"Thank God." I collapsed against the banister, still pressing a hand to my chest. "Then why are you here? What's wrong?"

"Nothing's wrong." He climbed the stairs and walked onto my porch. His gaze drifted to the left, toward my new rocking chair, before sliding back to me. "I just wanted to talk to you for a minute."

"So talk." I swallowed. "Does Chris know you're here?"

"No." He cocked a brow and touched my birdfeeder, tracing it with his pointer finger. "Is that going to be a problem?"

I shook my head. "He's not here anymore. We're . . . done. So if you were planning on hurting me to get to him, I'm afraid you'll be disappointed."

"I told you. I'm one of the good guys."

"Someone once told me that you being a cop didn't make you a good guy."

Scotty snorted. "Let me guess. Chris?"

"Maybe." I shifted. "But like I said. We're done now."

"Yeah, I know." He leaned on my banister and crossed his ankles. The collar of his leather jacket stood up straight, and he wore a pair of ripped jeans with brown leather boots. "He told me."

My heart sped up again, and I stepped down off the stairs. I wasn't sure why he was here, but if it was something shady . . . I needed to be able to run. "Then why did you come? What do you want from me?"

"Easy now." He held his hands up and took a step closer, removing his sunglasses so he could meet my eyes. His dark reddish brown hair framed those gorgeous green eyes perfectly, but something told me he liked to use that innocent charm that he exuded to his advantage. A lot. "I'm not here to hurt you. You know what I am. Who I am. Why would I hurt you?"

"I also know what Chris did to your brother." I gripped the railing of the banister and stepped behind it. "He told me everything. I also know he's looking to atone for the things he did, and you're taking full advantage of that."

Scotty tugged on his jacket. "He's been a great asset to me. I'm quite surprised by it all, to be honest. In just a few days, he's gotten me further than I did in a couple of years. I'm still not sure whether to trust him or not, but time will tell."

"You can trust him," I said slowly, not liking his attitude toward Chris, even though I understood where it came from. But I knew firsthand just how committed to keeping Scotty safe he was. "He's telling the truth. I swear it."

"No offense, but I've known Chris a long time. A lot longer than you have." Scotty pinched the bridge of his nose. "The thing about him is, he's always playing an angle, even when you think he's being sincere."

"Not this time." I crossed my arms and frowned. "He's dead serious about making it up to you and Lucas. He's prepared to do anything—*anything*—to make sure he does."

"Yeah. I kinda gathered as much." He shrugged and looked at the water before turning back to me. He rubbed the back of his neck and ducked his head down, grinning at me mischievously. But underneath that grin was a dedication to his job that couldn't be ignored, now that I knew his secret. He was the type of guy who would stop at nothing to get his way. Just like Chris. "Can I come in? Guys in my line of work generally don't like hanging around in the open, since it makes us easy targets, and I need to ask you a few questions. I swear I'm not going to hurt you. Or him."

I swallowed, trying to get a better read on him. I was ninety-nine percent certain he was genuine and didn't intend to do me any harm, but that one percent . . .

"Yeah. Sure." I shifted on my feet and dropped my arms back to my sides. "I can make you some coffee, if you'd like."

He smiled. "I never turn down coffee—especially when it's being offered by a beautiful woman. My ma taught me better than that."

"Oh yeah?" I walked by him and right into my house. Buttons came to the foyer to greet me, but once he saw Scotty, he took off for the bedroom upstairs. "And your father?"

"Never knew him." He shut the door. "Never cared to."

So he was *that* kid, the one who didn't know his dad and probably acted out in class to get attention. The one who sat in the last row and spit spitballs in girls' hair. "Ah."

He cocked a brow. "Ah?"

"Yeah." I shrugged and headed for the Keurig. "Caramel coffee okay?"

"Perfect." He sat down at the island, settling in Chris's favorite stool. It left him facing the front door, which was probably why he chose it. Just like Chris. "Thank you."

I nodded, slipping the K-Cup in the machine and pulling out a mug. "So, what did you want to talk about?"

"Chris." He rested his elbows on the gray granite, watching me closely. Too closely. "What happened between the two of you?"

I stared at the coffee as it brewed. Once it was finished, I set it in front of him, leaned over, and positioned myself the same way as him. "I don't really see how that's any of your business. Sugar? Cream?"

"You're right. It's not." He wrapped his hands around his coffee and picked it up. "And, no, thank you. I drink it black."

I nodded once. "If it's none of your business, why say anything? What's *your* angle?"

"I don't have one," he said, laughing. "But I've known him a long time."

"So you said," I answered dryly. "And yet, you still seem to think the worst of him. Was he always a guy you couldn't trust, or is this a recent development?"

"Recent." He blew on his coffee. "But do you blame me for being hesitant? He did a shitty thing. In my world, that makes you a shitty person."

"So you've never done something shitty?"

"I never said that. Of course I have." He gave me that easy grin that was way too perfect not to be fake. "And I'm a shitty person. I freely admit that. So does Chris."

"That's not all he is," I said defensively. "He's pretty amazing, once you get to know him. Did you know he draws? Like, really well?"

Scotty blinked at me. "No shit."

"It's true." I tipped my head toward the frame I'd hung up last night while half-drunk. Still, it was straight, so I took pride in that, thank you very much. "He did that one."

Scotty set his mug down and walked over to it slowly. Almost as if he was scared it might bite. He looked out the window, looked at the drawing again, and whistled through his teeth. "Damn. I had no idea. Though it does explain a few things."

"Like what?"

He lifted a shoulder. "That's his story to tell, not mine."

"He's not telling me any stories anymore." I leaned against the fridge, ignoring the pain that the truth sent coursing through my veins. "He left, and he's not coming back."

"He's been back." He smirked. "I helped him put that chair on the porch, though he refused to tell me why he got it for you or why it took him twenty damn minutes to write a single line in a card."

My fingers twitched and my eyes stung, and suddenly I wanted nothing more than to open that card. "Why are you really here, Scotty? What do you want?"

"I've known him a long time." The second I opened my mouth, he held up a hand. "Yeah. I know I already said that. Let me talk, dammit."

I frowned but remained silent.

When it became clear I'd let him speak, he continued. "I've seen him with a lot of women and I've seen him leave a lot of women. He goes from one bed to another without even blinking. I've never seen him care or act like he regretted leaving a single one. And he never goes back for seconds."

. . . And there went the urge to read the card.

"Wow. Thanks for telling me he's already moved on." I shoved my hair behind my ear. "I'm *so* glad you stopped by."

"Glad to see you still care." He picked his coffee up again. "But I'm not finished. Like I was saying, I've never seen him do any of those things . . . until you."

I cleared my throat. "What?"

"I don't know what went down between you guys, or how bad it was." He ran his hand through his hair again. "But he misses you. If you could let him come back, if you could forgive him for whatever bullshit he did—"

My heart had sped up the second Scotty said Chris missed me, but really, it didn't make a difference. He still wouldn't leave the gang, and I still couldn't be with him. He couldn't give me the type of life I needed, and quite frankly, I didn't think I could give him the kind of life he deserved, either. I'd never be content with sitting back and watching him ride out into danger. I'd never be that girl.

"He didn't do anything wrong." I pressed my lips together. "So there's nothing to forgive."

Scotty raised a brow. "There's always something to forgive."

"Not this time. I'd have to be angry with him to forgive him." I held my hands out. "I'm not. I never was. There's no anger or betrayal between us. I . . . I love him."

"Then why did he leave?"

"That's between him and me." I wrapped my arms around myself. "Why do you care so much, anyway? I thought you hated him. Didn't trust him."

"He's practically my brother." He took a sip of coffee. "I could never hate him, and neither could Lucas. It's why he let him live that day, and why I agreed to it, too. Though Chris might not realize it, we understood why he did what he did, to some extent. With a dad like his, who could blame him for being a little fucked-up in the head sometimes?"

My heart dropped to my stomach. "What do you mean?"

"His dad is, and always has been, an abusive asshole. He just hides it well."

I bit my lip. "You know this for a fact?"

"Yeah." Scotty set the coffee down. "Well, Chris never admitted it or told anyone, but come on. A boy only gets so many bruises on his own. Every other week, he came into school with a fresh cut or a black eye. He always had an excuse, but Chris isn't exactly a clumsy guy."

So my suspicions were correct. He didn't get birthdays. Didn't have fun. And had literally been *beaten*. That had been all he knew. Hatred, pain, and death. No wonder he didn't know how to love anyone, or even *want* to love anyone.

He didn't even know what love *was*.

"That son of a—" I broke off, biting my tongue. "His mother didn't do anything to help him? Didn't stop his father?"

Scotty snorted. "No. He spent more and more time at our place after he got older, but even so, there's no escaping an abusive father, no matter how far you run."

I stared at nothing at all, my mind on Chris and all he'd endured. He'd said he didn't form attachments or care about anyone, and I got it now. He made perfect sense.

"He thinks he doesn't deserve to be happy or to be loved. Everyone who lives the kind of life we do feels that way. How could you not when we do the shit we do?" Scotty set his empty mug down. "Anyway. I'll go now. I have to meet him at the docks."

"Is he okay?" I wrapped my arms around myself. "Like, is he getting shot at daily?"

Scotty snorted. "They're shooting, but they keep missing. He's fine. Reggie is laying low, but he'll show up sooner or later." He paused. "Be careful, Molly. Take care of yourself."

"I will. Make sure he takes care of himself, too."

"I'll try, but he's miserable without you." He walked past me and grabbed my shoulder, squeezing. "And you don't look so good yourself."

I didn't say anything.

Really, what was there to say? He was right. I did look, and feel, *awful*. I missed Chris, too. I missed everything about him—everything except his imminent death.

As soon as the door closed behind him, I locked it and stared out the window. The black sedan was back, but Scotty didn't seem to be worried. Maybe it was one of his guys, helping out by keeping an eye on my house or something like that.

Dropping the curtain back into place, I went into the kitchen and pulled the envelope Chris had left on the chair out of the drawer I'd shoved it in. I stared down at it for a second, took a deep breath, and ripped it open. Inside, it had two lines this time:

> *Because you were there, and I knew I would do*
> *anything to make you happy.*
> *I'd let you go. Even it if killed me.*

I held the card to my chest, breathing unevenly as I blinked back tears, because despite my thoughts and the millions of times I'd told myself it was better this way, that our futures didn't mesh well together, I still missed him and loved him.

So. Much.

CHAPTER 25

CHRIS

I came out of the florist holding a bouquet of yellow roses and pink tulips and pushed my sunglasses up into place. It had been a long day at the warehouse, showing Scotty the ropes—how he needed to handle sales, what to do when inventory fell low, and security measures for this end of things. He was getting the hang of it quickly, like I knew he would, and it wouldn't be long until I wasn't needed anymore. And to be honest, I couldn't wait.

This past week without Molly in my life had shown me something.

Life was too short to lose someone because you were too scared to be honest. I'd let her go because I thought it was best for her, but who the hell was I to decide what she should or shouldn't have? Who was I to subtract myself from her life without telling her the whole story and giving her a chance to make her own choices?

Yeah, I was a killer. Yeah, I was an asshole.

But I loved her, and I would love her better than any other asshole out there.

I was already making changes in my life to make sure she wasn't risking too much if she let me in. I'd never be an office, nine-to-five type of guy. But I had a five-year plan in place. If shit went as planned, the gang would be dead, I would be free, and I'd finally get to be the man she deserved.

She'd just have to stick it out until I was.

And if she let me love her, I'd do my best to make sure I didn't get my fool self killed in the meantime. I couldn't make any promises, but who could? At any given moment, a fucking meteor could fall out of the sky and kill us all. Life was uncertain.

Short. Cruel. Crazy.

But together, it would be a hell of a lot less ugly.

"Son."

I stiffened, the flowers in my hand a telling weakness that I didn't want my father to know a damn thing about. "Pops."

"Who are those for?" he asked, frowning at them.

"Lucas's grave." I shrugged. "Thought it would put on a good show."

"A show, huh?" He scratched his neck and shook his head. "Yeah. I'm not buying that."

I stiffened. "Not buying what, exactly?"

"I heard what you did the other night. You were offered Lucas's position, but you told Tate to give it to Scotty instead— and saved his life instead of letting him die." Pops shook his head. "What the hell were you thinking?"

"I was thinking it would be a good play for the long run." I pulled my phone out and checked the time. If I left now, I'd be at Molly's Cape house at sunset. "I know what I'm doing, Pops. I've got a plan."

"You've got nothing." He tightened his fists. "I should

have beat some more sense into you as a kid. Maybe then you'd have taken the position. Damn fool. You have no idea how to play this game properly. You could be raking in money right now, but instead you're too busy kissing Donahue's ass. Do you wipe it for him, too?"

"Maybe I do," I said dryly.

Pops flushed. "Should have known better than to think that you could actually do something to make me proud."

Once upon a time, those words might have hurt me. But not anymore. I was over it. Over him. "I don't give a damn if you're proud of me or not, because you're nothing but an old man. Time's running out, Pops. And you know who will be taking over when you're gone? *Me*. I don't play like you do. I'm done trying."

As a kid, I'd tried for so long to make him approve of me, to somehow earn his love, as if it mattered at all. As if he was capable of it. He wasn't. But *I* was.

Molly had shown me that.

It was time to move on. To forget about this asshole and all the bullshit he brought with him. He might be my father, but he wasn't my dad. He wasn't anything.

I was done with him. With Ma, too.

He grabbed my shoulder as I passed. "You ungrateful little prick. Maybe I should beat some more sense into you before you go."

"You're welcome to try." I pulled free, rolling my shoulder, and set the flowers down on the hood of my Mustang. "Go on. Hit me. But fair warning: I'm not a scared little kid anymore, Pops. I'll hit back."

I stared at him, waiting to see if he'd follow through.

He, of course, didn't.

Instead, he shuffled back on his feet and shook his head, spitting between my boots. "Prick."

"Like father, like son," I said, grabbing my flowers and opening my door. "Have a nice life, Pops. See you around the clubhouse. Beyond that? Leave me the hell alone."

As I shifted the car into reverse, he slammed a hand on the open window. "What about your ma? You can't abandon her."

"Why not? She abandoned me long ago."

I stepped on the gas and left my father in the parking lot. He watched me go with a frown, looking like he was about to spit nails, but I felt light as a fucking feather. Grinning, I pulled onto the highway and made my way to Molly. She'd be heading back to work in a couple of days, and if all went well, I'd be with her.

For the first time, I had hope for the future.

I was going to have Molly, because I loved her, and I wasn't giving up on us. When we were together, the world made sense. Everything worked. But when we were apart, it all collapsed and the world became a shit storm.

That was love.

If she wanted to date other people while I was still in the gang, I'd accept that. I wouldn't like it, but I'd accept it. I'd still come by her place, bring her poems and presents, and I wouldn't even scare the fuckers off as they left her house.

I'd let them have their fun. Let them think they were going to be happy with my Molly. In the end, she'd be with me. I didn't need to be her only lover—

But I intended to be her *last*.

The drive to her place passed pretty quickly, and before I knew it, I pulled into her driveway. I sat in the car, staring at her house, and took a deep breath.

It was time to open myself up to her. To let her in. I was ready for this. I was. I really fucking was. But—what if she laughed at me when I told her I loved her?

What if she thought the idea was so ludicrous that a guy like me thought a woman as perfect as she was could even debate loving me back? If she did, I'd set her straight.

I didn't really think she could love me. I didn't expect her to. I loved her enough for the both of us. She was scared to care about another person again, to lose someone like she had her father, so I had the perfect solution for that.

I'd never leave her side.

But first, I had to go tell her I loved her, and that was the hard part.

Swallowing, I flexed my fingers on the wheel, staring at the front door. It was the only thing that stood between me and my Molly. She wouldn't laugh at me. And if she did? Then whatever. I'd be fine. It wouldn't be the first time someone had laughed at me.

However, it would be the first time that shooting them in the head wasn't an appropriate response. Squaring my jaw, I let go of the wheel, grabbed the flowers, opened the car door, and got out. When I was halfway up the walkway, the door opened.

I froze, not sure if she was about to tell me to fuck off or not.

"Thanks for dinner." The asshat with pleated khakis came out the door instead of Molly. That Mitchell guy. I'd never forget the fucker's name. Not in a million years. "It was delicious."

"Anytime. It was nice having someone to talk to," Molly said, hugging her sweater closed and leaning on the doorjamb. Her back was to me, so she hadn't noticed me yet. "See you in the summer?"

"You know it." Leaning in, the man kissed her temple and hugged her. Molly patted his shoulder. "I wouldn't miss it."

I gritted my teeth. Looked like I was going to get some early practice at standing to the side as she dated some asshole who didn't deserve her.

He turned around, still smiling—until he saw me.

I wore a pair of jeans, my leather jacket, and a red T-shirt. He could maybe see some of my ink, but not a whole lot, and he had no idea I had a gun behind my back, tucked into a holster. Even so, he looked scared.

Good. He should be.

If he so much as harmed a hair on Molly's head, he'd be answering to me. And I didn't knock nicely on doors. I came in with guns and fists.

He stepped in front of Molly protectively. "We don't have any money on us."

I snorted. I couldn't help it. We both knew they did.

"What?" Molly asked, confused.

"Go back inside," Mitchell said. "Lock the door."

"Why? What's—?"

"I didn't come here for money," I gritted out. "I came here for her."

"But—" Mitchell's focus shifted to the flowers and his eyes widened with recognition. *No shit, Sherlock. I don't rob people and give them fucking flowers.* "Oh."

"Yeah. Oh."

Mitchell stared me down.

Molly had frozen the second she heard my voice, but now she slowly faced me. When her eyes locked with mine, my chest hollowed out. It was like someone took a spoon and scooped my heart out. She looked tired. Beautiful, but tired. "Chris?"

"Yeah." I tightened my grip on her flowers and inclined my head. "Hi."

She stared at me.

Mitchell frowned. "Chris? As in the artist?"

"Y-yes." Molly's cheeks flushed. "Chris, meet Mitchell. Mitchell, meet my . . . friend . . . Chris."

Friend. I walked forward and held a hand out to him, even though I'd rather punch him in the gut and laugh as he fell to the ground wheezing. My nose was mostly healed now, but I still had bruising under my eyes. He was, of course, impeccably groomed. Asshole. "Nice to meet you, man."

"Yeah." Mitchell shook my hand, meeting my eyes and not letting go. "I saw your artwork. You do lovely work. Some of the best I've ever seen."

I side-eyed Molly. She blushed. "And you know this because . . . ?"

"The drawing Molly hung up." He let go of me and glanced at Molly. "She told me you were new to the artist scene but that you'd drawn it for her. That you two were . . . together."

I could see the confusion in his eyes, because he couldn't picture a girl like Molly with a guy like me. I didn't blame him. She was all sundresses and babies and the girl next door, while I was leather and guns and a gangbanger.

On paper, we just didn't make sense.

I inclined my head. "I see."

"I'd love to talk to you about commissioning a piece from my house. Like you drew for her." He smoothed his shirt and looked at Molly again. "Maybe over dinner sometime, once you guys are back in town?"

Seeing as I wasn't even sure if she'd let me come back, I wasn't sure how to answer that. "Maybe."

"Excellent." Mitchell cleared his throat. "You good?"

Molly nodded. "Yeah."

"All right. See you this summer." As he passed me, he frowned. "Nice meeting you."

"Likewise." I walked right up to the door and stopped just

short of entering. I was a couple of steps from the woman who held my heart in her hands, even if she didn't know it. The second we were alone, I said, "I'm sorry that I broke my promise. I swear it's the only promise I'll ever break to you, but I couldn't stay away for another second."

She swallowed and didn't look at me. "Why *did* you come back?"

"I had to." I held the flowers out, locking eyes with her. "I'm sorry."

She stepped back, not taking the bouquet. "For what?"

"For letting you think I don't care about you." I held the flowers out more. "I do. I always have. I always will. You're the one exception to my rule. It's why I've always left you presents and poems and a cat. It's why I could never stay away from you, no matter how hard I tried, and it's why I'm here now, holding flowers yet again, with another line to my poem."

Her gaze dipped down to the bouquet, and she took it, lifting it to her nose to inhale. Then she looked at me, and I couldn't read her. "Chris . . ."

"Let me talk. I have a lot to say. Things I should have said all along, but I was too much of a pussy to do it." I stepped closer to her. "Not anymore. I refuse to hold this in another second. I said I don't love anyone, and I said I never would, but I lied. The thing is, I never really knew what love was. Not until the first time I saw you, and you literally stole my breath away, like in one of those corny movies you see."

She covered her mouth, eyes wide, with tears in them.

Well, at least she hadn't laughed . . . yet.

"I know I'm not a sure bet and that I live a crazy life. But I'm working on that. Aside from helping Scotty, I have a five-year plan. I'm going to do my best to keep my head down, kill as few people as possible, avoid starting any more gang wars, and help Scotty take down the gangs in Southie. All of them." I rubbed my jaw. "I'm officially a paid informant, with immunity and all that shit, and every single penny I make is going into funding an arts community center for kids in the middle of Steel Row. I'll have to be a secret investor, because if Tate finds out, I'm dead, but I'm going to have people there, teaching kids to draw and maybe learn computers, and basketball courts, and anything else I can think of to keep the kids out of gangs. To give them more choices than I had."

"That's wonderful," she said, her voice sounding choked.

"And I know you don't love me and probably never will. Hell, I don't blame you. And I know you're scared that if you let me in, it'll hurt when I die. So don't let me in. Don't love me. Don't need me. Just let *me* love *you*." I took another step closer. One more, and she'd be in my arms. And if she agreed to let me love her, she'd never leave them again. "You don't need to love me or pretend you do or ever give me your heart. Just let me give you mine, and hold on to it, and I swear on the sun and the moon and the stars that I'll do my best to make you happy. That I'll never let you go again."

"Chris." Dropping her hand, she shook her head. "I already l—"

I saw it out of the corner of my eye, barely. A black sedan slowly pulled up, which wasn't unusual. Lots of cars drove slowly here. But what was abnormal was the fact that the window rolled down—and a fucking gun came out. "This is for Phil!"

Reggie. Fucking Reggie. *"Shit."*

And he pulled the trigger on the AK-47.

CHAPTER 26

MOLLY

It all happened so fast.

One second, Chris was telling me he loved me and had always loved me, and the next he was throwing himself at me. I didn't even know why until I heard the unmistakable boom of a gun being fired, followed by fast repeats that I'd only ever heard in movies. As I hit the porch, glass exploded behind me and the siding blew out as bullets littered the front of my house like darts in a dartboard.

Chris landed on top of me, covering my body with his. As we fell, I heard a bullet hit something soft, and Chris groaned. I couldn't see who was shooting at us, or where from, but I knew one thing. It sounded like one of those bullets had hit Chris . . .

And he wasn't *moving*.

I arched my neck, trying to see where the threat came from, but he pressed me into the porch more firmly. *Thank God.* He wasn't dead. But he was shot.

There was a short break in the shooting, and Chris lurched up, yanking a gun out from behind his back and firing off a shot at the same time as his feet hit the ground. I looked over just in time to see a man driving a black sedan—the same black sedan I'd seen outside my house a few times—fall onto the steering wheel, his skull and brains painting the window to his left.

The car kept driving before crashing into Mitchell's BMW, which was parked in front of his house. Chris collapsed against the house, breathing heavily. His gaze slammed into mine. "Are you hit?"

"I . . . I . . . no. I don't think so." I swallowed hard and struggled to sit up, but my body was trembling too badly. I stared at his left arm, which was rapidly soaking his jacket in dark blood. "But you are."

"It's nothing. Just a flesh wound." He scanned the road and pulled his phone out, dialing quickly. "Scotty—I got hit outside of Molly's Cape house. It was Reggie, and he was working alone. I'm going to call Tate and put a spin on it." A pause, and then: "He's finished, and I took a bullet to the arm. I'm fine, and so is she."

Mitchell came running out of his house, taking it all in and grabbing his hair as he stared at his car. I'd probably have to apologize for that. A nervous laugh escaped me, bubbling out of me in a way that couldn't be contained, because *this was my life now.*

"I need to call Tate before the Boys get here." Chris shot me a look as he swept his finger over the screen of his phone. "You all right, Princess?"

"Y-yeah. Sure."

He eyed me skeptically but lifted the phone to his ear, anyway. "Sir, I was visiting my girl's house to make sure everything was okay, and Reggie from Bitter Hill showed up. He's dead, and I took a bullet to the arm, but there will likely be more retaliation. Since I'm in the Cape area, the Boys are gonna show up any second now, but I'll make sure this doesn't fall on us." When Mitchell came running over, Chris turned his back to us and lowered his voice. I couldn't make out what he said anymore, but I was past paying attention, anyway.

"Molly!" Mitchell skidded to a halt at the bottom of the stairs. "Are you okay?"

"I'm f-fine. He's shot, though." I pointed to Chris. "In the arm. You should look at it. Make sure it's okay."

Mitchell didn't even look at him. He took the steps two at a time and knelt beside me. "You're not fine. You're in shock."

"Oh." I laughed again, staring at the blood-splattered car. We'd almost died, and I'd thought Chris had. "Can't imagine wh-why."

Mitchell grabbed my hand. "Molly? Look at me."

I didn't. I couldn't look away from that *car*. "He was outside of my house the other day, too, just waiting to shoot Chris. Just *waiting*. Who does that?"

Chris hung up and came to my side, too, kneeling there. "Hey. Princess."

"Yeah?" I asked, finally looking away from the car.

Sirens blared in the background, already responding.

"The Boys are almost here," he said softly.

Should he run? Hide the gun? Hide himself?

I jumped, whipping my head to him. "You're shot and you killed him, and the cops are coming. You have to go. Go. Now."

"I'm not leaving you ever again. And I can't go. People saw us." He looked at Mitchell pointedly and gently cradled my face in his hands before kissing me. I curled my hands around his wrists, not letting go, tears running down my face. When he pulled back, I strained to get closer. "I'm going to get taken in, but it's okay. I'll get out by tonight. It'll be fine."

"No." I shook my head, tears blurring my eyes. "They can't arrest you."

"I'll come back. I swear it." He leaned in and rested his forehead on mine, his fingers tightening on my skin. "I'll always come back to you."

Mitchell cleared his throat and stood. "I'll go fill the cops in on what happened and give you guys a minute."

"Thank you," Chris said, not taking his eyes off me. "I'll be right here."

Mitchell walked toward the cops, his hands raised in the air.

"I don't want you to get arrested." I clung to Chris and closed my eyes. "He shot at us, not the other way around."

"I know, but I shot back, and I'm not supposed to have a gun. It's against my parole." He pulled back and smiled at me tenderly. "But we have guys in the Boys, and I have Scotty, too. I'll be out in a few hours. I promise."

I took a deep breath and nodded. "All right."

He kissed me again. I tasted my tears on him, and I didn't want to let go. What if he was wrong and they didn't let him out? What if he was in jail for years? What if something happened to him in there? What if he got taken out on the inside?

"Are you Chris O'Brien?" a cop asked.

Chris pulled back and ended the kiss but didn't let go of me. "Yeah. That's me."

"Release the woman. Slowly." The cop walked toward us cautiously with his hand on his weapon. Another walked behind him, gun already drawn. "Stand up nice and easy, hands up where I can see them."

Chris kissed the tip of my nose and let go. I felt empty

immediately. "All right, Officer. I'm not resisting. I do have a gun I'd like to inform you about, and it's in my holster on my lower back. I won't be reaching for it."

"Thanks for letting me know," the officer said. "And the girl? Is she permitted to leave of her own free will?"

Chris smirked. "Yeah. I'd never try to stop her from doing what she wanted to do. I know better. When she's angry, she makes you guys look like teddy bears with water guns."

I swallowed hard, not moving, unable to believe that Chris had guns pointed at him and he was cracking *jokes*. The cop looked at me with a wrinkled brow. Another officer pulled out his weapon, too, aiming it at Chris's back.

"He's kidding," I said quickly. With two guns pointed at the man I loved, I didn't want to upset the balance. "And he wasn't holding me hostage, Officer."

"Good to know. Just stay down, miss." The second cop came closer. "Hands on your head. Turn around."

"Yes, sir." Chris winked at me and did as he was told. He looked about as concerned about his arrest as he might be if he had dropped a meatball on the ground, or something equally unimportant. "The gun is in the middle of my back, underneath my jacket."

"What happened here?" The officer asked, cocking his head to a third policeman, who came up behind Chris, reached under his jacket, and took his gun. "You kill someone today?"

"Yeah, but only because he was trying to kill me and my girl." Chris stood completely still as the officer patted him down. "That's the only one."

The officer didn't pause in his inspection. "You'll forgive me if I don't take your word for it."

"You could at least buy me dinner first," he joked.

The officer laughed. *Laughed.* He handed the gun off to

another officer, dropping it into a big clear plastic bag. It was immediately toted off. "Do you have a permit for that gun I just took?"

"No." Chris side-eyed me. "I don't."

"Then you know what comes next."

"All too well," Chris said dryly.

"You have the right to remain silent. Anything you say can and will be used against you in a court of law." The cop closed cuffs over one of Chris's wrists, and I swallowed hard. "You have the right to an attorney. If you cannot afford an attorney, one will be provided for you. Do you understand the rights I have just read to you? With these rights in mind, do you wish to speak to me?"

Chris flexed his jaw. "Yes, sir."

"All right." He rotated Chris's hands behind him and locked the second wrist. "Something tells me this isn't your first arrest."

Chris laughed. "You'd best go play the lottery, because it's your lucky day, Officer."

The policeman shook his head but smiled. "Off we go."

"I meant every word I said," Chris said as he was led past me. "I love you."

"Yeah, yeah," the officer said, nudging him forward. "Let's go, Romeo."

I covered my mouth, watching as they led him to the car. They slid him into the backseat and slammed the door, and Chris ducked his head to look at me. The way he watched me, as if I was his everything, stole away any doubts I had about being with him.

After literally almost losing him, and watching him get carted away by the cops, I knew one thing. He might not be perfect, and he might break my heart, but I didn't care.

He was mine, and I loved him.

Even if he got himself killed, it would be worth every second I spent in his arms. Even if he would break me, I'd still choose the same. I'd still pick him. And I wouldn't regret a thing. To be honest, I'd probably have a much easier life without him in it. There would be no cops. No shootings. No guns. And I'd probably never have to watch another man die again . . .

But I wouldn't have *Chris*.

And that wasn't a life I wanted to live.

I stood up, my legs trembling badly enough that I had to hold on to the banister for support. "Where are you taking him?"

"To the precinct. He'll be printed, processed, and we'll go from there," the policeman to my left said. "If I were you, I'd start choosing your friends better."

I stiffened, not answering.

This judgment was something I'd have to get used to.

Mitchell came up to my side, staring at me like he didn't even know me. "This is the man you want to be with? A guy who gets shot at, almost killed, almost gets you killed, and admits he has a gun illegally?"

When he said it like that, it sounded crazy. I gripped the banister tighter. "Yes. That's the man I love with all my heart."

Mitchell shook his head. "God help you."

"I don't need help." Bending down, I picked up the flowers Chris had gotten me. They'd miraculously managed to remain intact. "I just need him."

"Miss? We'll need to bring you to the station for questioning."

I nodded. "Of course. But I have to check on my cat."

The officer gave me a weird look but motioned me inside,

anyway. I found Buttons under my bed, gave him a kiss, made sure he had food and water, and followed the officer outside. Before I knew it, I was alone in the back of a cop car, and we were headed to the police station.

The next couple of hours passed in a blur of statements and cops asking me a million questions. Chris was nowhere in sight. Every time I asked where he was, I got a different answer. He was in questioning. In booking. In a cell. With a lawyer. The answer constantly changed. And I just wanted to go home.

With Chris.

The door to the interview room opened. I glanced up, exhausted and sore and just done. "Can I go home—? *Scotty.*"

"Yeah. It's me." He shut the door behind him. He wore his dark leather jacket and a pair of jeans. "Tate sent me here to get Chris out."

So he wasn't here as a cop today. "Is he okay?"

"He's fine. I just saw him a little while ago, shooting the shit with some of the officers." Scotty walked over to me, grabbed my chin, and lifted my face. "How are you doing, though?"

"Tired," I admitted.

"I'm sure." He let go of me and cocked his head to the door. "They're done with you, so you can go home and sleep if you want. Do you need a ride home?"

I stood up and tucked my hair behind my ears. "I'm not going home. I want to wait for Chris."

"All right. He'll be a little longer, though. The Southie Boys are talking to these guys, so he won't be out for another couple of hours yet."

"I don't care." I picked up the bottle of water an officer had given me. "I need to talk to him."

Scotty opened the door and cocked a brow. "Good or bad? 'Cause he's had a pretty shitty day already."

I didn't answer. After we left the room, Scotty led me outside. It was dark out, and we were far away from the water now, but I still drew in a deep breath of fresh air. "God, I don't know how you guys do this."

Scotty cracked open the top of a Monster Energy drink. "Do what?"

"Break rules. Commit crimes. Answer questions." I gestured toward the closed double doors. "Be in there, in general."

Scotty snorted, his bright green eyes standing out in the moonlight. "Because it's what we do. There's really not much of a choice in our life."

His words reminded me of Chris's plans to open a youth center, to give kids the choices they had never had. "You know about Chris's plans?"

"The youth center?" He took a sip. "Yeah. He asked for my help with getting it set up the second he agreed to be on the payroll."

I swallowed hard. "If they find out . . ."

"They won't." He met my gaze, and for once, the dancing laughter was gone from his eyes. "I'll make sure of that. I promise."

It wasn't enough . . .

And yet it was all I would get.

CHAPTER 27

CHRIS

Half a day later, I stumbled out of the precinct, rubbing my eyes at the dawn sun. It had taken a lot longer to get out of there than it would have if I'd been taken in on Steel Row territory, since we had to play a lot of politics to get me out, but Tate came through, like always, and I was short a good pistol, but I was now a free man.

As I stumbled outside, I took out my phone. Just as I was pulling up Molly's number, someone walked in front of me. "You're out."

I lifted my head and grinned at Scotty. "Yep. For now."

"Good." He rocked back on his heels and shoved his hands in his pockets. "All fixed up?"

He wore his jacket, while mine was still in a bag—and covered in my blood. They'd removed the bullet from my arm and stitched me up, but my jacket would need some TLC again. It had been nice not having to stitch myself up for once, though. I glanced down at my bloody shirt. "Yeah, it wasn't too bad. I've had worse. Like, three times last week."

Scotty snorted. "You'd think you had a death wish."

I typed a quick text to Molly. Still at your Cape house?

"At one point, I kinda did." I glanced at Scotty. "After Lucas."

Scotty's amusement faded. "It was a shitty thing to do."

"Yeah. I know."

Scotty stared at me and nodded. "I forgive you. And I'm sure he does, too. That's why you're alive."

"Yeah." I shoved my phone away and swallowed hard. "Even if I don't deserve that forgiveness, he gave it to me. That's the kind of guy he is."

"And now you're ready to do whatever it takes to make it up to him." Scotty shifted on his feet and looked over his shoulder. We were outside alone, with no one in sight, but he still dropped his voice. "Even die for me."

I stiffened. "If need be."

"Well, you're not allowed. What I do, I do because I'm willing to risk it. I'm willing to take that chance with my life." He placed a hand on his chest. "That's my choice to make. If I get hurt, that's on me. Not Lucas. Not you. *Me.*"

I shrugged with my left shoulder, pulled my phone out, and checked for a reply from Molly. I had nothing. Great. The shoot-out had finally sealed the deal on us. She obviously wasn't willing to risk her life to be with me, and I didn't blame her one little bit. But that wouldn't stop me from loving her. "Doesn't mean I won't do my best to avoid that happening. I owe it to Lucas."

"No, you don't." Scotty frowned. "You owe it to him to stay alive. That's what he wanted. It's why he let you live. He'd want you to go to Molly, kiss her, and do your best to make your life a good one. You can bet your ass that's what he's doing."

I cleared my throat and averted my gaze. I'd had no sleep and was tired as hell, and my arm stung like a bitch, but it hurt more to have this conversation than all of those things combined. "He'd want you alive, too."

"Yeah. And that's on me."

I stared at him, my jaw ticking. "All right."

"And . . ." He dragged a hand through his hair and sighed. "If you want out of our arrangement, I'm okay with that. I can help you get out of this town, if you want. I can maybe even help you fake your death. Get you a new start."

"What about you?" I asked, scratching my head. "Don't you think Tate will begin to get suspicious?"

"That's for me to worry about." He shrugged. "Not you."

I closed my eyes, because he was offering me an out. A week ago, I might have taken him up on that offer, but not now. Too much had changed. Hell, too much inside of *me* had changed to take the cop-out. "Thanks, but no thanks. I want in."

Scotty eyed me with respect and nodded. "On one condition."

"Yeah?" I asked.

"Stay alive." He glanced at something over my shoulder. "For her."

I turned around, and my heart raced faster than an M60 shot bullets. *"Molly."*

Sometime during the night, she'd changed into a clean, soft knit dress with an open oversized sweater over it. She hugged her sweater closed and gave me a small smile. The sun rose behind her, bathing her in a soft yellow glow, and her hair looked almost red in the dawn. She was pale and had big bags underneath her eyes and looked as if she hadn't slept a wink last night, like me. Still, she was the prettiest thing I'd ever seen.

And she'd never stop making me want to be a better man.

"Hey." Scotty grabbed my shoulder. "Say it."

"I promise." I shrugged his hold off. "But you better do your best to stay out of shit, so I can keep that promise, too."

He laughed. "Deal. Now go get your girl. I helped her get her car, so you're free to go."

"Thanks, man." I locked eyes with him. "For everything."

Scotty nodded and walked off, whistling under his breath, smoothing his hair as he headed back toward the station.

I made my way over to Molly, my heartbeat increasing with each step I took. The closer I got to her, the faster it went. If I didn't hurry the hell up, I might die of a fucking heart attack before I got to her. I still had blood all over me, so I stopped short of touching her. "I'm sorry I'm late, Princess."

She let out a little laugh. It was like music to my ears. "I'll forgive you . . . this one time."

"I have so much to tell you. So much to say." I glanced over my shoulder. "If we don't get shot at, that is." I paused again. "I'm sorry for that, too."

"I know." She ducked her head down, hiding her face from me. "How's your arm?"

"Stitched up, by a real doctor this time."

Another nervous laugh. This time, she glanced over my shoulder. "Is Scotty gone?"

"Yeah." I swallowed hard. The way she was acting, and the way she kept avoiding my eyes, told me all I needed to know. She'd chosen to be smart. To not be with me. "I know you'll never love me, and I get that, I do, but I'll never stop loving you. I love you so damn much, Molly. And I just had to say that, one time, before I left you alone."

"Chris . . ." She hugged herself tighter. "I—"

"I know," I said quickly. "I just wanted you to know. I just had to say it one last time. That's all. I love you, Molly."

"I know. And I *hate* you, Chris." She closed her eyes and swallowed hard, her chin trembling. "I really do."

I winced, not even bothering to pretend that her words didn't hurt. "I know."

"No. You don't get it."

"I think it's pretty loud and clear," I answered slowly. "But feel free to elaborate if you want. I deserve it."

"I hate you because I didn't want to love you. I didn't want to care." She opened her eyes and smiled. I held my breath at the beauty that stared back at me. "I didn't want anyone to hold that power over me. To make me need them. But I do. I love you, Chris."

I didn't move for a second. What she was saying wasn't possible. Why would *she* love *me*? How could she? "No, you don't. I told you, you don't have to pretend to love me. I don't need it. All I want is you. That's enough for me."

"Too bad." She closed the distance between us, resting her hands on my chest. "Because I already love you. I love you so much it hurts, and it scares me, but I don't care anymore. I love you too much to fight it. You asked me to let you in. You swore to love me forever, no matter what I chose to do. Well, now I'm swearing the same thing. To love you forever, no matter what happens, or who you are, or what you do. *I love you*, and you're just going to have to deal with that."

I shook my head, my whole body reeling from her words. And, dammit, my throat ached in a way I'd forgotten it could ache. I hadn't cried in years, after I'd accepted the fact that my father was an asshole and nothing I did would stop him from beating me.

I'd sworn never to cry again.

But here I was, seconds from fucking tears, and I couldn't even be angry, because Molly loved me. Actually loved me. I'd never in a million years thought I would get this.

That someone would *love* me.

I wasn't that guy.

"Shit." I covered my face and let out a nervous laugh. I rubbed my eyes, trying to play it cool, because I was a fucking guy. I didn't do emotions. "You love me?"

"I do." She smiled up at me, tears rolling down her cheeks. "So much."

I closed her in my arms, hugging her tightly. So tightly she squealed. "I promise to do my best to give you the life you deserve. I promise I'll be out of this life, and once I am, I'm going to fucking marry you." I framed her face with my hands. "And I'm never gonna hurt you ever again. I promise that, too. And I'll give you lots of orgasms. Every day. As many as you want."

She let out a happy laugh, her cheeks pinking. *"Chris."*

"I mean it. Every word." I kissed her, my mouth lingering on hers. She clung to me, not seeming to want to let me go, either. "Someday, I'll be free. Even if it means that I have to lie low for a while, living off my savings before I can find a new, respectable way to provide for myself, I'll do it. I'm going to be that guy for you."

"You can be any guy you want to be," she whispered, hanging on to my shirt with both fists. "As long as you're *my* guy."

"Forever." I lowered my face to hers, stopping just short of kissing her. "I fucking promise."

"Take me home?" she whispered.

"Gladly."

I captured her hand and walked with her to her car. She smiled up at me, running her thumb over the backs of my knuckles. "We're really going to do this."

"Yep." I smiled. "Regrets already? It's too late. You said you loved me, and I said it, too, and I'm not going to let you forget that."

"No. No regrets."

I actually believed her. "There's something you should know, though."

"What?"

I unlocked the car and walked to her door, opening it for her. "Scotty offered me an out. He said he could kill me off and I could start over again."

She froze halfway into the car. "What? He did?"

"Yeah." I held a hand up when she opened her mouth. "But I said no."

"Why?" she asked, frowning.

"I want to stay, to help clean up the city. I want to help make up for the stuff I did." I leaned in the open door of the car, hoping she'd understand. "I have to play the part of a gang member and do bad things to keep my cover. But I'm not that guy anymore. I changed, and that's because of you. Of what you did for me. And I want to help Scotty in his mission to clean up the streets of Steel Row."

She swallowed hard and reached up, running her fingers over my cheek. "Then you'll have to do it. I love you for who you are, and if it's important to you, it's important to me, too. Let's clean up Steel Row."

Leaning in, I kissed her, unable to help myself. And if we hadn't been in the parking lot of a police station, I wouldn't have stopped there. I'd have her naked, in my arms, screaming my name for all to hear—because she *loved* me.

When I finally pulled back, she held on to my shirt, not letting go.

"Can you promise me one thing?" she asked breathily.

I swallowed hard. "What?"

"Can we go home, close the door, and not get shot at for twenty-four hours?"

I laughed. "Yeah. I think I can promise you that. Tate said I don't have to come in until tomorrow morning."

"Thank God." She drifted her hand down my chest, tugging on the waist of my jeans. "Because the things I need from you . . . they're going to require some peace and quiet."

"Oh yeah? And what are these *things*?"

"You. Me." Her hand dipped lower, and she cupped my hard cock, squeezing with just enough pressure to make my eyes roll back in my head. "And a bed."

"Just a bed?" I kissed the side of her neck and teased the curves of her cleavage with my fingertips. "Not a wall? Or a shower? Or the floor?"

She let out a breathy moan. "My terms are negotiable."

"Good." I nipped the skin right over her racing pulse. "Because I plan on making love to you in every room of that house, in every way possible, till you're too weak to stand. And I'm going to take you one more time, in your bed, so you can fall asleep in my arms. And I won't let you go."

She swallowed so hard I heard it. "Well, what are we waiting for? Take me home, Chris."

"Gladly." I slid my hand between her legs, pressing up against her clit. "But first . . . ?"

"Hmm?" she asked, her lids dipping down and her breath hitching in her throat.

"I need to do something for you." I traced the curve of her inner thigh. "Open your legs for me, Princess."

"Now?" she asked, her nostrils flaring. "Here?"

"I'll be quick. Less than thirty seconds. No one will ever know." I urged her thighs apart, locking eyes with her as my fingers dipped under her dress and inside her panties. The second I touched her hot pussy, I thrust my fingers inside of her, because she was already wet for me, pressing my thumb against her clit. "I promise."

She moaned and spread her legs more, her cheeks flushing. I pulled my fingers out and thrust them back in, hitting the spot guaranteed to drive her crazy. *"Chris."*

I moved my hand in between her thighs, still leaning in the car as if we were having a conversation. She bit down on her lip, her cheeks coloring more with each thrust of my fingers. When her pussy tightened around me and her breaths came faster and she cried out, muffling the sound with her hand, I grinned with satisfaction.

True to my word, I'd gotten her off in less than thirty seconds.

She collapsed against the seat, gripping my hand that was still between her thighs. "God, I love you."

"And I love you." I leaned in and said, "But just so you know, that orgasm you just felt?" I rolled my thumb over her clit, and she tensed. "The pressure building in your stomach even now, after I already made you come? That's mine. And I plan to collect more of those the second I have you home. I'm going to strip you naked, drop to my knees, and taste your sweet pussy. And I won't stop till you come so many times you forget your name."

"Now, that's a promise I can handle," she murmured, smiling.

I kissed her . . .

And the world felt right again.

EPILOGUE

CHRIS

Three months later

I juggled the keys, my phone, and a bottle of wine, trying to open the garage door to my and Molly's new home. We'd moved in a little over a month ago. Being next to my father didn't work so well when I was trying my best to avoid him and all the shit he brought with him. We'd made a new start here.

A good one.

Scotty and I were still doing our thing over in Steel Row, and we'd even managed to bring down a few rival gang members. After the attack on me, and Reggie's death, both sides had sort of cooled their heels. An eye for an eye left everyone satisfied—for now. It didn't change the fact that we were still locked in a heated war with Bitter Hill, and it was far from over, but we were on the winning side.

And I was still alive.

So there was that.

My youth community center was moving along nicely, and it was only a matter of time until I was actually making a difference in this shitty little city. Of course, no one could know, because I'd be a dead man, but still. It was something.

I finally managed to get the door open, kicking it shut behind me and locking it. I entered the code to the security system, the code only Molly and I knew, and flipped the kitchen light on. "Princess? I'm home."

No answer came back.

Her car had been in the garage, so she was here.

"Molly?" I yelled out, setting the wine down. "Answer me!"

Still nothing.

Buttons came into the kitchen, sitting and staring at me. He didn't have blood on his paws or look as if he was upset—but she wasn't *answering* me.

I pulled my gun out of my holster and stalked through the kitchen, my heart pounding and my stomach churning. If something had happened to her—

Hell, I wouldn't be around much longer.

I refused to live without my Molly.

Halfway through the living room, I froze. Molly had ordered an old-fashioned fainting couch the other day, and I'd rolled my eyes but helped her pick out a pretty print, anyway. If Molly wanted something, she'd damn well get it. Anything.

But if I'd known what she planned for it?

I would have bought twelve.

Swallowing hard, I lowered my gun. "You didn't answer me."

"I know." She lifted a naked leg, uncrossed it, and let it drape over the side of the chair. "I wanted to surprise you."

I laid the gun on the table and shrugged out of my jacket, gaping at all that naked skin and her perfect body sprawled across the beige chair. "Well, consider me surprised. To what do I owe this honor?"

"Remember when I made you watch *Titanic* last week?" She pulled on a piece of hair and glanced at me through her lashes. "And I told you how much the scene with Jack drawing Rose turned me on?"

My heart pounded so hard it was a miracle it didn't jump out of my chest and splatter on the hardwood floor. I started unbuttoning my shirt. If she was naked, it was only fair I be, too. Equality in the home, and all that shit. Her hair played peekaboo with her hard, pink nipples. She was deliciously, gloriously naked—and I couldn't take my eyes off her.

"Yeah. And I told you it made me horny as hell, too." I smirked. "And I showed you just how horny it made me."

"Mm-hmm." She bit down on her lip, staring at me mischievously. "Look behind you."

"I'd rather look in front of me." I unbuttoned my shirt and shrugged it off, letting it fall to the floor. "Actually, I'd like to do more than look. I want to touch."

She held up a finger and wagged it. "You will. But not yet. Turn around."

"Princess. You're *killing* me." Impatiently, I did as I was told. "What is—?" Reaching down, I picked up the heart necklace, letting the chain dangle between my fingers. They itched with the need to touch her, but even more strongly with the need to *draw* her. "Does this mean what I think it does?"

Her grin widened. "I want you to draw me wearing nothing but this."

"Fuck yeah." I swallowed hard, and it felt like a box of nails went down my throat. Stalking across the room, I knelt beside her. "Let me set you up properly first."

She stared at me—all hazel eyes, creamy skin, and long brown hair with a hint of pink nipples. "Anything you say, sir. I'm all yours."

"Don't say that," I growled, drifting my hands over her bare shoulders. Her smooth skin was like silk under my rough fingers. "You'll never get drawn if you tease me like that."

"I'm all yours, however you want me." She shrugged. "Whatever you want."

"I want this." I skimmed my knuckles over her nipples, watching them pull in and tighten, and tugged on her hair ever so slightly. "All of this."

Her breathing increased. "It's yours."

"I know. But first?" I leaned in and kissed her, pulling back after a few seconds. "I want to draw you. All of you."

Her tits rose and fell rapidly, and she nodded. "Put me where you want me."

All sorts of images—the most prominent one being her bent over, holding the couch, so I could draw her from behind—flashed through my mind. But there was one pose she'd like the best, and I wanted to make her happy, so I went with that.

I draped the necklace over her neck and pushed her back so she reclined against the cushions. Working from the memory of a movie I had only half paid attention to, I made it so she lay just like the actress in the movie had, complete with nipples peeking out of her long hair. I positioned the necklace between her breasts, raised her hand over her head, and nodded, satisfied with my handiwork.

"Fucking gorgeous." When I stepped back, all of my blood rushed south, hardening my cock, and I stared. She looked just like the actress in the movie, only a million times prettier. "Don't move."

Her lips twitched. "I won't. But I expect to be duly rewarded when this is over."

I pulled up a chair, grabbed the drawing pencils she'd

placed on the table, flipped open the pad, and stared at her for another second. "Oh, you will. Now shut up and let me work."

A small laugh escaped her, but she lay still, not moving so much as a muscle. I let my fingers take over, closing my mind off to everything but her and the paper in front of me. I started with her face, sketching out each line with perfect memory, not even needing to look at her. I'd drawn her hundreds of times by now.

But when I got to her tits and her thin waist, it took a hell of a lot more concentration to keep on going and not toss the book aside to take up a more personal approach to appreciating the artwork that was her body. My hands flew over the paper, and she watched me the whole time, her eyes glowing with love and desire.

It was a combination I'd never get enough of.

As I rounded out the pink buds of her nipples, the last finishing touch to my drawing, I slammed it on the table, stood, and undid my pants. "Done."

She bit her lip, still not moving. "I want to see it."

"You will. I plan on hanging that fucker in our bedroom." I let my jeans hit the floor, and I lay on top of her, settling between her legs, where I belonged. "But first? I need to touch you. Kiss you. Love you."

"God, yes." She curled her legs around my waist and her arms around my neck, threading her fingers into my hair and grabbing hold. *"Now."*

Nodding, I melded my lips to hers, and I thrust inside of her, not bothering with foreplay. Her warm, wet pussy claimed me, like it always did, and I groaned into her mouth. She was so fucking wet, and so tight, that I was close to coming already.

Each stroke of the pencil, each lingering gaze, had been like me stroking her skin. I'd seen her desire building with each passing moment, with each ragged breath, and mine was out of control at this point. Pulling out of her, I slammed back in, angling my hips. She dug her nails into my scalp and cried out, coming. I swallowed her cries, thrusting into her with a wild abandon only she brought out in me.

She was with me for every stroke, and when her pussy clamped down on my cock and she screamed out my name in pleasure, I was right there with her.

Holding her.

"Chris." She tightened her hold on me, kissing my shoulder. "I love you so much."

"I love you, too." I reared back, meeting her eyes. "I never thought I deserved this, and I still don't, but every day, I fall more and more in love with you. You are my life. My love. My heart. And I thank God every day—even though I don't believe in him—that you found me in that alley."

She gave me an emotional smile and smoothed her hands through my hair. "Me, too, Chris. Me, too."

Tugging me down by my hair, she kissed me, and I started moving inside of her again. Once wasn't enough with her. It would never be enough. Not with how much I loved her. Part of me was ninety-nine percent certain she would never understand exactly how much she meant to me. How much I loved her. What I would do for her.

She was my heart, my body, and my soul . . .

And she *completed* me.

CHAPTER 1

SCOTTY

A bullet flew by my ear with a soft *whizz*ing sound, sounding deceptively softer than its hollow-point reality, which would rip through flesh without mercy. I squeezed the trigger of my gun as sweat rolled down into my eyes and watched a Bitter Hill asshole fall to the ground, clutching his chest, blood bubbling out of his mouth as he breathed his last gurgling breath due to my bullet.

Shit.

That was going to be a lot of paperwork.

The Bitter Hill men had come at us when no one had their pistols drawn, giving them an advantage against us—one that hadn't lasted long. Chris O'Brien, the only other man on this side of the law who knew my secret, moved to my side, squeezing off shots without even a sign of hesitation. "You okay, Scotty?"

I nodded once, wiping my forearm over my forehead,

and scanned the alley for more of the assholes. "Where the hell did these fuckers come from?"

Another one came around the corner, and Chris and I simultaneously fired. Mine hit him in the chest directly over the heart. Chris's was dead center in the forehead. He liked head shots and was one of the only men I knew who could consistently nail them. Blood sprayed behind the man and he was dead before he hit the ground.

"I don't know," Chris shouted back, his eyes locked on the opening of the alley where they'd cornered us, just like mine. We'd come a long way, me and Chris. If someone had told me he would try to kill my brother, but then we'd become closer because he failed, I would've laughed in his face—or shot him.

"But they picked the wrong day to attack. Tate's pissed as hell."

I looked over my shoulder, eyeing the man in charge of the Sons of Steel Row. Tate looked seconds from pulling a grenade launcher out from behind his back and going all kamikaze on the Bitter Hill scum who dared to attack us when we were on our way to a funeral for one of our older members, Gus. May the fucker not rest in peace.

He didn't deserve it.

The Sons was the most influential gang in Southie, and up until recently, that title had gone undisputed. But then my "dead" brother, Lucas, started a war with Bitter Hill over a chick he was into and everything had gone to shit afterward.

Now, we were waging a full-fledged war with Bitter Hill . . .

One we just might lose, if we didn't play our cards right.

A bullet hit the wall next to my head with a poof of brick dust, and Chris growled angrily, squeezing his trigger in rapid succession at the fucker who'd tried to take me out. I couldn't get a shot on him since he was out of my line of fire. A groan sounded to the left of us as one of our men went down, taking a hit to the shoulder. Next went Roger, staggering back and clutching his arm. Cursing, I tried to find the shooter—and finally did. He was coming around the corner, aiming for Chris . . . who had just fired his last bullet.

Luckily, it had taken the other guy down.

Biting back a curse, I aimed and took the second shooter out before he could take out my friend, shooting directly over Chris's shoulder. For a second, he looked like he thought I'd been aiming for him. He was the only other man who knew I wasn't just another street thug, but was in reality in the DEA. Maybe he thought I was trying to kill the only man who could blow my cover. Not that I would do that, but I could understand the logic.

The man I shot fell to the ground, convulsing as he, too, died. My aim had been true.

Great. Even *more* paperwork.

After glancing over his shoulder with wide eyes, Chris turned back to me, breathing heavily. "Thanks, man."

I nodded, not saying anything.

It was my job, my *duty*, to keep him alive.

He had a scrape on his temple and blood trickled down his face from the wound, but besides that, he looked okay enough. His fiancée, Molly, would still be upset. I'd promised to return him unharmed. After all, we were only going to a funeral. But still, with tensions high between us and Bitter Hill, we'd suspected something like this might happen.

So we'd come prepared. Thank God.

Tommy, another lieutenant, called out, "Everyone alive?"

"Yeah," Brian growled, nodding at me from the brick doorway he'd taken cover at.

Frank nodded, his blond hair in his eyes. "Yeah, man."

Me and Chris called out, too, and then we all came out of cover when Tate said, "We're good. Everyone, reload in case they come back."

I slowly lowered my Sig, eyeing the carnage in front of us as I pulled out my extra mag. I'd taken down three, Chris as well. Who knew who had taken down the rest? We all reloaded silently. It had been twelve Bitter Hill guys against nine Sons. Not a fair fight for them. None of us had been killed, a gift given only by the grace of God. They'd come at us when we'd been backed into a corner, a strategic move that didn't pay off well for them. They should have known never to back a Son into a corner.

We always came out swinging.

Tate, scowling at the dead bodies in front of him, tucked his pistol into his suit jacket, his red hair immaculately styled, the gun battle not budging a strand. "Leave them for the Boys or for Bitter Hill. I'm not cleaning up their damn mess for them this time."

We tucked our guns away, nodding and murmuring consent. I nodded at Chris, who nodded back. It was time to go.

Before we could head for his Mustang, Tate came over to Chris, clapping him on the shoulder. "Nice shot, Chris."

Chris grinned and gestured to the corpse we'd taken down together. "Thanks, sir. I was particularly proud of that one."

Tate snorted. "Me, too. Nice teamwork, guys."

"We should go," I said quickly, tipping my head toward the corpses. "Before more come."

Tate hesitated, but nodded. "Roll out, boys."

We got into our cars, watching for another ambush. I was halfway into the passenger seat of Chris's Mustang when Tate called out, "Donahue?"

I froze, my hand on the roof of Chris's car. "Yes, sir?"

"Ride with me." He gave me a hard look. "We need to talk. Now."

Well, *shit*. That couldn't be good. Not when I was living a lie right under his nose. Most of the time, when Tate singled out a man like this, he didn't come back. "Sure thing, sir."

"Both of us?" Chris called out.

I appreciated the effort and all, but if I was going down, I wouldn't be dragging him down with me. Molly would fucking kill me. "Just me," I said, my voice hard.

"Yep, just him," Tate said, frowning. "Ready, Donahue?"

I mussed up my hair, grinning like I didn't have a care in the world. "Yes, sir. Whatever you want."

Chris cleared his throat as I closed the door, latching gazes with me over the roof of his car. "Everything okay?"

"I hope so," I muttered, smoothing my suit jacket over my abs. The only way Tate could have been told about me was if someone knew, and the only other person who knew was staring at me with concern. I was pretty damn certain he hadn't ratted me out. "It should be."

Chris nodded once, flexing his jaw. "Be smart."

"Always," I murmured, walking toward my boss with long, carefree strides and shoving my hands in my trouser pockets. As I slid into his town car, which was being driven by Tommy, I plastered an easy grin on my face, playing the part of Lucas's charming younger brother I'd been cast into years ago. "What can I do for you, sir?"

Tate closed the door behind us, tapping on the window that separated Tommy from us. The car pulled forward immediately. "You look young enough to be in college. How old are you?"

I blinked. "Sir?"

"Your age." He cocked a reddish brown brow at me. "What is it?"

Out of all the things I'd expected him to ask me, this was not it. "Twenty-five, sir."

"Hmm." He rubbed his jaw, looking me up and down. "You look half-decent in a suit."

I swallowed, having no clue where the hell he was going with this, but pretty damn certain I wouldn't like it. "Thanks . . . ?"

"How are your acting abilities?" he asked distractedly, staring out the window as we drove. "At playing a part that no one would expect you to play?"

Well, if that wasn't a trick question, considering my secret life, I didn't know what was. If I said yes, he'd wonder if I was playing a part right now—and I was. If I said no, I wouldn't be as valuable to the gang, and I'd lose any head-way I'd gained over the years. So I chose silence instead. "What do you need from me, sir?"

"I'm getting there. What I tell you can't leave this car. If it does, I'll know it was you, and I'll act accordingly for the breach of trust." He squared his jaw, finally turning back to me. He looked seconds from pulling out a gun. "Understood?"

I nodded once. "Yes, sir."

"Good." He cleared his throat. "I have a sister."

I blinked at him, taken aback. I'd done my research on Tate long before I officially became a Son. Before I was formally a DEA agent, too. I never entered anything blindly. That was a fucking death sentence. And yet I'd never found even a damn hint about Tate having a sister. "You do?"

"Yeah. She's twenty-three and in grad school." He leaned back in the seat, staring straight ahead at the tinted window. "She's not like us. She's good. Does charity work all the time and has no clue what kind of life I lead."

So the apple fell far from the tree? I found that hard to

believe. More likely than not, she put on a good front. "I see. And you're telling me this because . . . ?"

"She thinks I'm the CEO of an investment firm—which I am, on all fronts—but that's all she knows. She doesn't know about my ties to the Sons of Steel Row, and thinks I'm like any white-collar thirtysomething. So she wants me to do a bachelor's auction for a Valentine's Day date for charity, to play nice with some spoiled, rich socialite who would probably want more than dinner and a bottle of champagne from me." He turned to me, looking about as happy as he would if he'd been shot in the ass. "But I don't play nice with women. Not like *you* do."

I stiffened, knowing where this was going now. And I'd been right—I wasn't going to fucking like it. I'd rather be strapped to an electric chair and pumped with a thousand volts than do what he was about to ask me to do. And the worst part? I wouldn't have a choice. "Sir?"

"Since I now have to deal with the mess of this shoot-out, you are going to go in my place. Tell her you're a grad student, like her, and interning at my office. I'm regrettably held up at the office with work, which I am now with this shooting, so I sent you in my place. I promised her I wouldn't leave her a man short for tonight, since she had a hard time finding men who would volunteer. That's where you come in." He gestured to me. "You're already in a suit and everything. You didn't get shot, right?"

"Not this time, sir." I half laughed, half groaned. "But wouldn't I be more valuable in the office with you, plotting our next move?"

He stared at me, his blue eyes cold. "No. I want you with her."

"Yes, sir," I said through my clenched teeth. "Anything you need, I'm your man."

"Good." Tate smoothed his tie over his chest. "When you're done paying your respects to Gus, you can go. The auction starts at six at the Lower Boston Country Club."

I stared at him. "Seriously?"

"Dead." He shrugged. "We're members there. The best way to blend into society is to pretend to be one of them, right? I also have a condo nearby, in the gated complex on the golf course."

We all knew about *that* apartment. Tate said it was a front, that he used it to launder money away from the watchful eye of the feds. All the guys joked it was his bachelor pad, where he took chicks he scored for a night of fun before ditching them to return to his place in Steel Row. But now I couldn't help but wonder if it was more. Maybe his sister also lived in that community, and every time we assumed he was banging some chick in his fancy place, he was, in all reality, going to see *her*. "Wow. I never pegged you as the country-club type, sir."

"It's just for Skylar. I never go," he said, even though I knew for a fact that he played golf there every Saturday at eight a.m.

"Right." I grinned. "Of course not."

"Like I said. No one knows she exists. I'm telling you because I think I can trust you to keep my secret." He gave me a hard look, and I knew if I showed the slightest sign of proving him wrong, I'd be done for. No big shocker there. "You're good at that, aren't you? At keeping secrets?"

I forced a laugh. "Uh . . . yeah. I can be, when the situation warrants it."

"I figured," Tate said dryly. "This one does."

I nodded. "Yes, sir."

"Wear that suit and be charming. Call yourself Scotty instead of Scott. It sounds more innocent and college student–

like. Remember: You intern at my company and go to grad school at Boston . . . University," he said slowly, eyeing my outfit. "No leather coat."

"Not Boston College?"

"No." He shot me a look out of the corner of his eye. "She goes there, so it will invite too many questions."

"Okay." I lifted a shoulder. "What's my major?"

"Marketing."

Nodding, I tapped my fingers on my thigh. "Got it, sir."

The car stopped at the funeral home, and I reached for the handle. As I grasped it, he grabbed my arm hard, stopping me. "And, Donahue?"

"Yeah?" I asked hesitantly.

"This goes without saying, but I'll say it anyway, just to be perfectly fucking clear on the matter. Touch Skylar"—he dug his fingers into my biceps—"and I'll fucking cut you into pieces and feed you to my saltwater fish for dinner. Understood?"

Touch Tate Daniels's *sister*?

I'd sooner eat uncooked liver.

"Completely."

ALSO AVAILABLE FROM
NEW YORK TIMES BESTSELLING AUTHOR
Jen McLaughlin

DARE TO RUN
The Sons of Steel Row

Lucas Donahue is not ashamed of his criminal past, but after a brief stint in prison, he's ready to go legit and live a normal life. The problem is, no one leaves the gang without permission—even if he is one of the boss's top men. Plus someone's placed a hit on him. And then there's that feisty little bartender who's going to cause him even more trouble.

Heidi Greene knows to keep her distance from a ladies' man like Lucas—even if she can't keep her eyes off him. When he rescues her from an attack in the alley outside her bar, she's forced to stay by his side for safety. But the longer she spends time with him, the greater her chances are for getting hurt in more ways than one.

"A fast-paced, sexy read with the perfect bad boy in Lucas. Warn your loved ones they will be ignored when you're reading *Dare to Run*!"
—*New York Times* bestselling author Erin McCarthy

Available wherever books are sold or at
penguin.com

S0652

the only time Barbra was heard was singing the movie theme as she had over the opening and closing credits. The second album, truly a Streisand album, consisted mainly of previously unreleased material from earlier sessions.

Barbra did go into the studio to record some fresh songs for the album that December, and Jon joined her for some of the sessions. And then suddenly one night he wasn't there. In the middle of recording a song, Barbra broke into tears. "She began to cry," a musician present told Shaun Considine, "she got on the phone, begging Jon to forgive her. She couldn't sing if he wasn't there. She pleaded with him to come to her. And meanwhile we're sitting around, something like forty musicians, listening to all this. Barbra usually was *tough* at the studio, but this guy got to her, and eventually
The songs she sang that night were 'Make
'Being at War with Each Other,' and
Appropriate

Indeed, you get curiouser and curiouser as this rhythmic, imaginative, and humorous hour unfolds, dominated, of course, by La Streisand, a consummate performer and brilliant architect of a stellar show business career." Despite lukewarm reviews and lackluster ratings, *Barbra Streisand . . . and Other Musical Instruments* would make a strong showing at the Emmys the following May. And CBS Records expected the television exposure to boost sales of her next album, trumpeting in a *Billboard* ad: "On Friday, November 2, forty million people previewed the new Barbra Streisand album."

When her exclusive contract with CBS expired in 1974 they did not renew. She was now committed to her career in movies

mirer, Frank Rich, admitted that his affec-
ded at an accelerating pace, but he still
"especially when she opens

One who was not completely pleased with the success of Barbra's album was Ray Stark, who was only getting a piece of the soundtrack album. He threatened to sue, and Columbia had to change the title to *Barbra Streisand: The Way We Were*. Still, there was no hiding the news that it contained Barbra's latest hit single, "The Way We Were," and it soon went gold. So did the soundtrack album.

That November 2, *Barbra Streisand . . . and Other Musical Instruments*, her fifth network television special, aired on CBS. Reviews and ratings were lackluster. The chief complaint was that it was over the top: "The program is well-made, and it certainly is expensive. But it is overproduced, over-orchestrated and overbearing to the point of esthetic nausea," complained John O'Connor of the *New York Times*. On the other hand, Kay Gardella of the *New York Daily News* loved it: "Miss Streisand guides us through a musical journey that's as exciting as *Alice's Adventures in Wonderland*.

and recording.

Her one-time adm▨▨
tion for Barbra had fac▨▨
found her intermittently exciting, ▨▨ especially when ▨▨▨
her mouth to sing, as in the movies of *Funny Girl* or *Hello, Dolly!* or even over the credits of *What's Up, Doc?*

"In *The Way We Were*, where she played the Marmelstein/Brice character in '30s radical drag, I found her affecting, funny, and even (in the bedroom scenes with Robert Redford) somewhat erotic."

"She is too totally honest and too candid for the world we live in, for the business she's in," Erlichman told Peter Evans of *Cosmopolitan* around that time. "I tell her, 'Barbra, make your interview like another scene. Have your big interview scene. I'll give you the right dialogue and attitudes and you can rehearse it like another role.' But she can't fake."

Although Erlichman was still representing Barbra, Jon was exerting more and more influence on her work. Barbra told Peter Evans: "I feel terribly guilty having to work. He doesn't want to be around when I'm working—and I don't want him to be because my concentration goes right out the window.

The other day he came to rehearsal, for instance, and the musical director asked me if I wanted three bars or four in a certain spot . . . and I didn't know and I didn't care. Yet if he hadn't been there, I would've known exactly. It's a terrible thing—but I actually enjoy being subjugated to him. Not in a personal or physical sense—I still need to be respected in my own right—but in terms of our work. It's far more important to a man's ego to have a career than it is to a woman's. I don't need to work anymore to feed my ego. I get all the ego nourishment I need from him."

ELLIOTT'S COMEBACK

And there was more good news: her ex-husband Elliott was pulling his career back together. For two years, no studio would risk hiring him. Now, his disastrous experience with *A Glimpse of Tiger* long behind him, United Artists approached him about starring in Robert Altman's *The Long Goodbye*. There was one stipulation: he was asked to submit to a rigorous psychiatric evaluation. "I took all the tests, and finally, they put nineteen needles in my head to study my brain waves. At last, I was certified sane. How many of us are certified by document as being sane?"

Unfortunately, *The Long Goodbye* proved a mixed blessing for Elliott's career. Altman, who had directed him in *M*A*S*H*, produced a hip, modern version of the Raymond Chandler detective story. Early reviews in New York and Los Angeles were negative and United Artists clashed with Altman over the release program and final cut of the film.

Eventually, Altman retrieved his picture, turned the advertising campaign around, and *The Long Goodbye* was re-released to excellent reviews, especially for Elliott Gould. "They opened it wrong the first time," Elliott insisted. "They did it inside-out."

FOR PETE'S SAKE

Characteristically, Barbra was already deep into filming her next picture, another in her long-term commitment to Ray Stark, when *The Way We Were* opened. Filming on *For Pete's Sake* began September 24, in Brooklyn. Having played a frustrated housewife in a serious drama, *Up the Sandbox,* and seen it suffer a quick death at the box office, Barbra next chose a similar role played for laughs: Henrietta Robbins, seeking money to finance her husband in law school, tries increasingly wacky schemes. Michael Sarrazin was cast as her husband and she retained British director Peter Yates and cinematographer Laszlo Kovaks. This was Marty Erlichman's first venture as a film producer.

Michael Sarrazin had heard of Barbra's reputation and, like most of her colleagues, found the real woman much more likeable. "I was expecting a prima donna, but she was real nice," he said. "She had this quality that made you want to take care of her. Sounds strange to say, what with the Streisand image, but she's rather tender. I mean, vulnerable. She does have a big ego, don't we all? But she gets to indulge it with close-ups and special treatment. She's somewhat shy, and keeps to herself mostly. I could see that sometimes she forced herself to be outgoing, to keep up morale on the set. She knew everyone was always staring at her, listening to her; she has this hypnotic effect on people. But she also had this good-trouper camaraderie, and she'd pull out of herself to make everyone feel at home, like they were contributing. That's good PR, but it's also kind."

Distinguished stage actress Estelle Parsons (who had her own Oscar for Supporting Actress in *Bonnie and Clyde*) played Barbra's greedy sister-in-law. She did not have Sarrazin's happy experience with Barbra. According to Considine, Barbra humiliated Parsons by refusing to say her lines directly

Barbra Streisand, 1965. Suddenly women all over America were copying her hair and eye makeup. (*Courtesy of AP/Wide World Photos*)

Barbra accepts flowers from Fran Stark, daughter of
Fanny Brice and wife of "Funny Girl" producer Ray
Stark, after the show opened in Boston. Barbra had
yet to prove she could carry a Broadway show.
(*Courtesy of AP/Wide World Photos*)

Barbra clutching her first Emmy, 1965. Already the
toast of Broadway, she had just conquered television
with her first special, "My Name is Barbra."
(*Courtesy of AP/Wide World Photos*)

Elegant Barbra, at the 1970 Oscars.
(*Courtesy of Ron Gallela*)

Clowning with Omar Sharif on the set of *Funny Girl*.
(*Courtesy of Photofest*)

Barbra in the "Swan Lake" scene in *Funny Girl*. (*Courtesy of the Everett Collection*)

More ballerina Barbra. In spite of her best efforts, the scene was cut from the film because of time constraints. (*Courtesy of the Everett Collection*)

Totally mod Barbra with Elliott Gould and baby
Jason, 1967.   (*Courtesy of Photofest*)

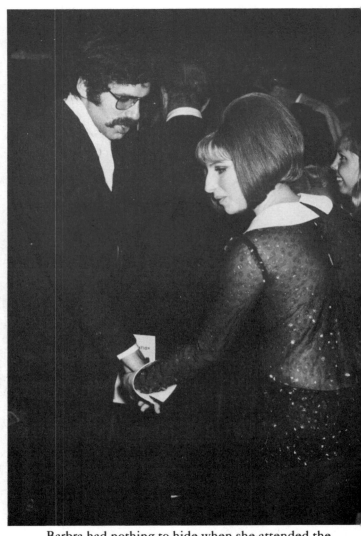
Barbra had nothing to hide when she attended the
1969 Academy Awards ceremonies and picked up her
Oscar for Best Actress for her role in *Funny Girl*.
(*Courtesy of Ron Galella*)

Barbra's favorite role: mother.
(*Courtesy of Photofest*)

Activist Barbra with liberal political leader William
Vanden Heuvel at a rally for Bella Abzug, 1970.
(*Courtesy of Ron Galella*)

One of the first photographs of Barbra with
Ryan O'Neal. (*Courtesy of Peter C. Borsari*)

Barbra and Ryan O'Neal in "What's Up, Doc?" She
never believed they were making a funny picture.
(*Courtesy of Photofest*)

Barbra and Kris Kristofferson rock in *A Star Is Born*.
(*Courtesy of Shooting Star*)

Barbra and Ryan—a love match.
(*Courtesy of Photofest*)

Barbra and Ryan reunited in *The Main Event*.
(*Courtesy of Photofest*)

Barbra and songwriter Paul Williams at the 1978
Grammy Awards. They collaborated on the theme
from *A Star Is Born*, "Evergreen."
(*Courtesy of Ron Galella*)

Accompanied by Pierre Trudeau, Barbra is honored
for her deep commitment to the Jewish community.
(*Courtesy of AP/Wide World Photos*)

Barbra and Robert Redford—
"The Way They Were."
(*Courtesy of the Everett Collection*)

Barbra and Don Johnson.
(*Courtesy of Photofest*)

Casual Barbra with Don Johnson.
(*Courtesy of AP/Wide World Photos*)

Grumpy Don with Barbra.
(*Courtesy of James Smeal/Ron Galella, Ltd.*)

Sharing Barbra with Don.
(*Courtesy of James Smeal/Ron Galella, Ltd.*)

Director Barbra with her co-star, Nick Nolte.
(*Courtesy of Anthony Savignano/Ron Galella, Ltd.*)

At the Oscars, 1991.
(*Courtesy of AP/Wide World Photos*)

Barbra and ice cream heir Richard Baskin, 1991.
(*Courtesy of B. Talesnick/Retna, Ltd.*)

Barbra with son Jason Gould at the premiere for
The Prince of Tides. (*Courtesy of Peter C. Borsari*)

Casual Barbra with Andre Agassi and Michael Bolton
at the U.S. Tennis Open, 1992.
(*Courtesy of Anthony Savignano/Ron Galella, Ltd.*)

Barbra arrives at the 1992 Academy Awards with
son Jason.   (*Courtesy of AP/Wide World Photos*)

Barbra directing her son in a scene for
The Prince of Tides.
(*Courtesy of John Barrett/Globe Photos, Inc.*)

Barbra and
Andre Agassi, 1992
(*Courtesy of Adam
Scull/Globe Photos, Inc.*)

Rare photograph
of Barbra with
longtime mentor
Marty Erlichman, 1992.
(*Courtesy of James
Smeal/Ron Galella, Ltd.*)

Barbra and her family: from left: mother Diana Kind,
Jason, sister Roslyn Kind. At the premiere for
The Prince of Tides. (*Courtesy of Peter C. Borsari*)

Barbra and Jon Peters, still good friends. (*Courtesy of Adam Scull/Globe Photos, Inc.*)

Barbra and Jon. (*Courtesy of Gregg de Guire/London Features Int'l. USA*)

Barbra with playwright and gay activist
Larry Kramer, 1993.
(*Courtesy of Anthony Savignano/Ron Galella, Ltd.*)

At the 1993 Academy Awards with Jack Nicholson.
(*Courtesy of Kevin Mazur/London Features Int'l. USA*)

Barbra's new hero: President Bill Clinton.
(*Courtesy of AP/Wide World Photos*)

Barbra at the Presidential Gala, 1993. At the peak of her powers. (*Courtesy of AP/Wide World Photos*)

to her on or off camera. "I've worked with difficult people, but she defies all," Parsons complained in *People*. "Her cruelty to coworkers, her director, and writers is unforgivable. It's sad." But she offered no specifics. Years later, however, when Barbra's film *Yentl* was shut out of the Academy Awards, Parsons would be one of her most vocal defenders.

For Pete's Sake wrapped in Los Angeles on December 11. Now Barbra was free to plunge into her romance with Jon. She joined him and his staff for their annual Christmas party later that month and then she and Jon took off for Vail, Colorado, where they learned how to ski.

Fourteen

Funny Lady

.

> "Jon and I have a perfect relationship. We're neither
> of us subjugated by the other. We exist as two equals
> who have mutual respect, love—and a helluva lot of fun."
>
> —Barbra

Barbra started 1974 on a roll. *The Way We Were* was shaping up as her biggest film yet, and the soundtrack album and her solo LP, both released in January, were headed for gold. Columbia had just announced that she would reunite with Ray Stark and Herb Ross for *Funny Lady*, a sequel to *Funny Girl*, continuing the life story of Fanny Brice. Shortly after New Year's, Lesley Ann Warren and Jon Peters announced their official separation and Barbra and Jon were now free to be seen in public. They arrived together at the Muhammad Ali-Joe Frazier fight in Madison Square Garden in January, dressed in identical western wear, only to find their seats taken. When the gate crashers refused to move and insulted Barbra, Jon exploded. "Pow!" he said later, "I let him have it. He's gonna hit my woman. I go crazy! They're pullin' me off him." Jon denied reports that he broke his wrist in the fight, however. According to Barbra, that happened at home: "Jon got so mad at something I said, he put his fist through a closet door. I'm so afraid he's going to hurt himself."

In February "The Way We Were" became Barbra's first number one single, and she was nominated for an Academy Award for her work in *The Way We Were*. Her co-star, Robert Redford, was nominated for his other big picture that year, *The Sting*. No sooner was Barbra nominated, however, than she was generating controversy.

She was invited to sing "The Way We Were" which had been nominated for Best Song, at the Academy Awards ceremony, but she declined. "I'm being honored for my acting," she said, "not for my singing." Peggy Lee was approached instead and cancelled a club date in Canada to do it.

Late that March, a week before the awards, Barbra changed her mind and wanted to sing. Jack Haley, Jr., who was producing the show, turned her down. A furious Barbra did attend the April 2 award ceremony with Jon anyway, but in protest she refused to sit with the audience, hiding out backstage to avoid cameras.

Because there were no cameras, no photographer captured Barbra's expression when dark horse Glenda Jackson was pronounced that year's Best Actress. Privately, a deeply disappointed Barbra dismissed the Academy Awards as a popularity contest, but the oversight rankled. Sure, she didn't go out of her way to win over the Hollywood establishment, but her work in *The Way We Were* was probably her best to date.

"YOU'LL HAVE TO DRAG ME INTO COURT TO DO THAT PICTURE!

The day after her disappointment at the Oscars, a very reluctant Barbra showed up for rehearsals for *Funny Lady*. In spite of their court battles, and although Barbra had already fulfilled her four picture deal with Ray Stark via *Funny Girl, The Owl and the Pussycat, The Way We Were,* and *For Pete's Sake,* she agreed to do a fifth. "The *Funny Lady* project was going on and off, on and off over many, many years," Marty Erlichman confirmed. " 'Let's do it.' 'Let's not do it.' 'Let's wait to see the script.' And that went back and forth before Barbra finally committed to do it."

Many were mystified by Barbra's decision. Some speculated that it was part of the 1967 out-of-court settlement, or that the original *Funny Girl* deal committed her to a sequel.

Others saw it as Barbra's move to stem rising competition from Liza Minelli who had won an Oscar the year before for *Cabaret.* Perhaps Ray Stark was sensitive to this when he assembled a first-class team of talent to keep Barbra happy, including Herb Ross, who had worked with her on *Funny Girl* and *The Owl and the Pussycat.* He also hired John Kander and Fred Ebb, best known as songwriters for Liza, and the screenwriter Jay Presson Allen, who had adapted *Cabaret* for the screen.

Funny Lady continued the life of Fanny Brice where *Funny Girl* had left off and focuses on her relationship with her third husband, the diminutive showman Billy Rose.

JAMES CAAN

Dustin Hoffman, Richard Dreyfuss, and Al Pacino were among the stars considered for the role of Billy Rose. A story circulated that Robert Blake, then at the height of his popularity on television's *Baretta,* wanted the part badly enough to visit Barbra in Malibu to talk about it. But the short-tempered Blake was so offended by Barbra's suggestion that they read a scene from the screenplay together that he insisted on reading not one scene but the entire script. When Barbra told him

he was wonderful he thanked her but declared he didn't want
the part after all and walked off.

In real life Billy Rose had been a notably short and unat-
tractive figure, but Stark had no intentions of pairing Barbra
with a troll. Instead he settled on James Caan, a handsome,
macho fellow New Yorker who instantly established a rapport
with her. Barbra was now so content with the leading men in
her personal and private life that she barely acknowledged the
return of Omar Sharif, who reprised the role of Nicky Arnstein
in a cameo appearance. The experience left Sharif sounding
a little wistful.

"For the first two or three days, she seemed a little different
to me," he said. "But then I'm sure I appeared somewhat
different to her, which is natural. *Funny Girl* was her very
first film, and she was married and had led a somewhat shel-
tered personal life. She has broadened considerably in the intervening years. I think it shows in her performing as well."
But he assured interviewers that they were still friends: "We
played some bridge between scenes. And another thing: now
she's almost as enthusiastic about horses as I am. She has her
own quarter horse and invited me to ride with her and some
friends at Malibu."

Nobody believed for a minute that Barbra wanted to make
Funny Lady, or that she enjoyed a single minute of filming.
She must have wondered whether she was going to have to
spend her whole life playing Ray Stark's mother-in-law.

"You can't capitalize on something that's worked before,"
she warned Stark when he sent her the first draft of the
script. "You'll have to drag me into court to do that picture!"

Yet once she had committed to *Funny Lady* and throughout the filming, Barbra was always the professional. She focused on what she had in common with Fanny Brice, starting
with a love of fine clothes and antiques. In the second half

of Fanny's life, Barbra felt that she had started to discover herself and finally let go of her illusions and fantasies about herself. Fanny grew up. And she opened up to someone who was like her, Billy Rose, just as Barbra had opened up to Jon.

Stark and Ross certainly put Barbra through her paces, demanding wild physical stunts from the notoriously sedentary Barbra. One scene filmed at the Olympic swimming pool in Los Angeles Stadium (standing in for Billy Rose's 1936 Cleveland Aquacade) had Barbra, dressed as a buxom clown in a pleated red shower cap and baggy swimsuit, frolicking in the water with a bevy of twenty-five synchronized swimmers. "It took her fifteen minutes to wriggle her big toe in the water," *Newsweek* reported. "She wouldn't go in until Ray Stark had heated the pool to eighty-two degrees." At the conclusion of the scene, Barbra playfully tried to pull Ross into the water, but he eluded her.

Yet another scene called for Barbra to fly in a 1937 open-cockpit, double-seater plane while singing "Let's Hear It For Me." The scene, a kind of mate to the tugboat scene in which Barbra sang "Don't Rain on My Parade" in *Funny Girl*, had been in the script from the beginning and Barbra had said from the beginning that she wasn't going to do it. Barbra protested strenuously, insisting the scene should be done in a studio. While Barbra was filming other scenes on location at the Santa Monica airport, Stark rented a plane and pilot and suggested she try it out. "It would look authentic," he said. "And think of the adventure," Ross added. Barbra agreed after she was assured that it could all be captured in one take.

The scene went off without a hitch, but as the plane descended, it got caught in sky traffic and the pilot had to circle the airport for a half hour while it was buffetted by headwinds. "The pilot was fiddling with the radio," Barbra recalled. "The first thing I thought was 'He's kidnapping me.' Then I thought 'The radio's dead; the guy can't land.' What happened was they radioed him he could not land because it was so crowded at Santa Monica Airport. Here I am risking my life for a movie!"

As they descended, a nauseous Barbra could see Stark, leaning on a truck, smoking a cigar. She swore at him, but Stark only smiled and waved. When they finally landed, Ross was the one who informed a furious Barbra that she would have to go up again to reshoot the scene.

It's possible that Barbra might not have continued if she had not had the support of Jon Peters. Certainly, Stark and Ross had reason to be grateful to him for getting her to the set each day. "He got her to work on time," Stark said later. "He said to her, 'Look, you're in business. I'm in business. We have to be on time.' And sometimes it worked." Jon obviously liked being on the set himself, he was enormously curious about every facet of the production and he would later demonstrate that he was a very good student. But his primary concern was Barbra and in interviews he made it clear that theirs was a *partnership,* and that neither of them dominated the other *all* the time.

"In some respects, she's a combination of the most difficult and the easiest person I've ever lived with," Jon acknowledged. "Because, when I feel like being very male and want her to be subservient to me, it's difficult because she doesn't buy that. She gives what she feels, as opposed to what's demanded of her. . . . But, on the other hand, she can be very loving. And absolutely great as a companion. I think I could say that besides everything else, she's the best friend I've got."

But Barbra's relationship with Stark was more of a love-hate tug-of-war than it had ever been. He believed in her talent and always had. "Barbra could do whatever she wants—and does," Stark said. "She could have been Joe Montana, H. Norman Schwarzkopf, Jonas Salk, Maggie Thatcher, or Barbra Streisand. I think she made the right choice."

"The thing that amazed me the most about her," raved co-star James Caan, "was that at 8:00 in the morning, after having Chinese food or something and her eyes just opening up she'd come into the studio and start singing like this incredible bird. I mean, it was just incredible."

But even Barbra's professionalism was tested by one very celebrated visitor to the *Funny Lady* set. Late in the filming Stark was informed that His Royal Highness Prince Charles was in Los Angeles on naval duty. The heir to the British throne was most anxious to meet only one person in Hollywood and that person was Barbra. "I'm sure they thought I'd say Raquel Welch," he told his valet, Stephen Barry, "but I said Barbra Streisand. I wanted to meet the woman behind the voice."

Barbra was totally unstrung when the big day came, full of nerves. Columbia executives and Ray Stark were delighted with the publicity potential, but she was terrified that she would say something awkward or tactless and the Prince would never buy another record.

The future King was introduced to Barbra on a cleared soundstage where she was dubbing dialogue. They shared coffee and small talk seemingly oblivious to the several hundred reporters and media people who were roped off a safe distance from them.

Barbra has never shared her impressions of the Prince, but it seems he was somewhat disappointed. "I think I caught her on a bad day," he told Barry that night. "She had very little time and appeared very busy."

It also must have pleased Barbra when her last television special, *Barbra Streisand . . . and Other Musical Instruments* garnered five Emmys that May. Although nominated for Outstanding Comedy-Variety, Variety or Musical Special, the pro-

gram lost to *Lily Tomlin,* but Barbra's director Dwight Hemion
was honored for Best Directing in Comedy-Variety or Music
and as Director of the Year—Special. Larry Gelbart, Mitzie
Welch, and Ken Welch were nominated for Best Writing in
Comedy-Variety or Music (Special Program) but the Emmy
went to the thirteen collaborators on *Lily Tomlin.* Jack Parnell
and the Welches did go home with Emmys for Best Music
Direction of a Variety, Musical or Dramatic Program and for
Musician of the Year. Brian C. Bartholomew was also honored
for Best Art Direction or Scenic Design (Musical or Variety
Program.)

FOR PETE'S SAKE

For Pete's Sake was released on June 26. David Begelman,
Barbra's former agent and the new president of Columbia,
announced that the company expected it to do as well as
What's Up, Doc? For Pete's Sake quickly established itself as
a summer hit, but it never reached the blockbuster status of
Doc. Today it is considered one of Barbra's lesser efforts.

The Los Angeles Times echoed most of the critics when it
reported that: *"For Pete's Sake,* a movie put together to honor
its star, Barbra Streisand, is an often boisterously old-time
farce. . . . Some of [the] material is fondly familiar; some is
in raucously bad taste. How long has it been since you've
seen a movie in which a woman has to hide in a closet when
a husband comes home early, or in which there's an ill-tem-
pered maid? That is, one who is black? *For Pete's Sake* courts
disaster, but most of the time manages to sidestep it."

And her once-devoted admirer Frank Rich was appalled.
He declared that his relationship with Streisand had hit rock
bottom and dismissed *For Pete's Sake* as "a compendium of
Vegas gags masquerading as a movie." He called it a "travesty" and complained that Barbra's original stage persona

"had metamorphosed into a hysterical caricature—a self-parody." The movie did well that summer, although it did not become the blockbuster that Begelman predicted. Produced by Marty Erlichman and based on his original idea, its artistic disappointment marked the beginning of the end of their relationship.

But Barbra had no time to dwell on negative reviews. She was deep into filming *Funny Lady* and working on a new album. By the time *Funny Lady* wrapped on July 9, Barbra was spending most of her free time with Jon at his Malibu ranch.

"Jon put Barbra more in touch with the mainstream of life," said one observer.

BUTTERFLY: "THIS IS POSSIBLY SOME OF THE BEST SINGING I'VE EVER DONE"

Jon had, in fact, begun to make himself indispensable, and he was about to produce Barbra's next album. Barbra vehemently defended Jon's growing influence over her career: "Do they think I would let Jon produce a record if I wasn't absolutely sure he could do it?" she said. "I believe in instinct. I believe in imagination. I believe in taste. These are the important ingredients, and they're all the things he has." Early in their relationship, Jon told Barbra that she reminded him of a butterfly. He later gave her an antique diamond and sapphire butterfly. Naturally, they agreed, the title of her next album—which Jon would produce—would be *ButterFly*.

ButterFly is the only Streisand album without a picture of Barbra on the cover. Instead, there is a photograph of an unwrapped stick of unsalted butter, with a fly perched on it—part of Jon's unique vision. On the back of the album is an equally tradition-busting portrait of Barbra, her hair lifted by a flock of butterflies.

ButterFly was a further move into contemporary material with Barbra moving from pop to reggae to country. Much of it is misconceived: Bowie called her version of "Life on Mars" "bloody awful." Yet there is a bold new sexiness in Barbra as she sings on "Guava Jelly," and "Let the Good Times Roll."

If Barbra had had her way, however, the album would have contained more traditional tunes as well. She recorded several standards, including "God Bless the Child," which was a favorite of Jon's. She also thought of pairing "A Quiet Thing," from Kander and Ebb's musical *Flora, the Red Menace* (which had introduced Liza Minelli) with "There Won't Be Trumpets," a song dropped from Stephen Sondheim's *Anyone Can Whistle.* Both songs told dramatic stories, which she loved.

But no one at CBS Records shared Barbra's enthusiasm and insisted that such songs did not belong on a "contemporary" album like *ButterFly.* Barbra went along, knowing in her heart that someday she would release the songs and she did, in her *Just For the Record* CD in 1991. In fact, recording that medley is what first got her thinking about doing a Broadway album.

ButterFly was released in October. Reviews were mixed, with a rave from the *New York Times.* But it was the *Los Angeles Times* critic who best captured the strengths and weaknesses of *ButterFly:*

"*ButterFly* is, in some ways her most daring album. That's not the same as saying it is her most successful . . . Streisand touches a wide variety of musical bases—from reggae to David Bowie to gospel-soul to country. Her voice is as lovely as it has been in years, often open and warm. But her interpretations are still narrow and unconvincing . . . The problem, I'm afraid, is that Streisand has no clear feel for interpreting contemporary pop music. She obviously enjoys the various musical styles represented on the album, but she has given us no new way to look at them or no emotion to feel over them."

Although the album would go gold four months later, the two single releases, "Guava Jelly"/"Love in the Afternoon" released in December, and "Jubilation"/"Let the Good Times Roll," released in April, failed to make the Billboard charts at all.

The controversial nature of Barbra's relationship with Jon Peters had already generated negative publicity long before the album was released. An angry Barbra told gossip columnist Joyce Haber: "This is possibly the best singing I've ever done. For the first time in my life, my work has become fun for me, and it used to be a drag. My attitude has changed towards people. I'm less afraid. That's Jon. It kills me to have him put down more than to have me put down."

Although the album received little support from Columbia it drew some surprisingly good reviews, including the *New York Times* whose critic called it "one of Streisand's finest albums in years."

It even looked as if her former husband's second comeback was underway. Elliott had followed his success in *The Long Goodbye* with the lackluster *Busting* and *S*P*Y*S*. But in the summer of 1974 he opened in a new picture, *California Split,* in which he and George Segal played fanatic gamblers who head for Reno, Nevada, for a big score. The reception was excellent.

Elliott seemed like a new man, a man at peace with himself. "I learned not to let anxieties get the best of me," he told interviewers. "I learned not to get over-anxious."

As Barbra closed out 1974 in the arms of Jon Peters, she could celebrate a year of continued achievement. Once again she was the Quigley Poll's Top Female Box-office Star. The success of *The Way We Were* had brought her international laurels, among them Italy's David DiDonatello Award for Best Foreign Actress, and India's International Film Festival's Silver Peacock Award for Best Actress. Her television special, *Bar-*

bra Streisand . . . and Other Musical Instruments had received the Silver Rose at the Montreux TV Festival. And her single, "The Way We Were," was recognized as Best Original Song by the Hollywood Foreign Press Association.

Fifteen

New Directions

"Someone like Barbra will always sound modern. Barbra doesn't need disco or new wave to be modern. Barbra is Barbra."

—Rupert Holmes

Secure in her relationship with Jon Peters, finally free of her youthful commitments to Ray Stark and the CBS network, Barbra faced 1975 with renewed energy. At Jon's urging, she was easing out her longtime manager Marty Erlichman. She may have blamed Erlichman for the disappointing *For Pete's Sake* and for the deal with Stark. In any case, Jon was taking up the reins. Between the two of them they were already planning the most ambitious project of her career.

Jon was confounding his detractors. That January *Butterfly*, the controversial album he had produced for Barbra, was certified gold. And it was Jon to whom Ray Stark turned when he wanted Barbra to help promote *Funny Lady*, just as he had turned to him to see that the reluctant star appeared on the set each morning in a cooperative mood.

RAY STARK

Once again, Ray Stark managed to maximize Barbra's star power to promote his blockbuster film. The March 9 world premiere of *Funny Lady* was scheduled to benefit the Special Olympics, a Kennedy family charity, at the Kennedy Center in Washington, D.C. Stark talked ABC-TV into broadcasting a live special built around Barbra and including figures from the worlds of politics and sports. It would be Barbra's first concert appearance in three years.

The show almost didn't happen, though, when Barbra's longtime conductor Peter Matz arrived in Washington with his musicians and discovered that TWA had lost their music. The airline representatives did not share Matz's alarm.

"Nobody was interested," Matz recalls. "We couldn't find anybody from TWA who was interested in helping us find our music that day. We kept getting referred from one office to another. They wanted time to track it down and we were saying, 'Wait a minute. We have an orchestra rehearsal at the Kennedy center this afternoon, and tomorrow we're going on the air *live!*'"

Matz finally turned to the all-powerful Ray Stark who was still at home in California. "Thank God he had the clout to put a tracer on it and they found the music in Las Vegas or Denver. He got a plane to pick it up and take it to Chicago where TWA agreed to bring it the rest of the way."

While Matz was frantically hunting down the arrangements, Barbra, Sue Mengers, and Jon attended a glittering party at the Iranian Embassy where Barbra danced with Senator Ted Kennedy and Jon danced with matriarch Rose.

Next night, Barbra appeared on the stage of the Kennedy Center and sang a medley and a duet of "It's Only a Paper Moon" with James Caan for a black-tie audience that included President Gerald R. Ford and Rose Kennedy. Boxers George

Foreman and Muhammed Ali joined Barbra on stage at the end of the show which came abruptly at 8:30 p.m. When the network shut it down, a surprised Barbra could be seen saying: "Oh, that's it? That's a live show for you." She went on to sing a rock version of "People" for those in the audience.

Committed to promoting *Funny Lady,* Barbra moved on to New York for another premiere to benefit the Hospital for Special Surgery. At a pre-show press conference she announced that this was her last public performance. "I had an anxiety attack backstage," she revealed. "I went cold, I felt faint, my throat closed up. I was scared to death. I was sure the audience would be uptight. It knocked me out when they weren't."

Stark praised his cooperative star: "She's changed like good wine. She's gone through those formative years, and she's come out of it magnificently. She's concerned, she's considerate. We fight like hell, but they're all fights about creative opinions on which I can be right or wrong and she can be right or wrong. She's just matured and become a lovely lady instead of a fiery, funny, kooky little girl."

When Barbra arrived swathed in red fox, outside Times Square's Astor Plaza Theatre, the street was literally mobbed with fans, barely controlled by police and private guards. Arthur Bell of the *Village Voice* reported that "they had fifty policemen and bodyguards on the street trying to get her from her limo into the theater. And I got a look at her face. She looked scared; *but* she was also reveling in it. She was playing both sides of the fence, 'Oh, I'm so frightened; I'm scared. Why do I have to do this?'—but she was also *thrilled."*

After the film Fran and Ray Stark hosted a midnight supper at El Morocco where Barbra was greeted by a standing ovation. In spite of that reception, Barbra lingered at a corner banquette with Jon.

Barbra and Jon opted to skip the Los Angeles premiere which featured a pair of gilded elephants and five thousand helium balloons, and instead headed for a Royal Film Performance in London.

A few weeks later, on St. Patrick's Day, Barbra made more waves at the London premiere. Queen Elizabeth and Prince Philip were to come backstage after the film to greet the performers. Barbra and others were briefed on royal protocol and the schedule for the evening. James Stewart, Lee Remick, James Caan, and Barbra were to be placed in a front row to be presented to the Queen. In a second row would be their spouses and lovers, including Jon. Barbra was deeply offended. She wanted Jon in front with her. She wanted him to meet the Queen when she did. Told that no one who was not directly connected with the show could be in the front row, Barbra held her tongue, but she was planning her revenge. Her chance came in the receiving line when she was presented to the Queen. Breaking protocol, which dictates that one waits for the Queen to speak first, she asked: "Your Majesty, why do women have to wear gloves and the men don't?" The stunned Queen replied: "Well, I don't really know. It's just tradition, I suppose." Turning to Jon in the row behind her, Barbra said aloud: "Well, I guess I still don't know."

"I think it's the men's sweaty hands that ought to covered, not ours." It was reportedly Jon who had goaded Barbra into posing the question. But Barbra was anxious to dispel any impression that she did not respect the royal family. "I like the idea of kings and queens," she told a radio interviewer. "It's like a storybook. It gives everyone an idea of honor and respect that we don't have in America. Now, Prince Charles and I have met and he is very sweet."

The aggressive publicity and marketing helped make *Funny Lady* an enormous financial success, but reviews were generally negative. The *Los Angeles Times* reviewer praised Barbra's singing and wrote that "What I find most impressive and likable about the performance is the softened, bittersweet maturity that Streisand let's us see in Fanny Brice. You sense that Streisand understands the star as well as she understood the impetuous young hopeful." But most reviewers agreed with the increasingly disenchanted Frank Rich who believed that "Streisand turned Fanny Brice herself into an overbearing, ruthless shrew."

AT THE ACTOR'S STUDIO WEST

Barbra now took time off to work on her acting and directing skills. She and Sally Kirkland worked on a scene from *Romeo and Juliet* which they presented for Lee Strasberg that May. Barbra was Juliet at fourteen, "a real horny kid" and Kirkland was her earthy, worldly-wise nurse. Barbra considered it the best acting she had ever done. She told Sue Mengers, her agent, that she wanted to play *Romeo and Juliet* and got Mengers to contact the networks about a possible special. There was no interest. Network executives all asked the same question: "Does she sing in it?" And "Who's Playing Romeo?" Barbra was discouraged, although she has never revealed who she saw as Romeo.

RUPERT HOLMES

In April a young New York-based singer-songwriter named Rupert Holmes received a call from Barbra Streisand's office in Los Angeles asking if he would prepare two of his songs for her because she was interested in performing them. "I thought it was somebody at the bowling alley playing a joke," Holmes said later. "A few hours later I was called again and asked if I would come to Los Angeles."

Holmes would later go on to fame for writing "Escape (The Pina Colada Song)," but he was then working in obscurity. His most recent album, *Widescreen*, also produced for CBS records, had sold slightly more than 10,000 copies. Later he would say that "The greatest thrill that I've ever experienced was the day I went to her home and she put the *Widescreen* album on. She sang most of the tunes, and she didn't have lyrics in front of her—she had memorized them. I couldn't believe it."

Barbra was so determined to work with Holmes that she put him up in her Beverly Hills home for six months, chauffeured him around Los Angeles to the recording studio and to her Malibu ranch where he stayed in the guest house. Holmes declared that "I'm trying to move her back to the sound that gave people shivers when they first heard her." He found working with Barbra a breeze once he understood her style. "The trick is to learn to hear in her voice when she's discussing something if her heart's really in it."

Most of Barbra's recent albums had been the product of many creative hands, but Holmes was the only arranger for *Lazy Afternoon*. This meant he was able to shape it in his image of the star. "I thought it would be possible to make a more traditional Streisand album without in any way making Barbra sound dated, and I think that works. Someone like Barbra will always sound modern. Barbra doesn't need disco or new wave to be modern. Barbra is Barbra."

They worked together so well that Holmes wrote several new songs for her. After she shared her memories of growing up without her father, Holmes wrote "My Father's Song." He also encouraged her to compose the music for "By the Way," the second time a song of hers was included on an album. (The first was "Ma Premiere Chanson" on the *Je M'appelle Barbra* album in 1966.)

They began recording for *Lazy Afternoon* in April with a forty-piece orchestra. Barbra picked most of the material and wrote the liner notes herself. Work was completed three months later.

Lazy Afternoon, with its cover photo of a barefoot Barbra in gypsy dress and scarf, became one of her favorites. "I can't bear to listen to my records until about ten years after they're out, and then when I do, it's usually agonizing," Barbra has said. "All I hear are the flaws, the things I could have done better." But *Lazy Afternoon* would become an exception.

"I love that album," Barbra said a decade later.

THE TONIGHT SHOW

Early in her career, Barbra had developed a close relationship with the *Tonight Show,* appearing on it seven times before her breakthrough performance in *Funny Girl* on Broadway. She had not been on the show since March 1963 and host Johnny Carson and his producer Freddy De Cordova had been pursuing her for years. At last, at Ray Stark's urging, she agreed to return to promote *Funny Lady* and her new record album, *Lazy Afternoon,* and the release of the first single from it, "My Father's Song." She even agreed to sing. Carson and De Cordova were more than accommodating: she could rehearse with the *Tonight Show* band the day of her appearance; she would be the first guest of the evening, perform two songs from *Lazy Afternoon,* chat with Johnny, and leave.

According to De Cordova, negotiations for her appearance were conducted with Ray Stark. Through him they agreed to allow Barbra to choose her own lighting technician, make-up person, and hairdresser. They promoted Barbra's appearance aggressively for days before the big night.

Then on the day of the show a call came in: Barbra would not appear after all. No explanation or excuse was offered.

That night Carson told his audience: "I was informed prior to going on the air that we'll have a cancellation tomorrow night. Barbra Streisand will not be with us. We don't know why. Nobody has been able to reach her. I think she changed her mind at the last minute. Although she doesn't owe the show anything in particular, we thought it only fair to tell you, so when you tune in, you don't get mad at us. I would rather you get mad at her. Streisand will not be here Wednesday night nor will she be here in the future. Over the years, we've had the reputation for delivering. We'll be here, though, and that's all there is to it."

Privately, Carson was furious at the perceived snub. He was a man who valued loyalty above everything else. It irked him that Barbra had not even given a reason for pulling out. The following night, he surprised his audience by introducing Barbra, who sang "People" very badly until he ordered her off his stage. "Barbra" then pulled off her wig and revealed herself as a female impersonator, generating much hilarity on stage and in the audience. Carson continued to take his revenge by making Barbra the subject of jokes in his monologue for weeks after.

But was Barbra wrong? She had cooperated fully with publicity for *Funny Lady,* taping an interview with Barbara Walters, performing live on *Funny Girl to Funny Lady* in Washington and giving press conferences in New York and London. Marty Erlichman tried to explain the thinking of his client: "In the early days of Barbra's career, she was able to get herself up to do all this. As she got more successful, a lot of anxieties came with it," he said. "There was tremendous anxiety over *The Tonight Show.* 'I don't want to do it. I don't want to do it.' 'Okay, I'll do it.' And a lot of people saying, 'Do it. It's good for this. . . . It's good for that.' "

In fact, Barbra was so nervous that she broke out in hives days before the booking. "You're better off saying no at that moment in time than you are going on the show and not being able to handle it in front of ten, twelve million people," said Erlichman.

He continued to defend his client: "It happens to all of us

on a daily, weekly, or monthly basis where we make decisions
that we know we just can't follow through on even though we
said we'd do it. . . . Barbra understood all of the effort that had
gone into the promotion of her appearance—which NBC had
gone above and beyond what they should have, and that's their
own problem for doing that. But she had to make a decision
predicated on her own well-being. Hers was a very severe emotional reaction that translated into a physical one. Barbra knew
at the time she said, 'I can't do it,' that there would be reper-
cussions. It wasn't like any of us hid from her the damage that
it could cause. It created a problem in the public's eye and with
Johnny directly, but she didn't know to what extent it would
go. . . . Then years later people are still talking about it. These
things happen in life. They just happen."

HER MOST CONTROVERSIAL PROJECT YET

With Jon's encouragement, Barbra was now ready to tackle
her most ambitious and controversial project yet: the remake
of *A Star is Born*. She would be able to draw on all she had
learned both in making movies and in her personal life, for
the plot of the classic movie had many parallels to her own
relationship with Elliott Gould.

There is no indication that Barbra and Jon ever considered
the most obvious candidate for the role, Elliott, but it is interesting to note that he did confide to columnist Earl Wilson
that he and Barbra and Jon had discussed teaming Barbra and
Elliott in a picture together "playing a romantic couple."

"The idea appeals to me," Elliott acknowledged, "though I
don't know whether it's anything very tangible. I don't know
Barbra as an actress, only as the mother of my son Jason, as
a woman, and as a GREAT singer."

Barbra must have had mixed feelings that fall when she
learned that Elliott's second marriage had fallen apart. That

October he was divorced in Los Angeles by Jennifer Bogart and was ordered to pay $2,500 monthly alimony and $1,400 monthly support for their children, Molly, now 3, and Samuel, now 2.

As Barbra closed out 1975, she could take pride in the fact that the Quigly Poll still listed her as the Top Female Box Office Star. She had also been honored by the Hollywood Foreign Press Association with a Golden Globe for "World Film Favorite—Female," and by the People's Choice Awards as "Favorite Movie Actress" and "Favorite Female Singer," and with a Photoplay "Gold Medal" Award as "Favorite Movie Actress." Three of her albums had been certified gold: *The Way We Were* (the original soundtrack recording), *Butter-Fly,* and *Funny Lady* (the original soundtrack recording).

Sixteen

A Star Is Born

"She can have any man she wants. So it is obvious she hasn't chosen me because I am a shmuck."
—Jon Peters

By the time Barbra and Jon teamed up to make *A Star is Born*, she had come to totally trust his judgment. Stories circulated in Hollywood that Barbra, long known for her fierce will, now deferred completely to Jon. One story had it that when a manicurist arrived at their Malibu home to do Barbra's nails, the star showed up in a cashmere sweater and suede pants. Jon told her that she was overdressed. She went upstairs to change into Jon-approved jeans and T-shirt.

The Hollywood community was mystified by this oddest of couples, but in fact, Barbra was only the first to see the qualities that would later establish Peters as one of the most important producers in the business. He in turn looked past the perfectionist with the iron will and saw the passionate woman inside.

Others in Barbra's inner circle—especially Marty Erlichman and her longtime agent, Sue Mengers—had ferocious battles with the newcomer. They discovered that fighting was hopeless. "He's like trying to withstand a hurricane," Mengers complained.

Yet it was Mengers who enlisted his help when she tried to convince Barbra to film *A Star is Born*. "I decided to go to my foe, Jon Peters, and see if he agreed with her or me," Mengers said. "He said, 'You're right and she's wrong.' "

The story had already been filmed three times: as *What Price Hollywood?* in 1932, directed by George Cukor and starring Constance Bennett and Lowell Sherman, and as *A Star is Born* with Frederic March and Janet Gaynor in 1936 produced by David O. Selznick and directed by William Wellman, and Judy Garland and James Mason in 1953, again directed by Cukor, with music by Harold Arlen and George Gershwin. The current project, conceived as a rock musical, had been first proposed by the team of Joan Didion and John Gregory Dunne who wrote the screenplay with James Taylor and Carly Simon in mind. They had long since bailed out and the project had been linked with other names before Warners picked it up as a vehicle for Barbra.

Jon had never heard of any of the previous versions. All he knew was that it was a great story that would showcase the young vibrant woman he loved. He wanted to capture the excitement of a live Streisand performance like the one he'd seen years ago at the Coconut Grove.

He did demand some changes in the script. He hated the ending. In all three previous versions, the self-destructive leading man kills himself, but Jon ruled that out from the beginning. *"No* suicide," he decreed. "Suicide is a downer. No guy with real balls would walk out on the woman he loves by taking his life." Instead, the leading man would die in an accident.

As for Barbra, when she was asked why she wanted to remake a classic, she answered: "Because there is a change in women's roles every twenty years. I am making this character very personal, very meaningful to me. I think this film will have a lot to say about the changing roles of men and women. Women are no longer afraid to confront the male society. Which is why, in the wedding scene in this movie, I'm wearing a man's suit. Now, I think that has a lot to say about the changing roles in today's society."

Jon had other creative suggestions and he was eager to produce and direct, although he has always denied that he was willing to play Barbra's leading man as well. That was a joke, he insists. "Barbra and I were kidding around at home reading the script, and I said, 'Hey! I can do this part. I got the looks and the energy.' And Barbra said, 'You can do *anything*, Jon.' And somehow that got picked up by some shmuck who printed it."

They had gone through seven versions of the script by seven different writers when they talked to Frank Pierson who had scored some success with the scripts for *The Anderson Tapes* and *Dog Day Afternoon*. Pierson agreed to work on the *Star* script if he could also direct. To the surprise of everyone concerned, Barbra and Jon agreed. Jon later explained his decision to pass up the directing job himself: "How could I direct her and keep our relationship? I had to decide which was more important, our love or the movie."

In retrospect, of course, Pierson does not seem an obvious choice. To begin with, he had never seen any of Barbra's movies. Now he began secretly screening them, and discovered that Barbra marched through her films "with her own clear force and direction regardless of what may have gone wrong or silly around her." He confided to his journal that "She is a primitive force and an elegant delight; I'm humble and amazed. What a fantastic picture we can make!"

Initially, all Barbra asked of Pierson was that he respect her. She could not bear to work with another Ray Stark, she explained. "Ray Stark used to bully me, the son of a bitch," she told him. "I made him, and he made millions from me, millions!" Barbra was determined that she and Jon would control this project and if there were millions to be made, they were going to make them. But even more than the money, she wanted the artistic credibility that would come with a first-class picture. She entered the relationship with Pierson with the highest of hopes and she was willing to take a chance on a first-time director. Sadly, at the conclusion of the filming she would feel he had betrayed her.

In their search for a leading man worthy of Barbra they even talked to Marlon Brando. "He was cute!" Jon said. "The son of a bitch, he wanted to screw Barbra—I was ready to kill him! I take him off and I kiss him! He's beautiful!"

But Pierson and, more importantly, the studio, had signed for a musical, and Brando was thus out of the question. They moved on to Elvis Presley, visiting him backstage at the Hilton International in Las Vegas. Elvis and Barbra had crossed paths several times in Las Vegas, but they really moved in two different worlds. He had not made a movie in years and although he was a sick, bloated travesty of himself, he still ruled in Vegas. Now Barbra tried to convince him the role she was offering him could garner him an Oscar and mark a creative rebirth.

"Elvis listened," a close associate recalled. "Elvis was a gentleman, through and through. He was also fascinated with Streisand. 'She's a star, a big movie star. What's she got?' He kept trying to figure it out. And the Peters guy, he kept shoveling it on. They tried to make his part sound like the Second Coming. Elvis would get the best lines, the best songs; they'd shoot the movie in Vegas or Memphis, wherever he was comfortable."

But Elvis knew his big screen days were over and he ruled out any more movies.

Next, Barbra and Jon focused on Mick Jagger and Kris Kristofferson. Peters pushed for Jagger, but Barbra wanted Kristofferson, with whom she had a brief fling after she separated from Elliott Gould in 1971. "He's an actor," she explained. "He's beautiful to look at. He can sing and play the guitar. And he's gentile, which seems to work with me—the Jew and the gentile."

Barbra and Jon signed up Kristofferson in September, 1974, and by mid-December Pierson had presented them with an acceptable script.

Kristofferson was a complex man. A former Rhodes Scholar, janitor, helicopter pilot, bartender, short story writer, military man, composer, folk singer, and actor, he had written such classic songs as "Help Me Make it Through the Night," "Sunday Morning Coming Down," and "Me and Bobby McGee," which was supposedly inspired by his relationship with the late Janis Joplin. And his marriage to up-and-coming Rita Coolidge mirrored some aspects of *Star.*

CLASSICAL BARBRA:
"IT DOESN'T MATTER WHAT PEOPLE THINK OF IT, WHAT MATTERS IS THE WORK ITSELF"

Filming was scheduled to begin in February, and CBS records, aware that Barbra would be too tied up with *Star's* tight schedule that year to provide them with any new material, finally agreed to release a collection of classical tracks she had recorded in 1973. Insiders had been hearing about this material for years, but until now the record company had been reluctant to release it. Their concern was that classical music buffs would not take Barbra seriously and her mainstream fans would be confused by the material. "Record companies haven't changed," Marty Erlichman explained. "The classical album was something they could live with, but certainly nothing they would foster." Barbra was still nervous about how the project would be received. It was beautifully packaged, with a photograph by Richard Avedon, liner notes by Leonard Bernstein, and released by Columbia's prestigious

"Masterworks" division, but Barbra wanted to include the line "This is a work in progress" in the jacket copy. Jon and Marty talked her out of it.

"Barbra did this with one hundred percent purity, and I don't want it to be bastardized," said Marty.

Reviews were generally cautious but positive. One that must have particularly thrilled Barbra came from composer Glenn Gould who confessed himself an ardent longtime admirer: "I'm convinced that she has a great 'classical' album in her."

"Musically, I've felt compelled to try everything," Barbra said, but she considered this her most difficult singing project yet because classical singing was such a disciplined art form. Not reading music, Barbra learned the classical lieder by listening to other singers' recordings. Even though she was not totally satisfied with it, she was happy she made it.

Classical Barbra performed modestly for a Streisand album, but Barbra was philosophical about it: "It doesn't matter what people think of it," she said, "what matters is the work itself. And, actually, it pleased a lot of people."

BARBRA'S INSTANT GRATIFICATION

While Barbra, Jon, and Pierson worked on the movie script, she and Jon also worked on their growing compound in Malibu, finishing one guest house and starting another. They purchased the house next door and began remodelling it to Jon's taste. Another property was acquired to be rebuilt in Barbra's Art Deco image. Frank Pierson saw a parade of trucks arrive daily with antiques, furniture, trees, and shrubs for the landscaping, cement for the new doubles tennis court and the swimming pool. "That's me," Barbra laughed when Pierson mentioned it. "Instant gratification."

"She's got her house to work on, I got mine," said Jon. "It cuts down on the fights."

She was also rehearsing with Kristofferson and working on the music for *Star.* As the score evolved, Barbra thought it would be interesting to have a number of artists contribute material. She had met Leon Russell through their mutual friend Gary Busey. One night Russell came to her house to play some music and overheard Barbra playing a little melody with a classical flavor that she had written years before but never finished. He started to hum a secondary melody that blew Barbra away. That was the beginning of "Lost Inside of You," and their creative conversation became dialogue in the film.

Barbra also had to learn to play the guitar. She admits she drove everyone crazy playing it morning, noon, and night. She would also test melodies on everyone. "How do you like this?" she would ask when a melody came into her head. "What do you think of these chords? What do you think of this bridge?" One of those melodies became "Evergreen." When she played it for Marty Erlichman, he said flatly that it would be a hit. Not just a hit, but number one. "On the one hand I thought he was kidding," Barbra says. "On the other—the hand that really excited me—Marty had made the same prediction for 'The Way We Were.' Happily, he was right again." Enlisting Paul Williams as musical director, she composed what would become the Oscar-winning theme for *A Star is Born.*

Barbra's style did not always mesh with Williams's and the question of credit for "Evergreen" has been the subject of much discussion over the years. Publicly at least, Williams has taken a philosophical, even humorous attitude: "When Babs got tough, we just tied her up and hosed her down until she cooled off," he joked. "Seriously, though, she's a perfectionist—and because of that, she's demanding." Barbra was not used to working with a lyricist who disappeared for days and arrived on the set with lyrics scrawled on a cocktail napkin.

"YOU THINK IT'S EASY, SOME DUDE MAKING LOVE TO YOUR WOMAN?"

Filming of *A Star is Born* began on February 2, 1976. It's likely nothing in her past experience could have prepared Barbra for the rigors awaiting her. Not only was she working closely in a high-stress situation with the man she loved, her leading man was in deep personal trouble and her writer/director was building up a resentment that would ultimately result in an act that she would regard as an unforgivable betrayal.

The one person who did not disappoint her was Jon. From the start, he demonstrated amazing instincts for filmmaking. He had a wonderful theatrical sense. His own role as lover/producer was a tough one, especially when it called for him to watch Barbra and Kristofferson make love. Jon made no secret of his jealousy.

One scene called for Esther Hoffman (Barbra) and John Norman Howard (Kristofferson) to make love in a marble tub, surrounded by candles. "For God's sake, find out if he's going to *wear* something," she pleaded. "If Jon finds out he's in there with nothing on, naked . . ." Pierson checked and learned that Kris was indeed planning to go natural. He quickly got him a pair of flesh-colored briefs. Barbra wore a flesh-toned top and bikini briefs.

That didn't restrain Kris, however. "Kristofferson had Streisand all but hissing 'stop' as he wound his legs around her, getting her hot and bothered in a nude bathtub scene . . ." Arthur Bell of the *Village Voice* reported.

"You think it's easy? Some dude making love to your woman?" Jon asked Pierson later. The director got the mes-

sage and after that, when Barbra and Kris rehearsed their love
scenes, the doors were kept open.

But a few days after the hot tub encounter a dramatic show
down came.

"WHEN YOU'RE IN LOVE EVEN A FIGHT IS A VERY INTIMATE THING"

Perhaps Jon's greatest contribution was the rock concert that
was the dramatic finale of the film. Pierson planned to use stock
footage of a concert, but Jon decided that they would stage a
real concert and charge admission. They set it up at Tempe,
Arizona's, Sun Devil Stadium and 70,000 people showed up.
They actually made money for the film.

Unfortunately, there would also be an incident at the concert
that touched off a wave of bad publicity about Barbra, Jon
and their film.

Much of the negative press arose because outsiders had
never understood the nature of their intense relationship. Barbra freely admitted that she drew on this for the movie. "The
characters in the movie, they laugh, they fight, lust like we
do," she said. "Jon and I had a spitting fight the other day.
Well, not a fight exactly. But we were in bed, and we were
kind of yelling and drooling all over each other. And you now
when you're in love even a fight is a very intimate thing." It
was this kind of intensity Barbra and Jon wanted to bring to
the film, but she was never sure that Pierson understood.

Yet the struggle only drew Jon and Barbra closer together.
"You know," she mused, "when I took the 'a' out of Barbra
and Jon took the 'h' out of John, we didn't even know each
other. Isn't it funny how an affectation can bring two people
together?"

But the Jon and Barbra show could be wearying for others
involved. Kristofferson was one who emerged battle-scarred.

from the experience. "It's the hardest thing I've been through since I jumped out of planes in ranger school," he told an interviewer on the set. "I'm writing a song about it—'It's Never Gonna Be the Same Again.'"

"What's never gonna be the same?" he was asked.

"My f—— head," he answered.

"How are things going between you and the director?" the interviewer continued.

"Who's the director?" he answered. "Barbra and Frank make me feel like a jackass between two stacks of hay. I don't know which one to go for."

But during the filming, Kristofferson was wrestling with his own demons. A studio chauffeur who was driving him to the set one morning told Kristofferson that he had read that the rocker had botched a concert. Kristofferson, who had been drinking all morning, immediately jumped to his own defense. "But I knew he was right," he said later. "I had given a bad performance because I was drunk."

According to *People* magazine, Kristofferson would arrive on the set at 5 A.M. with a couple of six-packs to chase his daily quart-and-a-half of tequila.

Kristofferson was used to working with directors like Martin Scorcese and Paul Mazursky or on free-for-all sets with Sam Peckinpah where the movie was almost incidental to the partying. He was not a trained actor. He relied on his director and his co-stars to give him direction—but in this case his director and his co-star were at odds. "Kristofferson is not a method actor, but he's been stoned or drunk since the day he arrived in Tempe," reported Arthur Bell of the *Village Voice*.

The blow-up came at the worst possible time—in front of a crowd of press.

Barbra and Jon were tense about the filming. They were filming a live concert and they had only one chance—it could not be reshot. The press was there to see the entire rehearsal.

"I was totally petrified and insecure about performing that day," Barbra told Lawrence Grobel. "I had to get up in front of 70,000 kids who had come to hear Peter Frampton and I didn't know whether I'd be booed off the stage."

They had flown in press junketers from Vancouver, Seattle, Cleveland, Chicago, and New York, to observe the filming of the concert, with Montrose, Frampton, Santana, and the L.A. Jets, all staged by Bill Graham.

Barbra had rehearsed her numbers with the band and taken so long she had used up Kris's time. Furious, he refused to come out of his trailer. "Goddamn it!" he said, "I've been trying to make this stuff sound like music. I've got to go out and play it in front of 60,000 people, but she doesn't give a damn."

Soon he and Barbra were trading accusations and insults—in front of an open mike over a sound system that could be heard five miles away.

"Look," said Barbra, "you're not doing what I tell you to do." Kris did not seem to be listening.

"Listen to me when I talk to you, God damn it," she shouted. Suddenly Kris was now listening. According to Bell: "He told her to go fuck herself." Barbra turned on her heels and stormed away.

An angry Jon Peters confronted Kris. "You owe my old lady an apology," he said. All of this carried over the sound system.

Kris responded: "If I want some shit out of you, I'll squeeze your head."

(A year later, a sober Kristofferson was unrepentant. "That has got to be one of the all-time great lines," he said to *Rolling Stone* magazine.)

In a white sweater and faded jeans, Barbra went on stage for the first time since her Los Angeles Forum concert four years earlier. Greeted by thunderous applause, she said shyly, "I didn't think you'd remember who I was." She went on to explain a bit about the concert and to introduce Kristofferson in character as John Howard Norman.

"The press asked me, 'Why make this movie again?' " she reported. "Just you wait until you see Kris in it. He's fabulous. . . . He's a star . . . and here he is. So, in the lingo of the movie, I say, 'All you motherfuckers have a great TIME!' " Allowing a pause for the thunderous applause to fade a bit, Barbra then yielded the stage to Kristofferson. Barbra returned to the stage to sing "The Way We Were," to a standing ovation. She continued with "The Woman in the Moon," and later in the evening came back with two backup singers to sing five more songs.

KRISTOFFERSON CLEANS UP

Kristofferson took one look at a rough cut of the film and decided to go on the wagon. But he defended Barbra: "All that crap about her was just crap," he insisted.

"In retrospect, I have a lot of gratitude to Barbra for some of the decisions she made," he would say years later. "Looking at the movie today, I can see a lot of opportunities she gave me, that weren't as obvious when I was drinking a quart and a half of tequila and a half a case of beer every day."

He told another interviewer: "I gained most of my confidence from *A Star is Born*. People who saw it came up to me and said 'You know, you got me right here,' pointing to their hearts. It proved to me that something I did in the picture worked. I saw moments in the film that made me feel good. It happened on screen the way I hoped it would. I don't dislike the film the way a lot of people did, and I feel I did a damn good job in it."

Kristofferson laid most of the blame for any *Star* shortcomings squarely on his director. "I used to think the endless changes on set-ups were because Barbra hadn't done her homework or just kept changing her mind," he said. "I didn't realize it was because Frank Pierson hadn't listened or remembered. He was out to lunch from the first day."

A clean and sober Kristofferson said: "I think we'd both find it easier to work with each other now, but I doubt that we ever will." (In fact, they did, in 1984 when Barbra asked him to appear in her "Left in the Dark" video.)

That March, while still on location with *Star*, Pierson received word that he had won an Academy Award for his screenplay for *Dog Day Afternoon*. Barbra called him that night to congratulate him, but mentally she had already written him off as a director. Directors Guild rules made it impossible to remove him, but Barbra had become convinced that it was up to her to get the picture made the way she and Jon envisioned it.

Jon was more open about his disappointment with Pierson. In one of their frequent flare-ups, Jon screamed "I'm sick of you. I'm waiting until the production is finished, then I'm going to punch you out."

A Star is Born wrapped that June, on schedule and under budget, but even Barbra acknowledged that making it had been a nightmare. The worst was yet to come: Barbra and director Pierson conflicted about the final editing and in keeping with the terms of his contract, Barbra took control of the film and proceeded to edit it to her satisfaction. She and Jon turned their pool house into an editing room and their tennis house into a fully equipped recording studio.

She worked there throughout the summer, taking a rare break in July to return to her Holmby Hills mansion to host a fundraising party for her longtime friend Bella Abzug. She also took time out to appear at the CBS records convention in Century City that August and tell them about the soundtrack album. Late that summer, as she was working night and day to cut the film properly, word reached her that the disgruntled

Frank Pierson had written a scathing article about the experience for *New York* and *New West* magazines. When Barbra saw an advance copy of the article she was stunned at what she viewed as his disloyalty, his breach of trust. "Pierson crucified an unfinished film!" she complained. She had always believed she was badly maligned by the press, but in all her years of dealing with reporters no other article had ever touched off such a deep sense of injustice in her.

She acknowledged that she wasn't always the most sensitive person on the set. "I have this problem with tact, I only know how to be direct," she told Pierson. But she had everything riding on *Star:* her career, her own money and Jon's, even their relationship. Together they immediately went into damage control and launched a publicity blitz to launch *Star* and counteract Pierson's article.

Even Kristofferson's wife, singer Rita Coolidge, lined up with the anti-Pierson forces. "Frank Pierson's story was an unethical betrayal of confidence. But worse than that, it was inaccurate," she charged. "It presented an image of Kris that had nothing to do with Kris. It seemed obvious to me that any stranger could read that article and tell that the man was wounded. He was so bitter from working with Barbra."

In October Barbra taped an interview with Barbara Walters at her Malibu ranch which would air on December 14. Barbra had first-rush approval, something no one else had ever gotten. Much of the segment was an extensive promotion for *A Star is Born,* including a few clips from the film. Walters took viewers on a tour of the rather small house, "This way we can clean it ourselves," Barbra told Walters. They visited Barbra's bathroom, "built with loving hands by Jon Peters," Walters noted.

But even Barbara Walters was impressed with their relationship. "Barbra's dog had run away and she was broken-

hearted," Walters told *People*. "He was very sweet and understanding."

In November, Barbra sat down with Lawrence Grobel for
an in-depth profile for *Playboy*. That November, Lawrence
Grobel reported in *Playboy* that he had watched Barbra edit
and dub the last seven minutes of her movie. "With her screen
image in front of us twenty feet high, Barbra fiddled inces-
santly with an electronic control board, bringing the drums
up, the guitars down, her voice out," he said. "She would stop
the film and have it run backward. She would hear things no
one else could—finding fault with a certain beat, a missed
stress. And although the engineers wanted to wrap up and go
on vacation, she remained and worked until exhaustion over-
took everyone." Barbra was full of fire and determined to
release the anger she felt at the way she had been treated in
the past. She was already braced for a backlash against her
and the movie because of Pierson's article.

"I have been accused of being ruthless," she said. "And, in
fact, it's my problem that I'm not ruthless enough. I *should*
have fired him." She ran into the age-old problem and complained: "I think that if a man did the same thing I did he
would be called thorough—while a woman is called a ball
breaker." She went on: "I am not a mean person. I don't like
meanness in anyone around me. Maybe I'm rude without being aware of it—that's possible."

"Why is the press so hostile to me?" she asked. At another
time she posed an even more complex question: "Why am I
so famous?" she asked him. "What am I doing right? What
are the others doing wrong?"

"I don't like the word superstar. It has ridiculous implica-
tions. These words—star, stuporstar, superstar, stupid star—

they're misleading. It's a myth, and the myths are a waste of time. They prevent progress."

Most of all, Barbra resented the way the press dismissed Jon as merely a hairdresser, merely her boyfriend. "I hired him because he's an excellent businessman who has great creative instincts," she insisted. "I'm no fool."

In fact, it was Peters who formulated the release and promotion strategy for *A Star is Born*. About her future with Jon, she was coy. When a journalist asked her how it felt to work with her husband, she smiled and answered: "Wonda-ful, but he's not my husband."

"Do you think he will be?" asked the reporter.

"He's not my husband *yet*," she said.

Was she hoping?

"Am I hoping?" Barbra smiled but did not answer.

"Is Jon hoping?"

"I hope so," she said.

But Barbra also insisted that "Marriage is not the most vital issue in our lives right now. Jon talks about it. I talk about it. But not at the same time."

STAR PREMIERE

Jon orchestrated the four million dollar publicity and marketing campaign to launch *Star*, beginning with the much-discussed photograph of the two stars by Scavullo. Jon was looking for "a kind of naked *Gone With The Wind*." According to the photographer, flown in to Los Angeles for the day at a cost of $50,000: "We tried it a couple of ways. Then they embraced and I told him to take off his shirt. Then I told her to lower her blouse . . ." One reporter said that "Scavullo made Barbra Streisand in the embrace of Kris Kristofferson look like a roman empress toying with her slave."

Columbia Records had planned to release the soundtrack

album in October, a month before the film came out. Jon talked them into postponing release to November to coincide with the premiere.

A Star is Born premiered in Westwood on December 18, and on December 23 at the Ziegfeld Theatre in New York. Among the guests was Muriel Choy, young Barbra's long-ago confidante. In between, Jon and Barbra also screened the film for a seminar at UCLA.

It received some pretty awful reviews: Pauline Kael called it "sentimental without being convincing for an instant," and Rex Reed dubbed it "a junk heap of boring ineptitude," but perhaps the most scathing assessment came from her one-time admirer Frank Rich. Now the drama critic for the New York Post, Rich declared that he put an end to his "love affair" with the star once and for all.

In a scathing essay, Rich wrote: "Even *Funny Lady* didn't prepare me for *A Star is Born,* the Streisand movie that recently rode into town on the largest wave of negative advance publicity to precede an American movie since *Cleopatra. A Star is Born* is truly the pits—it's the work of a madwoman. As I sat in the Ziegfeld Theatre watching this film, I realized that the image of Barbra Streisand on screen had lost all connection to the nineteen–year-old woman I'd first seen on stage almost fifteen years ago."

But unlike many others, Frank Rich did not blame Barbra's new lover. "Miss Streisand's behavior in her new film (her horrifying disembowelment of co-star Kris Kristofferson's winning performance through judicious editing, for instance) is exactly the same kind of behavior I saw her exhibit on stage in *Funny Girl*—well before she knew from hairdressers."

"Maybe she'll get away with this too . . . but for me everything valuable about Barbra Streisand has been lost. Not only is she an incompetent filmmaker, but she's throwing herself away as a performer."

Barbra was devastated. "I was in shock," she said. "It was like: Who's crazy? Can people call the movie brilliant, and can the same movie be called a piece of trash? Well, the audience is the only one who knows, the only one who can't be bought."

In fact, she was so upset that she didn't think she could face the post-screening party at New York's Tavern on the Green. It was Kristofferson himself who convinced her to go. During the festivities she slipped away for an interview with Geraldo Rivera, her Malibu neighbor who had become a close friend. The chat would air on his "Goodnight America" program on the ABC-TV network. "Pierson's article was so immoral, so unethical, so unprofessional, so undignified, with no integrity, totally dishonest, injurious," she said. "If anyone believes it, without examining who that person is, to try to put a black cloud over a piece of work before it's even released: that's the most important indication of who that person was." Pierson's article had united the three principals, and to celebrate, Jon gave Barbra a brooch with "Star" spelled out in diamonds.

In the end, Barbra and Jon had the last laugh. *Star* grossed $140,000,000 worldwide. In spite of terrible reviews, it would go on to become Barbra's biggest box-office success ever. "People are discovering the film for themselves and saying that the critics were all wrong," boasted Jon.

As the year 1976 ended, the soundtrack album for *A Star is Born* entered the *Billboard* charts a week after the film's release. Barbra's first platinum LP, the album sold over eight million copies, far more than any previous soundtrack albums, and it remains her biggest selling album to date.

MARRIAGE

Jon and Barbra could have chosen to cap their fairy-tale romance and generate even more publicity for *Star* by taking this time to get married, but they chose not to. According to Jon, he had already proposed twice and Barbra had turned him down. "I'm sure someday we'll get married—probably if a child comes along," he said. "She can have any man she wants. So it is obvious she hasn't chosen me because I am a schmuck."

Barbra considered marriage the ultimate trust, "a beautiful, romantic gesture." But she wanted to do it right. "It's the ultimate commitment, and if it happens, I want to be married in a beautiful antique, white dress; when I married Elliott, it was in Nevada and I wore a cotton dress."

They proposed to each other all the time, Barbra revealed, but it was always when the other wasn't in the mood to get married. "Jon and I don't discuss marriage," she said. "If it happens, it happens. I'm not particularly eager to rush into anything. Not because I'm anti-marriage or anything, but simply because I believe in leaving well enough alone. As far as I'm concerned, I've got everything now!"

Seventeen

Streisand Superman

"You've just finished playing a Jewish girl, now you want to play a Jewish boy?"
> —David Begelman's reaction to his client's wish to film "Yentl, the Yeshiva Boy."

After two years of intense concentration on *A Star is Born,* Barbra could afford to dedicate most of 1977 to personal growth.

Her life settled into a comfortable domesticity. She spent the week at her Holmby Hills mansion, and weekends at the Malibu ranch with Jon. Afternoons, she would pick up Jason after school in her Jaguar. Always restless, she was continuing to add to the Malibu property and to look at other houses as well. She even considered buying Gregory Peck's mansion in Brentwood and was impressed to see that he had her albums. When she noticed that the section label misspelled her name she was observed taking out a pen and crossing out the third A.

She studied philosophers like Krishnamurti and sought to

improve her mind and body through meditation, exercise, and nutrition. She rarely watched TV except for the nightly news and never read the newspapers, but she had begun to develop a deep concern for the state of the environment.

"THERE IS NO TRUTH. IT'S YOUR REALITIES VERSUS MINE"

Through Jon she had come to acknowledge her own reality as well as that of others. "There is no one truth," she proclaimed. "It's your realities versus mine and what we have to learn is to respect one another's realities and boundaries so that when you start arguing with someone, it's not an argument because each person sees it from his own point of view and you have to respect each other's reality." Together they were seeing a therapist Barbra considered a genius.

Barbra and Jon could comfortably go their separate ways and often did. His second film, the stylish *The Eyes of Laura Mars* would star Faye Dunaway and Tommy Lee Jones in a thriller about a fashion photographer with a psychic connection to a murderer. The picture was filming in New York early that year and Barbra often visited the set until it wrapped in March.

"NO MATTER WHAT I'VE DONE, MY ROOTS ARE IN THE MUSIC BUSINESS."

1977 would be the year that Barbra reestablished herself as the top pop singles female artist, with the *Star* soundtrack album moving into *Billboard*'s number one album spot that February and remaining in its Top 100 for the rest of 1977. "Evergreen," Barbra's second gold single, became her first international hit since "The Way We Were," and she recorded it in French, Italian, and Spanish.

At the Grammy Awards that February, Barbra presented the award for Record of the Year to George Benson for "This Masquerade." As she walked on stage she was greeted by thunderous applause. She told the audience how happy she was to be there, "because no matter what I've done, I feel my roots are in the music business."

In April she went back into the studio to begin recording her next album, *Streisand Superman,* and she released a new single, "My Heart Belongs to Me," that May.

Streisand Superman was released that June and went platinum by August. Jon's touch was all over this album, especially in the photos on the front and back covers that featured Barbra in short shorts, socks, and white T-shirt with the Superman logo across her chest.

The fetching cover photograph of Barbra was blown up for a giant billboard on Sunset Boulevard. Unfortunately, the sign became the target of tasteless vandals. In one episode a CBS records spokesperson reported that an archer had "shot an arrow with unerring accuracy into a rather unmentionable part of Barbra's anatomy." In November other hooligans splashed paint on the sign. There was still something about Barbra that left no observer indifferent.

RAY STARK

Ray Stark had sent Barbra several scripts to consider directing. Barbra had denied most of the quotes attributed to her in Frank Pierson's article, but she had been especially concerned about some comments about Ray Stark. Pierson quoted her as saying "Ray Stark used to bully me, the son of a bitch. I made him and he made millions from me, millions!" Barbra later told *Playboy,* "I don't want to hurt Ray. He got so hurt by one line that Pierson attributed to me, I felt terrible. We go through periods where we love and hate each other. He's a real character, an original."

It was now Barbra's turn to demonstrate her loyalty. In the decade since *Funny Girl,* Ray Stark had racked up a record as one of the most consistently commercial producers in Hollywood. He was still most closely associated with Columbia Pictures, which had distributed all his pictures with Barbra.

Stark's great friend, David Begelman, had also prospered. After representing Barbra for several years, he left the agenting business to become a film producer, but remained on good terms with Barbra. He and his wife Gladyce accompanied Barbra and Jon on the publicity tour for *Funny Lady,* and they were his guests at Columbia's Gala Fiftieth Anniversary party earlier in the year. He had green-lighted Jon's new non-Barbra project, *The Eyes of Laura Mars.*

So close was Begelman that he was one of the few who could tease her about her growing obsession with filming *Yentl.* After reading the short story in 1968, Barbra immediately called Begelman, her agent, to tell him that she had found her next film. When he heard the story's title—"Yentl, the Yeshiva Boy," there was a deadly silence at the other end of the line.

After Begelman recovered he said, "You've just finished playing a Jewish girl (Fanny Brice), now you want to play a Jewish boy?" Undeterred, Barbra would continue to develop her *Yentl* project while Begelman prospered as a producer.

That fall, however, Begelman's entire world was suddenly shaken when it was revealed that he was embroiled in a check forgery scandal. His longtime friend Stark and his former protégé, Sue Mengers, mounted an effort to salvage his reputation and his job. While Stark concentrated on the Columbia board, Sue Mengers lobbied the "creative community." According to David McClintick, author of "Indecent Exposure," which detailed the case, "Mengers urged her clients, friends, and acquaintances to send telegrams" to Columbia's chairman and board of directors. Barbra came through for Begelman, for Mengers and for Stark.

OSCARS/NEIL DIAMOND

That March 28, Barbra returned from Europe where she was still promoting *A Star is Born* to attend the Academy Awards. Although the film had scored a paltry number of nominations, mostly in the technical categories, she graciously agreed to sing "Evergreen." With her usual perfectionism, Barbra was the only performer who insisted on running through her entire number, testing lights and camera angles the day before the telecast.

This was the first time Barbra had performed at the Academy Awards and she also became the first woman to sing her own song there.

Moments after Barbra left the stage, Neil Diamond, her fellow Brooklynite and former classmate at Erasmus Hall, took the stage to present the Oscar for Best Original Song.

"Before I mention the winner," he said, "about three weeks ago I was talking to Barbra and I said, 'You know, I love your song so much that no matter who wins I'm going to read your name,' but I have to cancel out on that, Barbra. So, if I call your name out you actually won it, and if I don't . . . you wrote a terrific song the first time out." He then proceeded to open the envelope and joyfully announce the winner was "Evergreen." A delighted Barbra and co-writer Paul Williams started walking up the aisle.

"In my *wildest* dreams I could never, ever imagine winning

an Academy Award for writing a song," Barbra said as she
accepted her Oscar. "I'm very honored and excited. Thank
you all very much." Later, at the backstage press conference
Williams announced that that very day "Evergreen" had gone
gold.

EXIT MARTY ERLICHMAN

That fall, CBS Records planned to release a special five-LP
set retrospective of Barbra's career, from a demo of "Zing
Went the Strings of My Heart" that she had recorded at fourteen, to early club appearances at the Bon Soir and the Hungry
i and rare recordings such as her televised duet with Judy
Garland. The project was conceived by Marty Erlichman who
knew the material better than anyone else. Then suddenly the
project was canceled and so was the seventeen-year relationship between Marty and Barbra.

Many observers had been expecting it. Jon had gradually
taken up duties that had previously been Marty's. For years
Marty had been Barbra's sole liaison with her movie studio
and record company. While making *A Star is Born,* however
Jon, as producer, had solidified his relationships with Warner
and CBS records. It was an amicable split between Barbra
and Marty because he recognized that there was nothing he
could do. But as he turned over the reins to Jon the two men
clashed repeatedly.

"She was family," Erlichman said. "We had been together
since 1961. During those years I was a terrific manager. I
was giving her twenty-four hours of my day. And I couldn't
do that anymore. I was single then, and she was my child.
Now I'm married. I have my own family. I stayed with her
through *A Star Is Born*. Maybe she needed new directions.
Barbra and I are still close. We speak on the phone once a
week. As for Jon Peters? Even before I left he was calling

himself her manager. My thoughts on what he does and how he does it, well, they're not for publication."

RENEWING WITH CBS

One of Jon's first steps as Barbra's new manager was negotiating a new contract with CBS that December. The new agreement called for five albums in five years, plus a "greatest hits" package. Barbra would receive a $1.5 million guarantee for each album. Each album had a specified completion date and a bonus if delivered on time. To celebrate, Columbia threw a party for her in New York.

At the end of the year, she released *Barbra Streisand's Greatest Hits/Volume 2*, which included "You Don't Bring Me Flowers" and "My Heart Belongs to Me." In a typical review, the *Hollywood Reporter* said "This is a terrific 'Best of' package from the golden-throated girl, including many of her big single successes in recent years like 'The Way We Were,' 'Stoney End,' and the incomparable 'Evergreen.' It all kind of serves to say Streisand has a lot more to sing about and we can expect an endless flow of material from here."

For the release of *Laura Mars*, Barbra recorded "Love Theme from *The Eyes of Laura Mars* (Prisoner)" which was released in July 1978. "Some people have said they were disappointed I had Barbra sing the title track," Jon told *Variety*, "but she's a great singer and the song fit her perfectly." Barbra did not attend the premiere in New York, though, because she was already deep into preproduction planning for her next film, *The Main Event*.

Eighteen

The Main Event

"People have been unfair to Barbra . . . She's a delicately made creature, a great lady, and I would never have done *The Main Event* without her."

—Ryan O'Neal

1978 would be the year in which some old chemistry failed to ignite again, but in which Barbra would become a disco star.

In May Barbra released *Songbird,* an album of mainly lush ballads and proved once again that nobody did it better. "Streisand's gift—one that Liza Minnelli, Bette Midler, Jane Olivor, and a host of theatrically bent chanteuses vainly try to capture—is to elevate the old-fashioned romantic cliches of pop to near-operatic pitch, then to sustain that pitch with a combination of pyro-technical skill and sheer chutzpah," wrote critic Stephen Holden.

STARS SALUTE ISRAEL AT 30

Barbra had long admired former Israeli premier Golda Meir and wanted to do anything she could to help celebrate Israel's thirtieth anniversary that year. On May 8, she got her chance when she joined other celebrities for "The Stars Salute Israel at 30," a gala benefit concert broadcast from the Los Angeles Music Center and beamed via satellite to 2000 guests in a ballroom at the Jerusalem Hilton. Barbra sang "Tomorrow" from her new *Songbird* album, as well as "Happy Days are Here Again," and "People." At the conclusion, Barbra spoke to Golda Meir by telephone. This was a major thrill for Barbra. She found Meir "a marvelous *hamisch* woman—motherly and down to earth." In the finale, Barbra sang the Israeli national anthem "Hatikvah" ("The Hope") in Hebrew while silent audiences in Los Angeles and Jerusalem held candles.

Meanwhile, Jon was anxious to establish himself as a talent beyond Barbra's adviser. "I'm a businessman," he told *Variety*. "She's a genius, and I am not." By July he was also managing Geraldo Rivera and two fledgling rock bands.

THE MAIN EVENT

Barbra did not begin her next film project until that fall. The script for what eventually became *The Main Event* by Gail Parent and former boxer Andrew Smith, had been recommended to her by her agent, Sue Mengers. Once again Barbra returned to romantic comedy, starring as a successful perfume manufacturer who suddenly finds herself broke. Her only asset is a retired prizefighter whom she decides to manage back into top-level contention. Barbra was never very enthusiastic about the property, but it was a way for her to discharge her commitment to First Artists. And she could work with Jon again. He would be producing.

Jon's confidence was increasing with his experience. "*A Star is Born* was a labor of love, and you can't push love," he said. "Right now Barbra and I are getting off on working together. It doesn't interfere with our relationship—it enhances it. Everyone should be so lucky. People say I got this strange hold over Barbra. I do. It's called love." He characterized *The Main Event* as "not your usual fight picture . . . more a Madison Square Garden-variety love story."

Filming began October 2. The director was Howard Zieff, whose previous comedy, *House Calls,* Barbra had admired.

Zieff knew that Barbra had a reputation for being demanding. "People look at you in amazement when you say you've just directed Streisand," he recalls. "It gets around. 'Hey, he can handle movie stars and still bring movies in on time and on budget.' That speaks for itself in this town . . . I went in knowing it had to be made and I told myself it might as well be me making it."

Barbra had once likened her own work to prize-fighting. In 1967, on the set of *Funny Girl,* she told journalist Pete Hamill: "I was trying to decide how to describe my life to you. All these people patting you, and talking to you, and working you over. It's like being a fighter. A fighter between rounds."

Ryan was very excited about working with his former lover again. "I like her energy," he said. "It's vibrant and beautiful, and I think one of the most dynamic aspects of her personality."

As for Barbra, she thought that Ryan had "that rare ability to combine romance with comedy. Ryan is really a talented comedian. He does these falls and looks—something Cary Grant was also the master of." Actually, the part had been offered to Ryan when it was being considered for Goldie Hawn and Diana Ross, but he passed it up. Barbra called him herself and urged him to take it on. "Because, Ryan, if you don't want to do the part, I don't want to make the picture."

"If you're in it," her old flame answered, "I'll do it."

Once more, Barbra was attracted to material with relevance to her early life. In this case, the world of boxing stirred up memories of her stepfather, Louis Kind. She had wanted so much to please him and never had. Now she confided in Ryan: "You like the fights? My stepfather liked the fights. I always wanted his approval. He never liked me. He used to sit in his undershirt, drinking beer and watching the fights on television. And, you know, one time I crawled underneath the TV picture when I went by so I wouldn't interfere with his view. He never even noticed. He would *never* see me, he just stared at the fights."

"I'll never forget her telling me that," Ryan said. "I said, 'Whatever happened to him?' She said, 'I don't know. One day he just left and never came back. I thought it was my fault, and so did my mother.' " Barbra never saw her stepfather again.

The only person who wasn't quite overjoyed about the casting was Barbra's longtime lover and producer Jon Peters. "Am I cool about it?" he asked. "Hell, no."

Ryan could see that the intervening years since their first film together had wrought changes in Barbra. "In *What's Up, Doc?* we did what we were told," he said. "Peter Bogdanovich ran the show. This time we tried all kinds of things. She played the Bogdanovich role. Howard Zieff was under lots of pressure; I think he held up pretty well."

But Ryan was excited about repeating the chemistry. "I've known her intimately for years. I've watched her grow up. Let's say, I have a combination to the electric gate to her house on the movie star maps. We have a certain Pat and Mike teamwork. The goyim-Jewish thing works."

"The Main Event" wrapped December 15.

THE MAIN EVENT: THE ALBUM

Paul Jabara was an actor-turned-composer who had known Barbra casually since they were both making the Broadway rounds and auditioned together for *The Sound of Music*. Although they had crossed paths infrequently in the years since, Jabara's own professional breakthrough had not come until

1977 when he wrote "Last Dance" for Donna Summer. From that came an Oscar and a writing contract with First Artists.

"The reason I joined First Artists," he said, "was because I knew Barbra owned the company. Donna Summer and I were in *Hair* together with Diane Keaton—but they were my peers. I wanted to work with Barbra. She was the reason I got out of Brooklyn. There were things she was fighting for that I was fighting for also. I had this fantasy that when we met and worked together I'd be embraced." Soon he was handed a map to Barbra's Malibu ranch and arriving there found himself and his collaborators, Bob Esty and Bruce Roberts, deep in conferences with Barbra, seeking to write a theme song for *The Main Event*. Barbra was still not sure she wanted to sing it. That November 1978 he teamed with Bruce Roberts to write and produce a demo of their song, "The Main Event." It was played for Barbra, but she was not enthusiastic.

She had been working on her own theme, a ballad, and the Bergmans and David Shire had been working on a third possible theme, another lush ballad. But Barbra and Jon came to believe that the comedy needed an upbeat theme, and with disco in its heyday, they decided it was a good time for her to try a dance tune.

Jabara, Roberts, and arranger Bob Esty journeyed out to Barbra's house in Malibu where they played the song for her again. She was still not enthusiastic, until she saw eleven-year-old Jason's reaction: he started singing along upstairs.

"He was the one who really sold it, he loved it and she listened to him," said Roberts.

Barbra's single of "The Main Event"/"Fight" would become her fourth gold single. It would also be her only contribution to the soundtrack album and CBS records executives were reportedly disappointed when they learned that the *Main Event* soundtrack album was a collection of work by Frankie Valli, Loggins and Messina, and some lesser known artists.

But they had underestimated Jon's marketing genius. Barbra's "The Main Event"/"Fight" single would be released in May, a month before the film, in a seven-inch format for Top 40 stations and record stores and a twelve-inch version exclusively for disco stations and disco and gay clubs. "The gays love Barbra," Jon declared. "They'll eat up the longer version; but they won't be able to get it in the stores." To get the disco version, fans would have to buy the soundtrack album.

After that experience, Barbra continued to trust Jason's judgment when it came to the new music. Her next project, "Wet," was a concept album in which all the songs related to water, from rain to tears. They included "Hurricane Joe," "Niagara," "Kiss Me in the Rain," and "I Ain't Gonna Cry Tonight." Jabara and Roberts wanted to team Barbra in a duet with Donna Summer. Once again, Barbra trusted young Jason, now twelve-and-a-half. The boy wanted to meet Donna Summer.

The resulting duet, "No More Tears (Enough is Enough)," teaming as it did two of the biggest female singers in the business, was released in October 1979 and went gold the following February.

BARRY GIBB: "GUILTY"

Barbra's next creative teaming would be with Barry Gibb of the Bee Gees. Fresh from the enormous success of the *Saturday Night Fever* soundtrack, Gibb was looking for new and more challenging projects as a producer and songwriter.

It took record executive Charles Koppelman and Jon two years to bring Barbra and Barry together.

At first Barry was not sure he wanted to get involved on an album with the legendary Streisand. He had heard the usual stories about the difficult and demanding superstar.

Gibb even checked in with Neil Diamond to get the real truth about working with her. Diamond had nothing but good things to say about Barbra, so Gibb decided to go forward. Actually, there was another reason, he admitted: "My wife told me to do it or she'd divorce me!"

With the songwriting help of his brothers Maurice and Robin, Barry gave Barbra a collection of new songs unified by the concept of love-as-trial.

That February 1980 they began recording. Barbra had never worked this way before. Barry did most of the instrumental tracks in Miami before they got together to record her vocals. This was a far cry from the recording techniques of the 1960s when Barbra sang live with an orchestra in an old desanctified church that Columbia Records had turned into a studio.

Barbra found Barry's lyrics much more abstract than those she usually gravitated toward, but the melodies were so compelling that she decided to go along with them, and with him.

"We treaded on eggs until we actually got to know one another," Gibb said, but he discovered that "working with her turned out to be wonderful. She wanted my ideas and she gave me a lot of leeway—but she also wanted me to listen to her ideas, which I was glad to do. . . . And she was a hard worker. She'd work from 7:00 A.M. until late into the night and during the breaks she'd be working on the script of Yentl."

According to Barry Gibb, his only problem with Barbra was keeping her "away from the food so she'd keep singing!"

Barbra and Barry were magic together and the first single off the album, "Woman in Love," on which Barbra sings alone, was released that August, selling two million copies. The album, *Guilty,* was released the following month and would go on to become her best-selling LP ever, until *The Broadway Album.* The album included two duets with Barry Gibb, one of which, "Guilty"/"Life Story," a duet with Barry, became her second gold single from the album.

"I wanted to produce her best-selling album, and I accomplished that," Barry Gibb said later. "But, to me, none of the

songs on [*Guilty*] match the greatness of some of the songs
she's done with the Bergmans or 'People' or 'Evergreen.' I
would love to work with her again." But although Barry had
a lot of ideas for Barbra and felt they would work together
even better because they knew each other better, they have
not collaborated again.

Guilty was nominated for a Grammy as Album of the Year,
and "Woman in Love" was nominated as both Record of the
Year and Song of the Year, Barbra was nominated for Best
Pop Vocal Performance for her work on it, and she and Barry
were nominated for Best Pop Performance by a Duo or Group
with Vocal. They took home nothing. Newcomer Christopher
Cross swept the awards with his debut album *Sailing*, and
Bette Midler garnered the year's best female pop singer for
"The Rose," the title song to her movie.

Barbra had no regrets. "I must say I had the best time *ever*
making this record, as well as the easiest. I even had fun doing
the photos for the album cover. Barry was a wonderful producer—also the cutest—and *Guilty* became my bestselling album to date. Thanks, Barry."

"YOU DON'T BRING ME FLOWERS"

The story behind Barbra's next hit single must be unique
in the annals of record history. The song was written by Neil
Diamond and Alan and Marilyn Bergmen as the theme for a
TV sitcom that never made it to the air. Diamond recorded it
and so did Barbra. But it was a Louisville, Kentucky, disc
jockey, Gary Guthrie, who noticed that Barbra's version of
"You Don't Bring Me Flowers" was in the same key as Neil
Diamond's version. By playing them together, the disc jockey
produced a "duet" and the station and record stores were del-
uged with requests for a record that didn't exist.

Soon Barbra and Diamond teamed up for real and recorded

it together on October 17. The single turned out to be Barbra's biggest hit ever.

As Barbra closed out 1978, she found herself more popular than ever. One of her longtime admirers, writer James Spada, even announced plans for a magazine, *Barbra,* that would "chronicle this remarkable career." The nationally circulated quarterly was intended to present "a fair and accurate account of one of the most fascinating women in theatrical history."

Nineteen

Barbra's Dream: *Yentl*

"Jon gave me the challenge. He told me straight out
I'd never make the picture."

—Barbra

Barbra started 1979 with an accolade from *Seventeen*
magazine: in January the magazine's readers chose her as
the woman they most admired.

That March Barbra attended the AFI Salute to Alfred
Hitchcock at the Beverly Hilton and was photographed with
Sean Connery.

June 20, Barbra and Jon gave Hollywood its first gasless
premiere asking guests at the opening to arrive by gasless
means, e.g. roller skates, bicycles, golf carts, etc. *The Main
Event* opened in New York two days later.

THE STREISAND DERRIERE

In *The Main Event*, fans and critics alike began to notice
an alarming focus on the Streisand derriere. "When she's
not chattering like a hypertensive chipmunk, she's fanny

waggling," complained a reviewer for the Akron *Beacon Journal*. "Although her rear end seems reasonably decorative and probably is quite comfortable to sit on, it does little to advance the plot and may slow it down a bit," said the Detroit *Free Press*. Critic James Wolcott claimed she "sodomistically bent over for the camera."

NUDE PHOTOS

Barbra was further upset that year when ten-year-old photographs from her never-seen topless scene in *The Owl and the Pussycat* turned up in *High Society* magazine. A furious Barbra filed papers seeking to block publication and sought $5 million in damages. The court ordered publisher Gloria Leonard to send out telegrams to her five hundred distributors asking that they tear the pictures out of the magazines.

YENTL

For the last ten years Barbra had also been examining ways she could turn "Yentl, the Yeshiva Boy" into a film. By now she was supposed to be a powerful woman and a bankable star, but her pet project was rejected by every major studio. "I guess I couldn't blame them," she acknowledged. "On the surface *Yentl* was anything but commercial—me, a first-time director telling a story about a Jewish girl at the turn of the century in Eastern Europe who dresses up as a boy in order to study Talmud!"

But for Barbra, it was much more than that. "It was about a woman's right to be all that she could be," she said, and she had to make it.

Very few others understood her vision, not even the author of the story himself.

"What do you know about Poland, the Talmud?" the elderly Issac Bashavis Singer told her. "You're an actress. Make a movie about acting!"

Undeterred, she had proceeded to commission a script. And another. And another. Since 1968 the script had been rewritten eight times. It seemed to take forever to get the screenplay she wanted. Singer's story was misanthropic and downbeat. Barbra envisioned a movie that would be feminist and uplifting. "A poem to my father."

This vision was not shared by the powers in Hollywood. By 1979 she had offered it to six different studios. They all turned her down. No one believed that the public would sit still for a film in which an Orthodox Jewish woman marries another Orthodox Jewish woman, or that Barbra, now 37, could play a teenage boy on the big screen.

Barbra found herself auditioning again. She and Michel Legrand and Marilyn and Alan Bergman put together a tape of their score to help studio executives better understand the project. Among the songs on the tape were: "Papa, Can You Hear Me?" which expressed Yentl's longing for her beloved father and asked forgiveness for the charade she was about to begin; "The Moon and I" (not included in the film) which grew out of Barbra's fascination with the idea of the moon exerting an influence on women, just as it does on the tides, and "A Piece of Sky" which made it to the film's finale when Yentl's search for a new life sends her to the New World.

It had been a Hollywood adage: "Give me Barbra Streisand and five songs, and I'll get a movie deal." But everyone turned down *Yentl* and Barbra was mystified. "You'd think because I've got a pretty successful track record they'd have agreed. I have produced or co-produced other movies that have been on budget. I don't have a reputation for going over budget. They were afraid of my perfectionism, I know that. And studio executives don't like the idea that actors also like to direct sometimes."

Barbra did not think that the fact she was a woman in a business run by men was the source of the problem. "I don't think it had anything to do with my being a woman," she said. "But I do think it had to do with being a first-time director and wanting to go off to make a period film in Eastern Europe. That would make anybody nervous."

Time was running out. She was nearing forty, and, she told Wayne Warga, "I was too tired to make it into a *should* do, or saying, 'If I had more courage, I'd do that.' It was time to put up or shut up. I finally realized that I had to tackle it. I wanted to take the full responsibility for its success or failure. I could no longer blame anyone but myself. There is no cop-out on this one."

By 1979 Barbra almost believed that her dream would never be fulfilled. And then, her father himself spoke to her.

"I had never seen my father's grave," she told *People* magazine, "until one day my brother took me there. After 35 years it was a strange experience. But that night I had a much stranger experience. My brother invited a medium, a nice, ordinary-looking Jewish lady with blond hair, to his house. We sat around a table with all the lights on and put our hands on it. And then it began. The table started to spell out letters with its legs. Pounding away. Bang, bang, bang! Very fast, counting out letters. Spelling M-A-N-N-Y, my father's name, and then B-A-R-B-R-A. I got so frightened I ran away. Because I could feel the presence of my father in that room! I ran into the bathroom and locked the door. When I finally came out, the medium asked. 'What message did you have?' and the table spelled out S-O-R-R-Y. Then the medium asked, 'What else do you want to tell her?' And it spelled S-I-N-G and then P-R-O-U-D.

"It sounds crazy but I know it was my father who was telling me to be brave, to have the courage of my convictions, to *sing proud!* And for that word S-O-R-R-Y to come out—I mean, God! It was his answer to all that deep anger I had always felt about his dying."

"After that I never wanted to go to a psychic again," Barbra has confessed. "It was enough for me somehow to believe my father was speaking to me, was telling me to make this movie. Who knows? It might have been my own energy wanting me to make this movie. I think if I'd made it any time before this, I would have been much more judgmental. I would have found a way of putting men down, somehow, or of expressing my anger that I didn't get to have my own father. And know that he didn't die because I was a bad girl or anything like that. He died because he was sick, and he loved me and he was proud of me. It took me a long time to realize that. It was as though making this film was a way of working out my relationship to my father. To me he now exists. I always felt during my life that I had taken on his persona, that I was carrying on my father's life by making something of myself. That's why I dedicated the film to him and to all fathers."

Once Barbra had contacted her father, everything began to fall into place. United Artists came up with a $14.5 million budget—which meant that she would be working for Director's Guild minimum. And Streisand the actress would be getting a mere $3 million for her services.

"I was terrified I would fail," she told people. "But I was tired of playing it safe. I had already spent $500,000 of my own on *Yentl.* How many things do you believe in with that kind of passion?"

Yet Barbra was also feeling tremendously conflicted. *Yentl* would be her homage to her late father. But it would impact on the two most important living men in her life: Jon and Jason.

If she made the film on UA's tight budget it would mean filming in England and Europe and that would mean more than a year away from Jason, now twelve. She asked her son: "If I make the picture, will you come with me and go to school in London?" Jason declined. He did not want to leave his school and his friends. Barbra's therapist told her it was a good time for him to separate from his mother. "I had to let go," Barbra says.

Making the film in Europe would also mean a separation from Jon Peters. They had been living together for nearly eight years and with the success of pictures like *Missing* and *Flashdance,* he had established himself as an important producer in his own right. Their relationship still fascinated observers.

"He's a predator," a former Peters colleague told *People,* "Sharp, imaginative, and vulgar. But he's been important to Barbra because he's said no to her. They fought like tigers. Most of the time they lived on an adrenaline high."

Barbra differed. "He's very strong," she said. "but he's also sensitive and creative. And he has a great zest for life. He loves to build things and so do I." They built five homes in different styles on their twenty-four acre ranch in Malibu. "We each built our own," Barbra explained, "because we fought too much when we built our first one together."

It was ultimately Jon's skepticism that galvanized Barbra to commit to filming *Yentl.* "Jon gave me the challenge. He told me straight out I'd never make the picture."

On the set, she amazed cast and crew with her energy. "She never got more than four hours sleep," said co-star

Mandy Patinkin, "and usually three. We were concerned for her. Yet she never flagged and looks wonderful on film. Some mysterious power sustained her." Barbra said simply, "It was my father. He watched over me."

ISAAC BASHEVIS SINGER

One man who did not share the general public's enthusiasm for Barbra's work was the author of the original story, Isaac Bashevis Singer.

Singer especially loathed the musical elements. "As a matter of fact, I never imagined Yentl singing songs," he wrote in the *New York Times*. "The passion for learning and passion for singing are not much related in my mind. There is almost no singing my works."

HEBREW STUDIES

With her immersion in *Yentl* came a deeper immersion in her own Jewish roots. As Jason approached his thirteenth birthday, Barbra decided that he should be bar mitzvahed and she and Elliott met with Rabbi Daniel Lapin of the Pacific Jewish Center to discuss it. The rabbi encouraged her to spend a year studying Judaism along with her son.

As part of her renewed interest in Judaism, that May 1980 Barbra donated a substantial amount to the Pacific Jewish Center, an orthodox synagogue in Venice, California. The unreported, but substantial, amount was enough to underwrite twenty percent of the congregation's budget for its forty-four-student day school for the next five years.

"Miss Streisand's generosity couldn't have come at a better time," said a synagogue spokesman. "We really needed the money."

In return for Barbra's generosity, the school was renamed
for her father, Emanuel Streisand. "This is a school of moral
and ethical excellence, and we're proud that my father's
name, his thoughts, and his life will be a part of it," said
a proud Barbra.

On January 5, 1980, a proud Barbra sat in the Pacific
Jewish Center synagogue in Venice as Jason Gould stood on
the *bima* with his father and paternal grandfather. A lavish
party followed at the Malibu ranch with one table of strictly
kosher delicacies and another table of Chinese. Diana Kind
sang for the guests.

Barbra was denying published rumors that she and Jon
had split up. The latest story, as reported by columnist Jack
Martin in the *New York Post,* claimed that they had last seen
each other just a few days earlier at Jason's bar mitzvah.

After the party, according to Martin, Barbra had driven
home to her Holmby Hills mansion, leaving Jon in Malibu.

"I don't know whether the split will wind up being permanent—it could last another week, a month—or possibly
forever," a close friend of Peters was reported as saying.

"But it's all quite amicable—they're not at each other's
throats."

In any case, Jon was doing all he could to help Barbra
get her dream project made, but by now even he was beginning to tire of it. *Yentl* was now in development at Orion
and when drastic cutbacks there put it in turnaround it was
widely assumed that the project would go to Polygram where
Jon had a production deal. But he didn't want Barbra to
make *Yentl,* he wanted to see her undertake an international
concert tour. She had just turned down a $2 million offer
to make a one-shot appearance at Wembley Stadium in En-

gland. Barbra insisted she wanted to make important films; Jon shot back that she could not make any such films without his help. It was the beginning of the end.

BERGMAN TRIBUTE

On June 1, with the aid of a swami backstage, Barbra temporarily conquered her stage fright and gave a rare public performance at an ACLU tribute to Marilyn and Alan Bergman at the Dorothy Chandler Pavilion in Los Angeles. As unofficial mistress of ceremonies Barbra opened the show by humming "The Way We Were," behind a curtain. As the curtain rose to reveal her, she paused to acknowledge two minutes of applause and shouts of "We Love You, Barbra," before launching into "After the Rain." "You really have to be in love to write lyrics like that," she said. "You're going to hear many more before the evening is out." At the conclusion of the evening Barbra returned to sing "Summer Me, Winter Me," accompanied by Michel Legrand at the piano. "Michel," she joked, "you write the most extraordinary melodies. If you were only Jewish, they'd have an evening like this for you, too!"

This was followed by three more songs before Barbra moved into her big surprise, singing a few bars of "You Don't Bring Me Flowers," before pausing and inviting Neil Diamond up from the audience.

ALL NIGHT LONG

The film that ended Barbra's relationship with Sue Mengers was *All Night Long,* a winsome comedy in which Gene Hackman was cast as the middle-aged manager of an all-night drugstore who has a romance with a sexy younger woman.

Filming had started on April 14. On May 13, Universal

announced that Lisa Eichhorn was being replaced by—Barbra Streisand. Director Tramont said only that "the part was too much of a stretch for Lisa."

The director, Jean-Claude Tramont, was married to Mengers, the star was Gene Hackman, and Barbra was paid a mere $4 million plus fifteen percent of the profits, for her supporting role; a role she only took as a favor to Mengers.

Twenty

A Brief Detour: *All Night Long*

"No one talks Barbra into doing *anything.*"
—Sue Mengers

Late in the summer of 1981, while she was deep in preproduction for *Yentl,* Barbra was approached by Columbia Records. The previous year had been a disastrous one for the record industry in general and Columbia had a number of disappointing releases. For the end of the year the company needed a guaranteed winner—a Streisand album. Of course Barbra complied, coming up with "Memories" what is essentially a "greatest hits" package that included mostly ballads and "Enough is Enough," plus a new version of "Lost Inside of You" (from *A Star is Born*), and two new ballads by Andrew Lloyd Webber: "Memory" and "Comin' In and Out of Your Life."

ALL NIGHT LONG

According to Considine, when Sue Mengers married Jean-Claude Tramont in 1973, Barbra hired a symphony orchestra and spent three days recording French and Jewish love songs. She made one copy of the session and presented it to the newlyweds. By 1981 agent and client had become synony-mous, inseparable. Barbra had not hesitated to step into a sup-porting role in *All Night Long* to help Sue and Jean-Claude out, but that was the beginning of the end of their relationship, personal and professional. And by the end of the year they would no longer be speaking.

By March, it was clear that *All Night Long* was a dud. After disappointing previews it was quietly sent into general release. Although some critics praised Barbra's work, the consensus was that she was miscast. Ads featuring a madcap Barbra slid-ing down a firehouse pole gave moviegoers the impression they were going to see a Streisand vehicle. When they dis-covered that she only had a few scenes they did not hesitate to ask for their money back. Soon word was out that Mengers was no longer representing Barbra.

"Barbra believed that Sue talked her into doing *All Night Long*," Liz Smith reported.

"No one talks Barbra into doing *anything*. She is a girl who makes up her own mind," replied Mengers.

It could have been the failure of *All Night Long*, it could have been that Barbra agreed to work for much less than her regular fee and to accept second billing, only to discover her agent was taking her full commission. It could have been Jon, who believed she didn't need an agent with him around. Jon, however, was not inclined to take advantage of the rift. "No one bats a home run all the time," he said. "Barbra took a gamble and it didn't pay off."

But the real reason for the rift was more likely Barbra's new obsession—Sue Mengers did not share Barbra's feelings about *Yentl*. And Barbra's drive to make the film had become so single-minded that there was no room in her life for anyone who didn't support it.

By now Barbra had a commitment from United Artists for her to write, direct, produce, and star in *Yentl*, with production to begin the following February. But she agreed to a spartan $14.5 million budget and had to yield script approval, some casting approval and the final cut.

By 1982 Jon had established himself in his own right. He had been associated with such enormously successful films as *Caddyshack, Missing,* and *Flashdance.* He had mellowed personally as well, which was clear that December when he and Barbra encountered photographers. "Now if you just hold still for a minute and let them get their pictures, they'll leave you alone," he told her when they were spotted arriving at the Mayfair Regent in New York, returning from the premiere party for his production of *Six Weeks,* which starred Dudley Moore and Mary Tyler Moore.

Much has been said about Peters' effect on Barbra, but few have recognized that she influenced him physically as well as professionally. He gradually metamorphosized into a well-groomed, clean-cut, and rather dapper businessman.

Barbra completed most of the *Yentl* soundtrack before the start of filming. She would be the only character singing and the musical numbers were intended to reveal what was going on inside Yentl's head.

Yentl started principal photography at Lee International Studios in Middlesex, England, on April 14, just weeks before she was to turn forty.

Far from being overworked, Barbra found that she thrived on wearing four hats. "I found that doing more than one job was beneficial," she said. "Each job served the other. Put it this way, there's four less people to disagree. Everyone gets along, you see? The actress doesn't fight with the director, the director doesn't disagree with the producer, the producer doesn't argue with the writer."

Her stars loved their director. "She was demanding, yet flexible and compassionate, with the gentleness of a woman," reported Mandy Patinkin. And Amy Irving, whose part re-

quired her to share a tender kiss with Yentl, said she was
"pretty excited. I mean, I'm the first female to have a screen
kiss with Barbra Streisand! She refused to rehearse, but after
the first take she said, 'It's not so bad. It's like kissing an
arm.' I was a little insulted, because I believed so much that
she was a boy that I'd sort of fallen in love with her."

Jon joined Barbra in Czechoslovakia where she shot exterior
scenes. He was appalled at the primitive conditions. "Barbra
never noticed," he said. "There were flies as big as beetles
but they never bothered her. She just swatted them."

Production wrapped in London that October. The film had
gone $1 million over budget and Barbra was under enormous
pressure to finish it or be forced to turn it over to the insur-
ance company which would then turn it over to another filmmaker to complete. By driving herself day and night she
managed to complete it in the six weeks she was allotted.
Returning to Hollywood, Barbra then immersed herself in editing the film.

Stephen Spielberg, then involved with Amy Irving, was
completing a film on the same lot and Barbra invited him, as
someone she greatly respected, to view a rough cut. When
Barbra told a reporter that he had advised her "not to change
a frame," this was misinterpreted and grew into a rumor that
he was editing the film for her.

With justifiable pride, Barbra had shared this story with an
interviewer from the *L.A. Times,* only to see it distorted in
print. The *L.A. Times* reported only that she had gotten 'advice' from Spielberg but not what it was. "I was so devastated
by what they did, by how they tried to diminish me as a
woman, that I did not direct a movie for eight years," Barbra
has said. "So devastated that I actually forgot it. . . . I forgot
the pain of it."

It would take a long time for that wound to heal.

Even years later, Barbra would say, "The pain was enor-

mous when I thought, 'How did they leave out the advice?'
It was like saying 'Well, this woman couldn't have done it
without the help of a man.' The man saw a finished movie.
You know what I'm saying? It just doesn't make sense."

"WE ARE THE BEST OF FRIENDS"

In March of 1983, when Barbra went off to London to
present the Best Picture prize to *Gandhi* at the British Film
Awards, Jon stayed behind in Malibu where Liz Smith found
him. He called the rumors that his relationship with Barbra
was at an end "lies," and said they still spoke four or five
times a day when they were apart.

"Our relationship is closer than ever," he assured Smith.
"We are the best of friends. We are still in business together
in some respects, but we are not living together. I love Barbra
dearly and I think she feels the same way about me. We've
been together ten years and we have raised two beautiful children together—her son, Jason, and my boy, Christopher."

Both he and Barbra kept heavy work schedules, but he assured Smith that Barbra was "having the time of her life working on *Yentl.*" He even hinted at plans to tape a live concert,
possibly in Madison Square Garden or Israel that October.

And in New York, where Elliott Gould was filming *My Dar-
ling Shiksa* with Shelley Winters and Sid Caesar, Barbra's former husband told a reporter that he wanted to team with her in
a screen version of the hit musical *They're Playing Our Song.*
"Isn't that a great idea?" he told Stephen Silverman of the *New
York Post.* "It's Neil Simon's." Simon had written the book for
the 1979 Broadway hit, loosely based on the love-hate personal
and professional relationship of the show's composer Marvin
Hamlisch and lyricist Carole Bayer Sager. No doubt Elliott saw
parallels with his own relationship with Barbra.

On October 12 a song from *Yentl,* "The Way He Makes

Me Feel," was released as a single but made small waves. This was followed by the soundtrack album, dedicated to "my mother for understanding the dedication to my father."

That October 29 Barbra returned to New York in Warner chairman Steve Ross's private jet and was escorted by Pierre Trudeau at the music industry's division of the United Jewish Appeal dinner at the Sheraton Centre in New York. She was honored as their Man of the Year for her deep commitment to the Jewish community.

After almost a year of post-production, *Yentl* premiered simultaneously at the Cinerama Dome Theatre in Los Angeles and in New York on November 16. Barbra attended the Los Angeles affair, arriving on the arm of Jon Peters. Reviews were mostly positive. Isaac Bashevis Singer was emphatic in his distaste: "The leading actress must make room for others to have their say and exhibit their talents," he decreed. "No matter who you are, you don't take everything for yourself. I must say that Miss Streisand was exceedingly kind to herself. The result is that Miss Streisand is always present, while poor Yentl is absent."

On the eve of the premiere of *Yentl*, Barbra was pensive. Releasing her movie would mean the end of a sixteen-year obsession. And she was thoughtful about the whole process of creation.

"To me, the most creative experience I've ever had was being pregnant," she told Wayne Warga. "This is the second most creative experience: directing a film. It is all a very strange feeling. When my son was inside my belly, he was only mine. As soon as he was born, he belonged to the world, he was his own person. It's the same thing with this movie. In a way, I wish I never had to show it."

She was also poised for some criticism—especially about the ending, which she had changed from Singer's original story.

END OF JON AND BARBRA

Barbra's relationship with Jon would become a casualty of filming. He had been closely involved with the project almost from inception. He had been one of the great champions of the film. But his own commitments and Barbra's growing independence changed things. Yet, even when she was shooting the film in Czechoslovakia, Jon would fly in from time to time to lend his support.

"We're separated," she told reporters. "But I look at it another way: We lasted nine years. In this town that's an accomplishment."

Barbra was candid about the separation when she sat with Geraldo Rivera for an interview on *20/20:* "I had to go away. I had to leave him. . . . I had to go away to Europe and be my own person and help myself, because Jon actually protected me a lot, kept me insulated. . . . I needed to protect myself; I needed to see if I was strong enough mentally, physically, emotionally to succeed in this project."

Asked if they might resume their old relationship, Barbra was vague. "I dunno," she told Rivera. "It's for the fates—you know?"

"By the time we had been together for eight years, our relationship had reached a turning point. We were butting horns because I was passionately involved in *Yentl* and neglecting him. We had also been too dependent on each other. And you come to resent dependency. We needed to be apart."

Barbra was philosophical about the end of the relationship. "Before I was afraid to be alone. There was a void inside me. Now I have *myself.* I feel filled from within."

Geraldo Rivera conducted the interview at the Malibu ranch and wrote later, "Actually, calling the place a 'ranch' is like Vanderbilt calling his Newport mansion a 'cottage,'" going on to describe a modern-day San Simeon: "a golf course-sized property that occupies the entire end of Malibu Canyon. There are five major structures on the spread, including the original ranch-style house, a peach-colored California contemporary, a Victorian-themed wooden house. Barbra's fabulously authentic art deco delight, and the property manager's house."

Although they no longer lived together, Barbra and Jon still talked every day and had many business and personal interests, including the ranch, in common.

Rivera asked Barbra, "What about you and Jon, Babs, did you have to make a conscious choice . . . ?"

"My work or my personal life?" she responded.

"Really."

"Yes, I did. And I chose my work."

"I DON'T LIKE MY PICTURE TAKEN"

"I don't like my picture taken," Barbra told Rivera on *20/20*. "I feel like the Africans—you know, who believe when somebody takes your picture they take a little bit of your soul. It makes me feel like an object, an image—things I think I am not."

In view of her loathing for picture-taking, it's interesting to note that many of the men in Barbra's love have demonstrated their love with memorable clashes with photographers. There was Elliott who was sued by a photographer. Ryan O'Neal. Jon broke a foot in another fracas.

Twenty-one

Barbra Goes Back to Her Roots

"Barbra Streisand has one of the two or three best voices in the world of singing songs."

—Stephen Sondheim

On January 28, 1984, Barbra received two awards at the 41st Golden Globe Awards for *Yentl:* Best Director and Best Musical film. But this was followed by Isaac Bashevis Singer's devastating critique in the *New York Times*. "My story was in no way material for a musical, certainly not the kind Miss Streisand has given us," he said. "Let me say: one cannot cover up with songs the shortcomings of the direction and acting." Singer especially loathed the ending. "Weren't there enough yeshivas in Poland or in Lithuania where she could continue to study?" he asked. "Was going to America Miss Streisand's idea of a happy ending for *Yentl?* What would Yentl have done in America? Worked in a sweatshop twelve hours a day when there is no time for learning? Would she try to marry a salesman in New York, move to The Bronx or Brooklyn and rent an apartment with an icebox and dumbwaiter?"

A deluge of responses followed, and most of them supported Barbra. "I was shocked to realize that Mr. Singer is a

mean-spirited, ungenerous, and cranky man. I am thrilled that
Barbra Streisand lives dangerously and breaks ground," she
wrote. "Why did you sell it to the movies? I love Mr. Singer's
work," she finished, "but I am dazzled by Barbra Streisand's
valor and passion and aspiration. It made my heart burst with
pleasure."

Support like that must have been a small comfort to Barbra
on February 16 when the nominations for the Academy
Awards were announced and she was ignored. *Yentl* had garnered four nominations: two for songs, one for score, and one
for Amy Irving for Best Supporting Actress.

February 22, Jon Peters sold Barbra all his interest in the
Malibu compound, sealing their break-up. But he continued
as her manager and urged her to get back into the recording
studio.

Barbra was in England promoting *Yentl* when the Academy
Awards were held that year, but when she learned that Michael
Legrand and the Bergmans had won she immediately sent
them a message of congratulations. In her acceptance speech,
Marilyn Bergman pointedly mentioned Barbra: "I'm very
grateful for this," she said. "I'm very grateful too for the
privilege and experience of having worked on *Yentl* which is
a story of a woman with a dream, a woman with a struggle.
And life has a way of imitating art in very interesting ways.
We worked in an atmosphere of creativity, of collaboration,
of excitement, energy, synergy . . . that allowed us to do our
best work, I think. And for that I thank Barbra Streisand."

Michel Legrand added: "We spent years of love, and I'm
ready to do it again anytime."

Meanwhile, Barbra traveled from London to Paris to Rome
to Hamburg and finally Tel Aviv, greeted by adoring crowds
everywhere.

That April, Barbra went to Jerusalem to open a new study
center at Hebrew University, funded in part by her and dedi-

cated to her late father, Emanuel. "I'm so glad that women can now study Jewish philosophy without having to disguise themselves as men," she joked at the ceremony.

Earlier, she had paid a courtesy call on Prime Minister Yitzhak Shamir and attended the Israeli premiere of *Yentl*. "In Hollywood, a woman can be an actress, a singer, a dancer—but don't let her be too much more," she said when asked about her failure to gain Oscar recognition for her efforts.

In June, Barbra watched with Elliott as Jason graduated from the progressive Crossroads High School in Santa Monica. Jason had just completed his first short, noncommercial film—starring his father. Jason filmed his home movie at Barbra's Holmby Hills mansion, and it included appearances by his mother, father, Grandmother Diana, Aunt Roz, and was titled *It's Up to You*.

RICHARD BASKIN: ICE CREAM HEIR

That September, Barbra cut her first rock video: "Left in the Dark," written by Jim Steinman. Although the lyrics were about a woman waiting in bed for her faithless lover, Barbra insisted, "I would never wait in bed for anyone I *knew* was cheating on me." The script was changed so that Barbra's character would find her lover in bed with another woman and leave *him* waiting alone in the dark. The lover would be played by Kris Kristofferson and the video was taped in Los Angeles on September 24. The single was released two days later and the video came out the following month. Results were disappointing, and "Left in the Dark" never made it into *Billboard*'s Top Ten.

That September, Barbra was photographed with the new man in her life, composer Richard Baskin, an heir to the Baskin-Robbins ice cream fortune. They met at a Christmas party shortly after the release of *Yentl*, and he was with her in London where they were making a video.

Baskin, a musician and a businessman, understood her. "She's been famous now longer than she was unfamous," he told *Vanity Fair.*

That March, she and Baskin joined those honoring Quincy Jones at the Century Plaza Hotel where the Los Angeles Urban League paid tribute to the composer and honored him with the 13th annual Whitney Young award.

That same month, Barbra attended a private dinner in honor of the Japanese director Akira Kurosawa who was honored by the Directors Guild of America Awards at the 41st Annual Dinner. Directors in attendance included John Huston, Sydney Pollack, and Paul Mazursky.

"BEFORE, I WAS DRIVEN . . ."

After the intensity and single-mindedness of *Yentl*, Barbra was ready to have some fun and replenish herself creatively. "In some ways, my father and I have merged," she opined. "He has passed his essence into me. I got the love I needed from him, and now have it to give. Before, I was driven; now I'm doing the driving. It's easier to be around me these days." She surrounded herself with a wealth of talent for her next album. Among those who worked with her on the project were Baskin, Richard Perry, Kim Carnes, and Jim Steinman.

Emotion, released in October 1984, became Barbra's first studio album to fall short of Billboard's Top Ten since *Songbird*.

"MY SON IS THE MAN IN MY LIFE NOW"

"My son is the man in my life now," she told Brad Darrach. "I'm trying to give Jason some of the love I got from my father."

Of Jon Peters she said, "We're not living together, but we're better friends than we ever were.

"We're much less competitive, more respectful. We've realized that we're both powerful people. I can't control him, he can't control me. We'd been taking each other for granted, the way people do when they live together for a long time. We don't do that anymore. What I want is a relationship between equals."

Barbra wasn't sure they would ever live together again. "We don't know what's in store," she said. "We're just trying to grow."

Barbra had also recently resumed her friendship with the Canadian Prime Minister Pierre Trudeau, but she did not consider the new relationship an important one. She spent the holidays that year with Richard Baskin in Aspen.

BARBRA ON MEN

The years with Barbra had mellowed her. "Thinking about men, I realize I'm much more compassionate toward them than I used to be. I'm not competitive now. I love our biological differences and I don't want to be a man. To be liberated women doesn't mean just to use our minds. We have wombs and hearts as well as minds."

GETTING BACK TO HER BROADWAY ROOTS WITH STEPHEN SONDHEIM

The disappointing commercial and critical reception to the *Emotion* album finally sent Barbra on a long-anticipated return to her roots. "Anybody could have done the songs on [Emotion] as well or better than I could have done them," Barbra told Stephen Holden in an interview for the *New York Times*. "It was time for me to do something I truly believed in."

"Barbra's contract with Columbia says she has to deliver X albums," Marty Erlichman says, "but they have to be approved albums—meaning most of them have to be contemporary albums. CBS never approved this album, it was not considered to be a pop album. Therefore, she didn't get the advance she was entitled to and it wasn't going to count as an approved album contract. Except if it sold 2.5 million copies—at that point it would automatically become an approved album whether they okayed it in advance or not."

The album was not exclusively Sondheim. There was, for example, Frank Loesser's "Warm All Over," from *The Most Happy Fella.* Barbra recorded it on a cavernous soundstage at the old MGM studios and she could imagine the ghosts of the many famous people who had created magic there in years gone by.

As she stood in the glass booth ready to record, it brought back memories of being nine years old and having her mother bring her to MGM in New York where they put her in a glass booth for an audition. She never knew what they thought of her, but obviously not much since they never called her back.

Columbia was not enthusiastic about the new project. Executives considered Broadway old-hat, they vetoed the double album package Barbra and Peter Matz proposed, insisting on a single slip LP and in fact, never actually approved the album before or during production. This made for some tense moments as the album neared release.

It's hard to believe that Barbra had never done an album of show tunes before. "I had been thinking about doing an album of Broadway songs for years," Barbra said. "When I finally got around to it, I called up Steve [Sondheim] and said I was interested in doing some of his songs. We hardly knew each other, and I had only recorded one of his songs, 'There Won't Be Trumpets,' which ended up not being released. It turned into a process that was so exhilarating, there were moments I was screaming with joy over the phone."

"This album gave me a chance to live up to the greatness of the material," she told William Friedkin, who directed the "Somewhere" video. "I never understood the opposition to this album. I still don't."

When Barbra teamed up with Stephen Sondheim it was a magic coupling that should have happened years earlier.

The Broadway Album contained fifteen songs spanning more than half a century of musical theater, from "Showboat" to "Sunday in the Park with George." The album contains classic show tunes that could have been written with her in mind, gorgeous ballads from Stephen Sondheim, Rodgers and Hammerstein, Jerome Kern.

Barbra being Barbra, she even managed to persuade Sondheim to rewrite three songs for the project, including "Send in the Clowns."

Of course, Sondheim wouldn't perform such custom work for just anyone. "Barbra Streisand has one of the two or three best voices in the world of singing songs," Sondheim observed in the *New York Times*. "It's not just her voice but her intensity, her passion and control. She has the meticulous attention to detail that makes a good artist."

Released in November, 1985 *Barbra Streisand—The Broadway Album* would become the biggest selling solo album of Barbra's career, debuting on the *Billboard* charts at number one. By January it had gone platinum. Ironically, Barbra had never counted on commercial success for this album. The words heard at the beginning of Stephen Sondheim's "Putting it Together" were words she heard from company executives who tried to discourage her from making the record. Barbra put them in the mouths of the "Executive Chorus:" "Why take chances?" "It's just not commercial;" "No one's gonna buy it." But they did, and it made Barbra feel good that so many people appreciated the songs as much as she did. For Barbra, the success of the album was sweet artistic justice.

REUNION WITH MARTY ERLICHMAN

Since their split, Marty Erlichman had gone on to produce a number of films, including *Breathless* and *Coma*. Then he and Barbra crossed paths again while skiing in Utah. Barbra made the first move and soon the old friends were working together again.

Erlichman had been with her so long, he understood her completely.

ONE VOICE

Barbra's "One Voice" political benefit in 1986 would be her last live performance for years.

After all Barbra's insistence that she did not want to sing in public any more, she sang. Chernobyl had erupted in lethal radiation, she was convinced that the arms race was bankrupting the nation and the world, and she wanted to add her one voice to demands for action. The occasion was a September 6 benefit dinner and concert staged at her home in Malibu, to raise money for the election of six liberal Democrats to Congress. (Five of them got in.) Guests like Jane Fonda, Bruce Willis, Goldie Hawn, Jack Nicholson, and Bette Midler shelled out $5,000 a ticket to sit under the stars and bask in her presence.

Barbra Streisand: One Voice first aired on HBO on December 27 and was subsequently issued by Sony in a video cassette. Proceeds from audio and video sales of the concert went to The Streisand Foundation, which supports a number of nonpartisan organizations committed to disarmament, civil liber-

ties, and the preservation of the environment. A highlight of
the evening was Barbra's "Over the Rainbow," which she
chose for its human lyrics and rarely heard verse. To Barbra,
it seemed perfect as an expression of hope for the future of
the planet. The song would always be associated with Judy
Garland, whom she loved, and to whom she dedicated it that
evening.

The concert revealed that Barbra was possibly the single
most powerful fundraiser the Democratic Party had and in the
future they would seek to maximize her value.

NUTS

In 1986 Barbra also began production on another controversial film, *Nuts*. Based on a play by Tom Topor, it is the
story of Claudia Draper, a $500-an-hour call girl who kills
one of her clients. She claims it was self defense. Her mother
and stepfather want her declared insane to avoid a trial. What
Barbra loved about the character was that "she speaks the
truth and gets in trouble."

After much wrangling over the script and casting, *Nuts* began filming on October 20 with Richard Dreyfuss as Claudia's
court-appointed attorney, Karl Malden as her stepfather, and
Maureen Stapleton as her mother. The director would be Martin Ritt.

Nuts wrapped on February 3, 1987. Subsequent disagree-
ments about the final editing between director Ritt and Barbra
led to Barbra exercising her right to the final cut. By June
she had taken over the editing and she spent that summer
working on the score. Yes, Barbra had added another string
to her bow. "For some time, I had dreamed of scoring a
movie," she explained. "When I produced *Nuts*, the dream
became a reality—after all, who else would hire me . . . or
fire me?!" As a courtroom drama, *Nuts* required very little

music, so Barbra decided to give it a shot. The end title music was written to convey a sense of freedom and personal triumph. Later, Alan and Marilyn Bergman added lyrics to it and the song became "Two People," which she recorded for the *Till I Loved You* album.

Barbra had originally written the melody for "Here We Are At Last" as a theme for *The Main Event,* then shelved it in favor of something more uptempo. Now, the melody was used to underscore a bar scene in *Nuts.* When Richard Baskin put lyrics to it, the song found a home on the *Emotion* album.

Nuts opened to mixed reviews on November 20, and performed dismally at the box office.

Disappointing as it was, friends believe that Barbra was even more rocked by a surprise at home: Richard Baskin, her quiet, low profile companion of three-and-a-half years, suddenly moved out.

Twenty-two

Don Johnson

"Don's the perfect man for me—I'm not going to let him go. He's got it all—looks, brains, personality. He doesn't need anything from me except love."

—Barbra

Reeling from the reception to *Nuts* and the departure of Richard Baskin, Barbra retreated to Aspen for the Christmas 1987 holidays. She stayed in a secluded house on Red Mountain and limited her skiing to the easy Buttermilk slopes. She met Don Johnson at a party there the day after Christmas. "He took me by the hand and led me away to talk," she recalled. "He is not Mr. Tough, he is very gentle, sensitive, and nurturing." Actually, according to Streisand biographer James Kimbrell, she first met the *Miami Vice* star at a post-Grammys party the previous February. In a fifteen minute talk during which each professed to be a fan of the other, Barbra said she had enjoyed his *Heartbeat* extended video. Earlier that evening, when Johnson had presented the best album trophy, Barbra was visibly dismayed when he mispronounced her last name on-camera.

Early in 1988 Liz Smith told readers of her syndicated gossip column: "Hollywood is going gaga over the Barbra Streisand-Don Johnson romance." But Barbra issued a statement denying rumors that she planned to guest star on *Miami Vice.*

Once again, Barbra chose an unconventional man, but a man with whom she shared a surprising number of things. Like Barbra, Johnson had survived a difficult childhood. Like her, he had an uneasy relationship with his mother. "Couldn't stand her," he told an interviewer. "I mean, I love her to death, you know, but I can't stand her." Unlike Barbra, his career had been decidedly rocky. Like Richard Baskin, Don Johnson was almost eight years younger than Barbra.

Born in the small farming community of Galena, Missouri, he had seen his life turned upside down when he was eleven and his parents split up. "In one instant, life changed," he told Nancy Collins in *Rolling Stone.* "Suddenly there were major choices I had to make that you shouldn't have to make when you're eleven years old. I realized then it was dog eat dog, every man for himself." Like Jon Peters, he was a self-described "hell-raiser" and spent time in a juvenile home. Like Ryan O'Neal, he was a "major party animal." Like Barbra, he was on his own at sixteen, and like her he knew that he wanted to act.

By the time Johnson got to Hollywood in 1969 he was being touted as a hot new talent, but early disasters like *The Magic Garden of Stanley Sweetheart* had stalled his career.

And then, after fifteen years of getting nowhere, after six flop movies and four bad TV pilots, he was cast in *Miami Vice* and became an international star. The show premiered in September 1984 and introduced a whole new style to television. It was stylish, it was daring, it was beautiful to look at. And most beautiful of all was Johnson himself.

Like Barbra, he wanted to be involved in every creative aspect of the show. Eric Bogosian, the actor and performance artist, played a pimp on one episode, and shared some of his insights with Johnson's biographer, Mickey Hershkovits: "Don Johnson has very strong opinions about where he thinks scenes should go," he said. "He makes it very clear, and I think that rankles people sometimes."

But Barbra was immediately impressed with Don's brash self-assurance. "If I want to meet people, I have to talk to them first because so many are intimidated by me. So if a guy does make the first move, he is already a step ahead."

Recognizing her kind of guy, Barbra invited Don to her New Year's Eve party.

Like Barbra, Don had an uneasy relationship with his fans and was known to hand them business cards that read: "Sorry you caught me at an inconvenient moment. Thank you for appreciating my work. If you would like an autographed picture, please write to Don Johnson Fan Club, 2895 Biscayne Boulevard, Suite 395, Miami, Fla. 33137."

Also like Barbra, Johnson knew the isolation of stardom. "Loneliness," he told an interviewer, "well, sometimes it's the price of success."

On January 22, Barbra and Don went public at the Holmes-Tyson fight in Atlantic City. She remarked, "It was the first I enjoyed my celebrity, because I wasn't having to apologize to the man for getting all this attention, because he got as much attention as I did."

Not everyone fell for Johnson's fabled charms. One who remained immune was activist actress Susan Sarandon who had just finished filming *Sweet Hearts Dance* with him. Sarandon told *Glamour* magazine that Johnson was "a small-town guy with a lot of charm. Any faults or bad habits Don has are because nobody asks him to be any different." When she was questioned as to whether Johnson had a way with women, she responded: "With women, or girls?"

Promoting *Nuts* to the foreign press, Barbra said that Don simply made her happy. "I have never been so happy before, so it's something I am learning as if I am a child again," she explained. "It is a new thing and I have to get used to it. I never knew what it was like to have fun when I was growing up.

"Don's the perfect man for me—I'm not going to let him go. He's got it all—looks, brains, personality. He doesn't need anything from me except love."

To another London reporter: "He loves taking chances, he's gentle, warm, and very, very considerate."

By February her romance with Don was sizzling. They were snapped as they arrived for a film trade show in Las Vegas.

And on February 26 she filmed an unheralded cameo appearance for an episode of *Miami Vice*. Barbra and Don exchange meaningful glances on the street. "It must be love," was how Barbra laughingly dismissed the appearance.

They were everywhere together, as at a March 14 surprise birthday party for Quincy Jones.

And Don was around to comfort her when the Academy overlooked her performance in *Nuts* and she failed to get an Oscar nomination for her acting.

Smith informed her readers that Don and Barbra had been seen at the Conservatory Restaurant in New York's Mayflower Hotel. "It was an off hour, and the cafe was fairly deserted," she reported. "They occupied a leather banquette and were seen getting so cozy that eventually they all but slid down out of sight of the few other diners. So it was something big and electric from the very beginning!"

And one result of their relationship was an artistic collaboration. Through all the ups and downs of his career, Johnson had never given up on music and always had a guitar nearby to pick up and strum. He had even co-written songs with his good friend, Dickie Betts, formerly of the Allman Brothers. Barbra and Don teamed up in the recording studio for a lush, romantic duet, "Till I Loved You," which was included on her new album of the same name.

Not everyone loved it. One critic complained that "If narcissism could be captured on tape, it probably would sound something like 'Till I Loved You.' The single came complete with an angelic, soft-focus picture sleeve of Don and Barbra.

Barbra also sang uncredited back-up on Don's new record album *Heartbeat*. And she appeared at the ShoWest Convention in Las Vegas where she was named "Star of the Decade," arriving late, escorted by Don. "Sorry I was a little late, but I was auditioning for a part on *Miami Vice*," she joked as she accepted the award.

Also on the dais at the ShoWest awards ceremony was Jon Peters. By racking up successes like *Batman, Rain Man,* and *Nine and a Half Weeks* on his own, Jon had long since justified Barbra's faith in him and they had remained close friends. No one could have been more pleased than Barbra when in late 1988 it was announced that Sony, which had just acquired Columbia Pictures and was desperate to hire managers to run it, hired Jon and his partner Peter Guber by buying out their company for $200 million. Somewhat less pleased was their mutual friend, Steve Ross of Warner, who had a contract with them to produce pictures for him. Ultimately, Sony paid Warners millions to get Guber and Peters.

That April 24 Don celebrated Barbra's forty-sixth birthday with a party at his home. Although Don was still shooting *Dead Bang* in Calgary and unable to attend, he sent Barbra a $25,000 Arabian stallion wrapped with a bow. Patti D'Arbanville, mother of his son, was there. Barbra had also befriended Pamela Des Barres, the ex-groupie who chronicled her adventures in a memoir *I'm with the Band,* giving special kudos to ex-lover Don.

In May, Barbra took a much-needed break from working on the sequel to her Broadway album to go to Calgary for a long romantic weekend with Don. He was in Canada making

the movie *Dead Bang*, directed by John Frankenheimer o
Manchurian Candidate fame.

Don and Barbra were still going strong in September wher
Don's romantic comedy *Sweet Heart's Dance* starring himself
Susan Sarandon, and Elizabeth Perkins, directed by Rober
Greenwald, premiered in Westwood at a benefit for the Make-
a-Wish Foundation. They arrived together and Barbra ever
managed a few smiles but generally seemed annoyed at the
attention and popping flashes. But as the year 1988 ended, so
did the affair.

"Barbra was willing to stay," Don said later. "We genuinely
tried to make it work. But we'd reached a point where we had
to make a commitment or let it go." Johnson, who had beer
seeing his ex-wife Melanie Griffith, since she was released
from rehab in July, gave Melanie a four–carat engagement
ring and marriage followed the following spring.

HUMAN RIGHTS NOW!

That September 21, Barbra turned up back on the arm o
Richard Baskin at the Amnesty International Concert which
was billed as "Human Rights Now!" and held at the Los An
geles Memorial Coliseum. The benefit featured performances
by Bruce Springsteen, Sting, and other rockers and drew a
star-studded crowd of celebrities.

A LEGACY FROM DON JOHNSON

Once again, Barbra emerged from a relationship richer thar
when she entered it. For by 1989 she and Don Johnson had
faded as a couple, but she came away restored, anxious to
direct a project again and with that project in mind. It would
be Pat Conroy's novel, *The Prince of Tides*.

That June came the first public hints of her interest in the novel. According to Liz Smith: "Screenwriter Becky Johnston has been practically living in Barbra's house, as have other aides who are working on this project."

After all the tsimmis involved with the making of *Yentl,* Barbra did not get involved in another project for several years. Then, while making *Nuts,* the music editor mentioned *The Prince of Tides* as a story that she ought to direct. Although Barbra was not familiar with the novel, Don was also deeply engrossed in *The Prince of Tides,* and according to Joe Morgenstern, he read passages to her aloud. Slowly, like so many things in her life, her commitment to Conroy's book took root.

It is easy to see why *The Prince of Tides* appealed to both Don and Barbra. It spoke of troubled parents and children in pain, and of the strides made through psychotherapy.

"The movie is not just about being flawed but about forgiving the flaws in yourself," Barbra said. "Because when you can do that, you can forgive others. How many people love themselves?"

Twenty-three

Love and Losses

"We're from different worlds, but we collided."
—Andre Agassi

For Barbra, the 1990s would bring renewed energy as she continued to enjoy a revitalized recording career with *The Broadway Album*. She threw herself into bringing *The Prince of Tides* to the screen. She would also come to enjoy an unlikely love affair with a man a few years older than her son and spark many rumors of a romance with a man who is arguably the most powerful in the world.

After a long estrangement, Barbra and Sue Mengers were once again friends. "My biggest contribution was nagging her," Mengers claimed. "She has no need for constant employment like other stars. I used to be flattered when she would ask my advice about some artistic problem she was having, until I found her one day talking to the gardener about the same thing. When Barbra works she becomes obsessive and it's the only thing she is able to focus on. I think that's why she doesn't do it as much as the rest of us would like her to. It's just too exhausting. She has less 'star mentality' in regards to 'What's-the-next-hot-project?-Get-me-a-role-in-it' than anybody I've ever dealt with."

Her years in Jungian analysis have taught Barbra to put great credence in her dreams. When she wakes from a dream, she writes her memory down. So, while she was deciding whether to do *The Prince of Tides* or to build an early American dream house, the dream she had was significant. She was also ready to tune into other signs from the universe.

She told Julia Reed of *Tatler* that she woke up in the middle of the night to find that the light above a painting in her bedroom had come on. She decided that the message was "Light up your art" and made the movie.

STRUGGLE TO MAKE *PRINCE OF TIDES*

Jon Peters pushed Columbia to back Barbra's new project, but making *The Prince of Tides* was still a struggle.

It was Nick Nolte who approached Barbra about casting him as Tom Wingo, the central character. He had read the novel and connected to the material immediately. Like Wingo, his relationships with women were troubled. Barbra was impressed. "I saw a lot of pain in his work, in his eyes," she said. "In talking to him, he was at a vulnerable place, ready to explore feelings, romantic feelings, sexual feelings, and deep, secretive feelings."

As for the role of psychiatrist Susan Lowenstein, Barbra cast herself.

Many admirers of Pat Conroy's novel were disappointed with the cuts in the original text, especially the way the characters of Tom's brother Luke and his troubled sister Savannah were whittled away, but author Conroy professed himself delighted with the adaptation.

CASTING JASON

One of Barbra's greatest dilemmas while preparing *Prince of Tides* was the question of casting her son. "I thought deep, deep down, well, it's dangerous," she acknowledged. "We could both get attacked for this, but the critics loved it."

Filming began that June on location in Beaufort, South Carolina, the very town where Conroy had grown up and which he had dubbed "Colleton" in the novel.

JUST FOR THE RECORD . . .

In September, CBS issued a CD boxed set, *Just for the Record* that provided an almost complete retrospective of Barbra's career. Included in the package was a four-color booklet that documented important moments in Barbra's career from her 1955 recording of "You'll Never Know," to the *Back to Broadway* album.

PRINCE PREMIERE

On December 11, *The Prince of Tides* had its West Coast premiere at the Cineplex Odeon in Century City, California. Barbra arrived with Jon Peters and sported a sleek white Donna Karan pantsuit. She wore the jacket open to show cleavage and lacy camisole.

The film was welcomed with almost unanimous raves. From *Daily Variety*: "*The Prince of Tides* has a quality not often found in contemporary American movies—passion—and a quality not usually associated with Barbra Streisand—self-effacement;" from Gene Shalit of *The Today Show*: "Streisand is an *outstanding* director. One gauge of her directorial gifts is the superb performances she has drawn from this notabl cast."

NO MAN OF HER OWN

But the close of 1991 would find Barbra alone. She was still seen occasionally with Richard Baskin, and, more recently, James Newton Howard, who composed the music for *Prince of Tides,* but there was no special man in her life. "Barbra has few relationships; they are quiet and they don't last too long," a friend told De Vries. Barbra was even considering adopting a child, "but I'm not too sure I want to do that as a single parent. It wasn't too hot for me, and I don't particularly want to do that to another child."

On January 18, 1992, Barbra attended the Golden Globes at the Beverly Hilton with Richard Baskin. A few weeks later, *Prince of Tides* was one of five pictures nominated by the Directors Guild of America for Best Picture. But in February the entire motion picture community was shocked when the Academy Award nominations were announced and Barbra was completely ignored. That is not to say that *Prince* was, for its nominations included Best Picture, Best Actor for Nolte, Best Supporting Actress for Kate Nelligan, Best Screenplay Adaptation and Best Cinematography. But its director seemed not to exist.

Ironically, the snub probably generated more publicity for the picture and sincere sympathy for Barbra. She stole the show on March 30 when she attended the Awards ceremony with son Jason.

A few weeks later, Jon Peters hosted a $200,000 fiftieth-birthday bash in her honor featuring fire-eaters, circus animals, a Velcro wall, and face painters.

REDISCOVERING THE BOYS

Barbra had still not become active politically. The largest grants from her Streisand Foundation had been made to endow two chairs: the Streisand Chair in Cardiology at UCLA (in memory of her father, Emanuel) and the Streisand Chair on Intimacy and Sexuality at USC.

It was time for Barbra to get back in touch with what had once been her core constituency, gay men. And they had never needed her more.

"Of all the celebrities who should have done more for gay men during the AIDS crisis it's Barbra," one industry heavyweight complained to Kevin Sessums. "Whenever you call Madonna or Bette or Liz Taylor, they're *there,* no questions asked. But what has Barbra done? She hides behind this stagefright crap, but she got up and raised millions for a bunch of politicians. We are the people who discovered her, who have loved her. Where is she? It's shameful."

SAYING GOODBYE TO AN OLD FRIEND AND WELCOMING NEW ONES

In the fall of 1992, Barbra would be more often, seen with her new friend, Andre Agassi. That September 5, Barbra was photographed watching him at the U.S. Open Tennis Championships at Flushing Meadow Park in Queens, New York. They had been introduced in Las Vegas after a preview of *Prince of Tides,* but they scrupulously avoided publicity.

And another new and potentially powerful man was about to enter her life. Later that September, Barbra gave a concert to raise funds for Bill Clinton's presidential campaign. It was the beginning of a mutual admiration society between the superstar and the ambitious Arkansas governor, sealed when he was elected President that November.

But she would experience losses, too. And perhaps one of the most painful came near the end of the year when her long-time friend and advisor Steve Ross, Chairman and CEO of Time Warner, died of cancer on December 20. Ross had merged

Warner Communications with Time Life just two years earlier. Private services for the mogul were held at Guild Hall in East Hampton and he was buried in nearby Green River Cemetery. Barbra and Richard Baskin were among the mourners who flew in from Los Angeles on the Time Warner plane and journeyed all the way out to Guild Hall in East Hampton. The parade of speakers included Quincy Jones, Steven Spielberg, and Beverly Sills. Singers' performances were interspersed throughout the program and they included Paul Simon who sang "Like a Bridge over Troubled Water."

Aboard the plane, Barbra had told Terry Semel, the Warner Bros. president, that she *could not* sing at the funeral, but she did, demonstrating her deep love for Ross by singing "Papa Can You Hear Me?"

Connie Bruck reported that: "Mark Ross noted, ruefully, that he had helped to decide the order of the speakers, and yet had allowed himself to follow Streisand—something, he knew, that his father, who planned such things with great care, would have advised against. "I can hear my father saying, 'Never follow Barbra!' "

Bruck also reported that Barbra announced she was dedicating her next album to Steve Ross. "Steve loved making people happy," she declared. According to Bruck, Barbra then told the following story:

"I lost a piece of sculpture, I bid too low at auction. I came back to the country almost a year later, after shooting *Yentl*—I got off the plane, and I needed to see some art. I went to an art gallery, and there, on Madison Avenue, was the same piece—three times as expensive. Being a nice Jewish girl, I couldn't buy it. Months after that, Courtney and Steve gave a dinner party. And at the top of the stairs was *this* piece of sculpture! And I thought how glad I was that people I love had it. I told Steve the story, about losing it at auction. He said, 'Look at the card behind it.' It was a gift for me, for finishing *Yentl*. How he found it, how he traced it!"

She paused, then added: "However, no gifts he gave could compare to his love and friendship."

"The Streisand story didn't exactly make sense," Bruck observed. "One had to ask how Ross knew that she had missed buying this piece of sculpture—until a friend of hers explained, later, that Streisand had lamented to Ross her having missed out on the chance to buy it. He, as one might have predicted, made it right."

One consequence of the death of Steve Ross was that Barbra no longer felt any sentimental ties to Warner Bros. Jon and his partner had already left for a lucrative deal to head Columbia Pictures, now renamed Sony Pictures. Jon soon departed to pursue his own projects, but not before wooing Barbra, who signed a $2 million deal in December 1992 to develop projects for Sony. The multimedia agreement also covered her music, for which she would be getting $5 million per album and a record-breaking forty-two percent royalty.

Her superstardom and growing political clout certainly made a big impression on President Bill Clinton. In fact, by early 1993, there would be whispers in Washington that the two were becoming *too* close.

CLINTON INAUGURATION

Barbra got the year 1993—and the Clinton administration—off to a great start by her appearance at the inaugural ceremonies that January. It had been reported that she insisted that unless she introduced Clinton, she would refuse to perform at the Inaugural Gala. When her big moment came, Barbra was gorgeous in a Donna Karan pin-striped suit with a slit up the long skirt and some cleavage visible from the low-cut neckline. Taylor Fleming in the *New York Times* dubbed it her "peekaboo-power suit." The *Times* never mentioned that CBS paid $8 million for broadcast rights just because Barbra had agreed to sing.

That March, as Hillary Clinton flew to the side of her dying father, Barbra arrived in Washington. The President had invited her to attend the Gridiron Club dinner and she spent the night in the White House.

Reportedly, when Hillary learned of this, she was enraged and refused to speak to him for two days.

Nevertheless, that April, Barbra returned to the nation's capital to personally deliver a copy of her new album *Back to Broadway* to Clinton.

On April 18, as part of her new commitment to battling AIDS, Barbra attended a benefit reading of Larry Kramer's landmark play, *The Normal Heart,* at the Roundabout Theatre in New York. The reading featured introductory remarks by Barbra, who was so moved to tears by the performance that she embraced Kramer after. She plans to direct the film adaptation and to play the role of a nurse in the drama about the early days of the AIDS epidemic.

In May a select group of insiders was invited to a truly unique unveiling, simultaneously the premiere of her long-awaited *Back to Broadway Album* and an AIDS benefit. They filled the Eugene O'Neill Theatre to listen to the first playing of the album. The star did not perform. Although she did graciously accept a huge plaque commemorating the release of her fiftieth album, she did not sing.

That August, *The Back to Broadway Album* hit the top of the *Billboard* charts and Barbra celebrated with fifty friends at a party given by songwriter Carol Bayer Sager. Sager even announced that Barbra would perform and the guest of honor disappeared as everyone took their seats in Sager's home theater.

The music began, the curtain went up and—the audience suddenly realized it had not been listening to Barbra but to Streisand impersonator Jim Bailey. Barbra joined the applause when he finished, and generously posed for pictures with him.

Barbra also seemed more confident about being seen with her new young lover. That July, Barbra, 51, was photographed at Wimbledon, cheering on Andre, 23. "We're from different worlds, but we collided," Agassi told one journalist. "From that moment, we knew we wanted each other. With some people, there's an instant connection. That's what happened to us."

"Andre is intelligent, sensitive, and far more mature than his years," Barbra said of the man three years older than her son.

The British press covered the couple relentlessly when they arrived in England for the tennis tournament. After checking into a posh London hotel, Barbra ducked out the back door, slipped into a limo and headed for Andre's rented mansion in Wimbledon. And when she showed up at center court she drew gasps from the crowd.

Observers reported that Barbra watched him intently as Agassi first seemed to be losing the match. When he turned it around, Barbra stood up and punched the air, shouting "One more baby, one more! Beautiful! Beautiful!" He lost anyway.

JUST THE FAX

Another new and close friend was New York fashion designer Donna Karan. During the summer of '93 Barbra stayed at the designer's summer house in the trendy Hamptons while Donna left for a business trip in Japan.

When Donna called to check on her houseguest, Barbra was struggling with the fax machine.

"Oh, I forgot to tell you, it's broken," said Donna. Barbra was upset. "What did I come here for? I've got business to do." Donna suggested: "Why don't you just go out and buy one? Thrifty Barbra replied: "O.K., but I want to be reimbursed when you return."

A DUET WITH SINATRA

That summer, a series of artists recorded "duets" for a new album with Frank Sinatra. It was something new for Sinatra: an album of duets on some of his classic songs with other world-renowned singers. Initially, Sinatra would record with a fifty-two piece orchestra at the Capitol Records Tower in Hollywood. The voices of the other halves of the duets would be added to the recordings later.

Participants included Julio Yglesias who joined him on Johnny Mercer's "Summer Wind," Tony Bennett on Kander and Ebb's "New York, New York," Aretha Franklin on Gilbert Becaud's "What Now My Love," and other classic pop songs with Natalie Cole, Gloria Estefan, Liza Minnelli, Anita Baker, and Kenny G.

The "duet" Barbra recorded with Frank Sinatra would become one of the highlights of *Duets*. This was Barbra's first collaboration with her longtime idol. They sang together on George and Ira Gershwin's "I've Got a Crush on You."

Barbra had recorded it only recently for her *Back to Broadway* album but did not include it in the finished recording. Sinatra had recorded it as early as 1947 with arranger Axel Stordahl, again in 1960 with Nelson Riddle and included it in his live "Sands" album with Count Basie and Quincy Jones in 1966.

Barbra was scheduled to record her part at the Todd-AO studio in Los Angeles on the afternoon of August 17, 1993. She arrived at the studio to find a huge bouquet of flowers and a handwritten note from Sinatra himself.

"Streisand was touched," reported David McClintick, "and pulled from her bag a nearly thirty-year-old note that Sinatra had written her after seeing her in *Funny Girl* on Broadway in the sixties. She photocopied it and enclosed it with a new note thanking him for the flowers."

Even at the recording session, Barbra continued to ask for rewrites and a new ending to the orchestration. She even added the phrase "You make me blush, Francis."

According to McClintick, the producers then went back to Sinatra and "asked if he would overdub 'Barbra' for 'baby' in the preceding line to balance the reference. After thinking it over, Sinatra made the adjustment on a digital tape recorder in his dressing room before a concert outside Chicago in August.

"Despite the piecemeal process which is common in recording duets nowadays, the result sounds as if Sinatra and Streisand are singing in each other's arms. . . .", McClintick reported. "Sinatra sings with tender, understated passion, as a man who has unexpectedly fallen in love late in life. Streisand sings with eager, forthright desire, as a younger woman who wants him urgently, in a way she has never wanted anyone else."

ACTIVIST BARBRA

Barbra had long been the Democrat Party's secret weapon, and had raised millions for the party. Now, with a Democratic president in the White House, she was reaping the rewards. Suddenly she seemed all over Washington: Advising the administration on how to market the plan for national health care; attending the Gridiron Dinner and stealing the show at the White House Correspondents' Dinner (ex-beau Richard Baskin was her date), and dining with Attorney General Janet Reno.

But even her finest moments were spoiled by criticism. Maureen Dowd of the *New York Times* reported that Barbra spent all her time at the White House Correspondents Dinner talking to Colin Powell about Bosnia. What Dowd didn't know is that Barbra already knew Powell, they had met at an American Academy of Achievement Awards banquet a year earlier, and "he's a guy from the Bronx, I'm a girl from Brooklyn," and in fact were friends making small talk. "I don't know about Bosnia," she declared, "and I don't talk about things I don't know about."

ASPEN BOYCOTT

That fall, Barbra spoke out against Colorado's anti-gay Amendment 2. "Now, I'm willing to go out on a limb, you know, and say what I believe. And if it turns some people off and people don't go to my movies or buy my records, then so be it. It has to do with my involvement in the real world," she told Julia Reed. "Just by my saying something about Amendment 2 it gets national attention."

And she seemed newly recommitted to her career. She had signed a new contract with Sony which gave her up to $60 million for movies she would produce, direct, and/or star in under her Barwood Films banner, as well as for eight albums. She was looking at projects like *The Normal Heart,* Larry Kramer's play about two men hit in the early days of the AIDS epidemic, which she planned to produce, direct, and star in.

She had also acquired the film rights to books about Jackson Pollock by Jeffrey Potter, about Diane Arbus by Patricia Bosworth, even the story of Lt. Col. Margarethe Cammermeyer, a lesbian who was forced to resign from the Washington National Guard. This might be her most controversial proj-ect yet.

And the most exciting news of all was that she was even contemplating a world tour.

She told journalist Reed, "The people have kept me a star for thirty-some years because there's a truth to my work and that's what they get. And if I keep telling the truth, I can't get hurt."

TAKING STOCK

But Barbra was always taking stock and preparing surprises. By now she owned a compound of five houses at Malibu. One of them was known as the art deco house.

In the summer of 1993, she sat for a lengthy story on her Malibu compound that would appear in the December issue of *Architectural Digest*. Barbra posed on the cover and the story inside offered a unique and intimate look at the star and the way she lived.

She took the interviewer through her showcase: the art deco house she had been meticulously remodelling since the 1970s. Only four colors were used throughout the house, which was used as a guesthouse/poolhouse: burgundy, rose, black, and gray. Part of her wardrobe of vintage clothing hung there, color-coordinated with each room. There was even a maroon 1933 Dodge roadster (like the one Nancy Drew used to drive) and a gray 1926 Rolls Royce.

Barbra still had the pink satin shoes she wore for her debut at the Bon Soir. A particularly poignant moment came when Barbra pulled out the ancient fox-trimmed karakul coat she had worn at her audition for *Wholesale*. "Look at that embroidery," she said, showing off the lining. "It's a wonderful metaphor for life, isn't it? That something should be as beautiful on the inside as it is on the outside—maybe even more beautiful."

But she also revealed that she was becoming fascinated by eighteenth-century America and studying such showplaces as Winterthur and Monticello. Jefferson's home had inspired her to repaint her Beverly Hills dining room a deep, rich ivory and she was buying up everything from primitive paintings and furniture to eighteenth-century American interpretations of Chippendale and Queen Anne.

Barbra was also contemplating building another house inspired by the great colonial and southern mansions she had seen in her travels.

MALIBU CONSERVANCY

In line with simplifying her life, Barbra donated her Malibu estate—the land and the buildings—valued at $15 million, to the Santa Monica Mountains Conservancy. The state agency will use the place for research in ecosystems as the Streisand Center for Conservancy Studies.

"I'll miss my gardens," she admitted, "and all those organic vegetables and scented cabbage roses."

Barbra may have also been re-assessing her career. Catherine Seipp reported in *Buzz* magazine that a discontented Barbra called her representative, superagent Michael Ovitz, that fall to scream, "You're doing *nothing* for me." Perhaps it was a feeling that her career was languishing that made her contemplate singing in public for the first time in years.

And that fall she was also reaching the end of the road with Andre Agassi. But, in the tradition of most of the other men in her life, he would remain a good friend.

Ever eager for self-improvement, Barbra had even joined her best friend designer Donna Karan in the popular "Get Juiced" program of supervised fasting developed by "fasting" specialists Pamela Serure and Nancy Sorkow. "W" reported that the program cost $400 for three days worth of juice and bouillon (hotel not included). Part of the treatment involved a daily walk and breathing exercises to help detox the body—on the beach in Amagansett where the program was held—but Barbra declined to complete that portion of the program, reportedly because she feared beachcombers would bother her for her autograph.

PHOTO APPROVAL?

Hillary Clinton, already angry about Barbra's frequent visits to Washington, was reportedly further outraged in late 1993 when the President attended a party without her at the Los Angeles home of Marvin Davis, and she learned that Barbra showed up there to croon a romantic version of "Bill" from the musical *Showboat*.

"She stood in front of Clinton and when she delivered the key line, 'My Bill,' she gazed into his eyes," reported an observer.

"It was an explosive moment. After the song Bill and Barbra disappeared together and were missing from the party for more than half an hour," the observer told journalist David Duffy. "When word got back to Hillary she exploded. Hillary told Bill, 'I don't want that woman near you again. And I never want to see her in the White House again!'"

The whole thing distressed Barbra deeply. She could not believe that Hillary Clinton could be threatened by her. "For Hillary to fear that Bill and I could be romantically involved is silly," she supposedly said.

Barbra's legendary perfectionism and need to control also made waves in Hollywood that December. As a memento of the Davis party, a $25,000-a-plate dinner for the Hollywood elite and President Bill Clinton, Marvin and Barbara Davis followed up with photographs of each attendee posing with the President. Most people were pleased with the keepsake, not Barbra.

The word was that Barbra had called up the Davises to chastise them for sending out a photo which she had not approved. She insisted it had been shot from her bad (right) side. She insisted they destroy the negative immediately and promise her it would not find its way into the tabloids.

Twenty-four

Barbra's Back on Stage

"Whatever's said about me is said, you know. I can't control it. If one does good work, that's what stands the test of time. That's what lasts. The rest doesn't matter."
—Barbra

As 1993 drew to a close, Barbra had been in the public eye since she was nineteen years old. She had been an acknowledged superstar for almost that long. After more than fifty years on the planet and more than thirty as a star there seemed to be nothing left that could surprise her millions of fans and her scattered detractors. Everyone knew that she was brilliant, talented, controlling, obsessed with perfection and beset by paralyzing stagefright. Everyone knew that Barbra would never perform on a concert stage again. And a nightclub was out of the question.

Suddenly, Barbra surprised everyone.

Early in the fall of 1993 it was announced that Barbra Streisand, superstar, would return to Las Vegas for two New Year's concerts to hail the dawn of 1994. After nearly three decades away from the concert stage, Barbra was preparing to ring in the new year in Vegas.

It was reported that a psychic had conjured up the ghost of Barbra's father and he urged the star to conquer her stage-fright. At yet another seance, the same ghost told Jason Gould, "Tell your mother to sing live . . . nothing to fear."

Once Barbra had decided to appear at the Grand, she characteristically threw herself into preparations. In addition to her longtime friends Marilyn and Alan Bergman, she also retained a freelance political humorist to script some patter for her. The writer, Mark Katz, who had written humorous remarks for President Clinton and David Gergen, met Barbra at a party following the White House Correspondents Dinner. Ultimately it was decided that the shows were an entertainment event, not a political one, and Katz's political humor was shelved.

There was another, even more interesting turnabout. Charlotte Hays of the *New York Daily News* reported that screenwriter Gary Ross, whose credits included *Big* and *Dave,* got a late-night phone call from Barbra. She wanted him to write some material for her, and she wanted to include a put-down of Linda Richman, the *haimish* cable-TV talk-show hostess played by comedian Mike Myers on Saturday Night Live. Linda Richman adores Barbra, whose singing and appearance are, to Linda, "like buttah." Ross talked Barbra out of such nonsense and convinced her to include Myers himself in her show, doing his Linda Richman routine as her opener.

Instead of political humor, Barbra's appearance would eventually be scripted along the autobiographical lines of a one-woman Broadway show.

That November, Barbra was in New York, working on material with Marilyn and Alan Bergman, and her musical director, Academy Award winner Marvin Hamlisch. They were rehearsing intensively at Barbra's Central Park West penthouse and Marvin's apartment.

Even at $500 to $1,000 a seat, the available Streisand tickets sold out instantly. In the first twenty-four hours after the con-

cert was announced, one million calls with ticket requests were
lodged. By opening night, the scalpers were getting $2,000 a
ticket.

It was reported that Barbra was being paid as much as $20
million for the two performances, but neither the star, her
publicist, Dick Guttman, nor the hotel would confirm a figure.

Four seats to her Saturday show were advertised for sale in
a local Aspen paper at $2,000 each. They sold within hours.
By opening night, Vegas scalpers were claiming they could
get $4,000 a seat for the Friday night show.

Ever the perfectionist, Barbra rejected a $20-million deal
to carry the show live on pay-per-view, opting instead to film
it and edit it into a special to air at a later date.

Barbra was, of course, installed in the hotel's lavish new
6,000 square foot, two-story, high-rollers suite. But she disappointed hotel sources by refusing to pose with Frank Sinatra.

The shows, on New Year's eve and New Year's Day, would
take place in the MGM Grand Garden arena, part of a new
$1 billion complex that opened on December 18. The complex
includes the world's largest hotel, a casino, and a theme park.
Frank Sinatra would also be playing the MGM Grand those
same nights—in a smaller theater.

All was not coffee ice cream, however. Labor activists
begged Barbra not to appear on the grounds that MGM Grand
chairman Robert Maxey had not allowed his workers to union-
ize. In another controversy, twelve congresswomen, including
Pat Schroeder (D-Colo.) and Eleanor Holmes Norton (D-D.C.)
asked Barbra to meet with former employees of the hotel to
hear their stories of alleged sexual harassment. Maxey denied
the charges.

A spokesperson assured the congresswomen that she "will
be contacting Congresswoman (Anna) Eshoo [sic] as soon as
Congress convenes again."

On the big night, fans lined up outside for a chance to have their photographs taken beside a cardboard cutout Barbara. Inside the complex, souvenir stands hawked everything from concert programs at $25 to $100 silver key chains, from signature bottles of champagne at $100 to $75 crystal goblets to pour it into. Ultimately fans would shell out $1 million for souvenirs alone.

Lucky ticketholders passed through metal detectors. Inside, among those spotted in the audience were Roseanne and Tom Arnold, Quincy Jones with Nastassja Kinski, First Mother Virginia Clinton Kelley and First Brother Roger Clinton, rapper LL Cool J, Richard Gere and Cindy Crawford, and Alex Baldwin and Kim Basinger. At the first show: Coretta Scott King and Prince. There were Barbra's former directors Sydney Pollack and Peter Bogdanovich, her former husband, Elliott Gould, and her former boyfriends Andre Agassi and Richard Baskin. Her new agent Michael Ovitz was seen in the green room. Agassi had encouraged Barbra to go through with the performance, reportedly telling her that "her gifts as a singer needed to be shared with others."

"Not since Elvis played Las Vegas have I seen such a main event," fitness guru and die-hard Streisand fan Richard Simmons bubbled to *People*.

Simmons, a lifelong fan, covered the event for the *Tonight Show* on New Year's Eve. Shortly after Barbra appeared in a spotlight at the top of the staircase, silencing the crowd with "As If We Never Said Goodbye," from Andrew Lloyd Webber's *Sunset Boulevard*, Simmons ended his report by breaking into tears and disappearing into the ladies' room. "TV doesn't get much better," observed Jess Cagle of *Entertainment Weekly*.

Hamlisch led the sixty-four-piece orchestra in a lengthy overture. Then, from the top of a staircase at stage left, descended Barbra, in a long black velvet dress with a cream satin inset she had designed herself, finished off with a brooch of pearls and diamonds. Gradually, she loosened up. "I don't know why I'm so frightened," she said, "I'm trembling now, I've missed you, I've come home again." As the spotlight went out on this first number, the audience broke into thunderous applause.

Modestly accepting this tribute, Barbra stepped onto an all-white Palladian stage and into a Monticello-inspired drawing room set that included a silver tea service. She tossed off a few not-so-kind remarks about the state of the hotel's rooms and other facilities. Occasionally, she sipped from a china teacup.

Her first set was dominated by a long skit-with-songs about shrinks she had known and the questions they had explored together, a natural lead-in for songs like "What is This Thing Called Love?" Barbra also gave her audience her standards, like "For All We Know," "Can't Help Loving That Man of Mine," "Lover Man," "People," "Evergreen," "The Way We Were," and "Since I Fell for You."

She joked that it had taken 2,700 hours of therapy and $360,000 before she could really sing "On a Clear Day You Can See Forever" with Alan Jay Lerner's lyrics of self-acceptance and told her audience that she had not been able to sing songs like "It All Depends on You" since she learned to control her own life.

For Act II Barbra changed into a striking white georgette floor-length suit and vest trimmed with white bugle beads. Her skirt, slit to the thigh, exposing white stockings. She showed clips of herself with Robert Redford in *The Way We Were* and talked about learning to like herself, and sang a rousing "Happy Days are Here Again," in front of a video of clips of her new hero, Bill Clinton.

Barbra closed her show with an encore, "For All We Know."

At the end of the first show, she bubbled: "I did it! I did it! I did it! I think I even enjoyed myself a little."

But Barbra being Barbra, she called an all-day orchestra rehearsal for the next day.

One person who was less than pleased with Barbra's performance was Frank Sinatra, who invited her to visit with him and have a photo taken together.

But Barbra canceled at the last minute, pleading that she was too nervous about her upcoming show.

On December 31, Barbra begged off again because she was upset about a seating problem in the concert hall. That was when she decided she couldn't have the distracting cameras during her show.

Then on January 1 she simply refused to have her picture taken with Sinatra, even though Barbara Sinatra had attended her show instead of Frank's.

The first try at a picture was set up for Thursday night, December 30, backstage at Barbra's rehearsal.

Did Barbra snub Sinatra? It seems unlikely. It is far more likely that she truly was immersed in preparations and couldn't spare the time. She wanted to give her fans and paying customers full value. The two have too much mutual admiration for any such misunderstanding to last.

Barbra's second show, the following night was, if possible, even bigger than New Year's Eve. Michael Jackson showed up, his security detail blocking everyone out of the men's room while he was inside. He sat with new best friend Michael Milken. Mel Gibson was there with wife Robyn. Elliott Gould returned with their son, Jason. The indomitable Diana Kind, now 85, was there and managed to get her photo taken with Virginia Kelley. She was so thrilled that she clutched the Polaroid all through the show. But Barbra saw none of this. She was busy backstage, still fine-tuning the show.

For the second night, Barbra decided to open with "Don't Rain on My Parade." But she blew the words to her own song, "Evergreen." The miscue was projected on a huge closed-circuit video screen, so even those in the most remote areas of the Grand Garden arena could see the startled look on Barbra's face as she realized her error.

But rather than freeze, she smiled sheepishly and joked, "And it's my own song." She then resumed her singing, this time relying on the TelePrompTer for correct cues.

Next day, the reviews came in. Some complained because Barbra mixed the professional with the personal. David Hinckley of the New York *Daily News* reported that "Midway through the first of Barbra Streisand's ambitious comeback shows here Friday night, it became clear this was an extension not only of her singing career, but her therapy." Hinckley called the result "a kind of artistic schizophrenia." He acknowledged that when she sang, "She sounded sublime," but carped that "between songs, we visited her couch so often she could have been addressing the American Psychiatric Association."

Director Peter Bogdanovich, who had been in the audience at Barbra's last Vegas concert in 1972, was able to compare the two shows more than a generation apart. "The other one was small, kind of intimate," he said. "This was colossal. It signifies what a legendary name Barbra has become over those years."

"It's great to hear music again," said Quincy Jones, "There's a lot of gruntin' and mumblin' going on, but it's not that many people who really sing anymore."

There were other rumors. Some claimed that "there were so many empty seats that honchos at the MGM Grand Hotel had to herd chambermaids into the 13,000 theater." Marty Erlichman denied this and assured reporters that both nights had been sold out. "As with any concert," he said, "we held one or two percent of the seats to relocate customers whose views were obstructed. We ended up needing fewer relocation seats than we anticipated. The hotel may have given those seats away to its own help. We would not object to that."

Other seats became available at the last minute because Barbra decided against the heavy camera equipment that would be needed for a broadcast taping. That decision was said to cost her $1 million, but according to Marty Erlichman, the cranes and other apparatus "would have compromised both the live performance and the TV show."

Barbra had permitted a small group of ten cameras which her people said was videotaping "archival footage." But once she had a chance to look at the tapes she was pleased and was considering using them again.

At a party after the close of the second show a radiant Barbra declared: "Tonight was the way I hoped it would be. Everything felt right."

There was a sad postscript to Barbra's Las Vegas triumph: a few weeks later, Virginia Clinton Kelley passed away.

Because of her deep admiration for the President and his mother, Barbra was the first contributor to a fund to fight breast cancer created in her memory. The Barbra Streisand Foundation donated $200,000 to the Virginia Clinton Kelley Breast Cancer Research and Education Fund at the Arkansas Cancer Research Center.

"I am so grateful for the time I was able to spend with her," Barbra said later. "She died as she lived, with grace and dignity, full of enthusiasm and the joy of life. This new effort to combat breast cancer is endowed with that glowing spirit."

Bill Clinton was deeply touched by Barbra's generosity, but according to journalist David Duffy, Hillary Rodham Clinton was convinced that it was simply another of Barbra's ploys to get closer to her husband. She refused to lift her ban and is supposed to have said: "Streisand is not welcome here at the White House as long as I'm first lady . . . and that's final."

This estrangement between Hillary and Barbra would be

tragic, if true, for both women share not only love and admiration for the President, but a deep and generous nature themselves. Barbra's Streisand Foundation has given away $7 million since it was established in 1986, mainly to charities involved with AIDS, the environment, and civil rights, all issues that are deeply meaningful to the First Lady as well.

If Barbra was concerned that an estrangement from the First Lady might stall her political ambitions, she could certainly take heart from the progress she was still making as an artist.

This year she would also release another album of show tunes: *Back to Broadway.* Patti LuPone was reportedly upset that the album included two of Andrew Lloyd Webber's songs from *Sunset Boulevard,* "With One Look" and "As If We Never Said Goodbye," before Patti got to sing them on the cast album. But Patti should have seen this coming. Lloyd Webber had refused to give her permission to sing them in her Los Angeles concert the previous summer.

Perhaps Patti Lupone could learn from Barbra about the value of patience. For Barbra, who had waited more than twenty years, finally had the chance to right what she had considered an artistic wrong.

That January her *Back to Broadway* album was nominated for a Grammy in the category of Best Traditional Pop Vocal. Barbra herself was nominated with Michael Crawford for "Best Pop Vocal Group/Duet."

Barbra had been deeply disappointed when the final version of *Funny Girl* was released with only snippets of her hilarious portrayal of the Swan Queen. But she finally had the satisfaction of presenting the entire scene that January 4. Barbra herself tracked down a tape of the choreography cut from *Funny Girl* for inclusion in a tribute to Herbert Ross at the Film Society of Lincoln Center's Walter Reade Theatre.

Ross also showed clips of dance scenes from some of his

other films, including *The Turning Point, Nijinsky,* and *Pennies from Heaven.*

Before presenting the "Swan Lake" number, Ross recalled that for the filming Barbra wore silk tights that Margot Fonteyn had given her. But that was where any resemblance ended. "Our version was the Swan Queen as yenta," he told Carol Lawson of the *New York Times.*

Since the inauguration, Barbra had grown closer than ever to President Clinton. In fact, it was rumored that a jealous Hillary Rodham Clinton had banned Barbra from the White House, because she feared the smitten superstar was trying to make a play for her husband.

It was said that Hillary had been concerned ever since Barbra stayed overnight at the White House while Hillary was away. Her concern grew when Barbra sang a romantic ballad for Bill at an exclusive Hollywood party that Hillary did not attend.

Bill and Barbra's friendship had been heating up since the 1992 fundraiser, just as Hillary's feelings about Barbra took on a chill. Hillary did not appreciate Barbra's comments to friends that Bill was the sexiest man she'd ever been around.

The impact of her new close friendship with Bill Clinton could be seen everywhere in Barbra's life. Even her New York apartment has a new look these days. The furniture is almost entirely Stickley. And, with a new interest in the work of Thomas Jefferson, she has been inspired by Monticello and is redecorating her dining room all in white.

As long ago as 1978 Barbra had been complaining that maybe, maybe, she had too many *things.* She had been an avid collector of art nouveau and art deco since her Greenwich Village cabaret days, but her interests had diversified into chinoiserie, fine lacquers, and silk embroideries. "They all add another layer of complexity to my life," she told *Architectural Digest.* "I've *almost* reached the point of saturation," she acknowledged, "and I'm beginning to feel a little weighted down." By 1994 she had decided to do something about it.

Now that she was simplifying her life, Barbra had decided to convert her worldly goods into some ready cash. It was announced that the entire "Barbra Streisand Collection of 20th-Century Decorative and Fine Arts and Memorabilia" would be auctioned off at Christie's in New York on March 3 and 4, 1994. The auction house expected to bring in $4 million and marketed the collection aggressively with a $65 two-volume boxed catalogue.

The *New York Post* called it her "junk sale." *New York* magazine reported that Barbra drove a hard bargain, forcing Christie's to waive its usual fees, transport many of the items for free and print up special stationery bearing Barbra's name at the top.

Besides selling her vast art deco collection which included Tiffany lamps and a Tamara de Lempicka masterpiece, Barbra also used the occasion to unload her old clothes, hairbrushes, teacups, and even used playing cards.

Christie's catalogue for its Part II sale of Barbra's collection of decorative pieces, fine arts and memorabilia, featured a smiling portrait of the star on the cover, followed by 10 full page pictures inside of Barbra in various poses.

"She didn't instigate this, but she was cooperative when we came to her," Roberta Maneker, head of public relations for Christie's, insisted. Through the viewings, from February 25 through March 2, a videotape of Barbra talking about her collection played at the Park Avenue showroom.

"It is hard to let go of these beautiful things that I have loved for so many years," Barbra said in the video, "but I want to simplify my life. I want only two houses rather than seven."

As she told *Architectural Digest:* "If you're not going to use something, you have to let it pass on, go on its way and live a life with somebody who will appreciate it."

The Barbra Streisand Collection was auctioned at Christie's on March 3, 1994 for $5.8 million, well above the $4 million the auction house had estimated the sale would bring. More than a third of the total, $2 million, came from the sale of a single painting, Tamara de Lempicka's "Adam and Eve" from 1932, a record by that art deco artist and well above Christie's top estimate of $800,000. The purchase was made anonymously and Christie's would not identify the owner.

"We screamed when the Lempicka price went over $1 million," Barbra said by telephone from Beverly Hills, where she remained during the sale. "I was working out with my exercise teacher and when the bidding went over the top I screamed. I paid only $135,000 for it ten years ago."

Christie's officials readily acknowledged that an awful lot of the success of the sale had to do with the fact that all these things had belonged to Barbra Streisand. "People wanted something from her collection, meaning the smaller lots brought higher prices than we normally see," Christopher Bruce, the chairman of Christie's in America, said. "The celebrity value means less on the important pieces."

The auction house considered a frequently photographed Lewis Comfort Tiffany "cobweb" lamp to be the major disappointment of the day. Oddly enough, this piece was one of Barbra's favorites. She had found the lamp in 1979, in the basement of a favorite Manhattan hangout, a shop owned by Lillian Nassau.

"I thought it was kind of ugly-great," Barbra said, adding that the price—$70,000—"seemed huge" at the time, but proved a bargain two weeks later when another lamp of this design brought double the price at auction. It only brought

$717,500, below Christie's estimate of $800,000 to $1 million.

But Barbra was content. "I made more than 10 times what I paid for it," she said. "My motto is "Be a bull, be a bear, but don't be a pig."

Twenty-five

Barbra: By Herself

"I am the old Barbra, and I'm the new Barbra. I'm all the Barbras."

—Barbra

As soon as Barbra completed her triumphant two-evening engagement in Las Vegas rumors flew about her plans. Among the juicy stories in the air were hints that she intended to go on a world tour, even stories that she planned to sing with Luciano Pavarotti, Placido Domingo, and José Carreras at Dodger Stadium this summer. "It's a matter of fitting the pieces together," said Marty Erlichman. "She can sell as many seats as she wants," concert promoter John Scher told Jessica Shaw of *Entertainment Weekly*. "It would be the event of a lifetime." Another Streisand spokesman, Michael Levine, assured the press that her MGM Grand concerts had "exceeded everyone's hopes on every level, artistically, spiritually, professionally. . . . It was the most exciting event in the history of Vegas."

Barbra initially would not say whether she planned another tour, but she did tell *Daily Variety* that her immediate plans were to develop two movie scripts, *The Mirror Has Two Faces* and *The Normal Heart*.

"I want to have more fun," she told Julia Reed. "I'm willing to take those chances now, you know, live life to its fullest."

But flush with the success of her two-night stand in Las Vegas, Barbra was ready to go back on the road. That March she delighted fans by announcing that she would commit to a tour for the first time in more than two decades. Barbra would begin the tour on April 20 with four London concerts, then return to the U.S. where, beginning May 10, she would start the first of her four-city domestic engagements in Washington. New York's Madison Square Garden June 20 to 26. Southern California's Anaheim Arena, for six nights beginning May 25. And San Jose. The top ticket was going for $500 in New York, but of course scalpers were getting much more.

Anxious for her fans to have access, Barbra arranged for several thousand tickets to be made available to twenty-two different charities, who could then sell them for a sizable markup—$1,000 on a $350 ticket, with the difference being regarded as a tax-deductible donation.

"A lot of these are very good seats," said Ken Sunshine, publicist for the show. "It's a way for Barbra to help causes which are important to her, and it will also cut down on scalping—because people who would have otherwise patronized scalpers can now get the tickets from legitimate organizations." In New York the lucky organizations were Teach for America, Environmental Defense Fund, Planned Parenthood Federation of America, LIFEbeat, the music industry's AIDS charity, and the Gay Men's Health Crisis. It was estimated that each of the charities stood to earn more than $500,000 apiece from Barbra's gesture.

"The gift speaks volumes for Ms. Streisand's legendary

generosity and commitment to social justice," said Robyn Stein of Planned Parenthood.

There was still some carping about the high price of the tickets. Marty Erlichman loyally defended his client from charges of price-gouging. He said he had polled hundreds of arena concert promoters about a reasonable ticket price. "Everyone told me we could charge as high as Vegas and it would be a sellout," he told *Entertainment Weekly*. "But Barbra and I opted not to go as high." Nevertheless, Bob Grossweiner of *Performance* magazine pointed out: "Her tour is designed to gross $2 million per show, which is greed. No one else has asked for this kind of thing."

Still, there were many others who thought Barbra had *under-priced* herself. And there was no doubt she was calling the shots.

After all, most of the estimated $45 million the tour was expected to gross would be going to her. "The promoters are not making much off the net prices," a San Diego promoter told *Entertainment Weekly*. "The bulk, if not 100 percent, of the increase is probably going back to Streisand." Even the $9.3 million that Barbra's people estimated would be going to the charities came into question. She had chosen twenty-two groups to benefit from the tour, but as *Entertainment Weekly* pointed out, it was not Barbra making the donations. "In what can only be described as politically correct scalping," wrote Dana Kennedy in the magazine, "the groups must pay $350 for each ticket. *Then* they can resell them for $1,000 each and keep the $650 for good works."

A spokesman for one of the charities defended her quirky gesture. "She never came out and said she donated them, so you can't really call her on that," the official told Kennedy. "We always like to get something for nothing. Still, it presented us with an opportunity to raise a million dollars in a couple of weeks, and there are very few chances to do that."

Sunshine insisted that Barbra "doesn't see the tour as for

herself. It's her way of giving back, to just try to show love and support and appreciation for the fans. I know it sounds schmaltzy, but it's true."

And the fans would be amply rewarded. At Barbra's insistence, all the arenas on the tour would be fully carpeted. Marvin Hamlisch and the 64-piece orchestra that had backed her in Las Vegas would accompany her. "You can be sure that the sound, the lighting, and every technical aspect will be state of the art," Sunshine told Kennedy, "I don't think ever in live concerts have we seen that kind of detail, all supervised by Ms. Streisand.

Marty Erlichman said that the concerts would follow her Vegas performances in style and song selection, but Barbra being Barbra there were sure to be changes every night. As for the potential stalkers and worse that had kept her off stage for so many years, Erlichman acknowledged: "There are a lot of off-center people out there and you have to watch out for them." But his greatest concern was still Barbra herself: "She still has that stagefright," he told Kennedy. "She bit the bullet in Las Vegas, and she was able to enjoy herself that second show."

Erlichman also reported that Barbra was "horrified" when she read about the brazen scalping of tickets. Entrepreneurs on the street outside New York's Madison Square Garden were reportedly getting up to $3,000 a ticket and the New York State Attorney General's office and the New York City Department of Consumer Affairs had both launched investigations into ticket gouging after the New York concert was reported sold out in thirty-six minutes.

But this would be more than a concert—it would be an event. "Barbra makes you wait, and the more you wait, the more exciting it is," Vernon Patterson, a contributor to the short-lived *Barbra* magazine told Kennedy. "The longer you stay away, the more they want you. That was Garbo's trick, and I think Barbra is very cognizant of that."

"A ROMANCE MADE IN HEAVEN"

There doesn't seem to be a man in Barbra's life right now. Her last serious beau, Andre Agassi, is now involved with Brooke Shields. This spring, Barbra was denying rumors that she was dating ABC Television Network Group president Robert Iger who was in the process of getting a divorce. At one point she was reported to be dating Gary Busey, her Malibu neighbor. And they were spotted holding hands at a movie in Century City and sharing a soda at the food mall. Next, she turned up in Manhattan with an old and important flame: Pierre Trudeau, who escorted her to a production of *Medea* starring Diana Rigg and was by her side at an Elie Wiesel Foundation for Humanity Dinner honoring Hillary Clinton at the New York Public Library. Hillary was presented with the foundation's Humanitarian of the Year award.

And yet Barbra can always pull a stunning surprise, especially when it comes to the men in her life. On June 13th, she turned up for a gala state dinner at the White House on the arm of ABC anchorman Peter Jennings, who has been called "the sexiest man on television." Journalist Patricia Towle reported that Hillary Clinton herself had arranged the match. A week later, Jennings was Barbra's special guest at her New York concert. Barbra fans will be watching this relationship closely.

Professionally, Barbra will continue to take on daring projects and she's readying her most controversial project yet: the story of a woman who was kicked out of the U.S. armed forces because she is a lesbian. Barbra plans to co-produce the two-hour drama for NBC with Glenn Close who will star as Col. Margarethe Cammermeyer, the highest ranking woman to be booted from the armed forces for saying she is a lesbian.

"I am very proud to be producing Greta Cammermeyer's courageous story," Barbra said. "It is one of the most important issues of our time."

Barbra is also working on *The Normal Heart,* a film based on the play about the early days of the AIDS epidemic.

But she will always sing. "I must sing again," she declares, "to do what I can to ensure a safer and better world."

Chapter Notes

1. THE TWO MEN WHO LEFT HER

"I thought I might die . . ." Darrach, Brad, "Celebration of a Father," *People* Magazine, December 12, 1983.

"I always felt . . ." ibid.

". . . decent, hardworking people . . ." ibid.

"From the day I was born . . ." Evans, Peter, *Cosmopolitan* magazine.

"Spanking . . ." Klemesrud, Judy, "Barbra and Rozie's Mother Used to Hope for Her Own Name up in Lights," *New York Times,* February 23, 1970.

"I remember his mother . . ." Morgan, Thomas B., "Superbarbra," *Look,* April 5, 1961.

"I remember their taking off my clothes . . ." Grobel, Lawrence, "Playboy Interview: Barbra Streisand," *Playboy,* October 1977.

"My association . . ." ibid.

"When my mother . . ." ibid.

"He taunted her . . ." Darrach, op. cit.

"He disliked me." Michaelson, op. cit.

"There was a blank screen . . ." Steinem, Gloria, "Barbra Streisand Talks about Her 'Million Dollar Baby,' " *Ladies Home Journal,* August, 1966.

"I used to say . . ." Steinem, op. cit.

"My grandmother . . ." Sessums, Kevin, "Queen of Tides," *Vanity Fair,* September 1991.

"I was a peculiar kid . . ." Michaelson, op. cit.

"When a kid grows up . . ." Grobel, op. cit.

"They had the best ice cream . . ." Michaelson, Judy, "Woman in the News: Barbra Streisand," *New York Post,* September 28, 1968.

"I was sitting . . ." Miller.

"I liked the high school girl . . ." Rivers, Joan, with Richard Meryman *Enter Talking,* Delacorte Press, 1986.

2. THE BOYS IN THE BARS

"always late . . ." Steinem, op. cit.

"I knew I was good . . ." Miller, Edwin, *Seventeen* magazine.

"We were the only people . . ." Gavin, James, *Intimate Nights: The Golden Age of New York.*

"Look, you can continue . . ." ibid.

"her first romantic involvement" Spada, James, *Streisand: The Woman and the Legend,* Dolphin Books/Doubleday, 1981.

". . . had a collection . . ." Sessums, Kevin, "Queen of Tides," *Vanity Fair,* September 1991.

"I have a feeling that Barbra . . ." Gavin, op. cit.

"When I won . . ." Sessums, op. cit.

"When she returned . . ." Rivers, op. cit.

"Because I can be imitated . . ." Sessums, op. cit.

3. MEETING MARTY ERLICHMAN

"When I saw her walk out on the stage . . ." Sessums, op. cit.

"Streisand was phenomenally successful . . ." Gavin, op. cit.

"Opening night . . ." Douglas, Mike, *My Story,* G.P. Putnam's Sons, 1978.

4. ELLIOTT GOULD AND OVERNIGHT STARDOM

"In our original script . . ." Weidman, Jerome, "I Remember Barbra," *Holiday*, November 1963.

"You were brilliant . . ." Alexander, op. cit.

"Barbra was the one I chose . . ." Globe, "Elliott Gould: I lost my virginity to Barbra," December 28, 1993.

"He didn't think she was pretty . . ." Sessums, op. cit.

"I was always a director . . ." De Vries, Hilary, "Streisand, the Storyteller," Los Angeles *Times* magazine, December 8, 1991.

"I had very mixed feelings . . ." Grobel, op .cit.

"One night, we heard . . ." Lewis, Richard Warren, "Playboy Interview: Elliott Gould," *Playboy*, November 1977.

"I now have to make the *painful* admission . . ." Griffin, Merv, *Merv*, with Peter Barsocchini, Simon & Schuster, New York: 1980.

"Barbra was unique . . ." DeVries, op. cit.

5. BARBRA THE BROADWAY BABY

"After we cast her . . ." Sessums, op .cit.

" 'Barbra, if you don't sing . . .' ibid.

"I would eat these huge Chinese meals . . ." Grobel, op. cit.

"There is only one way . . ." Sesums, op. cit.

"Barbra is basically . . ." Lewis, op. cit.

"Once they froze the show . . ." Grobel, op. cit.

"I was scared . . ." Morgan, op. cit.

"I sang for Kennedy . . ." Grobel, op. cit.

"Everyone was telling me . . ." Swenson, Karen, *Barbra: The Second Decade*, A Citadel Press Book, Carol Publishing Group, Secaucus: 1990.

"Look, this was my first . . ." Carlsen, Peter, "Architectural

Digest Visits: Barbra Streisand," *Architectural Digest*, May, 1978.

6. BARBRA GOES TO LONDON AND MAKES A BABY

"As an artist . . ." *Newsweek*, "Barbra," March 28, 1966.
"This pregnancy . . ." Steinem, op. cit.
"I always knew I would be famous . . ." Morgan, op. cit.
"Kids stand downstairs . . ." *Newsweek*, op. cit.

7. BARBRA HITS HOLLYWOOD AND MEETS OMAR SHARIF

"He's great . . ." Carroll, June, "Latest little Gould rules roost," *Christian Science Monitor*, March 28, 1967.
"In terms of Hollywood standards . . ." Robbins, Fred, "Tape to Type," *Photoplay*, January, 1971.
"I just got off . . ." Hallowell, John, "Funny Girl Goes West," *Life*, September 29, 1967.
"The first impression . . ." ibid.
"It got so I couldn't wait . . ." Kimbrell, James, *Barbra: An Actress Who Sings*, Volume 2, Branden Publishing Co., Inc., 1989: Boston.
"I did feel that *Dolly* . . ." Morgan, Thomas B., "Barbra Streisand: On a Clear Day You Can See Dolly," *Look*, December 16, 1969.
"*Dolly* takes place . . ." ibid.

8. FEUDING WITH RAY STARK AND WALTER MATTHAU

"She steps on your head . . ." Kimbrall, op. cit., vol II.
"I really don't think about reviews . . ." Michaelson, Judy, "Woman in the News: Barbra Streisand," *New York Post*, September 28, 1968.

"Willy Wyler really screwed up . . ." Pierson, Frank, "My
Battles with Barbra and Jon," *New York,* November 15, 1976.

"I had an arrangement with Ray Stark . . ." ibid.

"Willfully and violently struck him," *New York Post,* October 30, 1968. Reuters.

9. ELLIOTT GETS HIS CHANCE

"heaven, just heaven . . ." Considine, Shaun, *Barbra
Streisand: The Woman, the Myth, the Music,* Delacorte Press,
New York, 1985.

"I think our divorce freed him . . ." Grobel, op. cit.

"We had screenings . . ." Considine, op. cit.

"I kept telling her . . ." ibid.

"I was amazed . . ." ibid.

"The year I took Barbra to the Academy Awards . . ." Lewis, op. cit.

"Barbra knew nothing . . ." Considine, op. cit.

"Barbra and I were . . ." Lurie, Diana, *Ladies' Home Journal,* August 1969.

"his life was too important . . ." Grobel, op. cit.

"It was fabulous . . ." ibid.

"I'm the hottest thing . . ." Klemesrud, Judy, "Now Who's
the Greatest Star?" *New York Times,* October 5, 1969.

"What are you fighting for?" Considine, op. cit.

"It's such a schlep . . ." Morgan, op. cit.

10. BARBRA CHARMS A PRIME MINISTER AND A "MASTER OF THE GAME"

"They're ugly . . ." Considine, op. cit.

"about having just bought a new house . . ." Bruck, Connie, *Master of the Game: Steve Ross and the Creation of Time
Warner,* Simon & Schuster, 1994.

"She acted like she was very upset . . ." Considine, op. cit.

"I know the film upset her . . ." Lewis, op. cit.

"She came up to me . . ." Considine, op. cit.

"It was almost a sermon . . ." *Rolling Stone*, June 24, 1971.

11. TEAMING UP WITH RYAN O'NEAL

"Barbra has always been appealing to men . . ." Considine, op. cit.

"frightened people on *Tiger* . . ." Hicks, Jack, "Elliott Gould: Trying to Doctor an Ailing Career, *TV Guide*, December 1, 1984.

"I was dying to do that picture . . ." Carroll, Kathleen, "Off Camera with Elliott Gould," *New York Daily News*, August 8, 1971.

"I was very unstable . . ." Hicks, op. cit.

"I owe Warners so much . . ." Flatley, Guy, and Tony Crawley, "Whatever Happened to Elliott Gould," *Game*, January 1975.

12. BARBRA'S FLOP: UP THE SANDBOX

"She is not difficult . . ." Considine, op. cit.

"I had the break of working with Barbra . . ." Kimbrall, vol. I, op. cit.

"I mean all my life I've been scared . . ." ibid.

"Both Warren and Barbra, when they wanted something . . ." Considine, op. cit.

"Julie had been out of town . . ." ibid.

"one of my flings." Grobel, op. cit.

"I had turned it down . . ." Kimbrall, vol. I, op. cit.

"You want to talk clothes and wigs here . . ." Considine, op. cit.

13. JON PETERS—THE MAN WHO . . .

"I proposed that since Barbra . . ." Considine, op. cit.

"No, because at the time I thought I was the biggest star . . ." Eisenberg, Lawrence B., "Barbra Streisand: Tough, Temperamental, Tremendous," *Cosmopolitan,* March 1977.

"I don't think that producing . . ." ibid.

"I took all the tests . . ." Hicks, op. cit.

14. FUNNY LADY

"In some respects, she's a combination . . ." Swenson, op. cit.

"Barbra could do whatever she wants," De Vries, op. cit.

"This is possibly the best singing . . ." Swenson, op. cit.

15. NEW DIRECTIONS

"Nobody was interested," Swenson, op. cit.

"In the early days . . ." ibid.

16. A STAR IS BORN

"How could I direct her . . ." Pierson, op. cit.

"The characters in the movie . . ." Eisenberg, op. cit.

"But I knew he was right . . ." Lardine, Bob, "Less Crazy after All These Years," *Sunday News Magazine,* November 28, 1978.

17. STREISAND SUPERMAN

"Ray Stark used to bully me . . ." Pierson, op. cit.

"She was family . . ." Considine, op. cit.

18. THE MAIN EVENT

"Because, Ryan, if you don't . . ." Swanson, op. cit.
"You like the fights? . . ." ibid.
"The reason I joined First Artists . . ." Considine, op. cit.

19. BARBRA'S DREAM: YENTL

"I had never seen my father's grave," Darrach, op. cit.
"It sounds crazy . . ." ibid.

20. A BRIEF DETOUR: ALL NIGHT LONG

21. BARBRA GOES BACK TO HER ROOTS

"My story was in no way material for a musical . . ."
Isaac Bashevis Singer, *New York Times*.
"She's been famous . . ." Sessums, op. cit.
"My son is the man . . ." Darrach, op. cit.
"Anyone could have done . . ." Holden, Stephen, *New York Times*.
"Barbra's contract . . ." Swanson, op. cit.
"I'm drawn . . ." ibid.
"Barbra Streisand has one of the two or three best . . ."
Holden, op. cit.

22. DON JOHNSON

"He took me by the hand . . ." Kimbral, op. cit, vol. I.
"Couldn't stand her . . ." Mickey Hershkovits, *Don Johnson,* St. Martin's Press, 1986.
"If I want to meet people . . ." *Long Beach Press Telegram,* March 9, 1988.

"Sorry you caught me . . ." Diana Maychick, *New York Post*.

"It was an off hour . . ." Liz Smith, *New York Daily News*, April 29, 1988.

"Don's the perfect man . . ." Kimball, op. cit., vol. I.

"Barbra was willing . . ." Judy Ellis, "Copy Again," *Life*, April 1989.

"The movie is not just about being flawed . . ." Morgenstern, Joe, "The Triumph of Barbra," *Cosmopolitan*, December 1991.

23. LOVE AND LOSSES

"I thought deep, deep down . . ." Reed, Julia, "Major Barbra," *Tatler*, January 1994.

"Of all the celebrities . . ." Sessums, op. cit.

"Mark Ross noted . . ." Bruck, Connie, *Master of the Game: Steve Ross and the Creation of Time Warner*, Simon & Schuster, 1994.

"The Streisand story," ibid.

"One more . . ." *Globe*, July 20, 1993.

"Oh, I forgot . . ." *Star*, July 13, 1993.

"He's a guy from the Bronx . . ." Reed, op. cit.

"You're doing nothing for me . . ." Charlotte Webb, *New York Daily News*, January 12, 1994.

24. BARBRA'S BACK ON STAGE

"Tell your mother . . ." *National Enquirer*.

"Tonight was the way . . ." Robert Hilburn, *Los Angeles Times*.

"As with any concert . . ." George Rush, *New York Daily News*.

25. BARBRA BY HERSELF

"Streisand is not welcome here . . ." *National Enquirer* 3/15/94.

"They all add another layer . . ." *Architectural Digest* 1978.

"We screamed . . ." *New York Times*.

"My motto . . . ibid.

Bibliography

Alexander, Shana, "A Born Loser's Success and Precarious Love," *Life*, May 22, 1964

Bell, Arthur, "Barbra Streisand Doesn't Get Ulcers—She Gives Them," *The Village Voice*, April 26, 1976

Bender, Marylin, *The Beautiful People*, Dell Publishing Co., Inc., 1968

Bruck, Connie, *Master of the Game: Steve Ross and the Creation of Time Warner*, Simon & Schuster, 1994

Carlsen, Peter, "Architectural Digest Visits: Barbra Streisand," *Architectural Digest*, May, 1978

Carroll, June, "Latest Little Gould Rules Roost," *Christian Science Monitor*, March 28, 1967

Carroll, Kathleen, "Off Camera with Elliott Gould," *New York Daily News*, August 8, 1971

Considine, Shaun, *Barbra Streisand: The Woman, The Myth, The Music*, Delacorte Press, 1985.

Crist, Judith, *Take 22—Moviemakers on Moviemaking*

Darrach, Brad, "Celebration of a Father," *People* Magazine, December 12, 1983

Devlin, Polly, "Instant Barbra," *Vogue,* March 15, 1966

De Vries, Hilary, "Streisand, the Storyteller," Los Angeles *Times* magazine, December 8, 1991

Douglas, Mike, *My Story,* G.P. Putnam's Sons, 1978, p. 226–7

Drew, Bernard L., "Elliott Gould New Superstar," *The Hartford Times,* June 28, 1970

Eisenberg, Lawrence B., "Barbra Streisand: Tough, Temperamental, Tremendous," *Cosmopolitan,* March 1977

Flatley, Guy, and Tony Crawley, "Whatever Happened to Elliott Gould, *Game,* January 1975

Gavin, James, *Intimate Nights: The Golden Age of New York Cabaret,* Limelight Editions, New York: 1992

Globe, "Elliott Gould: I Lost My Virginity to Barbra," December 28, 1993

Goldman, William, *The Season: A Candid Look at Broadway,* Limelight Editions, 1984

Graham, Sheila, "$1,500 a Month and No Shower," *New York World-Telegram and Sun,* April 8, 1966

Graham, Sheila, "Barbra's Spouse Burns," *New York Post,* November 30, 1967

Griffin, Merv, *Merv*, with Peter Barsocchini, Simon & Schuster, New York: 1980

Grobel, Lawrence, "Playboy Interview: Barbra Streisand," *Playboy*, October 1977

Haddad-Garcia, "The Lady is a Champ," *Cue*, July 6, 1979

Hallowell, John, "Funny Girl Goes West," *Life*, September 29, 1967

Hershkovits, David, *Don Johnson*, St. Martin's Press, 1986

Hicks, Jack, "Elliott Gould: Trying to Doctor an Ailing Career," *TV Guide*, December 1, 1984

Hinckley, David, "Babs: The Way She Is" *New York Daily News*, January 2, 1994

Kimbrell, James, *Barbra: An Actress Who Sings*, Volumes 1 and 2, Branden Publishing Co., Inc., 1989: Boston.

Klemesrud, Judy, "Now Who's the Greatest Star?" *New York Times*, October 5, 1969

Klemesrud, Judy, "Barbra and Rozie's Mother Used to Hope for Her Own Name up in Lights," *New York Times*, February 23, 1970

Lardine, Bob, "Less Crazy after All These Years," *Sunday News Magazine*, November 28, 1978

Lewis, Dan, "Gould is 'Free,' " Sunday *Record*, September 8, 1974

Lewis, Richard Warren, "Playboy Interview: Elliott Gould," *Playboy,* November 1977

Life, "Barbra Streisand Hits the Top," September, 1963, unsigned

Lurie, Diana, *Ladies' Home Journal,* August 1969

Maychick, Diana, "Getting Hooked on Don Juan Johnson," *New York Post,* October 25, 1985.

McClintick, David, *Indecent Exposure: A True Story of Hollywood and Wall Street,* Morrow: New York, 1982

McClintick, David, "Sinatra's Double Play," *Vanity Fair,* December 1993

Modern Screen, "Separation Blues," June, 1969

Morgenstern, Joe, "The Triumph of Barbra," *Cosmopolitan,* December 1991

Mothner, Ira, "Mama Barbra," *Look,* July 25, 1967

Photoplay, "Elliott Gould: Crackup!" June 1971

Maslin, Janet, "Street Smarts, Says Jon Peters, Are What Make a Producer," *New York Times,* January 29, 1978

Michaelson, Judy, "Woman in the News: Barbra Streisand," *New York Post,* September 28, 1968

Morgan, Thomas B., "Superbarbra," *Look,* April 5, 1961

Morgan, Thomas B., "Barbra Streisand: On a Clear Day You Can See Dolly," *Look,* December 16, 1969

Newsweek, "Barbra," March 28, 1966

Norwich, William, "America's First Voice," *Interview,* April 1993.

Pierson, Frank, "My Battles with Barbra and Jon," *New York,* November 15, 1976

Prideaux, Tom, "Funny Girl with a Frantic History," *Life,* April 7, 1964

Reed, Julia, "Major Barbra," *Tatler,* January 1994

Reuters & UPI, "Barbra Stuns Queen," March 18, 1975

Reuters, "Barbra's Husband Sued for $200,000," November 7, 1968

Rich, Frank, "The End of a Love Affair," *New York Post,* January 15, 1977

Riese, Randall, *Her Name is Barbra,* Carol Publishing Group, 1993.

Rivers, Joan, with Richard Meryman *Enter Talking,* Delacorte Press, 1986

Robbins, Fred, "Tape to Type," *Photoplay,* January, 1971

Sessums, Kevin, "Queen of Tides," *Vanity Fair,* September 1991

Shah, Diane K., "The Producers," *New York Times Magazine,* October 22, 1989

Siegel, Micki, "Barbra Streisand—Passion and Pleasure" *Modern Screen,* August 1974

Siskel, Gene, "Grand Dame," *Entertainment Weekly,* January 14, 1994

Spada, James, *Barbra: The First Decade: The Films and Career of Barbra Streisand,* A Citadel Press Book, Carol Publishing Group, New York: 1974

Spada, *Streisand: The Woman and the Legend,* Dolphin Books/Doubleday, 1981

Star, "Barbra Streisand Took My Virginity in Wild Night at Hotel," Elliott Gould, December 28, 1993

Streisand, Barbra, "Funny Girl Talk," *Playbill,* November 196

Swenson, Karen, *Barbra: The Second Decade,* A Citadel Press Book, Carol Publishing Group, Secaucus: 1990

Taylor, Curtice, "Follow a Star," *Seventeen Magazine,* January 1965

Thomas, Bob, *Liberace,* St. Martin's Press, 1987

Time, "Streisand: The Year in Tantrums," January 17, 1994

Travis, Neil, "Barbra Bares Her *Really* Bad Side," *New York Post,* January 3, 1994

Viladas, Pilar, "Architectural Digest Visits: Barbra Streisand, *Architectural Digest,* December 1993

Webb, Charlotte, "Charlotte's Web," *New York Daily News,* January 12, 1994.

Weidman, Jerome, "I Remember Barbra," *Holiday,* November 196

Filmography

1. *Funny Girl.* (1968) Omar Sharif, Kay Medford, Anne Francis, Walter Pidgeon. Directed by William Wyler. Produced by Ray Stark. Musical numbers directed by Herbert Ross. Original music by Jule Styne, Lyrics by Bob Merrill. Columbia Pictures and Rastar Productions. Academy Award nominations for Best Picture, Best Score of a Musical Picture (Walter Sharf), Best Song (Jule Style and Bob Merrill for "Funny Girl"). Co-star Kay Medford won an Oscar for Best Actress in a Supporting Role. Barbra shared her Oscar for Best Actress in a Leading Role with Katharine Hepburn (who won for *The Lion in Winter*).

2. *Hello, Dolly!* (1969) Walter Matthau, Michael Crawford, Louis Armstrong, E.J. Peaker, Tommy Tune, J. Pat O'Malley. Directed by Gene Kelly. Produced by and screenplay by Ernest Lehman. Dance and musical numbers staged by Michael Kidd. Music and lyrics by Jerry Herman. 20th Century Fox. Academy Award nomination for Best Picture. Garnered Oscar for Best Score of a Musical Picture (Lenny Hayton and Lionel Newman).

3. *On a Clear Day You Can See Forever.* (1970) Yves Montand, Bob Newhart, Larry Blyden, Jack Nicholson. Directed by Vincente Minelli. Produced by Howard W. Koch. Paramount Pictures Presents a Howard W. Koch-Alan Jay Lerner Production.

4. *The Owl and the Pussycat.* (1970) George Segal, Robert Klein, Allen Garfield. Directed by Herbert Ross. Produced by Ray Stark. A Ray Stark and Herbert Ross Production. Columbia Pictures and Rastar.

5. *What's Up, Doc?* (1972) Ryan O'Neal, Kenneth Mars, Austin Pendleton, Sorrell Booke, Stefan Gierasch, Michael Murphy, Madeline Kahn, Randy Quaid, M. Emmett Walsh. Produced and directed by Peter Bogdanovich. Warner Bros.

6. *Up the Sandbox.* (1972) David Selby, Jane Hoffman, George Irving, Joseph Bova, Isabel Sanford, Paul Dooley, Conrad Bain, Anne Ramsey, Lois Smith, Stockard Channing, Conrad Roberts, Sully Boyer. Director: Irvin Kershner. Produced by Irwin Winkler and Robert Chartoff. Screenplay by Paul Zindel. A First Artists Presentation of a Barwood Film. A National General Pictures Release.

7. *The Way We Were.* (1973) Robert Redford, Bradford Dillman, Lois Chiles, Patrick O'Neal, Viveca Lindfors, Murray Hamilton, Herb Edelman, Sally Kirkland, James Woods. Directed by Sydney Pollack. Produced by Ray Stark. A Rastar Production. Columbia Pictures. Barbra was nominated for an Academy Award for Best Actress in a Leading Role.

8. *For Pete's Sake.* (1974) Michael Sarrazin, Estelle Parsons, William Redfield, Molly Picon. Directed by Peter Yates. Miss Streisand's hairstyles designed by Jon Peters. Produced by Martin Erlichman and Stanley Shapiro. A Rastar Production. Columbia Pictures.

9. *Funny Lady.* (1975) James Caan, Omar Sharif, Roddy McDowall, Ben Vereen. Music and lyrics to original songs by John Kander and Fred Ebb. Directed by Herbert Ross. Produced by Ray Stark. A Rastar Production. Columbia Pictures.

Four Academy Award nominations: Cinematographer, Sound, Song, and Original Song Score.

10. *A Star is Born.* (1976) Kris Kristofferson, Gary Busey, Paul Mazursky, Marta Heflin, Sally Kirkland. Directed by Frank Pierson. Executive Producer: Barbra Streisand. Produced by Jon Peters. A Barwood/Jon Peters Production. Warner Bros./First Artists. Academy Award nominations: Best Cinematography, Sound, Original Song, and Original Song Score and/or Its Adaptation.

11. *The Main Event.* (1979) Ryan O'Neal, Paul Sand, Patti D'Arbanville. Directed by Howard Zieff. Produced by Jon Peters and Barbra Streisand. Warner Bros./First Artists.

12. *All Night Long.* (1981) Gene Hackman, Diane Ladd, Dennis Quaid, Kevin Dobson, William Daniels, Terry Kiser. Directed by Jean-Claude Tramont. Universal Pictures.

13. *Yentl.* (1983) Mandy Patinkin, Amy Irving, Nehemiah Persoff. Produced and directed by Barbra Streisand. Screenplay by Jack Rosenthal and Barbra Streisand, based on "Yentl, the Yeshiva Boy" by Isaac Bashevis Singer. A Barwood Film. United Artists. Five Academy Award nominations including: Best Supporting Actress (Amy Irving), Art Direction. Oscar went to Michel Legrand and Marilyn and Alan Bergman, for Best Original Song Score. (Their original songs "Papa, Can You Hear Me?" and "The Way He Makes Me Feel," were nominated but did not win.)

14. *Nuts.* (1987) Richard Dreyfuss, Karl Malden, Maureen Stapleton. Directed by Martin Ritt. Produced by Barbra

Streisand and Cis Corman. Screenplay by Darryl Ponicsan and
Herb Sargent.

15. *The Prince of Tides*. (1991) Nick Nolte, Kate Nelligan,
Melinda Dillon, Jason Gould. Directed by Barbra Streisand.
Based on the novel by Pat Conroy. Academy Award nomina-
tions for Best Picture, Best Actor (Nick Nolte), Best Support-
ing Actress (Kate Nelligan), Best Screenplay Adaptation and
Best Cinematography.

Discography

(For reasons of space, only a limited number of key contributors to each album can be named.)

Albums:

1. *I Can Get it for You Wholesale,* Columbia Original Cast Recording, 1962. Album produced by Goddard Lieberson. Barbra is heard on "I'm Not a Well Man," with Jack Kruschen; "Ballad of the Garment Trade," with Marilyn Cooper, Bambi Lynn, Elliott Gould, Harold Lang, Ken LeRoy, and the Company; "What are They Doing to Us Now?" with Kelly Brown, James Hickman, Luba Lisa, Wilma Curley, Pat Turner, and the Chorus. She solos on "Miss Marmelstein."

2. *Pins and Needles,* 25th Anniversary Edition of the Musical Revue, Columbia, 1962. Music and Lyrics by Harold Rome. Recording supervised by Harold Rome. Produced by Elizabeth Lauer and Charles Burr. Barbra is heard with Harold Rome, and others on "Four Little Angels of Peace," and solo on "Doing the Reactionary," "Nobody Makes a Pass at Me," "Not Cricket to Picket," "Status Quo," and "What Good is Love?"

3. *The Barbra Streisand Album,* Columbia, 1963. Produced by Mike Berniker. Arranged and conducted by Peter Matz, liner notes by Harold Arlen. Includes: "Cry Me a River," "My

Honey's Loving Arms," "I'll Tell the Man in the Street," "A Taste of Honey," "Who's Afraid of the Big, Bad Wolf?" "Soon It's Gonna Rain," "Happy Days are Here Again," "Keepin' Out of Mischief Now," "Much More," "Come to the Supermarket (in Old Peking)," and "A Sleepin' Bee."

4. *The Second Barbra Streisand Album,* Columbia, 1963. Produced by Mike Berniker, arranged and conducted by Peter Matz, additional materials by Peter Daniels. Liner Notes by Jule Styne. Includes "Any Place I Hang My Hat is Home," "Right as the Rain," "Down with Love," "Who Will Buy?" "When the Sun Comes Out," "Gotta Move," "My Coloring Book," "I Don't Care Much," "Lover Come Back to Me," "I Stayed Too Long at the Fair," "Like a Straw in the Wind."

5. *The Third Barbra Streisand Album,* Columbia, 1964. Produced by Mike Berniker. Arranged and Conducted by Ray Ellis, Sid Ramin, Peter Daniels, Peter Matz. Cover Photo by Roddy McDowell. Liner notes by Sammy Kahn. Includes: "My Melancholy Baby," "Just in Time," "Taking a Chance on Love," "Bewitched (Bothered and Bewildered)," "Never Will I Marry," "As Time Goes By," "Draw Me a Circle," "It Had to be You," "Make Believe," "I Had Myself a True Love."

6. *Funny Girl,* Capitol Records Original Cast Recording, 1964. Album produced by Dick Jones, conducted by Milton Rosenstock. Barbra is heard on "I'm the Greatest Star," "Cornet Man," "His Love Makes Me Beautiful" (with the Ensemble), "I Want to Be Seen with You Tonight," (with Sidney Chaplin), "People," "You Are Woman," (with Chaplin), "Don't Rain on My Parade," "Sadie, Sadie," (with the Ensemble), "Rat-tat-tat-tat," with TK Meehan and the Ensemble, "Who Are You Now?" "The Music That Makes Me Dance."

7. *People,* Columbia, 1964. Produced by Robert Mersey. Arranged and Conducted by Peter Matz and Ray Ellis. Accompaniment by Peter Daniels. Includes: "Absent-Minded Me," "When in Rome (I Do as the Romans Do)," "Fine and Dandy," "Supper Time," "Will He Like Me?" "How Does the Wine Taste?" "I'm All Smiles," "Autumn," "My Lord and Master," "Love is a Bore," "Don't Like Goodbyes," "People."

8. *My Name is Barbra,* Columbia, 1965. Based on the TV Special. Produced by Robert Mersey, arranged and conducted by Peter Matz. Includes: "My Name is Barbra," "A Kid Again/I'm Five," "Jenny Rebecca," "My Pa," "Sweet Zoo," "Where is the Wonder?" "I Can See It," "Someone to Watch over Me," "I've Got No Strings," "If You Were the Only Boy in the World," "Why Did I Choose You?" "My Man."

9. *My Name is Barbra, Two,* Columbia, 1965. Produced by Robert Mersey, arranged and conducted by Peter Matz and Don Costa. Includes: "He Touched Me," "The Shadow of Your Smile," "Quiet Night," "I Got Plenty of Nothin'" "How Much of the Dream Comes True," "Second Hand Rose," "The Kind of Man a Woman Needs," "All That I Want," "Where's That Rainbow," "No More Songs for Me," and a medley of "Second Hand Rose," "Give Me the Simple Life," "I Got Plenty of Nothin'," "Brother, Can You Spare a Dime?" "Nobody Knows You When You're Down and Out," "Second Hand Rose," and "The Best Things in Life are Free."

10. *Color Me Barbra,* Columbia, 1966. Soundtrack of her TV special. Produced for television by Joe Layton and Dwight Hemion. Includes: "Yesterdays," "One Kiss," "The Minute Waltz "Gotta Move," "Non C'est Rien," "Where or When," "C'est Si Bon, "Where am I Going?," "Starting Here, Starting Now," and a medley of "Animal Crackers in My Soup," "Funny Face," "That Face," "They Didn't Believe Me," "Were

Thine That Special Face," "I've Grown Accustomed to Her Face," "Let's Face the Music and Dance," "Sam, You Made the Pants Too Long," "What's New, Pussycat?" "Small World," "I Love You," "I Stayed Too Long at the Fair," and "Look at That Face."

11. *Harold Sings Arlen (with Friend),* Columbia 1966. Produced by Thomas Z. Sheppard. Barbra sings one solo, "House of Flowers," and duets with Arlen on "Ding-Dong! The Witch is Dead."

12. *Je M'appelle Barbra,* Columbia, 1966. Produced by Ettore Startta, arranged and conducted by Michael Legrand. Cover photo by Richard Avedon, liner notes by Maurice Chevalier and Nat Shapiro. Includes: "Free Again," "Autumn Leaves," "What Now, My Love?" (arranged and conducted by Ray Ellis); "Ma Premiere Chanson," "Clopin Clopant," "Le Mur," "I Wish You Love," "Speak to Me of Love," "Love and Learn," "Once Upon a Summertime," "Martina," "I've Been Here."

13. *Simply Streisand,* Columbia 1967. Produced by Jack Gold and Howard A. Roberts, Arranged by Ray Ellis, Conducted by David Shire. Liner notes by Richard Rogers. Includes: "My Funny Valentine," "The Nearness of You," "When Sunny Gets Blue," "Make the Man Love Me," "Lover Man," "More Than You Know," "I'll Know," "All the Things You Are," "The Boy Next Door," "Stout-Hearted Men."

14. *A Christmas Album,* Columbia 1967. Produced by Jack Gould, Side One Produced and Conducted by Marty Paich, Side Two Produced and Conducted by Ettore Stratta and Arranged and Conducted by Ray Ellis. Includes: "Jingle Bells?" "Have Yourself a Merry Little Christmas," "The Christmas Song (Chestnuts Roasting on an Open Fire)," "White Christ-

mas," "My Favorite Things," "The Best Gift," "Silent Night," "Ave Maria," "O Little Town of Bethlehem," "I Wonder as I Wander," and "The Lord's Prayer."

15. *A Happening in Central Park*, Columbia 1968. Album produced by Jack Gold. Recorded live at Central Park concert, summer 1967. Includes: "I Can See It," "New Love is Like a Newborn Child," "Folk Monologue/Value" "Cry Me a River," "People," "He Touched Me," "Marty the Martian," "Natural Sounds," "Second Hand Rose," "Sleep in Heavenly Peace," "Happy Days are Here Again."

16. *Funny Girl*, Original Soundtrack Recording, Columbia, 1968. Music by Jule Styne, Lyrics by Bob Merrill, Musical numbers directed by Herbert Ross, Musical Supervision by Walter Scharf. Barbra is heard on "I'm the Greatest Star," "I'd Rather be Blue over You (Than Happy with Somebody Else)," "His Love Makes Me Beautiful," "People," "You Are Woman, I am Man (with Omar Sharif)," "Don't Rain on My Parade," "Sadie, Sadie" (with Sharif), "The Swan," "Funny Girl," "My Man."

17. *What About Today?* Columbia 1969. Produced by Wally Gold, Arranged and Conducted by Peter Matz, with Don Costa and Michel Legrand. Album photos by Richard Avedon. Liner notes by Barbra Streisand. Includes: "What about Today?" "Ask Yourself Why," "Honey Pie," "Punky's Dilemma," "Until It's Time for You To Go," "That's a Fine Kind of Freedom," "Little Tin Soldier," "With a Little Help from My Friends," "Alfie," "The Morning After," Goodnight."

18. *Hello, Dolly!*, Original Soundtrack Recording, 20th-Century Fox, 1969. Produced by Ernest Lehman and Directed by Gene Kelly, Music and Lyrics by Jerry Herman, Musical numbers staged by Michael Kidd, Conducted by Lennie Hayton

and Lionel Newman. Barbra is heard on: "Just Leave Everything to Me," "It Takes a Woman," "Put on Your Sunday Clothes," "Dancing" (with Michael Crawford and TK Lockin), "Before the Parade Passes By," "Love is Only Love," "Hello, Dolly!" (with Louis Armstrong), "So Long Dearie."

19. *Barbra Streisand's Greatest Hits,* Columbia, 1970. Produced by Robert Mersey, Ettore Stratta, Jack Gold, Warren Vincent; Arranged and Conducted by Peter Matz, Michel Legrand, Don Costa; Cover photograph by Lawrence Schiller. Includes: "People," "Second Hand Rose," "Why Did I Choose You?" "He Touched Me," "Free Again," "Don't Rain on My Parade," "My Coloring Book," "Sam, You Made the Pants Too Long," "My Man," "Gotta Move," "Happy Days are Here Again."

20. *On a Clear Day You Can See Forever,* Original Soundtrack Recording of a Paramount Picture, Columbia, 1970. Music by Burton Lane, Lyrics by Alan Jay Lerner, Arranged and Conducted by Nelson Riddle. Barbra is heard on "Hurry! It's Lovely Up Here!" "Love with All the Trimmings," "Go to Sleep," "He Isn't You," "What Did I Have That I Don't Have?" "On a Clear Day."

21. *The Owl and the Pussycat,* Columbia, 1971. Comedy highlights from the screenplay by Buck Henry, and music from the motion picture soundtrack performed by Blood, Sweat and Tears. Barbra is heard, but acting, not singing.

22. *Stoney End,* Columbia 1971. Produced by Richard Perry; Music arranged by Gene Page, Perry Botkin, Jr., Claus Ogerman. Includes: "I Don't Know Where I Stand," "Hands off the Man," "If You Could Read My Mind," "Just a Little Lovin' " "Let Me Go," "Stoney End," "No Easy Way Down,"

"Time and Love," "Maybe," "Free the People," "I'll be Home."

23. *Barbra Joan Streisand,* Columbia, 1971. Produced by Richard Perry. Includes "Beautiful," "Love," "Where You Lead," "I Never Meant to Hurt You," "One Less Bell to Answer/A House is Not a Home," "Space Captain," "Since I Fell for You," "Mother," "The Summer Knows," "I Mean to Shine," "You've Got a Friend."

24. *Live Concert at the Forum,* Columbia 1972. Produced by Richard Perry, conducted by David Shire, Vocal direction by Eddie Kendrix, Background by the Eddie Kendrix Singers. Includes: "Sing/Make Your Own Kind of Music," "Starting Here, Starting Now," "Don't Rain on My Parade," "On a Clear Day," "Sweet Inspiration," by Carol King; "Didn't We?" "My Man," "Stoney End," "Sing/Happy Days Are Here Again," "People."

25. *Barbra Streisand . . . and Other Musical Instruments,* Columbia, 1973. Soundtrack of television special, Produced for television by Gary Smith and Dwight Hemion; Album produced by Martin Erlichman, Musical materials written and arranged by Ken and Mitzie Welch, Musical direction by Jack Parnell. Includes: "I Got Rhythm," "Johnny One Note/One Note Samba," "Glad to Be Unhappy," "People," "Second Hand Rose," "Don't Rain on My Parade," "Don't Ever Leave Me," "By Myself," "Come Back to Me," "I Never Has Seen Snow," "Auf dem Wasser zu Singen," "The World is a Concerto/Make Your Own Kind of Music," "The Sweetest Sounds."

26. *The Way We Were,* Columbia, 1974. Solo album. Produced by Tommy LiPuma, Marty Paich, and Wally Gold; Arranged by Nick DeCaro, Maryt Paich, Peter Matz, and Claus Ogerman. Later retitled *Barbra Streisand/The Way We Were.* In-

cludes "The Way We Were," "All in Love is Fair," "Pieces of Dreams," "How about Me?"

27. *The Way We Were,* Original Soundtrack Album, Columbia, 1974. Produced by Fred Salem, Arranged by Marvin Hamlisch. Barbra is heard on "The Way We Were" (a slightly different version from the one on her solo album, this is the version she sang over the opening and closing credits).

28. *ButterFly,* Columbia, 1974. Produced by Jon Peters, Arranged by Tom Scott and Lee Holdridge. Includes: "Life on Mars" by David Bowie, "Love in the Afternoon," "Guava Jelly," "Let the Good Times Roll," "Jubilation."

29. *Funny Lady,* Original Soundtrack Recording, Arista Records, 1974. Album coordinator: Peter Matz; Arranged and Conducted by Peter Matz. Includes: "How Lucky Can You Get," "Let's Hear it for Me," "If I Love Again," "More Than You Know," "Am I Blue," "Isn't This Better?" "Great Day."

30. *Lazy Afternoon,* Columbia, 1975. Produced by Jeffrey Lesser and Rupert Holmes, Arranged and Conducted by Holmes. Includes: "Moanin' Low," "My Father's Song," "Letters That Cross in the Mail," "Widescreen," "You and I," "Shake Me, Wake Me," "Everything," "A Child is Born," "Lazy Afternoon" (suggested by Francis Ford Coppola), "Better," "I Never Had it so Good," and "By the Way."

31. *Classical Barbra,* CBS Masterworks, 1976. Produced by Claus Ogerman, featuring the Columbia Symphony Orchestra under the direction of Ogerman. Jacket photos by Francesco Scavullo, liner notes by Leonard Bernstein.

32. *A Star is Born,* CBS Records, 1976. Produced by Barbra Streisand and Phil Ramone. Includes "Evergreen" (duet with

Kris Kristofferson), "Lost inside of You," (another duet with Kristofferson); "Everything," "Woman in the Moon," "Watch Closely Now."

33. *Streisand Superman,* CBS Records, 1976. Produced by Gary Klein. Includes "Answer Me," "Love Comes from Unexpected Places," "New York State of Mind" by Billy Joel, "My Heart Belongs to Me," "Lullaby for Myself," "I Found You Love."

34. *Songbird,* CBS Records, 1977. Produced by Gary Klein. Includes "Tomorrow," "A Man I Loved," "I Don't Break Easily," "You Don't Bring Me Flowers."

35. *Eyes of Laura Mars,* Original Motion Picture Soundtrack, CBS Records, 1977. Produced by Gary Klein. Barbra is heard on title track.

36. *Barbra Streisand's Greatest Hits/Volume 2,* CBS Records. Includes "You Don't Bring Me Flowers," duet with Neil Diamond; "Songbird," "Sweet Inspiration," "Where You Lead," "My Heart Belongs to Me," "The Way We Were," "Stoney End," "Evergreen."

37. *The Main Event,* Original Motion Picture Soundtrack, 1974. Produced, arranged and conducted by Bob Esty. Barbra's only contribution: the title song written by Paul Jabara and Bruce Roberts which Barbra renders both ballad and disco versions.

38. *Wet,* Columbia Records, 1979. A "concept" album inspired by the outdoor jacuzzi that Jon Peters built for Barbra, is made up of a collection of songs with water themes including "Hurricaine Joe," "Niagara," "Wet," which Barbra cowrote with David Wolfert and Sue Sheridan, and Barbra's duet with

Donna Summer, "No More Tears (Enough is Enough)," "Kiss
Me in the Rain," and "Splish Splash."

39. *Guilty,* Columbia Records, 1980. Producers and arrangers
included Barry Gibb. Includes: "Woman in Love," "What
Kind of Fool," "Carried Away," "Secrets," "Guilty."

40. *Memories,* Columbia Records, 1981. Collection of old and
new Streisand. Includes her never-before-recorded versions of
"Memory" and "Comin' In and Out of Your Life," produced
and arranged by Andrew Lloyd Webber; a newly recorded version of "Lost Inside of You" (which she wrote with Leon
Russell for *A Star is Born*), "Enough is Enough," other material
included previously recorded ballads 1974–1980 includes: "The
Way We Were," "You Don't Bring Me Flowers," "My Heart
Belongs to Me," "Evergreen," "No More Tears." Export album,
sold abroad as *Love Songs,* included "Kiss Me in the Rain," "I
Don't Break Easily," "Wet," and "A Man I Loved."

41. *Yentl,* Original Motion Picture Soundtrack, Columbia Re-
cords, 1983. Produced by Barbra and Alan and Marilyn
Bergman; Associate Producer: Michel Legrand; Post-produc-
tion supervised by Phil Ramone. Includes: "Papa Can You
Hear Me?" "Where Is It Written?" "This Is One of Those
Moments," "No Wonder," "No Matter What Happens," "The
Way He Makes Me Feel."

42. *Emotion,* Columbia Records, 1984. Producers include
Barbra, Richard Baskin, Richard Perry, Kim Carnes, and
Jim Steinman. Includes: "Left in the Dark," "Heart Don't
Change My Mind," "Make No Mistake, He's Mine" (duet
with Kim Carnes).

43. *The Broadway Album,* Columbia Records, 1985. Producers
include Barbra, Peter Matz, Richard Baskin, and Paul Jabara.

Includes ten songs by Stephen Sondheim, among them: "Putting it Together," "Pretty Women/The Ladies Who Lunch Medley," and "Send in the Clowns," also: "If I Loved You," "Can't Help Lovin' That Man" (with harmonica accompaniment by Stevie Wonder), "I Loves You Porgy/Bess You Is My Woman Now" medley.

44. *One Voice*, Sony/Columbia, 1986. Live recording of Barbra's "One Voice" concert at her home in Malibu. Includes "Somewhere," "Over the Rainbow," (which Barbra dedicated to Judy Garland), "America the Beautiful," and "Happy Days are Here Again."

45. *Nuts*, Warner Bros., 1987. Soundtrack album. Barbra does not sing, but she composed the film score, including "Theme from Nuts."

46. *Till I Loved You*, Sony/Columbia, 1988. Includes "Two People," formerly "Theme from Nuts," with lyrics by Alan and Marilyn Bergman. Title track is Barbra's duet with Don Johnson.

47. *Barbra Streisand—A Collection!* Sony/Columbia, 1988. "Greatest Hits and More."

48. *Barbra Streisand: Just for the Record*, Sony/Columbia, 1991, boxed set. A four CD retrospective spanning more than three decades and including ninety-four tracks of which sixty-seven were previously recorded but unreleased and only one new recorded song. Opens with recording of acetate of "You'll Never Know" that Barbra made in 1955. Closes with the mature Barbra of today dueting with herself. Other highlights: early recordings, among them Barbra's appearance on the *Judy Garland Show,* and dueting with Neil Diamond on "You Don't Bring Me Flowers" at the 1980 Grammy Awards.

48a. Highlights from *Barbra Streisand: Just for the Record,* Sony/Columbia, 1991. A CD appetizer produced by Barbra Streisand and Martin Erlichman. Consists of both vintage and contemporary versions of "You'll Never Know," "Cry Me a River," and "Papa, Can You Hear Me?"

49. *Prince of Tides,* Soundtrack album, Columbia, 1991, includes Barbra singing "For All We Know," which was not included in the film.

50. *Back to Broadway,* Sony , 1994. Barbra sings Stephen Sondheim, Andrew Lloyd Webber.

51. *Frank Sinatra Duets.* Capitol, 1993. Frank Sinatra performs thirteen classic songs with other world-class singers. Teams with Barbra for "I've Got a Crush on You." Other artists include Charles Aznavour, Anita Baker, Tony Bennett, Bono, Natalie Cole, Gloria Estefan, Aretha Franklin.

52. *Barbra Streisand: The Conccert,* Sony, coming soon.

Singles (all released on Columbia Records, unless otherwise indicated):

"Happy Days are Here Again," single. B side: "When the Sun Comes Out." (1962)
"My Coloring Book," with "Lover, Come Back to Me" (Columbia) (1962)
"People" (1964)
"Stout-Hearted Men" (1967)
"Sleep in Heavenly Peace (Silent Night)" (1967)
"Stoney End" (1970)
"If I Close My Eyes" (Theme from *Up the Sandbox*) (1971)
"The Way We Were" (1973)
"Guava Jelly"/"Love in the Afternoon" (1974)

"Jubilation"/"Let the Good Times Roll" (1975)

"My Father's Song/By the Way" (1975)

"Shake Me, Wake Me" (1975)

"Love Theme from *A Star is Born* (Evergreen)" (1976) Also recorded in French, Spanish, and Italian.

"My Heart Belongs to Me" (1977)

"Songbird"/"Honey, Can I Put on Your Clothes" (1978)

"Love Theme from *Eyes of Laura Mars* (Prisoner)" (1978)

"You Don't Bring Me Flowers" (duet with Neil Diamond) (1979)

"The Main Event"/"Fight" (1979)

"No More Tears (Enough is Enough)" duet with Donna Summer (1979) (released as a single (Columbia) and a 12-inch (Casablanca), each of which sold over 1,000,000 copies.

"Kiss Me in the Rain"/"I Ain't Gonna Cry Tonight" (duet with Donna Summer) (1980)

"Woman in Love" (1980)

"Guilty"/"Life Story" (1980) (duets with Andy Gibb)

"What Kind of Fool"/"The Love Inside" (1980)

"Comin' In and Out of Your Life"/"Lost Inside of You" (1981)

"Memory" (1981)

"The Way He Makes Me Feel" (1983)

"Papa, Can You Hear Me?" (1984)

"Left in the Dark"/"Here We Are At Last" (1984)

"Make No Mistake, He's Mine" (Duet with Kim Carnes) (1984)

"Emotion"/"Here We Are At Last" (1985)

"Somewhere"/"Not While I'm Around" (1985) Barbra pledged to donate proceeds from this single to PRO-Peace (an antinuclear organization) and the American Federation for AIDS Research.

"Send in the Clowns"/"Being Alive" (1986)

"Till I Loved You" duet with Don Johnson (1988)

Theatrical Performances

Another Evening with Harry Stoones, Music and Lyrics by Jeff Harris, Musical direction and accompaniments by Abba Bogin, Choreography by Joe Millan, Entire production staged by G. Adam Jordan, Presented by Stenod Productions, Inc. Cast included Diana Sands, Dom De Luise. Barbra sang: "Value," "Jersey," "Butterfingers," and duet with DeLuise, "Miss Heinshlinger." Opened October 21, 1961, Gramercy Arts Theatre. Closed October 21, 1961.

The Insect Comedy, Karel and Josef Capek. Barbra portrayed a butterfly. Opened May 1960, three performances, Jan Hus Theatre.

I Can Get it for You Wholesale, Book by Jerome Weidman, based on his novel; music and lyrics by Harold Rome; Musical staging by Herbert Ross; Directed by Arthur Laurents, Produced by David Merrick. Cast included: Elliott Gould, Marilyn Cooper, Lillian Roth, Sheree North, Bambi Lynn, Harold Lang, Luba Lisa. Barbra sang "Miss Marmelstein" and "What Are They Doing to Us Now?" Opened March 22, 1962, Sam S. Shubert Theatre. Closed December 9, 1962.

Funny Girl, Music by Jule Styne, Lyrics by Bob Merrill, Book by Isabel Lennart, Musical Numbers staged by Carol Haney, Production supervised by Jerome Robbins, Directed by Garson

Kanin. Cast included Sydney Chaplin, Lainie Kazan, Kay Medford, Jean Stapleton. Barbra sang: "If a Girl Isn't Pretty," "I'm the Greatest Star," "Cornet Man," "His Love Makes Me Beautiful," "I Want to Be Seen with You Tonight," "People," "Don't Rain on My Parade," "Rat-tat-tat-tat," "Who are You Now?" "The Music That Makes Me Dance." Presented by Ray Stark. Opened March 26, 1964, Winter Garden Theatre. Barbra was nominated for a Tony Award as Best Actress in a Musical, but lost to Carol Chaning in *Hello, Dolly!*

Funny Girl in London, cast included Kay Medford, Michael Craig. Choreographed by Larry Fuller, directed by Lawrence Kasha. Presented by Bernard Delfont. Opened April 13, 1966, Prince of Wales Theatre. Barbra was voted Best Foreign Actress and *Funny Girl* was named Best Foreign Musical.

Cabaret, Concert, and Television Performances

June 1960
 THE LION

August 16-30, 1960
 The Boy Friend, Fishkill, N.Y. Cecilwood Theatre. Small part as the French maid. Sang one short song—with a French accent.

September 9, 1960
 BON SOIR debut. Engagement extended and reextended into December.

March-April, 1961
 CIRCUS CLUB, Detroit (extended)
 CRYSTAL PALACE, St. Louis.

April 5, 1961
 The Jack Parr Show (NBC-TV); 11:15 PM-1:00 AM; Other guests: Phyllis Diller; B. sang: "A Sleepin' Bee"; Her network debut.
 P.M. East, host: Mike Wallace.

July 1961
  Winnipeg, Canada.

November 1961
  Debut at the Blue Angel, days before her audition for *Wholesale,* opening for Pat Harrington, Jr.

January 1962
  New Orleans, Miami, and Chicago.

May 22, 1962
  Bon Soir.

July 16, 1962
  Blue Angel, now headlining.

December 16, 1962
  The Ed Sullivan Show. Sang "My Coloring Book" and "Lover, Come Back to Me".

March 5, 1963
  The Tonight Show, Barbra's seventh and final appearance with host Johnny Carson.

mid-March-March 27
  Eden Roc Hotel's Cafe Pompeii, Miami, Florida. Shared billing with Sergio Franchi.
  The Hungry i. San Francisco, California. Shared bill with Woody Allen. Three week engagement.

April
  Mr. Kelly's, Chicago, Illinois. Shared bill with Jackie Vernon.

April
   The Chateau, Cleveland, Ohio. Co-hosted *The Mike Douglas Show* the same week.

May 12
   The Dinah Shore Show, NBC-TV network.

May 13
   Basin Street East, New York, N.Y. Shared bill with Benny Goodman.

June 9
   The Ed Sullivan Show.

June 25
   The Keefe Brasselle Show CBS-TV network (premiere). Sang "Soon It's Gonna Rain."

July 2
   The Riviera Hotel, Las Vegas, with Liberace.

August 21
   Coconut Grove, at the Ambassador Hotel, Los Angeles. Sold-out three–week engagement through September 8.

September 27
   Chrysler Presents a Bob Hope Special.

April 12, 1964
   What's My Line? with Arlene Francis and Dorothy Kilgallen.

July 12, 1964
   Forest Hills Tennis Stadium concert.

April 28, 1965
  My Name is Barbra, CBS-TV network special.

March 30, 1966
  Color Me Barbra, CBS-TV network special, her first in color. Director: Dwight Hemion; Choreographer: Joe Layton; Musical Director: Peter Matz; Costumes: Ray Diffen. Filmed at Philadelphia Museum of Art.

July 30, 1966
  Newport Music Festival

August 2
  John F. Kennedy Stadium, Philadelphia

August 6
  Atlanta Stadium

August 9
  Soldiers Field, Chicago

June 17, 1967
  Central Park concert

July 9
  Hollywood Bowl

October 11
  The Belle of 14th Street, third television special, CBS-TV network. (Taped April 26-30)

July 26, 1968
  "Entertainment Event of the Year": Hollywood Bowl benefit for the "Poor People's Camp."

September 15
  A Happening in Central Park special

September 18
  Don Rickles's Brooklyn

July 2-30, 1969
  International Hotel's Showroom International, Las Vegas, Nevada.

April 19, 1970
  Tony Awards, accepted "Star of the Decade" award.

December 22
  A World of Love

March 14, 1971
  Burt Bachrach Special

December 24-January 13, 1972
  Las Vegas Hilton

March 9, 1975
  Funny Girl to Funny Lady, ABC-TV. Produced by Gary Smith and Dwight Hemion; Directed by Dwight Hemion; Executive Producer: Ray Stark; Written by Herb Sargent; Musical Conductor: Peter Matz; Audio Consultant: Phil Ramone. Among the guests on the live program: Dick Cavett, Muhammad Ali, James Caan. Barbra sang "The Way We Were," "Don't Rain on My Parade," "My Man," a duet with James Caan for "It's Only a Paper Moon/"I Like Her (Him)"
  A one-hour special preceding the premiere of *Funny Lady*.

March 14, 1976
  AFI Salute to William Wyler. (pre-taped) Barbra donated

her honorarium to the Institute to help establish an exchange program with the Soviet film industry.

March 20, 1976
Live concert at Arizona State University's Sun Devil Stadium, Tempe, Arizona. Staged for *A Star is Born* by Bill Graham and Jon Peters, other acts included Peter Frampton, Santana. Barbra's numbers included: "Evergreen," and "People."

December 14, 1976
Barbra Walters Special, ABC-TV, She interviewed Barbra and Jon for thirty minutes; the second half of the show was devoted to President and Mrs. Carter.

February, 1977
With One More Look at You. Documentary syndicated to local TV stations. Produced by Kaleidoscope Films. A behind-the-scenes look at the making of *A Star is Born.* Includes Barbra sharing her thoughts about acting, stardom, critics, and being a woman.

March 28, 1977
1977 Academy Awards. (ABC-TV) Barbra sang "Evergreen." Minutes later, Neil Diamond opened the envelope and announced Barbra and co-writer Paul Williams the winners for the Best Original Song.

April, 1977
"My Heart Belongs to Me." Promotional video produced exclusively for 1977 Columbia Records convention.

May 8, 1977
The Stars Salute Israel at 30. Stars from Mikhail Baryshnikov to Sammy Davis, Jr., gathered at the Dorothy Chandler Pavilion on the afternoon of May 7, 1978 for a gala celebration,

simultaneously held in the Grand Ballroom of the Hilton Hotel in Jerusalem. Barbra sang "Tomorrow," "People," and "Happy Days are Here Again," and "Hatikva" ("Hope") accompanied by the Los Angeles Philharmonic, led by Zubin Mehta. A 2-hour collection of highlights of the event, which included a phone conversation between Barbra and Israel's Prime Minister Golda Meir, aired May 8 on ABC-TV.

1979

The Mike Walsh Show Australia three-part exclusive interview.

1979

Getting in Shape for "The Main Event," Behind-the-scenes documentary, syndicated to television, thirty-minutes, includes interviews with Barbra and Ryan O'Neal.

February 17, 1980

1980 Grammy Awards Barbra and Neil Diamond performed their "You Don't Bring Me Flowers" duet live at the ceremony.

June 1, 1980

"ACLU Tribute to Marilyn and Alan Bergman." Fundraising event for ACLU. Barbra was unofficial host for the evening, opening the show on stage and singing "The Way We Were." She returned to close the show with "Summer Me, Winter Me," accompanied by Michel Legrand.

March 21, 1982

"I Love Liberty," (ABC-TV) Barbra filmed a video "America the Beautiful," backed by the U.S. Air Force marching band, especially for this special, produced by Norman Lear and his foundation, People for the American Way. Barbra's "special guest taped appearance" was shown at the taping on

February 22. Among the stars who performed live that night were Melissa Manchester, Gregory Hines, and Kenny Rogers.

April, 1982
"Memory," promotional video of a recreated Streisand recording session. Released in Great Britain only.

November 17, 1983
20/20 (ABC-TV) For the first time, the show devoted an entire hour to one star.

1983
"A Film is Born." (BBC) Forty-minute documentary of the making of *Yentl*.

October 1984
"Left in the Dark," video directed by Jonathan Kaplan.

January 1985
"Emotion," video directed by Barbra and Richard Baskin.

November 1985
"Somewhere," video directed by William Friedkin.

January 1986
Putting it Together: The Making of The Broadway Album (HBO) Video of the first recording session for the album. Later released by CBS/Fox for the home video market.

FUN AND LOVE!

THE DUMBEST DUMB BLONDE JOKE BOOK (889, $4.50)
by Joey West
They say that blondes have more fun . . . but we can all have a hoot
with THE DUMBEST DUMB BLONDE JOKE BOOK. Here's a
hilarious collection of hundreds of dumb blonde jokes—including
dumb blonde GUY jokes—that are certain to send you over the
edge!

THE I HATE MADONNA JOKE BOOK (798, $4.50)
by Joey West
She's Hollywood's most controversial star. Her raunchy reputation's brought her fame and fortune. Now here is a sensational collection of hilarious material on America's most talked about
MATERIAL GIRL!

LOVE'S LITTLE INSTRUCTION BOOK (774, $4.99)
by Annie Pigeon
Filled from cover to cover with romantic hints—one for every day
of the year—this delightful book will liven up your life and make
you and your lover smile. Discover these amusing tips for making
your lover happy . . . tips like—ask her mother to dance—have his
car washed—take turns being irrational . . . and many, many
more!

MOM'S LITTLE INSTRUCTION BOOK (0009, $4.99)
by Annie Pigeon
Mom needs as much help as she can get, what with chaotic schedules, wedding fiascos, Barneymania and all. Now, here comes the
best mother's helper yet. Filled with funny comforting advice for
moms of all ages. What better way to show mother how very much
you love her by giving her a gift guaranteed to make her smile
everyday of the year.

*Available wherever paperbacks are sold, or order direct from the
Publisher. Send cover price plus 50¢ per copy for mailing and handling to Penguin USA, P.O. Box 999, c/o Dept. 17109, Bergen-
field, NJ 07621. Residents of New York and Tennessee must
include sales tax. DO NOT SEND CASH.*